Crossing the Line

PREVIOUS TITLES BY KIMBERLY KINCAID

The Cross Creek Series

Crossing Hearts

Crossing the Line

KIMBERLY KINCAID

Montlake
Romance

Text copyright © 2017 Kimberly Kincaid
All rights reserved.

No part of this book may be reproduced, or stored in a retrieval system, or transmitted in any form or by any means, electronic, mechanical, photocopying, recording, or otherwise, without express written permission of the publisher.

Published by Montlake Romance, Seattle

www.apub.com

Amazon, the Amazon logo, and Montlake Romance are trademarks of Amazon.com, Inc., or its affiliates.

ISBN-13: 9781542046503
ISBN-10: 1542046505

Cover design by Jason Blackburn

Cover photography by Regina Wamba of MaeIDesign.com

Printed in the United States of America

This book is dedicated to my three daughters, who never say no when I ask if they want to go to the farmers' market and (almost!) always eat their veggies.

CHAPTER ONE

Eli Cross was about to be in a shit-ton of trouble. But since he wasn't exactly pioneering new territory by landing himself in hot water, he might as well take it like he usually did—with a shrug and a smile and great big steaming mug of *here we go again.*

"Have you seriously not loaded any of these crates for tomorrow's farmers' market yet?" His brother Owen pinned him with a steely stare as he gestured to the six dozen wood-slatted crates stacked in neat columns against the barn wall. Kind of hard to believe Owen was only five years older than him, what with the whole thirty-two-going-on-grumpy-old-man thing the guy was rocking. For Chrissake, Owen bossed Eli over every last one of their 750 acres even more than their father did, and Tobias Cross had run the farm since his own father had left it to him more than three decades ago.

Not that Eli actually listened to his brother much.

He rolled a slow glance over the obviously empty crates, inhaling a lungful of humid, late-summer air before working up his trademark drawl. "It appears that way."

Despite his carefree cover, guilt panged low in Eli's gut, just above the top button on his beat-to-hell-and-back Levi's. It was true that he hadn't loaded the crates with produce from the fields and greenhouses like he was supposed to, just like it was true he'd known Owen was expecting him to get the job done. What he *had* been doing, though, was harvesting as much sweet corn as he could get to before their old man got done repairing the irrigation system in the north fields. Not that their father couldn't do the work—hell, he was as salty as they came, and Eli would bet good money the man could harvest sweet corn easier than he could spell his own name. But he'd also suffered a not-small bout of heat exhaustion only two months ago. No sense pickin' a fight with fate. Especially not in the dog days of a Virginia summer, and double especially not when Eli could do the work instead. After all, Owen already thought Eli was a screwup, and Eli had to admit, most of the time, his brother wasn't wrong. But taking some extra heat to save a little bit of their old man's pride? Hell, that was worth every last one of Owen's legendary eye rolls.

"I've got a little time to burn," their middle brother, Hunter, said from his spot in front of the barn door, throwing on the easy-does-it peacekeeper face Eli knew all too well. "I don't mind helping you load the crates for the farmers' market, E."

Owen's snort killed the offer before it had finished echoing off the wide, wooden walls. "It's the height of the worst season we've seen in a decade, and a Friday afternoon to boot. There's no such thing as 'time to burn.' We're all up to our eyeteeth trying to get ahead before the weekend kicks off. Except for Eli, of course, who might as well be on vacation."

For a hot second, Eli was tempted to pop off and tell Owen that he hadn't exactly been sitting on his ass pontificating about the meaning of life all afternoon. But telling his brother why he was running behind would just be a moot point, because even if Eli forked over the truth now, Owen would still only hear what he wanted—an excuse. Provided he even listened at all.

Yeah. Time to just get good and comfy on the hot seat. It was, after all, the only place at Cross Creek Farm where Eli really belonged.

"It's cool, Hunt." Eli lifted his shoulders up and around in a move so well practiced it was probably stamped into his muscle memory for life. "I've got this. I'll just throw the crates in my truck and fill 'em now, nothing doing."

"No, you won't."

Owen's voice halted Eli midstep on the packed dirt beneath his Red Wings. "I'm sorry?"

"Been hearing that a lot from you lately. Not that it does much good when your work doesn't get done," Owen said, and the words sent Eli's molars together hard enough that his jaw considered crying uncle. But before he could unhinge the thing to deliver the verbal ass-kicking Owen had been gunning for since he'd clapped eyes on the crates in the first place, Hunter stepped in, both hands lifted as if he could literally stuff the tension back with his palms.

"Come on, you two. We're still trying to bounce back from the crazy weather and both me and Dad being out of commission for part of the summer." Hunter rolled the shoulder he'd spent most of June rehabbing after going ass over teakettle out of their hayloft. "If we want to get this farm back in the black, you need to be working together. Not trying to knock each other's fucking blocks off."

As usual, Hunter wasn't wrong. But of course, Owen's heels were dug in good and hard. "No one wants to make up for this weak season more than I do," Owen said, a frown marking his darkly stubbled face. "But you and Dad and I can't work together with Eli when he won't work at all."

Oh, for Chrissake . . . "I just told you I'd load the crates," Eli pointed out.

"When, exactly?" Owen shot back. "The farmers' market opens up at seven tomorrow morning, all the way in Camden Valley, which means the truck's gotta be loaded in time to roll out of here by five. We've got maybe two more hours of good daylight to get these crates filled and ready to go."

3

Eli looked out the double-wide barn door, measuring the slant of the sunlight with a glance. "I know how much daylight we've got left."

Which sucked, because in this particular case, Owen happened to be right. Eli would have to put the pedal to the floorboards in order to get all the produce prepped and packed for transport before he lost enough daylight to do the job, and even then, he'd probably have to grab some floodlights in order to finish. Not that he'd give Owen the satisfaction of saying so.

His brother arched one dark-brown brow high enough for it to disappear beneath the hair tumbling over his forehead, and shit, looked like Owen didn't need the out-loud satisfaction to keep pushing. "Then you know at this point, it's a two-person job."

"I'm good for the help," Hunter said, but the buffer bounced off Owen like a pebble hitting a tractor tire.

"Thank God somebody is." He pivoted on the heels of his work boots, beelining directly for the crates. "Let's get these up to the greenhouse, Hunt. Between me and you, we should be able to fill 'em fast enough to get you home for dinner with Emerson."

Shock merged with all the irritation pumping through Eli's veins. "And what is it you want me to do, then?"

Owen paused before saying, "We need baling twine for the hay in the east field. The co-op's open for another hour."

Freaking stellar. He'd just been reduced to errand boy. Shit couldn't get any worse. "Fine," Eli said, although he slapped the word with enough of an edge that it came off like a different F-word altogether. At least the trip into town would buy him some space so he could get his no-big-deal attitude back into place.

"And stay out of trouble, would you?" Owen called after him, the words making Eli's muscles tense beneath his work-damp T-shirt. "The last thing we need around here after the season we've had is more heartache."

4

"Kiss my heartache," Eli mumbled, stowing the words under his breath as he gave Owen the rest of his back. Walking the rest of the way to his dust-covered pickup, he gripped the door handle hard enough to make his knuckles protest before yanking the door open and pulling himself into the driver's seat. A fresh sheen of sweat formed beneath the brim of his work-worn baseball hat, and Eli adjusted the thing against the glaring, late-afternoon sunlight.

He reeled in a deep breath, but still, his frustration lingered like the smell of old, stale smoke. He might not have an *all*-work ethic like Owen or feel like he'd been born to farm like Hunter and their old man, but he wasn't a degenerate. He did his share on the farm—maybe not as often or as hard as everyone else, but he still knew how to put in a long day just like the rest of them.

Man, the days had felt as if they'd each lasted a week lately. And the labor was the least of the hardship.

After all, hard work was a whole lot easier if you were actually meant for what you were doing.

Eli's chin snapped up, the thought jamming his chest chock-full of *don't go there* before he mashed down on it completely. Yeah, he might be the odd man out at Cross Creek, and yeah again, tensions were at an all-time high from all the unforeseen circumstances they'd been fielding lately and the slower-than-usual business they'd seen as a result. But he'd been born and bred on Cross Creek soil, just like his brothers, his father, and his grandfather besides. He'd never even set so much as a baby toe outside the state of Virginia, for God's sake.

He couldn't exactly tell anyone he knew he didn't belong there. And he sure as hell couldn't tell anyone where his true, fire-in-the-belly passion lay.

Not when it was far, far easier to just grin, do the bare minimum at the farm, and cover the rest up.

Eli turned the key in the ignition, sending the F-150's engine into a low rumble. All of this scrapping between him and Owen was just making him stupid. What Eli really needed was to forget about his brother's sky-high expectations and just go through the motions of getting back to normal.

Until their next argument, anyway. Then it would be rinse and repeat all over again, and dammit, he needed more than a little distance to get his mind right.

He needed Shakespeare.

Eli angled his truck over the two-lane road leading into Millhaven proper, tapping the touch screen on the F-150's sound system until *A Midsummer Night's Dream* started rolling through the speakers. Yeah, he knew the Shakespeare thing was weird—enough so that he went to great lengths to hide it from his brothers and his buddies and pretty much anyone with a pulse. Most folks around Millhaven were content to blow off steam the old-fashioned way, with a cold beer or hot sex, and Eli had to admit, he wasn't unhappy to go that route, either. But when shit got really critical, the best way for him to get right side up again was to hit the classics. Shakespeare. Twain. Hemingway. He'd loved to read since middle school. And writing? Even freaking better.

Fire, meet belly.

The trip into town was short but scenic, and Eli's truck ate up the dozen or so miles of sun-drenched farmland in about as many minutes. The two-lane ribbon of faded asphalt became Town Street about a half mile from downtown, which was probably a misnomer, although with the highly limited travel in Eli's past, he couldn't really say with any authority. But the neatly kept cobblestone walkway lining the four blocks of "downtown" Millhaven had always seemed right nice to him, even if they weren't fancy. The town had the essentials—The Corner Market, Clementine's Diner (Best. Cheeseburger. Ever.), Doc Sanders's office, and the fire station, plus a handful more businesses to round out the bunch. The farming co-op sat smack in the middle of things on the corner of the second block, and Eli was careful to switch his sound system over to the local country station before pulling within earshot of the place.

"Freaking great." A sour taste filled his mouth at the sight of the dusty, rusty Chevy Silverado parked front and center by the co-op's main entrance. While under normal circumstances Eli had no problem engaging in the ongoing pissing contest he'd had going with Greyson Whittaker since about puberty, he *so* wasn't in the mood to tangle with the only son of Cross Creek Farm's biggest rival today. Maybe he'd get lucky and Greyson would be in the back, placing an order for feed or fertilizer. Better still, maybe the stars would align, and the guy would just sense Eli's utterly shitastic mood and leave him be for once.

Or maybe Greyson would be leaning against the front counter with a toothpick tucked into one corner of his mouth while the other side kicked up into a smirk that broadcast very bad things on the immediate horizon, and shit, shit, *shit*. Eli needed this like he needed a prostate exam with a tax-audit chaser.

His heart kicked at his sternum as he lifted his chin at Billy Masterson behind the counter, ignoring Greyson altogether. "Hey, Billy. I need to grab a half dozen bales of Poly Baler."

"Sure thing, Eli," Billy said, shifting a nonsubtle glance at Greyson before turning toward the computer system set up behind the counter. "So how's it going?"

It was a bit of a loaded question, coming from Masterson. The guy was cool enough, but he also had a thing for lighting up the small-town grapevine like a fifty-foot spruce on Christmas Eve.

"Alright," Eli said, jamming a thumb through the belt loop of his jeans. Greyson's smirk felt like an army of hornets buzzing over him, just waiting for an excuse to attack, and yeah, today had officially hit the redline on his Suck-o-Meter. "You want me to pull around back to help load them?"

"Hang on a sec." Billy's brows lowered for just a second beneath the brim of his John Deere baseball cap before his expression grew uneasy. "Did you want to put these on Cross Creek's line of credit?"

Hell of a weird question. They'd used the farm's account at the co-op for the past . . . well, ever, as far as Eli knew. "Yeah. Why?"

"Because it looks like y'all have reached your limit. There's a hold on your account until the balance is paid off."

Eli's pulse hopscotched through his veins. That couldn't possibly be right. The Cross men might be way better farmers than number crunchers, but no way would they have missed something as big as paying off their co-op tab.

Before Eli could say so, though, Greyson butted in with a snort. "Jesus, Cross. Haven't you got anyone over there at that two-bit operation to run your books for you?"

"Shut up, Greyson." The adrenaline pumping through Eli's body was putting a hard limit on his creativity, but at least the directive got his point across.

Unfortunately, Greyson didn't budge, his dark eyes turning junk-yard-dog mean as he narrowed them on Eli. "Who's gonna make me? You?"

Billy's stare went wide, moving back and forth between Eli and Greyson as if he were watching a testosterone-soaked tennis match, and Eli struggled to pull a breath past his tightening lungs. His laid-back attitude only stretched so far. He needed to get Greyson out of his face so he could fix the misunderstanding with Billy, get the baling twine he'd errand-boyed himself out here for, and get the hell out of Dodge before the last of his patience hit the skids.

Knotting his arms over his chest, Eli fixed Greyson with the most bored up-and-down he could possibly muster. "Your village called. They're missing their idiot, so why don't you run along home."

"That's rich, coming from someone who can't even keep his books straight." Greyson paused to raise one black brow. "Or is it more than just the books? Don't tell me there's trouble in paradise over there at precious Cross Creek Farm."

The words made a direct hit in the center of Eli's sternum. "Everything's fine at Cross Creek," he snapped.

But dammit, the response came out too sharp and too fast, and for as big of a dick as Greyson Whittaker was, he sadly wasn't stupid. "Bullshit."

"What did you say?" Eli asked, his heart thundering in his ears as he clung to the last thin thread of his control.

"I said bullshit." Greyson took just enough of a step forward over the linoleum to back up the taunt in his voice. "I see what everyone else around here sees. The crap weather might be affecting all of us, but with the way you Cross boys have been droppin' like flies and can't pay your bills now on top of it . . . I'm calling you out. I think your business is going under."

Eli's composure vanished in a white-hot instant, all the tension of the day, the week—hell, the entire fucking season—cranking his jaw and turning his hands into fists. He was in Greyson's dance space before his brain had fully registered the movement of his legs, but not even the sight of Billy's shock in his peripheral vision or the fact that Greyson actually met him halfway for a chest bump could make him stand down.

"You're as dumb as you look," Eli bit out, each syllable more bitter than the last.

"Put your money where your mouth is and prove it, asshole."

Shock replaced the tiniest bit of the anger pulsing through Eli's veins, and Greyson took full advantage of the pause to tack on, "I'll bet you all the money on that tab of yours that Whittaker Hollow brings in more business than Cross Creek between now and Fall Fling."

Whoa. The challenge was a hell of a step up from their normal shit slinging. Millhaven's town-wide harvest celebration was second only to the Watermelon Festival that kicked off the summer season, and Eli's old man had five grand on the farm's line of credit. But far be it for him to balk if Greyson wanted to let his attitude write the check that would pay it off.

Still . . . "Like I'm going to trust you to give up honest numbers," Eli said. Integrity had never been Greyson's strong suit, and the Whittakers had been trying to best Cross Creek Farm for frigging decades. No way would Greyson take the honesty path if he thought that was in his reach. Which it wasn't, but—

"My mom could be the judge," Billy offered. "She does both y'all's business taxes anyway, right?"

Both Eli and Greyson turned to look at the guy, whose mother was the only accountant in Millhaven.

"Yeah," they said simultaneously.

Billy nodded, his head moving up and down on his beefy neck. "So she could figure out which farm brings in more revenue over the next four weeks without disclosing any business details, and she's impartial."

"Perfect," Greyson drawled, squaring his shoulders and settling himself right back in Eli's face. "So what do you say, Cross? Are you ready to prove once and for all which one of us has the better farm?"

Adrenaline, impulse, and something a whole lot deeper that Eli couldn't name pushed the words out of his mouth before he could think twice.

"Hope you've been saving your pennies, Whittaker, because I'm about to take them. You've got yourself a deal."

CHAPTER TWO

Scarlett Edwards-Stewart needed a shower. No, check that. What she really needed was a steamy, two-hour bubble bath followed by an equally long massage and enough sleep to make people wonder whether she was still breathing. She might love her job the way most people loved spouses or sports teams or anything else that could be invested in with a sheer ton of energy, sweat, and devotion, but even she had physical limits. Spending her day trekking through three different international airports and twice as many time zones with thirty pounds of photo gear slung over each shoulder after three weeks of nonstop of work?

Apparently her ticket to finding them. At least temporarily.

She lowered the duffel bag she'd been living out of for the better part of the month to the threshold of her Upper East Side apartment, following it with the gear case holding her lenses, rechargeable batteries, and portable tripods. Keeping the well-padded, bright-red bag holding her primary camera (aka Baby) on her hip, Scarlett moved through her living room, her five-inch platform wedges clack-clacking against the hardwood floors as she tugged open the blinds to reveal the gorgeous New York City skyline.

"There. That's better." She grinned. Three weeks in Europe—first to shoot a photo documentary in Spain, then to cover the last two legs of the Tour de France before finishing up with a weeklong independent film festival in which an A-list Hollywood star was making his producing debut—had made her miss the city. Of course, as soon as Scarlett spent a week, maybe two, in the Big Apple, she'd be antsy to get up and go someplace else. That was the best thing about being a photographer, really.

There were great images all over the world just waiting for her to frame them up and capture them forever. Bright, brilliant colors. Nuances of black and white. Snapshots hidden in plain sight, some existing for milliseconds, some outlasting time itself, each one waiting to be seen.

All she had to do was hit the ends of the earth to uncover them.

Scarlett placed her camera bag gently on one end of the walnut dining table that doubled as her desk space whenever she was in New York. Even though this was the only apartment she kept on a permanent basis, calling it "home" never felt quite right since she was gone more often than not. Yes, her adoptive dads still lived in New York, and they'd raised her happily in their Brooklyn brownstone, less than ten miles from the spot where she currently stood. But as far as Scarlett was concerned, the concept of a place to settle down in and call home was more like a unicorn than anything else.

It might be magical for some people, but for her? It was just a great, big, sparkly myth.

Her cell phone sounded off in a buzz-and-chime combo that sent her heartbeat into the ozone layer and her awareness on a straight shot back to reality. Reaching into the back pocket of her vintage 501s, she slid her iPhone into her palm, a fast and easy smile lifting the edges of her mouth at the sight of the name on the caller ID.

"Mal!" Of course, her best friend's built-in sonar would be pinging like mad now that Scarlett was back on New York soil.

"I wasn't sure if you'd be on the ground yet," Mallory said, her voice oddly muffled.

A thread of guilt stabbed through Scarlett's belly. Dammit, she should've known Mallory would be worried about her flying. Not even twenty-one years could erase the fact that her best friend's parents had been killed in a plane crash. God, Scarlett could still remember how sad and scared Mallory had been that first night in foster care.

"I'm so sorry I didn't text you when my flight landed. Customs took forever, and they went over every last piece of my gear." Thankfully, Scarlett had the whole hand-check-the-bags, these-are-my-credentials thing down to an art form. "But yes, I landed safe and sound about ninety minutes ago, and you have great timing because I literally just walked into to my apartment. So what's up? Did I miss anything juicy in the last three weeks of city life?"

Mallory paused. "Oh, you know. Not too much."

Nope. Sadly for Mallory, Scarlett had a titanium-reinforced bullshit meter, and right now, the thing was going apeshit. "What's the matter?"

"Nothing, really."

"What is this, Opposite Day? We're not nine anymore. Spill it, Parsons."

"Fine. I . . . I'm just having a little trouble at work," Mallory started. But she didn't elaborate, and jeez, what *was* that sound in her voice?

"Trouble at work," Scarlett repeated gently. Mallory ran an online food magazine that, while relatively small, was the product of her heart and soul and more than half a decade's worth of sleeves-rolled-up effort. "Okay. So on a scale of ice cream to chick flick movie marathon, how bad is it?"

Mallory's exhale wobbled over the phone line. "Tequila." Pause. "Top-shelf. Bottomless glass."

"Holy shit." Scarlett's pulse tripped in her veins, and she pulled a chair from beneath her dining table-slash-desk, planting herself over the bright-turquoise-and-gold cushion. "Talk to me, Mal."

Thankfully, the prompt was all her best friend needed. "Things have been kind of bumpy at *FoodE* for the last four or five months."

"Four or five months?" Scarlett pressed her teeth into her bottom lip, too late. But subtlety had never been one of her strong suits, so screw it. She added, "Why didn't you say anything?"

"At first, I thought it was just a normal slowdown in the market. You know how publishing is," Mallory said.

Although Scarlett was on a different side of things as a freelance photographer, she definitely did. The publishing world had more ups and downs than a carnival roller coaster on crack. "Being a smaller publication in a sea of online magazines *is* tough," she admitted. "But *FoodE* has such a great vibe with the whole farm-to-table focus."

"Yeah, but unfortunately it's not entirely unique," Mallory sighed. "A lot of the big-name publications have caught on to the fact that people don't just want a meal, they want a food experience. There's a ton of competition. With all these other magazines upping their emphasis on digital distribution and online subscriptions lately, we've really been struggling for visibility."

Realization trickled into Scarlett's brain, her shoulders growing heavy against the back of her dining room chair. "And lower visibility means less advertising dollars." *Dammit.* Those dollars were a huge part of how Mallory's business stayed afloat, from covering her costs to paying salaries—including her own.

"Exactly. I've cut every corner I can think of, but our site hits are at an all-time low, and our subscriptions are even worse. *FoodE* is hemorrhaging money. My reserves are as shot as my nerves." Mallory grew quiet, to the point that Scarlett wondered whether the call had dropped. But then her friend whispered, "I lost my last big advertising client about an hour ago. Without a high-impact, high-velocity spread to start generating major buzz ASAP, I don't think I'll be able to stay in business."

Scarlett's heart pitched against her rib cage, but oh no. *Hell* no. No way was she going to sit by and let her best friend's business go under. Not without one hell of a knock-down-drag-out.

"Well, I guess that leaves us with only one option," she said. "We need to find you a blockbuster."

Mallory's laugh was all disbelief. "Are you kidding? No big-name locales are going to want to waste their time hosting a dying magazine for a layout article. In fact, the only nibble of interest I've had in weeks is from a farm in the foothills of the Virginia Shenandoah. I don't even think the town has a mapdot. Truly"—Mallory broke off, her voice wavering in earnest now—"I have no idea how to fix this."

An idea formed in Scarlett's head, brash and bold and absolutely perfect. "Send me."

"Send you where?" Mallory asked, taking a full three seconds to connect the dots before she gasped. "To the mapdot? Scarlett, that's crazysauce!"

"Maybe," Scarlett agreed. "But we're still going to do it. This farm. What's it called?"

"Cross Creek."

"Right." The idea snowballed in her head, gaining both speed and momentum. "They reached out to you for coverage, didn't they?"

"Yeah. Their business manager, Emerson . . ." Mallory paused, the soft tap-tap-tap of laptop keys clicking on the other end of the phone. "Got it! Emerson Montgomery. She and one of the farm's operators, Hunter Cross, sent me an e-mail about a week ago asking if I'd like to visit to write an article. I'd put off answering because I didn't know if I could pay a freelancer to cover the story. Now I know I can't."

"But you checked the place out, right? And it's a location you'd normally feature." Although Scarlett hated to admit it, no matter how hard the two of them worked, if the farm didn't mesh with *FoodE*'s theme, all the articles on the planet wouldn't garner interest.

But Malory said, "Yeah. They've got seven hundred and fifty acres of combined agriculture, with both produce and livestock. It's the biggest family-run farm in the area, and they're transitioning to a lot of specialty produce and ecologically conscious farming. To be honest, between that and the agritourism market they're trying to build on, there's probably enough subject matter there for an entire series of articles."

Eeeeeeven better. "Email them back and tell them today is their lucky day. You're not going to do *an* article. You're going to do *bunches* of them."

"Bunches of them." Doubt and disbelief clung to Mallory's answer, but Scarlett met both head-on.

"You just said there's a ton there. Why not go big? I can go down to the farm and shoot a series of photos, do the hands-on fact gathering and interviews, and send it all to you. Then you can turn the information into articles, recipes—the sky's the limit, really." Scarlett popped to her feet, pacing out the excitement thrumming through her veins. "Ooooh! You said people want the whole experience, right? If this is a family-run place, why not play up the personal-interest angle along with the food? I could do an immersion-type thing with video clips if you want. You know, to give a real-life depiction of what true, hands-on, farm-to-table looks like, but with a reality TV–style twist. It's freaking click fodder."

"People *do* love video," Mallory said slowly. "It gives a stronger sense of personal connection, and I bet our readers would love to see the people behind the process. But still, we're talking about weeks to shoot something like this, and not one or two. I couldn't possibly ask you to cover this story. I don't even know how I'd pay you."

Scarlett shook her head even though Mallory couldn't see the gesture. "I don't want you to pay me."

"Um. Spoiler alert. You're one of the most in-demand photographers on the East Coast. Possibly in the entire United States. Since when do you work pro bono?"

"Since now. Look, if it makes you feel any better, you can consider it an advance for when *FoodE* becomes a household name."

Scarlett paced her way to the foyer, sending a glance from her duffel to the view of the city, where the sun was just beginning to set behind a backdrop of brick and glass. Okay, so the turnaround time was a little bit tight, but she wasn't exactly a stranger to living out of her duffel. She didn't have anything set in stone on her schedule for another six weeks—hello, Brazil—plus, she'd covered everything from end zones to war zones. Other than having to tough out not having a Starbucks on every corner and the fact that her hosts were likely to count overalls as a positive fashion statement, how hard could an extended shoot and some videos at a farm be, for God's sake?

Mallory loved her online magazine, and Scarlett loved Mallory. Her best friend had always been there for her. Even when no one else had.

And now Scarlett was going to return the favor.

"Mal," she said softly. "I haven't taken more than a week off total in the last two years. I have the time and the ability to cover this story for you, and I really want to help. So what do you say?"

For a heartbeat, then another, then a dozen more, Mallory said nothing, and Scarlett's gut filled with unease.

"Mallory—"

"Okay." Mallory's answer collided with Scarlett's, and the single word was enough to send an ear-to-ear grin over Scarlett's face. "I'll send you to the farm," Mallory said. "But *only* if you agree to let me pay you as soon as I'm able."

"Done!" Scarlett could fight that battle when they got to it. "Just give me twelve hours to do some laundry and a little research. I can be on the road tomorrow."

"You want to go so soon? Tomorrow's Saturday."

But Scarlett just laughed. "You need a blockbuster ASAP. There's no time like the present to get you one."

CHAPTER THREE

Eli walked down the aisle in the horse barn with an apple in one hand and a plastic gallon jug of water in the other. Compared with yesterday evening's near brawl with his brother and mouthy throwdown with Greyson freaking Whittaker, today had been pretty quiet, although a large part of that was probably owed to the fact that Owen, their old man, and two of their farmhands had left for the farmers' market in Camden Valley at the whip-crack of dawn. The Cross men usually rotated farmers' market duty between among the four of them, but Owen had been so gung ho about specialty produce lately that he'd been taking Eli's turn more often than not. *I just want to keep my finger on the pulse of the competition and make sure we're offering the very best of the best,* had been the excuse du jour.

Of course, while Eli might be a lot of things, a dumbass wasn't one of them. He heard the translation as loud and clear as the Fourth of July fireworks over Willow Park.

I don't trust you to know or care about farming trends the way the rest of us do.

Eli shook his head, loosening the twinge of tension that went with the thought. Owen's disdain wasn't exactly a news flash, and in truth, Eli was more fine than not with taking a pass on the farmers' market. It allowed him a whole hour to write on Saturday mornings; plus, he was used to odds-and-ends duty around Cross Creek. No sense in thumbing his nose at what worked.

Speaking of which. He brought his boots to a stop on the hard-packed dirt floor in front of the horse barn's last—and biggest—stall, sending his gaze over the one animal in the entire structure who, ironically, wasn't a horse.

"Hey, pretty girl," Eli said, the sight of Clarabelle, his fourteen-year-old Jersey brown cow, making the corners of his mouth edge up into a grin. "Sorry it took so long for me to get to you today. I've been playing catch-up since I *got* up."

He stepped into the stall and offered up part of the apple he'd halved before heading down here, the muscles in his back throbbing with the threat of a labor strike. He'd run the gamut with scut work today, from mending fences in the east fields to hauling hay down to the back half of the farm where they kept their cattle, to site-mapping the corn maze they'd be putting together in the next couple of weeks as part of the agritourism side of their business, complete with apple and pumpkin picking as the weather turned. While he put in the work because he had to, the nine hours of manual labor in the dropdown heat was putting his body to the test.

The feeling of unease that had been sinking hooks in his gut all too easily lately? Definitely wasn't doing him any favors in the chill department, either. All the Shakespeare in the galaxy couldn't change the fact that sooner or later, this roller-coaster ride with Owen was going to go off the rails.

And when it did, Eli had no idea where he'd be left standing.

The thought brought his chin up with a snap, his awkward laugh bouncing through the dusty, musty space of the horse barn. Damn, this heat must really be getting to him if he was getting all torqued up over yet another stupid fight with his brother. He needed to shake it off and cover it up with a cocky smile and an even cockier "whatever" just like he always did so he could get back to normal.

Blowing out a breath, Eli rolled his aching shoulders beneath his T-shirt. His muscles began to loosen as he fed Clarabelle the other half of the apple, double-checking to make sure she had enough feed and clean hay before pouring some of the water over her back.

"Feels good, huh?" he asked, his grin growing in both size and intensity when Clarabelle chuffed in reply. "I know. It's hell-hot out here." He paused to rub the cool water into the silky hair on Clarabelle's back and sides, inhaling the earthy, slightly sweet scents of fresh hay and sunbaked barn boards. "That's August for ya. But don't worry. I've got you covered."

Eli continued Clarabelle's rubdown, which was no small feat seeing as how the old girl was pushing twelve hundred pounds. He'd no sooner upended the last of the water over her butterscotch-colored back than the two-way radio clipped to the waistband of his Levi's let out a staticky crackle.

"Eli, what's your location?" Hunter's normally laid-back voice carried a thread of seriousness that slid right between Eli's ribs.

"Just finished up in the horse barn. Everything alright?" His pulse picked up the pace against his throat. God, ever since their father had gone and had that scare with heat exhaustion, every call on the two-way gave Eli the fucking shakes.

"Yeah," Hunter said slowly, allowing Eli to let go of the breath that had been trapped in his lungs. "But if you're done in the barn, can you come on up to the main house?"

Eli stuck his head out of Clarabelle's stall, examining the angle of the sun through the barn's double-wide entryway. While there was no such thing as a Saturday off in the busy season, they usually managed to start early and finish early, giving all four men the opportunity to carry on the Cross family tradition of a weekly supper together. It was still a little early to chow down, but Hunter probably just wanted a hand in the kitchen to prep.

"Roger that," Eli said into the two-way. "I'll see you in a few."

Hooking the radio back over the faded denim at his hip, he stepped out of Clarabelle's stall, triple-checking the latch on the chest-high swinging door before heading toward the exit at the far end of the barn. Although the sun was starting to drop lower in the cloudless blue sky, the heat still hit him like a wrecking ball gone bad, and by the time he'd finished the five-minute walk to the white, two-story Colonial that served as his father's residence and Cross Creek's central hub, he'd broken his four hundredth sweat of the day.

Eli turned the corner from the side of the house, a pop of surprise working its way up his spine as he caught sight of his brother standing on the wide-planked porch steps.

"Oh, hey, Hunt. Did you want some help getting some stuff together for dinner, or . . ."

The rest of Eli's question met a quick end in his throat as he realized both Owen *and* their father stood two steps up on either side of Hunter, and when the hell had they even gotten back from Camden Valley?

More importantly, why did Owen look like that vein in his forehead was about to go ground zero?

As usual, his brother didn't dispense with any pleasantries. "You bet Greyson Whittaker five *thousand* dollars we'd bring in more revenue than Whittaker Hollow by Fall Fling? Are you out of your fucking *mind*?"

Eli blinked, his brain tilting in an effort to catch up with Owen's obvious anger. "Who told you that?" Christ, that stupid wager wasn't even twenty-four hours old, and not that big a deal, to boot.

"Well, let's see." Owen lifted a hand to start ticking off his list, finger by finger. "Daisy Halstead was first, followed by Harley Martin and Mrs. Ellersby and—oh, right. Can't forget Moonpie Porter. By about noon, I'm pretty sure every damned vendor at the farmers' market—along with more than half the regular patrons from both Millhaven and Camden Valley—had heard all the gory details, because guess what? Amber Cassidy posted them all over her Facebook page. At this point,

I'd be shocked if there's anyone left in the county who doesn't know all about this high-dollar, higher-profile bet you seem to have made . . . except for me and Hunter and Dad."

Oh. Shit.

Eli's gut dropped like a stone in still water before tightening in defense. "Greyson was being a total dick yesterday at the co-op, giving me a raft of crap because we'd maxed our line of credit without paying the balance."

"What?" Hunter asked, his brown brows winging upward. "I dropped that payment off yesterday morning."

"Yeah, well I didn't know that when Greyson was all up in my grill, jawing about how Cross Creek was going under." Of course, getting to the bottom of the payment mix-up had been Item Number One on Eli's to-do list this morning. Not that knowing there'd been a lag in processing the payment helped him now. "Anyway, *he's* the one who popped off with the bet. Not me."

"But you accepted," Owen said, the words slipping between his teeth as he stood straighter on the porch boards. "Jesus, Eli. You and Greyson have been at each other since grade school. How could you take that kind of bait *again*?"

Anger flashed, hot and reckless in his chest. "Right. Because I'm sure if Greyson had been in your face, mouthing off at you with a bunch of horse shit about how Whittaker Hollow's so much better than Cross Creek, you'd have given him your prettiest smile and told him to have a right nice day."

"No, but I damn sure wouldn't have bet him our entire co-op tab that we'd do more business than him, either!"

Eli fought the urge to roll his eyes, choosing instead to shoot a glance at their old man. He stood a half step behind Owen, his expression as readable as the Great Wall of China as he took in the argument wordlessly, per usual. Their father was the sort of man who watched and listened about four times as much as he spoke. But whether he was waiting for Owen to get all the pissiness out of his system before stepping in to mediate or biding his time to dish out his own verbal ass-whupping, Eli couldn't quite be sure, so he dialed up a cover-everything-including-your-ass smile and returned his attention to his brothers.

"Look, this isn't that big of a deal. Greyson and I talk smack all the time." Okay, so this particular brand of shit slinging was a pretty amped-up version of the norm, but still. This bet was hardly anything to shit crab apples over.

Hunter crossed his arms over the front of his T-shirt, the frown taking over every feature on his stubbled face marking his disagreement. "This hardly sounds like a little smack talk, E. You really bet him the whole five grand we'd bring in more revenue?"

"What was I supposed to do?" Eli asked, incredulous. "Not defend the farm?"

Hunter tipped his head in a nonverbal *okay, decent point.* "Still. You've got to admit, taking a bet that big when business has been iffy at best? In front of Billy Masterson? That was a pretty dumb-shit move."

"Wait . . ." The sweat trickling between Eli's shoulder blades grew cold as realization slammed into him without remorse. "You're seriously going to side with Owen on this? Are you kidding me? It's just a stupid bet!"

"I'm not siding with anybody," Hunter answered, although his voice held an edge that sure said otherwise. "All I'm saying is—"

"That you're siding with him," Eli snapped past the hammer of his heartbeat. Un-be-fucking-lievable.

But funny, Hunter had no problem snapping right back. "I'm not *siding* with anyone, you ass. But we've had our backs in the corner all damn year, fighting to get out, and Emerson's been workin' real hard on getting us right side up with our marketing. So, yeah. You making a stupid, trash-talking, potentially expensive-as-shit bet that puts all those long, hard hours in jeopardy? I'm not doing fucking cartwheels, Eli."

The mention of Hunter's girlfriend, who happened to be one of the nicest people going, and, oh by the way, also just happened to have multiple sclerosis but helped them out with PR in her spare time anyway, tagged Eli right in the solar plexus. "It was just a bunch of lip service, Hunt. What's the big deal?"

"The big deal?" Owen repeated, his voice pinching in disbelief. "First of all, this bet is bound to churn up no less than ten tons of drama and gossip, none of which will have anything to do with what matters—namely, farming. It's a public-relations nightmare."

Okay, so Millhaven was small, and people around here tended to live in each other's pockets more often than not. Still . . . "Come on. Don't you think you're overreacting just a little bit?" Eli asked.

But Owen barreled right on over his protest, so, yeah, guess that was a solid *no*. "Secondly, there's the money. I'm assuming you don't have five grand tucked away to cover the tab of your runaway mouth."

The temptation to remind his brother what happened to people who made assumptions burned brightly on Eli's tongue. But since he couldn't exactly 'fess up to the fact that he'd funneled damn near every dime of his savings into secretly getting his undergraduate degree online in a field that had nothing to do with their family business, he held back on the urge to let the insult fly. "No. I don't have the five grand."

"Right," Owen barreled on. "Another thing you don't have is any idea what sort of business Whittaker Hollow has been doing this season. For all we know, between their local produce contracts, the business they bring in with the farmers' market and their roadside stands, plus their pick-your-own, they could be out-earning us already."

Eli let out a snort. At least this part was a no-brainer. "Whittaker Hollow is over a hundred acres smaller than Cross Creek, and our roadside stands have always been better than theirs. Plus, they've been dealing with the same terrible weather we have."

"But not the same staffing setbacks," Hunter interjected.

"Or the same soil compositions and planting ratios," Owen added.

"*Or* the same field rotations," Hunter said, and something deep in Eli's belly snapped in two.

"For fuck's sake! Can I get you some pom-poms to go with that? Since when did you two become Whittaker Hollow's biggest cheerleaders?"

"Since your common sense went on a complete goddamn walkabout, that's when!" Owen jammed his hands over his denim-covered hips. "This isn't something you can fix with a cocky smile and that half-assed attitude of yours. Christ, Eli. When are you going to get your head out of your ass and use the thing for actual thinking?"

The words sent Eli's blood racing even faster through his veins, prompting him to take a swift step forward over the stone pavers leading up to the porch.

"I was thinking just fine—"

"You *never* think—"

"It *was* a stupid move, Eli—"

"Oh, screw *both* of you—"

"That's enough!"

Their father's voice cracked through all three arguments, his boots thumping over the porch boards as he descended the stairs to spear Eli and both of his brothers with a steely stare chock-full of *shut up and listen*. "All this bickering ain't gonna change the fact that Eli made the bet and everyone in town knows about it."

Eli scraped for a deep breath before meeting his father's gaze head-on. "I thought Greyson was just being Greyson." God, the guy was such a douche canoe! He'd probably had all that crap preloaded and ready to launch the second Eli had walked into the damned co-op. "I didn't know Billy Masterson would flap his gums so hard, or that the bet would turn into such a production."

"Hate to say so, son, but that don't change the fact that it did. The money part is bad enough." His father paused, his wince sending a fresh flare of unease through Eli's gut. "But your brothers are right. This bet is a bigger deal than you bargained for. Putting a good spin on it with the gossips in town is gonna be a tough row to hoe."

"Not when we win," Eli pointed out. That'd earn them bragging rights until pretty much the end of time. Slam, meet dunk.

"And what if we don't?"

Shock forced Eli's feet into a step back. "What?"

A small, irony-laden smile moved over his father's sun-weathered face. "I'm not sayin' I don't think Cross Creek is the better farm. But that's not what you bet Greyson, now is it?"

Eli's pulse stuttered, and his words followed suit. "No. I, ah . . ." Shit. *Shit*. "No."

"Truth is, as far as this bet goes, we *don't* know what we're up against," his father said. "We don't know what kind of resources the Whittakers have got, and we don't know how they're planning to use 'em for the final harvest. Yes, every farm in the county has had to deal with the same weather, but this is the hardest season Cross Creek has seen in decades. Losing a bet like this, with odds we can't predict, when we're already strugglin'? That could hurt more than the win would help."

Ah hell. "I was just trying to stick up for Cross Creek," Eli said, his shoulders growing heavy as his father's words sank in, nice and deep. "I didn't think of things that way."

His old man lifted a hand, presumably to defuse the statement Owen looked to be working up. And thank God for that, because seriously, Eli'd had enough of Saint Owen to last till he was 104.

"Don't reckon you did. This bet still has us in a jam, though, and it ain't a small one."

Ever the problem solver, Hunter said, "Okay, Pop. So how do we fix it?"

"Well." Their father swung his gaze from Hunter to Eli, not even squinting in the intense late-afternoon sunlight. "Come hell or high tide, I guess we're gonna have to win us a bet."

Eli ran a palm over his crew cut, letting his hand rest on the back of his neck. Okay, so maybe this bet had gotten bigger than he'd expected, and definitely he was going to have to work his boots into the ground for the next four weeks in order to be sure they won. But he couldn't let Greyson Whittaker get the last word. Cross Creek was the better farm.

He owed it to his old man to do whatever it took to prove that.

"Okay," Eli said, punctuating the word with a nod as he nailed his resolve into place. "Our contracts with suppliers are already set, so we're going to have to do a lot of local business with our farm stands and the agritourism stuff, like pick-your-own, in order to win. I guess we'll need a strategy to bring as many people out here as possible between now and Fall Fling."

"You think?" Owen sent his gray stare skyward. "You're going to have to come up with something more than that. Hunter and I have been strategizing all summer. Yeah, we're bouncing back a little with things like the farmers' market, but rebuilding after a bad season takes time."

"Unless some kind of miracle falls into your lap," Hunter pointed out, and great—they were already reduced to hoping for miracles.

Frustration sent a flare of heat up the back of Eli's neck. "I was kinda hoping for something tangible."

The sound Owen let out was part sarcasm, part snort. "Probably you should've thought of that before opening your yap."

"I'm trying to figure out a way to fix this," Eli grated. But before he could tack on the "you great big freaking jackass" that Owen truly deserved, he was interrupted by the clatter of footsteps on the porch boards and a familiar, feminine voice loaded with excitement.

"There you all are!" Emerson broke into a grin, her curl-filled ponytail swishing over the shoulder of her pale-pink top as she descended the porch steps to meet the four of them on the pavers with their family's black-and-white mutt, Lucy, hot on her heels. "You'll never believe this! I'm not even sure *I* believe it yet, but I . . ." She trailed off suddenly, her gaze moving from Owen to Eli to their father before settling in on Hunter's and going wide. "Seem to be totally interrupting. I apologize."

"No." Hunter speared both Eli and Owen with warning stares that proved that while he might be laid back about nearly everything else, he was 100 percent fierce when it came to Emerson. "We could use a break in the conversation. What's up?"

The tiny "V" between her coppery brows broadcast her doubt at Hunter's claim, but then her excitement reappeared to cancel it out. "I just got off the phone with Mallory Parsons."

Mallory Parsons, Mallory Parsons, Mallory... Eli searched his mental batch files, all to the tune of nada.

Fortunately, Hunter didn't come up so empty. "The editor of that online food magazine based in New York City?"

"That's her!" Emerson said gleefully. "She was really enthusiastic about our invitation to visit the farm for an article."

All at once, the dots connected in Eli's head with a snap. Hunter and Emerson had talked about reaching out to a bunch of newspapers and magazines when they'd done their business rundown over Saturday supper a couple of weeks ago. At the time, Eli had thought the idea had been a Hail Mary with a whole lot of long shot on top, especially given how tough it was to get so much as a toe in the door with most publications. That fact was the first thing he'd learned when earning his degree in journalism . . . not that he could fork over *that* little gem.

Apparently, he'd have done well to remember that tough wasn't synonymous with impossible. "So does this woman want to publish an article featuring Cross Creek?"

Emerson's smile went for broke. "Even better. She wants to publish a whole series of them!"

"Are you serious?" Owen asked, clearly as gobsmacked as the rest of them.

"As a sledgehammer." Emerson paused to cross her forefinger over her heart before continuing. "So Mallory's online magazine is called *FoodE*—"

"Foodie?" Eli wrinkled his nose. It sounded a little fancy for their brand of farming. And by "a little," he really meant "a fuck-ton."

"Yes. It's pronounced 'foodie,' but she spells it f-o-o-d-capital E," Emerson said, and ugh, even better. "Anyway, she features a lot of organic food with a big focus on farm-to-table cooking and dining. Environmental sustainability, chic cuisine—"

"Chic what?" This was getting weirder by the second.

Emerson let out a laugh that was all humor. "Chic cuisine," she repeated, not that it made any more sense the second time around. "It's basically another way of saying 'trendy food.'"

Now it was Eli's turn to laugh, only his emerged with a heavy layer of doubt. "Cross Creek is hardly trendy." Or chic, but hell if he could push the froufrou word past his lips.

"I don't know," Emerson politely disagreed. "There's an increasing demand for good, natural, straight-from-the-earth food in a lot of consumer markets now. Mallory thought a lot of the specialty produce you've been growing in the greenhouses, plus some of the newer farming methods you've started to employ to make Cross Creek more eco-friendly, were all a great fit for an extended series of magazine features, including personal-interest pieces and online video blogs. Four weeks' worth, to be exact."

Owen's jaw dropped, and funny, Eli knew just how his brother felt. "She wants to come here all the way from New York City to feature the farm on her site for four weeks?"

"She does! Well, her photographer does," Emerson said. "Mallory has to stay in New York to run the magazine, but her photographer is going to work with us on this end to gather all the information and take the photos and videos, then Mallory will use the information to write the articles and publish them in biweekly installments. But that's not even the best part!" Emerson paused to wave her hands in another burst of excitement, and good Christ. How could there be more?

"Okay," Hunter prompted, and Emerson took the one-word lead and ran.

"Mallory wants to publish everything with as little lag time as possible, so Cross Creek will start getting online exposure almost immediately. In fact, she said our features would be her number-one priority."

"Starting when?" Hunter asked, and Emerson's smile faltered, her sandal scraping over the sun-warmed stone beneath it as she shifted her weight.

"So that's the only catch. I guess she tried to call my cell a couple of times today, but you know how service is around here." Emerson paused to make a face that looked as if she'd taken a big ol' bite out of a lemon, and yeah, that pretty much summed up the quality of cellular service in Millhaven. "We played a bit of phone tag before finally connecting just now, and her photographer is really excited to go ahead and get started on the project. Apparently, she's one of the most well-known photographers in the Northeast."

"Sounds pretty highbrow." Eli looked down at his very favorite pair of Levi's, which were currently streaked with dirt and likely smelled like the horse barn.

Nothing about this could end well.

"Well, she's definitely ambitious," Emerson ventured. "Also, she's, ah. Going to be here soon. Tonight, actually."

Eli exhaled in a hard burst of you've-got-to-be-kidding-me. *"Tonight?"*

Emerson nodded, shifting her gaze from Eli to his father. "I'm sorry, Mr. Cross. I know the short notice isn't ideal. But landing a four-week magazine spread with a photographer of this caliber is like winning the lottery. I was worried if I said we needed more time, Mallory would reconsider."

"No, no. You did the right thing, telling her to come on out now, darlin'."

His old man's words—coupled with the pair of nods Owen and Eli were giving up—sent Eli's shock straight over the line into disbelief.

"You want to let some fancy-pants photographer from New York City come in here and have her way with Cross Creek for an entire month while we do the final harvest of the season?" Eli asked.

Hunter shot Eli a look that clearly questioned his sanity. "If it'll get us the exposure we need to get business booming? In a word, yes."

Still, Eli was unconvinced. "Millhaven's hardly a luxury destination. Where on earth will this woman even stay?" The closest lodgings that didn't have the words "Motel" or "Economy" attached to them were a good hour and a half away in Lockridge, for cripes' sake.

"I still have three months left on my lease at the Twin Pines," Emerson said, half-question, half-offer. "All my personal stuff is at the cottage now that I've moved in with Hunter, but the apartment is mostly furnished. You're welcome to use it."

The Twin Pines was the only apartment complex in Millhaven, although calling the place a "complex" was a gift and a half. It was more like thirty-two units better suited for Matchbox cars than people. Eli knew, because he'd lived there for a decade.

"That's awful kind of you, Emerson," Owen said. Turning to look at Eli, he added, "Anything else you wanted to argue, here?"

"I'm not trying to argue," Eli . . . well, argued. But come on. They might need a strategy for bringing in business, but a photographer they'd never even met, from the largest city on the Eastern Seaboard, who wanted to get all up in their business with intrusive photo sessions and video blogs? No fucking thank you. Especially not now that they'd be busting their asses times ten to get ahead of this bet.

Eli shook his head to nail down the thought. "All I'm sayin' is maybe we should think this photographer thing through. What if she doesn't even like the place?"

"What's not to like?" Owen asked, his genuine confusion at the question and Hunter's expression that matched it sending a hard twist through Eli's gut. Of course, not wanting to spend forever and ever, amen on the farm had never occurred to either of them. But Lord knew a woman who was used to enjoying her "chic cuisine" in the concrete jungle was going to stick out a country mile around Millhaven. Shit, he gave her three days—four, tops—before she took off running.

But hell if that opinion didn't make Eli the odd man out at Cross Creek yet again, so the best thing to do—the only thing, really—was the thing he did best.

Deflect. Slap on a cocky grin. And forget about it.

Eli lifted his hands, forcing his shoulders into a shrug and his mouth into a smile even though both moves took more than a little effort. "Whatever y'all say. Far be it for me to step in the way if you think hosting this photographer will help bump up business."

"Glad you feel that way," his father said, pinning him with a no-bullshit stare. "Because someone's going to have to show this woman around the place. Really sell her on Cross Creek."

Unease collided with the shock pumping through Eli's veins. No way. No *way*. He might be the closest thing the farm had to an extra, but this was outer limits. "You want me to babysit the city girl?"

"No." His old man's tone turned the answer into a warning. "You ain't gonna babysit anybody. You're going to work up all that charm of yours and be a good host."

"For a month." God, it was the ultimate damned grunt chore.

"You'll have plenty to do around here besides," his father said, tipping his head toward the fields in the distance. "We've got our work cut out for us, and we need all the manpower we can scrape up to get us to Fall Fling. But you got us into this tangle, needing good PR. You're gonna be the one who gets us out."

"Pop," Owen started, clearly trying to choose his words with care. "Are you sure Eli's the best, ah, choice for this?"

Well *that* figured. But for once, Eli agreed with his oldest brother wholeheartedly. "Owen's right, Pop. He'd be way better at showing this woman the farm, and—"

"No." Their old man's tone brooked zero argument. "When that photographer arrives, anything she wants or needs is up to you, Eli. For the next four weeks, we'll all play host, but as far as these articles and all this video stuff goes? You're gonna make good and represent this farm. She's on *your* hip."

Eli's mouth burned from the weight of the protest welling up from his chest. In front of a camera was the last place he wanted or needed to be, and really, the irony of him being the face of the farm? Yeah, it would've been laughable if it didn't sting so bad. But *dammit*, with the way Hunter was nodding in agreement and the look of don't-even-think-about-it tacked to his old man's face, Eli would be shot down faster than a plastic target at the county fair if he let it loose.

Deflect. Slap on a cocky grin. And forget about it.

Letting out a slow exhale, he asked, "When's she supposed to get here, exactly?"

The words had no sooner slipped past his lips when a bright-yellow Volkswagen convertible came whipping up the dirt path leading to the front of the house, rap music blaring from the speakers and a tattooed platinum blonde caterwauling along at the top of her lungs.

CHAPTER FOUR

Several thoughts whizzed through Scarlett's brain upon pulling to a stop in front of the homey-looking white clapboard house at Cross Creek Farm, the first of which was that if there was a bright, bustling heart of civilization, she was as far from it as a girl could possibly get. Second of all, she sure hoped Mallory wanted a lot of pictures of corn, because Scarlett had just found the goddamn mother lode.

Thirdly . . . whoa. Where was the funeral?

Scarlett eyeballed the group of people gaping at her from the walkway in front of the farmhouse, grateful as hell for the Dolce & Gabbana aviator sunglasses covering half her face. An educated guess said the redheaded—and only—woman in the group was the business manager who Mallory had been trying to get ahold of this morning when Scarlett had packed the last of her camera equipment into the adorable convertible she'd grabbed from the car rental agency. The four men varied in age, one of them clearly the patriarch who ran the place, with the other three looking to clock in at about her age, if Scarlett had to guess. The website she'd scanned last night while clacking out some preliminary notes on her iPad had listed Tobias Cross's sons as the other operators of the farm, and yep, the three men currently giving her the wide-eyed, drop-jawed routine bore enough resemblance to one another to fit the bill.

Make that handsome, rugged, just-enough-muscles-to-make-a-girl-sit-up-and-take-notice-oh-hi resemblance.

And not one pair of overalls in the bunch.

"Right. Here goes nothing," Scarlett whispered, inhaling to counter the flush of warmth creeping over her cheeks and tugging a hand through her shag cut in an effort to tame the worst of the windblown look. Plastering a smile to her face, she hopped out of the Volkswagen, lifting her chin up high as she cut a path toward the spot where her not-so-welcoming committee stood at the bottom of the porch steps.

"Hi. I'm Scarlett. From *FoodE* magazine," she added, reaching out to shake the hand of the older man. God, the whole scene was straight-up Norman Rockwell, right down to the family dog sitting at the man's feet.

"Tobias Cross." His eyes traveled the length of the loose silver bangles and assorted bead bracelets stacked halfway up her forearm, pausing over the pop of dark-red and pink and green that made up the cherry-blossom tattoo etched across her nearly bare shoulder before landing on her face. "Sure is nice to meet you, ma'am."

Scarlett bit back her laugh as she shook the hand he'd extended, but only just. "Oh, wow, no. Scarlett is fine." She threw a quick glance at the rest of the group, who seemed to have traded in their shock for curiosity. Well, all except for the broody-looking guy with the dark-blond crew cut. *He* was giving her a double dose of you've-got-to-be-joking with those ocean-blue eyes of his.

Fine by her. She wasn't the one living in a frigging time warp. She hadn't been able to get a single bar of cell service for the last fifteen minutes of her drive, for God's sake. She didn't even want to get started on the fact that her last Starbucks sighting had been nearly an hour and a half ago. Where else was a girl supposed to get an iced coconut milk mocha macchiato?

You came here to do a job. Focus. Scarlett gestured to the fields around them, where despite the small breeze moving over the wide-open terrain, it had to be conservatively eleven billion degrees. "I have to admit, I wasn't expecting you to all be out here waiting," she said, and the redhead flushed for a second before recovering with a smile.

"Oh! Well, it wasn't quite intentional, but I'm glad we were here to meet you. I'm Emerson Montgomery. I spoke with Mallory on the phone just a little while ago."

Surprise worked a path up Scarlett's spine. Guess things really were a *lot* slower way out here in the sticks. "Ah. I thought Mallory would've been able to touch base with you this morning. I hope I'm not catching you all too unaware."

"Not at all," said the guy in the baseball hat standing next to Emerson, his nice-and-easy smile and handshake almost canceling out crew cut's small-but-definitely-there nod. "I'm Hunter Cross, and these are my brothers, Owen and Eli. We're happy to have you here at Cross Creek for the next four weeks to work on these articles."

The reminder of why she was here, of how important her purpose was, threw Scarlett's determination back into gear. "I'm excited to get the ball rolling. I'd love to go ahead and grab my camera so I can get some first impressions of the farm, if that's okay with you."

Owen's shocked stare followed her gesture toward the endless fields of green. "You want to get started right now?"

"Sure. I'm not really a sit-still kind of woman." The farm might be pretty and all, but she definitely wasn't here to vacay. Mallory needed the goods, the faster the better.

Emerson cleared her throat gently before giving up a small smile. "I think Owen's concern is that we haven't really been able to prepare anything for you to photograph just yet."

"Oh. *Oh*." Scarlett waved a hand through the ultra-humid air. "That's okay. This first round of photos would be for my frame of reference more than anything else. Anyway, what I'm really interested in is capturing Cross Creek authentically, so I'd like to immerse myself in day-to-day operations and interactions right along with you. As a result, most everything I shoot will be candid."

"Wait." Eli, aka Mr. Personality, leveled her with a tight frown. "So *we're* all going to be the main focus in these pictures and articles? Not the food or the farming?"

"Well, the articles are all going to include multiple aspects of farm life, but human-interest pieces tend to garner the highest reach. You do run the place, so yes. There's a large probability the five of you will end up in many of the shots and stories, and definitely in all the videos."

"So you basically want to turn us into an online reality TV show?"

Note to self: Mr. Personality might be hot, but he sure knew how to work the hell out of a scowl. Not to mention being unusually perceptive about her media angle. "That's a pretty condensed way of looking at it, but I suppose it's accurate. I'd like to focus on the personal aspects of farm life as much as possible, which means capturing a fair amount of reality. Is that a problem?"

"Not at all," Tobias said, tipping his light-brown Stetson first at her, then at Eli, who looked none too thrilled with his father's answer. *Innnnnteresting.* "Eli, why don't you show Scarlett around the place so she can get the lay of the land? It'll give the rest of us a chance to finish up in the greenhouse and get another place set for supper."

"Then I can run into town and get your room set up with fresh linens, too." Emerson capped off the words with an enthusiastic nod, and holy crap, the down-home hospitality was a serious kick in the pants.

"Oh, you don't need to feed me or worry about a room," Scarlett said. "I can just grab some takeout on my way to the nearest hotel later, really." Granted, she'd have to head the opposite direction from her drive in if she wanted to find either of those things, but surely there was *something* around Millhaven other than the single stoplight she'd passed about ten minutes before arriving at the farm.

Owen shook his head, but not before shooting Eli a lightning-fast glance that—funny—seemed to promise murder. "It's our pleasure to put you up for the month in the local apartment complex a little ways from here. As for supper, we wouldn't be very good hosts if we didn't offer you a firsthand taste of what Cross Creek has to offer. We can talk a little bit more about what you have in mind for your articles and the logistics of your visit while we eat."

"Okay," Scarlett agreed, albeit tentatively. Although having an actual apartment sounded kind of nice the more she kicked it over in her mind, crashing their family dinner (okay, *anyone's* family dinner, or anyone's family anything) didn't rank too high on her list of "Yay! Let's do that!" But she was here to soak up story ideas so Mallory could put *FoodE* back on the digital map, and getting her eyes—not to mention her taste buds—on the food probably wasn't a terrible idea. Plus, observing their family dynamic might give her a lead or two on the more personal end.

Hunter pulled a key ring from the pocket of his faded jeans, the plastic casing around the fob and keys clacking softly in his hand. "Great. I'll take Emerson into town and help her out with the apartment, and we can all meet back here at six for supper. Sound good, E?"

Eli lifted one shoulder in an approximation of a shrug, although the move seemed more forced than fluid. "Six. Got it."

Holy brotherly tension, Batman. Scarlett's curiosity sparked, but she tucked that little nugget away in favor of doing her job, which right now meant taking reference pictures with more than just her mind's eye. "So, guess you're my tour guide, huh?" she asked, turning toward Eli.

A muscle tightened across his clean-shaven jaw as the rest of the group dispersed, but he covered it with a smile that didn't come within a mile of those baby blues. "Looks that way." He dropped his eyes to her suede, block-heeled booties, his sudden frown completely discordant with the firm, full mouth shaping it. "You're going to want to change your shoes before we start."

Scarlett's brows took a one-way trip up. "What's wrong with the ones on my feet?" It was just a quick walk around the farm, for God's sake. She'd cruised all over Manhattan in these babies, and half of Brooklyn besides.

Funny, Eli looked just as dubious as she felt. "Nothing. If you want to break your ankle before we even make it to the henhouse, that is."

Scarlett took in the network of unpaved pathways spiderwebbing out from the spot where they stood, and hell. Even though she was more than a little tempted to stay as she was just to prove she'd be fine, pulling off a four-week shoot in an air cast because she'd gotten chippy with karma was so not on her itinerary.

"'Kay. I've got a pair of flip-flops in the car," she conceded, and one corner of his mouth lifted in an unnerving little half smirk.

"Not sure that's going to be any better, but suit yourself, I guess."

Just like that, her patience skipped a beat. "I usually do."

The answer seemed to get him, or at the very least, make him keep his disdain for her footwear to himself. Scarlett fast-tracked her way back to the Volkswagen, swapping out her booties for the pair of bright-orange flip-flops she'd stowed on the floor mats as a last-minute why not. Unbuckling her primary camera bag from the passenger seat, she slung the strap over her shoulder, ducking to pull the padded fabric crosswise over her body and squeezing her muscles to maneuver the gear over her hip, safe and secure and ready to go.

"Okay," she said, freeing first the Velcro closures, then her Canon 5D Mark IV from the center storage well. Popping the cap off the 35mm lens—a bit standard with all this sprawling landscape, but for now she'd make it work—she clicked Baby to life and looped the camera strap around her neck. "All set. Lead the way."

Eli's feet remained as unmoved as the rest of him looked. "Are you going to have that thing out all the time?" he asked, his eyes on her camera as if the thing were a murder suspect.

"It's sort of why I'm here." Scarlett laughed. "And by 'sort of,' I mean 'totally.' Why, does the camera make you uncomfortable?" He certainly wouldn't be the first person to get a little wiggy at the sound of the shutter snapping, although God, nothing soothed her more.

"No," Eli said, his shoulders lifting in a spray-starched shrug. "I'd just hate to see anything happen to it. Between the elements and the manual labor around here, things can get a little rough."

Translation: too rough for you. She barely bit back the scoff brewing in the back of her throat. "This camera and I have both seen plenty of action in the field. I'm sure we'll be just fine."

"If you say so."

But still, Eli didn't budge from his spot, and yeah, okay, Scarlett had officially hit her limit. "Is there something going on here that I should know about? Because you seem awfully determined to give me a hard time."

"Not at all, ma'am," he replied, the word sending her free hand on a straight shot to the denim wrapped around her hip.

"Scarlett." Her camera shifted against her breastbone as she straightened, the familiar weight comforting her, and she inhaled on a five-count. "I'm ready whenever you are."

With zero hesitation, Eli turned toward the nearest footpath, kicking up clouds of dust that hung low in the hazy sunshine as he started to stride away from the main house. The dirt-and-gravel path wasn't quite wide enough for them to move side by side without the risk of touching, so Scarlett walked a half step behind him for a minute, stealing the opportunity to take him in.

The dark-blond hair and Caribbean-blue eyes she'd already caught sight of were ruggedly handsome, and now that she could see Eli's face in closer profile, she mentally catalogued the nuances in his features. His strong jawline was offset by that ridiculously sexy mouth, along with the slightest sign of a dimple on his left cheek, although the jury was still out on its definite presence because he had yet to fork over a genuine smile. His light-gray T-shirt hugged a frame full of muscles— not so tight that it was indecent, but snug enough to outline the thick swell of his biceps, a pair of shoulders that would fill the better part of a doorframe, and holy shit, those frayed and faded jeans might be far from clean, but they were doing all sorts of favors for his ass. Dropping her chin, Scarlett craned her neck for a better look, watching the denim press over the perfect curve-to-hard-muscle ratio of Eli's rear view with every step . . .

The masculine timbre of a throat clearing hooked into Scarlett's well-hellllooo-there reverie, and her eyes darted back to Eli's just in time to catch him catch *her* staring.

"Oh!" Her cheeks prickled with warmth at the same time her girly bits prickled with something decidedly naughtier. *Way to keep it suave, girl.* "Sorry. You were saying?"

Eli arched a brow, lifting it even higher at Scarlett's you-got-me smile, but busted was busted. She might as well own it.

"There are a couple of things you're going to need to know if you want to make it past day one around here," Eli said—apparently for the second time—and the heat in Scarlett's veins morphed quickly into surprise. She'd covered breaking news in more volatile situations than she could count on both his hands and hers. Was this guy for real?

"I'm pretty sure I can handle myself," she replied. They were on a *farm.* She'd have to be halfway to sleeping to not keep up.

But either he hadn't heard her or he seriously doubted her claim, because he kept right on talking. "The heat around here is no joke. You'll need to hydrate. A lot. It's not optional."

Okay, so that wasn't an entirely stupid rule. Even if he was treating her like an entirely stupid idiot.

"Fine," Scarlett said through her teeth. "What else?"

"You're gonna need sunscreen." Eli's bright-blue stunners flicked over her fair skin and her tattoo, landing on her spaghetti-strapped halter top and denim cutoffs. "And jeans. Also, shirts with longer sleeves."

He had to be kidding. It was hotter than hell's hinges out here. "I thought you just said I'd need to stay cool."

"No, I said you'll need to stay hydrated. But the second you get into the hay barn or out in the middle of one of these cornfields where's there's no shade to be had for a quarter mile, you're going to be sorry you left all that skin exposed. You and I are gonna be spending nearly all our time together outside, and I can't have you keeling over from too much exposure to the sun."

Her pulse kicked in a burst of realization. "You're going to be my point of contact for the whole four weeks?"

Looked like she'd unknowingly managed to piss off karma after all. But come on. She needed a blockbuster, not a ballbuster. She had to be stuck with the cockiest Cross of the bunch?

That unsettling smirk worked its way back over Eli's mouth. "Yes, ma'am."

Greeeaaat. "Scarlett," she said. "And I'm not going to keel over from heat exhaustion." She was hardly a delicate freaking flower.

Eli lifted one shoulder halfway before letting it drop. "That's what everyone says right up till they do it. But just because you don't plan on something doesn't mean it isn't gonna jump up and bite you on the . . ."

"Ass?" Scarlett supplied, filling in the obvious blank from where Eli had abruptly trailed off. No, really? They didn't even swear all the way out here in God's country? Fuck, she was *hosed.*

Chagrin flickered over his sun-bronzed face, there and then gone. "Yes, ma'am."

"Scarlett," she reminded him, pulling a breath full of hot air into her already tight chest. *Story. Story. You're here for a story.* "Okay. Any other house rules I should know about?"

"We start early 'round here." He angled his boots over a branch on the path, heading toward a long, skinny barn-looking structure.

Wait . . . "How early?"

His smile paved the way for his answer. "Five thirty."

Oh, *ow.* "You do know that's inhuman, right?"

"You do want the 'authentic experience' of farm life, right?" Eli volleyed, slinging air quotes around the words she'd used earlier, and shit. Shit, shit, sleepless shit. He kind of had her there.

Not that she was conceding defeat of any kind. "So no flip-flops, hydrate, cover up, and be ready to roll at o'dark-thirty. Is that all?"

The slight lift of his dark-blond brows was the only betrayal of his surprise. "It'll serve for now."

"Excellent, because I've got a couple of rules of my own." Scarlett jammed her flip-flops to a halt on the path, staring Eli down even though he stood a solid foot taller than her in those banged-up boots of his. "I'm here to do a job, and I don't intend to take any half measures, which means, yes, I'm going to take a lot of pictures, and yes, I do want to experience farm life authentically. I'm fine with hard work, and also fine with any suggestions or guidance you're willing to offer while we get that hard work done. What I'm not cool with"—she lifted a finger to send her point all the way home—"is you underestimating me. These features are going to do a lot for your farm, and I'm a damned good photographer, not to mention a pretty smart woman. Now, are we going to play nicely together for the sake of this magazine layout, or are you going to keep leading the way with your cocky attitude? In truth, I'm fine with either, but if you want to go the arrogant route, be forewarned. I bite back."

A beat passed, then another, with nothing but silence and an epic staring contest passing between them. Eli's smirk was gone, but the expression he wore now was completely unreadable, and Scarlett's heart corkscrewed behind her breastbone. No, she hadn't been wrong about Eli's Rock-of-Gibraltar-sized ego, and yes, the articles really would be a boon for Cross Creek as much as for *FoodE*. But Eli ran the farm with his family, and as such, he could still send her packing without so much as a single photo.

Dammit, she needed those photos.

"Listen, Eli—"

"I'm sorry."

Her plea crashed into his apology, and she blinked in an effort to recalibrate. "What?"

"I didn't mean any disrespect," he said, and even though the words sounded as if they'd just rolled off a teleprompter, they were way more stiff than disingenuous. "Spending time on the farm can be a tough adjustment for folks who aren't used to it, is all, and the heat can get downright dangerous. I wanted you to know there can be serious risks for safety's sake. I apologize if I came off rude."

"Oh." Talk about the farthest thing from what she'd been expecting. Still, she knew much better than to mess with karma twice in one day. "Okay, then. What do you say we start over, no harm, no foul?"

Eli gave up an all-business nod and a polite, barely there smile to go with it. "Yes, ma'am."

"Scarlett," she insisted, and all of a sudden, she got the sinking feeling that the next four weeks were going to last forever.

CHAPTER FIVE

Eli took the slowest possible path to the compost bin behind the main house after dinner, wishing like hell he was anywhere other than Cross Creek even though he'd never *been* anywhere other than Cross Creek in his entire twenty-eight years. But between the familial fallout from that dumbass bet and the smart-mouthed, sharp-eyed photographer he'd been saddled with as a result, Eli would take a one-way ticket to Timbuktu over his current situation.

Even if, with her wild, platinum-and-dark-blond-streaked hair and her olive-green eyes and her petite-yet-still-plenty-curvy frame, said photographer was hotter than homemade sin.

Turning the corner toward the three-sided alcove that housed the trash cans, the blue plastic recycling tubs, and the compost bin, Eli lifted the lid to the latter, the rough-hewn wood scraping across his palm as he dumped the contents of his bucket in with a thunk. After his showdown with Scarlett in front of the henhouse a few hours ago, he'd gone the deflect-and-forget-about-it route, keeping their tour to just the facts despite the million and two questions she'd asked and the billion and two pictures she'd snapped, then done his level best to park himself as far away from her as possible during dinner. Scarlett had been all business, too, touching her meal only to push her fried chicken and mashed potatoes over her plate as she'd chattered on and on in that heavy New York accent of hers about the endless list of things she wanted to know about and immortalize on film.

The woman seemed allergic to either shutting up or sitting still, and God dammit, being in charge of this stupid project was going to suck up every last ounce of Eli's time, energy, and sanity. He needed to be working now more than ever, not tasked with the shit job of baby-sitting a brash blonde with enough nosy questions to sink a fucking battleship—especially not when even money said she was going to hate the very place she was supposed to be promoting and the very place he needed to be working hard to save.

"Guess the look on your face pretty much answers the 'how's it going' question."

The sound of Hunter's voice dumped Eli back to the reality of the dusk-covered yard behind the main house, his chin winging up just in time to catch sight of his brother heading toward the alcove with a black plastic trash bag in one hand.

"Hey," Eli said, slapping his smile together even though it fit about as well as a miniskirt on a moose. "Sorry, I checked the trash before I came out here. The bag wasn't even half-full."

Hunter popped the lid on the trash can and swung the suspiciously flabby bag inside. "I know. But I needed an excuse to come out here and see if you're alright, so . . ."

A hard squeeze worked its way through Eli's gut. Time to duck and cover. "Damn. A guy finds a serious girlfriend and all of a sudden we're hugging it out and talking about our feelings around the campfire."

Hunter grinned, although likely more at the mention of Emerson than at Eli's humor. "Fuck you. How's that for feelings?"

"Better." A genuine laugh fell from Eli's lips, loosening the tension that had tangled beneath his sternum. "But as cool as she is, I still think living with Emerson has left you addled."

"Look at you, using the twenty-five-cent words. Frigging brainiac," Hunter popped back.

Careful, Eli's pulse warned, and he amped his cocky factor up another notch. "Hey, I can't help it if smart is the new sexy and I'm the king of both."

Hunter snorted before slipping his thumb through the belt loop at his hip, looking out over the shadowy outlines of the flower garden that had remained unchanged since their mother's death twenty-four years ago. "Seriously, though. I know today has been a bit of a bitch. You okay?"

His permanently laid-back tone curved around the question, making it all too easy for Eli to twist the truth in response.

"Yup. I'm right as rain, brother." He pulled in a deep breath of finally cool evening air, pivoting on his scuffed-and-scarred Red Wings to head back to the house when Hunter stopped his cut and run dead in its tracks.

"I'm not trying to come down on you, E, but this bet you made has the potential to really jam us up."

Eli's heart took a whack at no less than four of his ribs before tilting toward his knees. "You don't need to remind me."

"Actually, I think I do," Hunter said. "Look, I get that Greyson was acting like a bucketful of dicks and that you didn't mean for this to go pear shaped. But it did. And like it or not, you're gonna have to make it right."

Oh, for the love of all that was sacred and holy. "I *want* to make it right, Hunt." Eli slashed a hand through the air in frustration. "I'd bust my ass to make it right if I could, but I'm going to be too busy playing cruise director for the city girl to get any real work done."

Hunter stood perfectly still, his face a tough read in the last scraps of daylight and the scant glow being thrown off from the windows on the back of the house. "Like her or not, that city girl could be the key to getting out of this mess."

"Or she could make everything worse by turning us into a reality show–style joke," Eli said, the words launching out before he could pull them back or pretty them up. "She tromped all over the farm in flip-flops, for Chrissake! And don't even get me started on the sunstroke I'm gonna have to save her from, even though she'll likely fight me tooth and goddamn nail while I do. She's bossy, brash, and a pain in the ass, not to mention she's a disaster waiting to go down with all this hands-on shit she wants to try and pull off for these stories. Hell, she's a city girl, through and through. She's probably not even going to *like* it here. How's any of that supposed to get us the business we need?"

"I don't know," Hunter admitted. But his expression was far from noncommittal as he added, "Here are a few things I *am* sure of, though. Scarlett's résumé reads like a Who's Who of badass publications, and despite her Manhattan zip code, this series she's shooting for *FoodE* does have the potential to bring a whole lot of people to our farm stands and pick-your-own fields, not to mention maybe land us some new contracts with distributors." He held up a hand to stave off the brewing argument that must have been showing on Eli's face. "You might not agree that Scarlett's being here at Cross Creek is a good thing, but you sure as shit still need to do whatever it takes not to piss her off so we can make the best of this PR."

Eli locked his molars together hard enough to make his jaw protest, turning his brother's words over in his mind even though he hated every last syllable. "You honestly think her buzzing around here at warp speed and asking a billion questions while she airs our personal shit all over the Internet like laundry on a line is going to help Cross Creek?"

"With this bet you made and the fallout we'll face if we lose, I think we need to do all we can to find out. And that means you"—Hunter paused, pointing at Eli through the twilight for emphasis—"are going to have to stop being pissy and start making Scarlett love it here."

Eli let out a long, slow breath, his shoulders sagging as he watched Hunter walk back to the main house.

Screw Shakespeare. Eli was going to need an outright miracle to make it through the next month.

◆ ◆ ◆

Eli stood on the concrete threshold of apartment 4A, blinking the sleep out of his eyes for the fifteenth time since he'd dragged himself out of the sweet haven of his bed as many minutes ago. Not even the day and a half that had passed since he'd walked Scarlett to this very spot and left her with a spare key, his contact information for emergencies, and a clipped-yet-polite "good night" had erased the unease from his gut over this month-long magazine mission.

The sight of Scarlett, her blond-on-blond hair wild from sleep and a bright-red toothbrush centered smack in the middle of her lush, smart mouth? Not fucking helping.

Keep it simple, stupid. You need to charm her, not make her think you're some sort of backwoods creeper. "Morning," Eli said, following her into the shoebox-sized apartment that had been Emerson's only a few short months ago. Damn, Scarlett had moved in quick. Or at least, her mess had. Stacks of books and magazines, errant hoodies and shoes, a laptop splayed open on the coffee table next to two—make that three— notebooks of various sizes and colored pens to match . . . and all that was before he got to the mile-high stack of camera equipment covering the kitchen table. How could one little convertible hold so much stuff?

"Unh," she replied, padding barefoot through the living space to the tiny, open kitchen. After a quick swish to rinse her mouth and toothbrush, she added, "If you say so, but as far as I'm concerned, if it's dark outside, nighttime should still apply."

"Not a morning person, I take it?" Well. At least they had *something* in common besides both being human. Not even the fact that Eli had been able to spend six blissful hours last night reading Hemingway and writing website updates and ad copy for Cross Creek—albeit under the guise of a freelancer who only existed in his gray matter—could change how hard the crack of dawn smarted in the here and now.

Ever tough, Scarlett lifted a noncommittal shoulder. "I'll have plenty of time to sleep when I'm dead. I'll be fine after I caffeinate." She reached for the space-age-looking travel mug on the counter, cradling the thing like a newborn before taking a long sip.

Eli took in the contents of the now-lowered cup clasped between her palms, absolutely wary. "What on earth is that?"

"Coffee." A little smudge of foam clung to the indent of her upper lip, and oh hell, Eli wasn't going to make it past sunup.

"No," he said, blanking the suggestion from his wayward cock while lifting the dinged and dented Thermos in his grip. "This is coffee. That is . . ." His gaze landed on the commercial-grade coffee maker taking over half the chipped Formica next to the utilitarian kitchen sink. "Where did you even get that thing?"

"Since yesterday was a day off at Cross Creek, I went exploring. I ended up in that little town ninety minutes from here." Scarlett waved her free hand as if she were already terminally bored with Millhaven. "If I had known that's where the closest Starbucks is, I'd have packed my cappuccino maker from home. This one doesn't have all the bells and whistles, but it'll do."

Eli's laughter emerged on a heavy huff of disbelief. "That little town ninety minutes from here? Do you mean Lockridge?" It had one of the highest populations in the Shenandoah Valley, for pity's sake.

"Mmm-hmm, that's the one," Scarlett said. "Cute place. And thankfully for my caffeine addiction, they have a supercenter."

She took another sip of her coffee (although the jury was still out on whether or not there was really any *coffee* underneath all that frilly, foamy stuff) wrinkling her nose and grabbing a carton of milk from the counter. Adding a splash to her drink, Scarlett handed over the carton before snapping the lid on the mug and turning to make her way back into the living room.

"I just have to grab my shoes and my equipment and I'll be ready to go. Help yourself if you're thirsty."

"Soy milk?" Eli dropped the carton back to the counter faster than if it'd been chock-full of rattlesnakes. At least those, he'd know what the fuck to do with.

Scarlett paused, midstep over the carpet. "Oh, yeah. Actually, I'm sort of vegan."

"You're what?" No way had he heard her properly, because he could have sworn she'd just said—

"Vegan," Scarlett confirmed, finishing her trip to the living room to scoop up her camera bag. "It means I don't consume any animals or animal products."

He resisted the urge to rub his suddenly pounding temples, although barely. "I've worked on a farm for my entire life. I know what vegan means. I've just never met anybody who actually is one." Guess that explained all the food maneuvering she'd done Saturday night at dinner. But seriously? No cheeseburgers? No butter? Christ, no bacon?

Who did that?

One platinum-blond brow arched. "I know this will shock you," she said, the beads around her wrist clacking together as she splayed her fingers wide against one hip. "But we vegans aren't all tree-hugging hippies who run around chanting and naked and smelling like patchouli."

Do not picture her naked, do not picture her naked, DO NOT . . .

An image of Scarlett, her creamy skin flushed with desire and her pretty, pink nipples begging to be tasted like summer fruit ripped through his mind's eye, and sweet Christmas Jesus.

Too late.

"Ooookay!" Eli barked out, gripping his keys hard enough to feel the metallic bite against his palm. "We need to go, or we're going to be late."

Scarlett blinked, but thankfully didn't question the swerve in subject. "I told you. Shoes and gear. I'm ready."

Tamping down the good-morning-to-*you* message coming from his dick, Eli looked at her more closely. "You're wearing that?"

"On the list of top ten things a woman will punch you for, that question is easily number three," she said, her stare as frosty as her words.

Shit. So much for not pissing her off. But the cherry-red Converse low-tops she'd just slipped into looked about as sturdy as a sapling, and while today she was actually wearing jeans, rolling them up to midshin and pairing them with a cut-to-*there* T-shirt didn't rate too high on the scale of one to practical. "All I meant was I'm not sure you're going to be comfortable."

"You said jeans, sleeves, and better shoes," Scarlett reminded him as she lifted her camera bag over her shoulder, and outstanding. Not only did her shirt reveal more of her chest than it covered, but it was also short enough to show off a sliver of skin between the hem and the waistband of her jeans.

Although it took effort, Eli stuffed back the argument brewing in his chest. While her feet might be crying uncle by lunchtime, nothing about today's outfit was an outright liability like those flip-flops, and anyway, they were already halfway to late. With how much work he'd need to bang out today to get a jump-start on this bet, he didn't have time to argue.

"Have it your way," he murmured. When she turned to lift another equally big, equally bulky camera bag, Eli's surprise took charge of his mouth. "Wait. How much stuff are you bringing, exactly?"

Scarlett dipped a look over her shoulder. "Oh. Well, any photographer worth her salt wouldn't be caught dead without a backup camera. Plus, it's a pain in the ass to switch up lenses all the time, so I prefer to work with two cameras at once. That way I can go back and forth, depending on what the shot calls for."

"You have *two* cameras?"

"Nope," she said, her smile going deep and wide and weirdly beautiful. "I'm taking two cameras with me today. And if you think that's a lot, I don't even want to tell you how much glass I brought from home."

"Glass," he repeated, and Scarlett gave her head a little shake.

"Sorry. It's photographer-speak. Lenses." She pointed to the kitchen table over his shoulder. "Most people think it's the cameras that matter, but in truth, it's the lenses we get all geeky for. Well, unless you're talking about a Hasselblad or something, but everything about one of those babies is totally outer limits."

Eli shook his head, trying to process. "And you just haul all of it around with you?" She couldn't be a hair over five foot four, for Chrissake.

Apparently, moxie counted double. "Of course." Scarlett shifted the bags on either hip, clearly comfortable despite the fact that, judging by the pull of muscles in both her biceps and her forearms, they couldn't be even close to light. "I'm not about to miss a shot because I couldn't carry my weight. Literally."

"We're going to be doing an awful lot of moving around," Eli said, because it was as diplomatic as he could get under the circumstances. Hell, some days in the busy season, it took all he had to drag himself around the farm.

But Scarlett just laughed. "This isn't my first rodeo, cowboy. I'll be just fine."

"Great," Eli mumbled. He crossed the carpet, holding the front door open for her as they made their way over the threshold and across the Twin Pines parking lot. Switching gears, he channeled his mental energy into organizing the tasks in front of him. God, there were no less than a hundred, and that was just what he could come up with off the top of his walnut.

As if she could see the wheels turning in his brain, Scarlett asked, "So what are we up to today?"

Eli popped the locks on his F-150, the truck's running lights flashing bright yellow in the predawn shadows of the parking lot. "There are a handful of daily chores that always have to get done no matter what. Those keep us busy for the first hour or so, and then my brothers and old man and I will hook up at the main house for breakfast to discuss the rest. And I, uh, guess you'll come, too," he tacked on.

What she'd eat would be a mystery, since bacon and eggs were a definite negative on the bound-to-impress-her list. Which was a crying shame, really, because for as much as Eli liked to rattle Owen's cage, the guy's culinary skills were seriously on point.

Scarlett didn't seem to give it a second thought, though. "Daily chores," she prompted, pulling an iPad out of one of her camera bags as she got situated in the passenger seat.

He gave the thing three hours before it overheated or she flat-out busted it, but hey, whatever blew her skirt up. "Checking the henhouse, inventory in the greenhouse. Pulling orders with all the local businesses we supply to prep them for processing. Making sure the equipment and irrigation systems are a go before we harvest hay, soybeans, and corn. Stuff like that."

Scarlett's fingers became a backlit blur over the screen. ". . . annnd hay, soybeans, and corn. Got it." She sat quietly for a second, sipping her coffee while Eli turned onto the road leading out to Cross Creek. Without looking up from her iPad, she asked, "So how come you don't live on the farm like everyone else?"

"What?" Shock made his brain logjam on the question, but Scarlett dove back in without pause.

"The other night, Emerson mentioned that both Owen and Hunter live in cottages on the property, and that she lives with Hunter. I was just curious as to why you don't live at Cross Creek, too."

Fuck. He needed something stronger than coffee for this.

Deflect and forget it. Eli dug deep into his arsenal, pulling out his most charming smile. "Because I live here instead."

"Yeah, I got that part," Scarlett said, apparently immune to his smile and hip to his dodging the subject. Figured she'd be as brazen about this as she was everything else. "But you guys have like miles and miles of land, right? Wouldn't it be easier to build another place at Cross Creek and be done with it?"

"No."

"No?"

Eli held steady as he flipped the tables on her in yet another evasive maneuver. "What about you? Do you live near your family?"

"Oh." Scarlett blinked through the scant light in the truck, and look at that. He'd managed to throw her. "Well, I'm not actually in New York all that much, but yes. My fathers live in Brooklyn, and I have a place in Manhattan."

Thankfully, there was *so* much about that he could tackle, and all of it would keep her busy talking about herself. "Your fathers?" he asked after a mental coin-flip. "As in, two?"

"Yes." Scarlett straightened against the passenger seat, her chin hiking up as she pegged him with a stare he could feel even though his eyes were mostly on the road in front of them. "I was raised by two men, who just so happen to be wildly in love and married to each other."

While a small part of him was tempted to take offense at her obvious assumption that he'd disapprove of her family, Eli worked up an answer that was as easy as hers had been defensive. After all, he needed to charm her. If he could keep the focus off his own family dynamic while he was at it? Triple-word score.

"You say that like you think I'm going to have something against the fact that your fathers are gay."

She paused for a heartbeat, then another, but man, that chin of hers didn't budge a millimeter. "Some people do."

"Well, I'm not one of them," Eli said, and he meant it. "It's far better to be curious than judgmental."

Her brows shot up for a single second before snapping together in a tight "V." "Did you just quote Walt Whitman?"

Eli's palms went slick over the F-150's steering wheel, his brain bouncing back and forth between a state of panic and a very strange, very serious shot of arousal. "I dunno, did I?" he drawled, leaning hard on his small-town country accent in an effort to cover his ass. "All I meant was that there's better stuff to be interested in than other people's business. Seems simple to me, but maybe . . . who was it? Walt Whitman? Maybe he felt the same."

Much to his relief, she shook her head. "Weird coincidence, I guess. And I'm sorry I assumed you'd judge. It's just that sometimes I get a lot of side-eye from people when I tell them I was adopted by two men."

"The only thing I judge a person by is whether or not he's an asshole," Eli said, the back of his neck instantly heating at the swear word he'd let slip. He was supposed to be winning this woman over, for Chrissake. "'Scuse my language."

Scarlett laughed, the throaty sound filling the truck. "Eli, we're going to be spending the next four weeks together, so please. Do me a favor. Unless the video camera is rolling, feel free to swear as much as you fucking like."

Shock arrowed through his chest, forcing his own laughter up and out. "Yes, ma'am."

"Oh for the love of . . ." She broke off, her arms threading into a tight knot over the spot where her seatbelt crossed her chest. "*Scarlett. My name is Scarlett.*"

He knew—he *knew*—he should just let her protest go and call her by her first name from now on like she preferred. But something deep in his belly put a mischievous smile on his face instead. "You know, 'round here we call those manners."

Eli hung the words with just enough levity, and wait for it . . . wait for it . . .

Gotcha. Scarlett's exhale was pure surprise. "You're not calling me 'ma'am' to bust my chops?"

"Nope." Okay, so it was only 85 percent true, but he wasn't about to split hairs. "Calling women 'ma'am' is just what we do here in Millhaven, whether they're eight or eighty."

"And no one finds it a little sexist?" she asked. But rather than being pushy or accusatory, her tone was genuinely curious, and hell if that didn't make Eli stop and think about the question all the more.

After a minute, he said, "No. I mean, I can only speak for myself, but I don't think using 'ma'am' is meant to be sexist at all. We tend to throw 'yes, sir' around just as much for men, and they're both terms of respect. Same goes for me not swearing in front of you. It's not that I don't think you can handle me dropping the F-bomb." She was a New Yorker, for God's sake. He was pretty sure they'd *invented* the F-bomb. "Guess I just believe language is powerful, is all."

Scarlett nodded slowly. "'Ma'am' makes me think of mothers. Which is pretty weird, seeing as I've never had one."

"Everybody's got a mother."

"I don't," she reiterated, her words growing steam but not teeth.

But two could square-dance to that song, and Eli had known the moves since he'd been four years old. "Yeah, you do," he said, unease strumming its way back between his ribs, slowly sticking him from the inside out. "Everyone comes from somewhere, just like everyone belongs somewhere."

Of course, Scarlett didn't budge. "Not me. I come from nowhere, and I belong all over the place." She turned to face him a little more fully, and even the small glimpse of her in his peripheral vision slipped right under his skin. "Anyway, what about you? What happened to your mother?"

Eli's pulse rushed in his ears, the hard, rapid thump-*thump,* thump-*thump,* thump-*thump* completely at odds with the sleepy pink-and-purple sunrise coloring the horizon through the windshield. Nope. Absolutely not. He'd suck up a lot of things to get off the Cross Creek hot seat and into Scarlett's good graces for the PR, but not this.

He wasn't about to tell some photographer who was there to show God and everybody with a connection to the Internet that his mother had died of breast cancer at only thirty-seven, devastating his father and leaving the man to raise three young boys on his own, and he *damn* sure wasn't going to tell her that the reason for his nondisclosure had more to do with the cold, hard truth than any warm, fuzzy emotions.

After all, it was tough to talk about a woman you knew you should love but couldn't even remember.

Oh, screw this. Eli needed to dodge, deflect, and forget about everything other than showing Scarlett the farm and *only* the farm.

He fixed her with a smile, as plain and polite and free of emotion as he could make it. "Where I live and what happened to my mother—hell, what color boxer shorts I pulled on this morning—none of that has anything to do with the magazine layouts you're going to shoot. We'll do best if we remember that and focus on what you came here for."

Her chin did that stubborn-lift thing again, and for a split second, Eli was certain she'd argue.

But then she set her shoulders, turning her attention back to her iPad as if the thing were far more fascinating than anything else in the county. "You're absolutely right. I came here to work. That's all that matters."

They spent the rest of the drive to Cross Creek in silence.

CHAPTER SIX

For as stubborn as she was, Scarlett royally sucked at the silent treatment. The whole thing drove her apeshit, really—stewing on your feelings only made it impossible to move on to the next ones. So the last twelve minutes of her life, sitting literal feet but theoretical leagues away from Eli Cross in total screaming silence?

Yeeeeeeah. Pretty much her definition of hell on earth. Not that Eli had been wrong about work being their number one priority, because truly, Scarlett wouldn't have spent more than half a day out here in BFE unless she was shooting a magazine spread that would help save her best friend's business. But she couldn't exactly do that if her entire daily agenda consisted of following him around like a puppy until quitting time, and she *definitely* couldn't do it if they didn't speak to each other.

Unfortunately, calling him a cocky, swagger-happy jackass probably didn't count.

"Oh," Scarlett said, her surprise getting the best of her and breaking the stalemate between them as Eli pulled his pickup truck to a stop in the empty gravel lot beside the main house. "Are we the first ones here?"

Eli examined the plum-colored skyline through the windshield. "More like the last." He shrugged off his seatbelt, although his shoulders still remained high and tight beneath his T-shirt. "My old man is at the back of the property, touching base with the guy who manages our cattle. Hunter's prepping the harvesting equipment in the barn by the cornfields, and Owen's in the greenhouse, doing inventory and organizing CSA orders."

It wasn't a landslide of engaging personal convo, but at this point, she'd take it. "How do you know?"

"Because unless one of them is missing a limb, that's where they start every day during the busy season. And unless one of them is missing two limbs, they're always in ahead of me. It's already five forty."

"Wow," Scarlett said. Pulling Baby out of its resting spot, she double-checked the battery and the memory card even though she knew they were both primed and ready to go, attaching a heavy-duty shoulder harness around the camera's frame before repeating the process with its twin. "Your father and brothers have some serious dedication."

Eli's laugh was as fast as it was humorless. "You have no idea."

"Bet I do, actually." After all, her life code was work first, everything else (including food, sleep, and sex, although not always in that order) next. But of those things, work was by far the best, and definitely the fastest paced. Why fuck around, really?

Scarlett scrambled out of the passenger seat with one camera at each hip and her backpack between her shoulder blades, falling into step next to Eli as he headed down the same dirt-and-gravel path they'd taken on their tour the other day. "So where do we start?"

"Henhouse," he said, although he didn't elaborate.

After a dozen steps, Scarlett caved. "Doing . . .?"

Eli gave her a sidelong glance that she couldn't quite read. "I'll give you three guesses, and the first two don't count."

Scarlett was less than a millimeter from pointing out—rather icily—that *he* was supposed to be the expert about that sort of thing when she caught the smirk playing belatedly over his lips. "Oh my God. Are you messing with me?"

"In my defense, you made it kind of easy with that question," he said, and she couldn't help it. She laughed.

"Fair enough," she admitted. "I take it you're going to feed the chickens?"

Eli nodded, and they paced off another half dozen steps before he asked, "You ever collected freshly laid eggs before?"

"No." Scarlett's pulse picked up the pace along with her feet. "You're actually going to let me help you?"

"You'll just be under my feet all day if I don't, right?"

His question held a three-to-one ratio of teasing to legit truth, so she answered with the same. "I hate to break it to you, but it's my job to be under your feet. A job *you* asked me to come do, might I add."

"Mmm." Eli swiveled his gaze over the flower garden behind the main house, then the fields of whatever the leafy-green stuff was farther in the distance to the right before turning his attention back to their spot on the path to the henhouse. His smirk coalesced into a smile that crept up toward his eyes, and oh Lord, that dimple she thought she'd spied the other day was actually a matched set. "You wanted a hands-on look at farm life. Might as well put you to work while I give it to you."

Scarlett nodded, tamping down the wake-up call those dimples were sending to her libido. "Okay, but—wait!"

He jerked to a stop on the path next to her, his boots crunching hard against the gravel and his blue eyes wide in the softly breaking daylight. "What's the matter?"

Heart pounding, she scrambled for her primary camera, scooping it up and letting the lens cap fly in one deft movement.

"Does the farm look like this every morning?" The deeper blue-black hues of just half an hour ago were quickly giving way to brighter pinks and golden-edged sunlight. Although the wood-planked boards and thick shingles of the henhouse still stood veiled in the heavy early-morning shadows, their textures stood out almost as if they were a relief painting, and no *way* was she passing this up.

"What, you mean the sky?" Eli asked, tacking on a half laugh. "I hate to be the one to tell you this, but that great big shiny thing poking up over the horizon there? 'Round these parts, it comes up every single day."

"Funny." But Scarlett didn't even think about tearing her eyes away from the scene in front of her, not even to roll them at Eli's sarcasm. Excitement combined with something deeper, something she couldn't name but knew by heart as she measured the light—*click*—the depth—*click-click*—the balance of all the elements—*click*. She metered her breath and her pulse to the sound of the shutter, everything else falling away except for the colors and nuances and angles of each shot.

This. *This* was her sanctuary. It didn't matter where she was, but with a camera in her hands and something new to aim it at, Scarlett was exactly where she belonged.

An idea slammed into her with all the subtlety of the A train at rush hour. "Oh God, you know what would be perfect?" *Click-click-click.* "Get in the frame."

Eli huffed out a shocked breath. "You want me in the picture?"

"I don't want you to jump in and yell 'cheese!'" she said, unable to keep a leash on her tart laughter as she calculated the variables of the lighting in her mind. "In fact, it'll be better if you don't look at the camera." But with him in the foreground in that white T-shirt and faded jeans, then the henhouse to the side, with that ridiculous sunrise as the backdrop? Talk about flawless composition with an evocative, personal hook. Not to mention click bait on Mallory's website.

Or it would be as soon as Eli found his internal clutch and got his ass in gear.

Scarlett tore her focus from the Canon. "Eli?"

"No, thanks." His smile was the polar opposite of the genuine version he'd given her a few minutes ago, although from the look of things, he sure was trying to match them up. "Hunter and Owen already give me crap for being the best-looking Cross brother. Proving it with photographic evidence would just be bragging."

She paused, her fingers going tight over the body of the camera. Eli had signed the consent waiver to allow her to take photos of him while she was here at the farm—all the Crosses had, and Emerson, too—and taking photos was what she was here for. Hell, it was what she *lived* for. If she was going to deliver the sort of personal-interest magazine spread that would bring Mallory's business back to life, she needed to come out swinging for the fences.

"You could just walk in front of me on the path," Scarlett suggested, framing up the shot in her mind. Not ideal with the scant light, but she was good enough to make it work. "Give up a little profile with a sideways glance. Easy."

"I'll pass."

His arms threaded over the front of his T-shirt in a living embodiment of the "no" he'd just given her, and frustration flared, hot beneath her skin.

"I'm here to take pictures and tell stories," Scarlett tried again, lifting the camera for emphasis.

"Of the farm." Eli gestured to the fields she'd just been shooting. "Not of me."

"Oh, come on. You're the perfect face for Cross Creek, and these stories are supposed to be personal. Plus, you signed the waiver."

Judging by the stubborn glint in his eyes, that little point of fact wouldn't garner any headway. But she'd already jumped in feet first for the penny. She might as well throw whatever she could at the whole damn pound.

Unfortunately for her, Eli threw back. "I signed the waiver," he agreed. "And if I end up in a shot or two that you take while we get things done, then I guess so be it. But I've got far too much work that needs done to play cover model, and I'm already behind. You want shots of the sunrise, or anything else on the farm, be my guest and take a thousand of 'em. I'll be in the henhouse when you're done."

Oh, Scarlett was tempted to push, and push hard. She didn't just need ho-hum photos of the landscape, as pretty as it was. She needed absolute showstoppers, with kick-ass story ideas to match.

But that was the rub. Eli was her point of contact for the entire time she was here at Cross Creek. She didn't just need the photos. She needed a connection to the farm. She needed a way to put the photos with stories that Mallory could turn personal and real.

Dammit, she needed *him*.

"Okay," she said, lowering her Canon back to her side even though the move grated like two-inch fingernails dug deep on a chalkboard. "Lead the way to the henhouse, then."

The slight lift of Eli's brows was the only sign of his shock, and it lasted for maybe a nanosecond before he did what she'd asked. After a few dozen more strides, they reached the entryway to the henhouse, and Eli tugged the door open on its squeaky hinges.

"The chores in here are pretty intuitive," he said, his tone testing the water with her as he flipped the light switch to illuminate the single, bare bulb set high in the center of the rafters. "Cross Creek isn't a poultry farm, but right now we've got about fifty birds here in the henhouse. Every day, they need eyes on them, just to make sure none of them look sick or hurt. We also need to refresh the hay, check the feed, and provide plenty of fresh water daily, along with grabbing whatever eggs have been laid since the last sweep."

"And you're going to let me do all of that?" Scarlett peered around the open, two-story structure. In truth, it would be at least another hour before there was enough natural light in here for her to take any usable shots, even with the henhouse door wide open and the overhead light pumping out all ninety of its watts. She might be good, but she wasn't a magician, and terrifying the poor animals with the camera flash definitely wasn't on her list of yep yep.

Eli handed her a wooden bucket with a scattering of hay in the bottom in reply. "If you think you can handle it, sure."

"I can handle it just fine," she promised, taking the bucket and giving back a smile sweet enough to give him a head full of cavities. Honestly, he must think she was an idiot.

At least, his half smile sure said so. "Then let's get to it."

He took a few more steps into the henhouse, and she followed him into the cool, shadowy space. For the most part, the interior looked like that of a small barn. The heady, musty-sweet scent of hay filled her nose, her pulse picking up the pace in her veins as Eli bent down low to scoop up a tawny, butterscotch-brown chicken just as easily as she'd lift her camera bag.

"Uh." Okay, it was less than eloquent, Scarlett knew. But park-bench pigeons were pretty much the extent of the wildlife she was accustomed to, and even then, she'd never gotten close enough to touch one, let alone pick it up.

Stories. Stories. You're here for the stories. She squared her shoulders. She'd worked with Pulitzer Prize–winning journalists on impossible stories under even more impossible deadlines. Certainly chickens weren't *that* hard to wrangle.

Eli sure made it look like child's play, anyway. "This here is a hybrid chicken, although we've also got some Rhode Island Reds and a coupl'a Leghorns thrown in for good measure."

Ah, wait. She'd need to Google those to make sure any photos she took later were labeled properly. "Hybrid chicken," Scarlett said, her camera banging awkwardly against her hip as she tried to maneuver her iPad out of her backpack.

The chicken in Eli's grasp fluttered nervously, clucking her displeasure at Scarlett's fumbling. "Need some help?" he asked.

"Nope. I'm all set, thanks." She balanced the finally free iPad over her fingers, tapping the screen to life with one thumb. "Hybrid, Rhode Island Red, and Leghorns. Check. What else?"

But for as quickly as Scarlett wanted to get to the feeding/watering/egg-gathering/fabulous-story part of things, Eli seemed content to slow-roll the tutorial. "You can pet her if you want. Since you wanted to go hands-on, and all."

"Oh. Okay." She eyed the hen, who was now chattering happily from her perch beneath Eli's sun-bronzed arm. Reaching out, Scarlett gave the bird a couple of quick pats on the back before returning her stare to Eli expectantly.

But instead of giving her something she could use, he laughed. "Seriously? That's what you're going with? Jeez, didn't you ever have a dog or anything when you were a kid?"

"I spent the first ten years of my life in foster care and the next eight after that traveling all over the world with my dads while they worked for a humanitarian aid organization," she said, laughing right back. "So, yeah. That's a 'no' on man's best friend."

Eli went bowstring tight from shoulders to shins. "Oh. I, uh . . . didn't mean to make you uncomfortable."

"That's okay. You didn't," Scarlett said truthfully. "Most of the foster homes were okay, even though I lived in a lot of them." She'd lost track after the third, or maybe it had been the fourth. "I mean, living with my dads was better, obviously, and things tended to be kind of crowded in foster care. But that's where I met Mallory, so it wasn't so bad."

"You've known Mallory that long?" Surprise lined Eli's face, but she met it with a shrug. He might want to go all zip-lipped with his personal details, but she'd never really minded sharing her own. Anyway, maybe if she got the ball rolling, she'd actually loosen him up. At least enough to snap a photo or two with him in the damn frame.

"Mmm-hmm," she said. "Her parents were killed in a plane crash when we were both nine. By then I was a total pro at the foster-care thing, so our caregivers at the time put us in a room together. Her adoptive parents ended up being the ones who hooked me up with my dads—they're all friends. So even after Mallory and I were both placed, we stayed close."

"So you two are kind of like sisters, then?" Eli ran a hand over the hen's feathers, and okay, he really did make it look easy.

Scarlett reached out and followed the path of his fingers at a safe distance, surprised at how soft the chicken was on the second pass. "I don't know about sisters. We talk often, and I love her. But I was turned over to the Office of Children and Family Services when I was twelve hours old. I don't exactly have a frame of reference for that sort of thing."

"Wow," he said, the ensuing silence drawing out for a heartbeat, then another, before he cleared his throat and took a step back toward the henhouse door. "Right. Anyway, each hen usually lays an egg a day, although sometimes they skip a turn here and there."

Damn. Eli's defenses: one, Scarlett: zero. Not that she'd be throwing in the towel after one tiny little setback. "And I just need to collect all of them, then make sure there's food and water?" Seemed pretty easy for her first assignment. She could probably finish in less than ten minutes. "That's it?"

"Yup," he confirmed. When he didn't offer up anything else, Scarlett turned on the heel of her sneaker. A set of wooden cubbies serving as nests spanned the right-hand wall, each hay-lined row stacked three high with a series of ramps and ledges serving as access points to the slots above floor level. Squatting down, she looked into the nest in front of her, which was thankfully unoccupied.

And also empty of anything other than a thick bed of hay and a scattering of honey-colored feathers.

Scarlett pulled back, doing a quick count of the cubbies. *Forty-six, forty-seven, forty-eight . . .* okay, so if each chicken delivered the goods once a day, where the hell was the egg?

Refusing to be bested by either a chicken or the cocky smile currently making a comeback tour over Eli's handsome face, she tried the next cubby. But slot number two, then three, revealed a whole lot of nothing, and finally Scarlett had no choice but to grit her teeth and ask, "Okay, what am I missing?"

"Besides the eggs, you mean?"

She bit her lip, but whether it was to keep from screaming or—worse yet—returning Eli's insanely contagious smile, she couldn't be sure. "Yes. Besides those."

"Nothing. You just have to slow down long enough to see what's in front of you."

But rather than being snarky or condescending, his answer was simply matter of fact, and he pushed off from the edge of the rough-hewn doorframe, lowering the hen in his grasp with surprising gentleness before walking over to her.

"There's no fixed real estate when it comes to the henhouse, and no fixed schedule, either. Not when it comes to laying eggs, anyway." Gesturing to the hens pecking and clucking their way over the packed dirt floor and out into the wider circle of space past the open door, he said, "Even though we keep them in here at night, these beauties are far more free range than not, which means you never really know where you're going to find their eggs. Case in point—" Eli nodded down to a mostly empty storage crate on the wall opposite the cubbies.

"Oh!" Unexpected laughter bubbled up on the heels of Scarlett's surprise at the sight of the three pretty, light-brown eggs tucked into the corner. She bent down to pick them up, but Eli stopped her midreach.

"Here. You're gonna need these," he said, dropping a trio of small wooden eggs into her palm.

Oooookay. "Sorry, I thought we were collecting the real deal."

"We are. But we also want the hens to remember where they're supposed to do their thing, otherwise the eggs will be scattered to the four winds of the farm. When the hens see the wooden ones here in the henhouse, they figure they're in the right spot. It's not a guarantee that they won't lay eggs wherever they please, but it helps to keep things mostly contained."

Scarlett slipped her hand into the next cubby in the row, her fingers closing over not one, but two eggs. "Is that why these eggs are together?" she asked, and Eli added a lift of his brows to his ice-melting grin.

"Look at you, making the logic leap after only one cup of coffee. I'm impressed."

She recognized the cocky words as the bait they were. But if he thought for even a nanosecond that she'd get distracted in the face of a little banter, he had another thing coming.

She needed a blockbuster. And she wasn't going to stop until she got it.

"You might want to raise those standards of yours," Scarlett said, stepping in toward him even though she had to crane her neck a little extra to fasten him with the full force of her sassy smile. "Because I get a whole lot more impressive as the day goes on."

Shifting back, she delivered the real eggs to the safety of her bucket, replacing them with the faux version before turning her attention back to the task at hand. Scarlett continued collecting whatever eggs she could locate while Eli took a head count of the chickens and replenished the food and water dispensers at the back of the henhouse. While he didn't hog the conversation, he didn't totally penny-pinch it, either, giving her some fairly interesting—if textbook—information on the different breeds of chickens and how they cared for them at Cross Creek. Grappling again with her backpack, she reclaimed her iPad from the spot where she'd stuffed it in the front pocket, squinting to make out the backlit screen against the harsh glare of the sunlight.

Eli tipped his head, his eyes lingering on her as she began to thumb-type. "You don't like to sit still much, do you?"

"What, so the world can go by me while I watch? No, thanks." God, the thought alone gave her a case of the shakes. Balancing the iPad in the crook of her elbow to keep it shaded, she tightened her grip on the handle of the bucket, jotting down ideas with one hand while adding to her stash of eggs with the other.

"That thing isn't going to last out here, just so you know," Eli said, jutting his chin at her tablet.

Please. This wasn't even high-level multitasking. "I appreciate the concern, but I'm used to juggling a lot of equipment. I'll take my chances."

"Okay." His dimples flashed for a split second. "But don't say I didn't warn you."

"You don't think my being here is a very good idea, do you, Eli?"

The question popped past her lips before she could alter its brash factor, and even though her pulse thrummed in the wake of her words, she still didn't take them back.

He gave her a slow up-and-down stare before answering with extreme caution. "We're all happy to have the opportunity to host you, and I'd be right glad to tell you anything you'd like to know about Cross Creek."

Oh, screw caution. Scarlett needed a story she could use, not some canned party line or tutorial on the care and feeding of chickens. "So you'll tell me all about the farm. Just nothing about you personally."

"Are you going to talk my ear off all day?" Eli asked, dishing up a smile that was pure charm. Which was interesting, really, seeing as it was also pure bullshit. Nobody made a habit of dodging questions with a smirk and a honey-covered drawl unless they had something they didn't want seen.

"That depends," Scarlett said. "Are you going to avoid my questions all day?"

His smile slipped, the glint in his eyes cooling to a steely blue in the growing daylight. "If we don't hurry up and finish in here, we're going to be late for breakfast."

A yes if she'd ever heard one. Time to pull out all the stops. "The rest of your family seems perfectly comfortable with me digging into the personal-interest side of farm life. What makes you so different?"

Eli closed the space between them in strides so fast Scarlett had barely registered his movement before he was as close as he could possibly be without touching her. For a second, he said nothing, just giving her a storm-colored stare that sent a bolt of unrepentant heat all the way up her spine. But despite the intensity in his eyes, he also looked far from angry or mean, and she didn't step back or stand down even though she had plenty of room behind her to do so.

Scarlett's heart slammed beneath her T-shirt as she tipped her face up to take that stare head-on. Eli's exhale coasted over her cheek, his voice soft yet serious as sin as he snapped their banter—along with any headway Scarlett had made with him this morning—cleanly in half.

"What makes me different is that I'm the one who's got to make up for all the time that gets lost standing here yapping instead of working like I need to be. So like I said, if you've got questions about Cross Creek, I'm happy to oblige. Other than that, if you want to get personal, you're gonna have to do it with someone other than me."

CHAPTER SEVEN

Although Scarlett would rather be raked across a mile-long bed of coals than admit it, farm life was kicking her ever-loving ass. Running a hand over her lower back—which was a lovely shade of tomato, thanks to the fact that she'd missed it with the sunscreen three days ago—she tossed her keys onto the counter in her borrowed kitchen, grabbing a bottle of water from the fridge before dragging herself to the couch in the living room.

"Ahhh. Home sweet home for now." The muscles in her legs let loose with a hallelujah chorus as she flopped back against the cushions, allowing herself a few seconds' worth of oh-hell-yes relief before reaching for the camera bag at her side. Carefully unearthing Baby from its heavily padded resting spot, Scarlett clicked the camera to life, sharpening her gaze over the display screen on the back as she scrolled through today's pictures, one by one.

Thoroughly meh. Again.

"Dammit," she muttered, her gut sliding south. She'd been here in the boondocks for five whole days, actively shooting for the last four straight. Cross Creek was a beautiful farm, with dozens of scenic views and endless opportunities to snap the perfect shot. But for some reason, even the best of her photos were missing that extra something that took them from "pretty" to "utterly compelling."

Some reason. Right. Make that a cocky, six-foot-four, close-lipped, muscle-packed reason.

Eli Cross was driving her insane without saying a word.

Okay, so technically, he wasn't giving her the absolutely silent treatment. He'd stuck to his promise of answering every question she'd had about the farm. But he'd also kept to his affirmation that getting personal wasn't anywhere near his agenda, putting his nose so hard against the Cross Creek grindstone instead that Scarlett had needed to dump all her energy into keeping up with even the small stuff.

Which was problematic, since what she really needed was a huge story concept.

"Okay," she said, shaking her head to re-cement her determination. Although the light had been iffy, she'd managed to get a few pictures of Hunter early this morning, before the Crosses had met to discuss their agendas over breakfast and then scattered to the four winds of the farm. She might—maybe . . . hopefully . . . *please, please, please*—be able to turn one of them into a good-enough image for Mallory to use. But before she could take out her laptop to make the best of today's shots, her cell phone did the jump and jangle from the back pocket of her these-have-been-cleaner jeans.

Scarlett smiled despite her exhaustion—*God*, Eli hadn't been kidding about the work being hard to get used to. "Hey, Mal. Please tell me you're drinking a four-shot soy-vanilla latte, because seriously, at least one of us should be."

"I'm on my second one in the last six hours," Mallory confirmed, the words making Scarlett both groan and laugh.

"You sure know how to kick a girl when she's down."

"Sorry. It's been a long day. Anyway, how's it going over there in the heartland?"

Scarlett's gut gave up a healthy pang, but she muscled past it. *Think positive, girl.* "I actually just got back from the farm a few minutes ago. I'm shuffling through the pictures right now."

"Of course you are." Mallory laughed, but only for a second. "So, what did you shoot today?"

"Lots of corn. I'm here to tell you, harvesting that stuff is harder than it looks." She sure had the muscle aches to back *that* up. But she hadn't been about to let Eli think she was some inept urbanite who couldn't hold her own. Scarlett had met every challenge he'd tossed in her direction. Except for getting in his good graces, anyway. "Did you get the photos of the hens and all the information on Cross Creek's specialty produce I sent yesterday?"

Mallory paused. "Mmm-hmm. I've got yesterday's photos in front of me right now. I finished mocking up the first round of introductory articles today, and they should go live at midnight. The farm looks really pretty."

The unspoken "but" hung heavy in her voice, and since Scarlett had never pulled punches in her entire thirty years, she gave the word voice. "But?"

"Look, don't get me wrong," Mallory said. "The pictures are great—your pictures are always great—and the information is all good. But the shots with people in them are kind of few and far between, and the articles read kind of like a travel brochure. I'm just not getting the really powerful sense of personal connection I'd been hoping for."

Sure. That was because the powerful connection Scarlett really wanted to make was the one between her foot and Eli Cross's very sexy, very stubborn ass. "Yeah, the point of contact I spend most of my time with is a little, um. Still a little camera shy."

Mallory let out a chirp of surprise. "Seriously? Emerson was so excited when I told her I was sending you. She practically bubbled over with that crazy hospitality thing small-town people do, telling me how happy the Crosses would all be to accommodate the personal-interest angle we wanted to pursue."

"No, no. Emerson has been great," Scarlett said in an effort to file the edge off the panic threading through Mallory's voice. "Everything's going to be fine. It's just taken a few days for the Crosses to adjust to having a photographer around."

Specifically, the one Cross with whom she spent 90-plus percent of her day. Dammit, a tiny handful of iffy shots of everyone else just wasn't going to be enough. Capturing one really great image either required a truckload full of luck or fifty shots you had to ditch first, and Scarlett was fresh out of both.

A pause extended from Mallory's end of the phone line. "But you think this guy will start opening up now that you've been there for almost a week?"

Crap. Time for a little smoke and mirrors. She could do this. She *could*. She just needed to figure out how.

"I think I'm going to come up with some more in-depth personal-interest stuff really soon. Look"—Scarlett took a deep breath, glancing down at the camera in her lap—"I managed to sneak in a few good shots of Emerson cutting flowers for the roadside farm stand today. I'll get them edited and over to you tonight so you can squeeze one or two into the first round of articles if you want."

"That does sound promising," Mallory agreed. "I can put those with the pictures of the specialty produce and a few recipes we've got in the archives. The photos of the heirloom tomatoes you sent yesterday look really pretty on-screen."

Hope pushed Scarlett's pulse a little faster in her veins, locking her resolve back into place. "Perfect. Tomorrow, I'll focus on shooting the first video segment. I can start with a welcome to Cross Creek sort of thing, nice and laid-back." At least, it would be, provided she could get Eli to agree to actually do it. But she'd cross that bridge when she got there. She was here to work. To do her best to save Mallory's magazine. If that meant she had to take more drastic measures to make these stories happen, then so be it.

"Trust me, Mal. The stuff I'm going to shoot tomorrow will be the best yet. You just wait and see."

◆ ◆ ◆

Eli slumped against the old wingback chair in the corner of the study-turned-office at Cross Creek's main house, absolutely convinced he was going blind.

"Is this all of them?" he asked Owen, holding up the list of weekly CSA orders that their ancient printer had just spit out.

His brother looked up from the hunt-and-peck job he'd been doing at their equally ancient desktop computer, his frown answering the question before he even opened his mouth. "Every last one. But just because they're a little thin this week doesn't mean we don't have to fill 'em."

The orders were more than a little thin—Christ, they were practically malnourished. But saying so would only make Eli the master of the obvious, along with supremely frustrated, so instead, he went with, "Alright. The henhouse is all set, and the last of those hay bales I harvested yesterday are in the loft, waiting to go up into storage. So I can get started on these right now."

"You've been busy today, huh?" Hunter stuck the paperwork for the delivery he'd just made to Clementine's Diner into the logbook by the door. His brows traveled up in question and curiosity, and Eli's gut twisted in response. He might not always do as much work as his brothers, but they didn't have to act so surprised when he was productive.

He covered his frustration with a haphazard shrug. "Like you said, the work needs done." Not that filling these CSA orders would take Eli long. Dammit, how could business still be lagging when he'd been busting his ass twice as hard as ever? "How are the blackberry fields looking?"

"Not too bad," Hunter said, although his tone tacked on a nonverbal *as long as your gauge for bad is being skinned alive with a spoon.* "Probably not enough there to put them in those CSA orders, but with some luck and maybe a good rain, we can likely squeeze in a decent round of pick-your-own early next week. How's it going with Scarlett?"

"Outstanding," he said, but the word carried none of the easy charm he'd meant to pin it with. Rolling his shoulders beneath the faded-red cotton of his T-shirt, Eli went for a do-over. "She's in the kitchen, taking pictures of some of the eggs she collected this morning. Said something about the butcher block being a textural gold mine with the juxtaposition of the late-morning sunlight in there. Or whatever."

While Eli tended to agree, he'd been all too happy to leave Scarlett to her own resources for a few minutes while he'd gotten caught up in the office. It had taken everything he'd had to dodge the overzealous *click-click-click* of her camera shutter over the last four and a half days and focus on drumming up enough strength and energy to keep his foot on the work pedal, full bore.

Not that the work was actually helping to ramp up business.

"Heard the Whittakers hauled in a truckload of peaches this week." Owen delivered the news with all the enthusiasm of a death knell, and great, now Eli had a cherry for the top of today's shit sundae. But peaches had always been the one crop they'd struggled to grow at Cross Creek, to the point that even Owen—who had studied every soil composition and complex fertilizer under the sun and stars—had even given up the ghost. Of course, Whittaker Hollow seemed to grow the damned things as easy as weeds. A late-season bumper crop would send everyone in town beelining to their tent at tomorrow's farmers' market, no question.

Still, the flavor of the gossip depended on the source, and some were more rotten than others. Especially where the Whittakers were concerned. "Who told you that?" Eli asked.

"Lane," Owen said, and so much for that. Lane Atlee might be a scary hulk of a dude, but he was Millhaven's sheriff, not to mention Owen's best friend, which meant the intel was sadly legit. "He overheard Harley Martin talking about it at the Corner Market yesterday. Apparently Greyson told his sister Kelsey, who told Amber Cassidy, who told everybody with a pulse. But she also posted pictures on both Facebook and Instagram, and their website says they even added special pick-your-own hours yesterday. So it looks like for once, Greyson's not full of piss and wind."

Unable to help it, Eli arched a brow. "Oh, I'm sure he still is. Just maybe not about the peaches."

"Yeah, well you'd better hope we catch a break, otherwise he's going to be full of piss and wind *and* bragging rights no one in this town will ever hear the end of. Plus five thousand dollars we don't have to give."

Hunter cleared his throat from his spot by the door, slipping into that easygoing let-it-slide thing he always did, right on cue. "Speaking of a few bragging rights . . . the first article went up on *FoodE's* website this morning."

"Yeah?" Eli threw some effort into keeping his increased heart rate far away from his expression. "Are we keeping up with the Kardashians yet?"

Hunter barked out a laugh, and bingo: attention averted. "No, jackass. They were mostly an overview, but Scarlett made the farm look nice. Gave up some Cross Creek history and featured Owen's heirloom tomatoes from the greenhouse."

Huh. Can't say he'd seen that coming. That sounded almost . . . normal. "I'll have to take a look when I've got a sec." Right about now, that'd be when he was ninety, but hey. He had work to get done, and not a little bit.

Work, it seemed, that Owen was determined to stir up with a monkey wrench. "There's a great shot of Emerson cutting flowers from the garden and some good ones of yesterday's farm stand," he said, his gray-blue eyes narrowing just enough to make Eli's pulse do the thump-thump-oh-shit in his veins. "But I noticed you're not in any of the pictures Mallory posted online, and you're not really quoted in any of the articles, either. You want to tell me why that is?"

Eli's defenses went on offense, pushing his smile to the forefront. "Because out of everyone on this farm, Hunter's girl is the only person prettier than me."

"Eli," Owen warned. "Just because you think these personal-interest articles are a bad idea doesn't mean they are. You can't slack off on this like you do everything else."

Christ, he needed to beat feet before this conversation turned into quicksand. "Whatever you say, brother."

"I say you need to make good and sure you don't piss Scarlett off."

The words carried just enough edge to send Eli's molars into a hard grind and Hunter's chin snapping up. "Owen—" Hunter started, but, yeah, Eli'd had enough.

"Trust me. If Scarlett's pissed, she'll let you know. Anyway, since there aren't enough blackberries for these CSA orders, I'd better hit the apple orchard so I can grab the early Jonagolds and Galas instead. See y'all later."

With only the briefest of pauses to snag one of the two-way radios from the charging stand by the door, he aimed his Red Wings toward the kitchen before either Owen or Hunter could say anything else. But come on. Scarlett might have surprised Eli a little (okay, a lot) by mostly keeping up with the day-to-day stuff, but now more than ever, he needed to be double-timing it to get ahead of the curve. Just like now more than ever, he needed to stay the hell away from Scarlett's camera. Between her sharp eyes and her even sharper wit, dodge and deflect was his only chance at survival.

He was already the black sheep of his family. He could not, under any circumstances, let her see any glimmer of the fact that he didn't belong at Cross Creek.

Because the camera never fucking lied, and his entire family—hell, everyone in the entire town—was clearly watching.

Stuffing the thought down as far as humanly possible, Eli cut a path toward the kitchen, where he found Scarlett behind the butcher-block island. Although her body faced his, her attention was lasered in on both the camera in front of her face and the shot in front of the lens, leaving her inevitably unaware of his presence. She hummed softly under her breath as she worked, the slim line of her shoulders strong yet relaxed and her motions fluid, and even without being able to glimpse her face, Eli would have to be a complete ignoramus to miss the reality right in front of him.

She looked perfectly, irrevocably, unapologetically comfortable in her own skin.

And wasn't *that* something he'd never once felt at Cross Creek.

"Sorry," he said, blinking back the nameless sensation slapping him directly in the sternum. "I don't mean to interrupt—"

Scarlett looked up from the camera, her face bright and her smile huge, and so much for losing that weird feeling that was now making itself nice and comfy between his ribs. "No, no, no. You have perfect timing! Come see."

Eli's legs had auto-piloted halfway over the kitchen tiles before his brain could consider any other strategy. "Okay. What am I looking at?"

She answered by way of tapping her way through the display screen on the back of the camera. "Your father just stopped in to grab some more water for him and Lucy before he went back out to get ready to harvest corn with your brothers, and when he was washing his hands at the sink, I had this idea." After a few more taps, she unlooped the camera strap from its resting spot around her neck and angled the screen so he could see the image she'd pulled up. "What do you think?"

Whoa. Eli leaned in close, his shoulder brushing against Scarlett's ever so slightly as he bent to look at the digital photo of three pale-green eggs cradled carefully between his father's callused, sun-burnished hands. The sight seemed like such a normal thing—a thing Eli had probably seen no less than a bazillion times in his life. Yet the way Scarlett had arranged the photograph, with the diffused sunlight all around and the contrast of the fragile eggs against the hardy ruggedness of his old man's hands, was so simple and at the same time powerful enough to jab him right in the gut.

Scarlett must not have sensed all the "holy shit" taking the fast path through Eli's veins, because she jumped in with a harder sell. "Don't get me wrong. The eggs look pretty all by themselves." She clicked back through the camera roll, and sure enough, the shots she'd taken of the eggs, both on the butcher block and in the hay-lined bucket she'd used to carry them up to the house, were kinda nice. "But I thought if your dad held them like this, with the eggs resting in his palms . . ."

"His hands would mimic a nest."

"Exactly! The personal element is subtle, but it takes the whole thing from good to perfect," she crowed, returning her pretty green gaze to the image with a smile.

No, smile wasn't exactly accurate. Scarlett was giving up a full-blown grin, her eyes sparkling and her nose crinkling in a way that was far sexier than it should've been. Eli was close enough to see the dusting of freckles on the bridge of her nose, the gold-tipped sweep of her eyelashes, the exact shade of her perfect pink mouth, and heat rushed over him on the heels of his quickening pulse.

She was really beautiful. And if he stood here any longer thinking so, he was going to be really, *really* screwed.

"Right." Eli cleared his throat, then did it again for good measure. Christ, all this stress over brothers and bets and peaches was making him loony tunes. "So, uh, how do you feel about picking apples?"

"Ummm, interesting segue," Scarlett said, tucking a few wayward strands of platinum hair behind one ear as she lowered her camera to the safety of the butcher block. "Apples sound great. Just let me get these eggs put away."

By the time she was done with the quick pickup and a tuck and slide of the cardboard egg crate back into the timeworn Kenmore in his old man's kitchen, Eli thankfully had his libido pretty much under control. Reorienting his thoughts, he ushered Scarlett past the back door and out into the yard of the main house.

"So, apples," she prompted in that both-feet-first manner he was quickly becoming accustomed to, and he kicked into Wikipedia mode as he led the way toward his truck.

"We grow a handful of different varieties, and there are about two hundred apple trees on Cross Creek's property in all. They're on the east side, way over by Owen's place, so we'll have to drive."

"Okay." Although she'd ditched taking notes on her iPad once the thing had overheated enough times on day one to turn it into the world's priciest paperweight, she still asked a truckload of questions, and Eli braced himself for the barrage that she was surely working up.

Only instead, she just opened the passenger door and climbed into the truck, and okay, yeah, that was officially weird. But since weird was better than death by questions, he pulled himself into the F-150's driver's seat, hitting both the automatic ignition and the control to lower the front-seat windows. The weather was still dry and hot—thank you, late August—and the run to the apple orchard wouldn't take long enough for the AC to cool the truck much.

"So," Scarlett said as he pulled out onto the dirt-and-gravel road leading away from the house, drawing out the word just long enough to trip his uh-oh sensors. "Now that it's nice and light out, I was thinking about shooting some video."

Eli used the entire length of his inhale to temper the slam of his heartbeat before throwing on a cocky smile. "Be my guest, but I have to be honest. That old adage about watching the grass grow is sadly pretty true."

"And that is precisely why I want to give people something more exciting to watch than the grass."

His knuckles tightened a fraction over the smooth leather of the steering wheel, and he tried a different tack. "I'm sure Hunter or Owen would be happy to oblige."

"Okay, but they're not here and you are," Scarlett pointed out, and jeez, how could her smile be so pretty and so merciless at the same damned time? "Plus, between all the work Owen does in the greenhouse on the other side of the property and Hunter's meetings with Emerson to develop marketing strategies, I barely ever see either of them in action, and I need a story today. Now."

For a brief second, Eli wondered whether Scarlett had a setting other than all-in-right-this-second. But as much as he hated it, he'd known that dodging the camera for the entire month was going to be impossible. Better this than copping to the fact that the reason they barely ever saw his brothers on any given day was that Eli always got the grunt work and extra jobs.

He went for a haphazard shrug. "If you need a warm body in a still shot or two, I guess I can stand in. But no video."

Scarlett's smile faltered, and she pushed her windblown hair from her face as he pulled the truck to a less than seamless stop in front of the footpath leading to the apple grove. "Shooting video is easy. All you have to do is talk about how much you love the farm. You can even pretend you're talking to just me if you want."

Translation: you can pretend you're pretzeling the truth for just me instead of the entirety of the Internet. No frigging thanks. "I've got too much work for this," he said, pushing his way out of the driver's seat and heading to the bed of the truck as a case in point.

Scarlett followed on the other side of the F-150, her falter turning into a frown. "Let's get something straight. Cross Creek is pretty and all, but I'm not out here for shits and giggles. I have a job to do, too."

"And I'm not keeping you from it," Eli reminded her. "All I'm telling you is that if you want someone to play reality TV, you're going to have to ask Hunter or Owen."

"But I'm here right now with you. *You're* my point of contact, Eli, and—"

Just like that, his frustration tipped. "Scarlett, I'm not changing my mind. I have enough work on my plate to keep three of me running all over hell's half acre, and believe me when I say that even if by some miracle I can get to all of it, there'll be plenty more waiting. So could we please stop wasting precious time here? These apples aren't gonna jump off the trees in surrender."

For a second, she said nothing, simply standing in front of him with her hands on her hips and her mouth flattened into thin, pale line. But then she let out a curt "Fine," turning toward the sun-strewn path leading to the apple grove, and halle-freaking-lujah. Maybe now she'd stop bugging him, and he could get a jump on this damned bet, once and for all.

Eli hooked a palm beneath the handle of one of the stepladders in the bed of his truck, grabbing a sturdy wooden crate with his other hand before following Scarlett down the path. Although she remained uncharacteristically quiet, he had zero doubt her brain was pinging a mile a millisecond, and that as soon as they reached their destination, both her body and her questions would follow suit.

Because they always did.

Taking a deep breath to nail down his resolve, Eli made his way toward the grove. A soft breeze cut through the sun's efforts to make the morning unbearable, rustling through the bright-green leaves of the trees in front of him and carrying just a hint of the crisp scent of apples. With the commonsense layout of eight rows of twenty-five trees each, the grove wasn't much to look at from the scenic standpoint. But the branches were studded with enough fruit to send a shot of fuck-yeah through Eli's blood, and finally, *finally*, a check mark for his utterly anemic win column.

He didn't waste any time crossing the grass and lowering both the stepladder and the crate in his grasp. "Yesssss," he murmured, 90 percent under his breath but still out loud. Reaching up into the low branches of the tree in front of him, he cupped a freshly ripe Gala in his palm, the skin of the apple smooth and warm from the sunshine hugging its red-gold curves. "So when you pick apples, the most important thing to remember is . . ."

But the rest of his tutorial fell prey to the fact that Scarlett had slipped past him and shouldered her way under the thick of the branches, headed directly to the tree trunk.

"What the hell are you doing?" Eli asked, even though it was painfully obvious that she was A) climbing the tree in front of them, and B) in all probability, insane.

Scarlett didn't even spare him a backward glance as she maneuvered higher into the network of branches. "I'm playing Tiddlywinks with manhole covers. What do you think I'm doing? If I want a great shot, I've got to go get it."

"You can't climb to the top to take pictures," he warned. Okay, so the trees were a few decades old, and the branches weren't exactly toothpicks. But they weren't indestructible, either, and even though she'd shrugged out of the backpack and second camera she normally lugged all over God's green earth, any abrupt shift in weight could spell danger. Not that a little thing like bodily harm would probably deter her.

Case in point. "Don't be ridiculous. Of course I can."

As if to prove her claim, she wrapped her fingers around the branch to her right, planting the sole of one bright-red sneaker, then the other, into a juncture of tree limbs to propel herself even higher into the lush foliage.

Dread crowded Eli's chest. How had she already made it ten feet off the ground? "I'm not trying to argue semantics, Scarlett. What I meant was—"

"You think it's dangerous, I could get hurt, blah, blah." She surprised him with a laugh that was more humor than heat, and for the love of Christmas, this woman's tenacity knew no bounds. "Seriously,

Eli. I know you think I'm some sort of brainless city girl who can't take care of herself, but trust me. I've done far worse than a little tree climbing to get a good shot. And God knows I need to send Mallory pictures of *something*."

Fuck if that one didn't land a direct hit. Still . . . "You need to stop climbing."

"What I need is to do my job. And I'm perfectly fine. See?" Scarlett turned her chin over her shoulder, her sassy smile holding enough brass for a marching band. "As a matter of fact, I bet if I go a little higher, I'll be able to clear this branch here and see half the farm."

Eli saw where she intended to go. Realized a split second later what lay hidden in the leaves directly beside it. And lurched forward with his heart in his windpipe.

"Scarlett, *stop!*"

The cut-glass tone of his voice must have gotten through her shit-stubborn determination, because—thank fuck—she paused. But in that moment, she must have also heard the soft, insidious buzzing of the yellow jackets in the softball-sized hive now just over her shoulder, because she whipped around, her eyes as wide as dinner plates. The shock on her face lasted for only a time-stopping instant before it morphed into pain. Scarlett yanked her arm from the tree branch with enough force to kill what was left of her already precarious balance.

And in the next breath, she tumbled all the way out of the apple tree.

CHAPTER EIGHT

"Scarlett!"

Eli's pulse hammered the word from his throat, and he moved out of pure, undiluted instinct. Stabbing his boots into the soft, uneven grass beneath the apple tree, he surged forward, his arms shooting out just in time for Scarlett to crash into them in a tangle of jerky motions and top-shelf curse words. The force made him stagger despite the crush of adrenaline sending his muscles into lockdown, and he squeezed his arms even more tightly around Scarlett's body as he fought to regain his balance.

"Camera," she gasped, her body curled in over the equipment still hanging by a miracle around her neck.

"Screw the camera," Eli bit out, but she struggled hard enough in search of the damned thing that he had to either relent or lose the footing he'd just fucking gained. "Okay, okay. Let's get clear of the tree so we can take a look." That he'd be looking at her just as closely as she'd surely look at the camera was beside the point. But shit, she had to have been stung at least once or twice, and no way had she fallen from that high without tagging a couple of branches on the way down.

If he hadn't caught her . . .

"Right." He smashed the thought before it could fully form. Setting her down in the grass about ten paces from the tree, he scanned her from head to heels for any obvious injuries, relief skidding through him when he found none. "Did you get stung?"

"I . . . um. Yeah, I think on my back." Scarlett's rapid-fire blink told him her adrenaline had kicked in nice and hard, but her voice stayed steady, tough. "I'm not allergic or anything, though. I'm fine."

Yeah, no. "You're not fine. Let me take a look."

She opened her mouth, and if past experience was any indicator at all, it was to protest. But Eli cut her off before she could even start.

"You fell ten feet out of a goddamn tree and got stung by some of the nastiest insects going. I know you're tough, Scarlett, but you're not indestructible. If you're hurt, you need to let me help you."

After a microsecond's worth of a pause, she nodded, and Eli would bet the concession smarted as much as the yellow jacket stings. Still, he wasn't going to sit around and wait for her to change her mind. He moved over the grass to kneel behind her, gently placing one hand on her shoulder and the other at the hem of her flowy black-and-white-striped top.

"Oh, *ow*," Scarlett cried out, arching away from his touch a mere second after his fingers skimmed up to make contact with the middle of her cotton-covered back. With good goddamn reason, too, Eli realized as he shifted her shirt away from her skin to get a better look.

"Jesus." Eli winced at the trio of furious red welts on the back of her rib cage, then again at the cluster of scratches below them, closer to her spine. "A yellow jacket must've flown under your shirt," he said, eyeballing the loose armholes beneath her short sleeves. "They're vicious bastards, good for multiple stings when they've got a mind for it. Looks like you banged into a branch on the way down, too."

"Great," she said, and although her toughness took center stage with that set of her chin over her shoulder, the way she had her lips pressed together betrayed the truth.

She was hurting, and not a little.

"Alright," Eli said, his gut going for a full corkscrew before his resolve took over. "We've got to get this scrape cleaned up and the welts treated with some baking soda before they get too swollen. Your back's probably going to ache like crazy for a day or two, but the good news is, I promise you'll live."

"Oh, no. I don't need all that first aid. Really, I'm fine." Scarlett shifted her weight over the grass, likely in an effort to stand up and prove it. "The light right now is perfect, and—" He'd moved back in front of her before his brain had fully registered the command to go. But she'd gotten hurt on his watch. Superficial or not, he was going to make damned sure her injury was taken care of. "And the longer we argue, the longer the first aid will take. Is your camera okay?"

She looked down to the equipment she hadn't let go of since the second Eli had put her down. "I think so. Yes."

"Good. Then we can get right back to business when we're done. But first, I'm taking you to the house to patch you up. Now are you coming, or do I have to carry you?"

Whether it was the dead certainty he'd pinned to the words or the promise to get straight back to work after he'd cleaned up her cuts, Eli couldn't be sure. But something propelled Scarlett to give in with a nod.

Gathering her backpack and spare camera took less than a minute, and the trip to his truck was equally short. After a quick drive back to the now (thankfully) empty main house, they got situated at the kitchen table, with Scarlett sitting backward in one of the Windsor chairs and Eli behind her, first aid kit in hand. Shifting forward, she dropped her hands down low to lift the hem of her T-shirt. But now that Eli's adrenal gland had slid back out of the stratosphere, he realized Scarlett would have to reveal a not-small amount of skin in order for him to treat her stings and scrapes, and whoa, yeah, that was definitely a bunch of petal-pink satin and lace wrapped high around her rib cage.

"Uh," Eli blurted, a bolt of heat laddering down his spine as he forced his focus to the cream-and-tan pattern of the kitchen tiles. "I can get you a towel or something. You know, to wrap around your shoulders if you want."

"I'm not uncomfortable, if that's what you mean. Not about that, anyway." She tucked the bottom edge of her shirt under her bra, baring the middle of her back down to the top of her jeans but effectively covering everything else.

"Yeah, I know the yellow jacket stings hurt," he said, slipping to the sink to wash his hands. Between the apples and the handful of different berries they'd taken to growing in higher quantities over the last decade, yellow jacket stings tended to be an occupational hazard around Cross Creek. Still, they hurt something fierce. Uncomfortable was probably an understatement.

Scarlett huffed out a laugh, humorless and soft, as she rested her arms and upper body over the back of the chair in front of her. "I didn't mean that, either. You can go ahead and say it."

"Say what?" Eli asked, moving back in behind her at the table.

The brows-up look she sent over her shoulder clearly outlined her disbelief. "I told you so."

Eli matched her laugh, only his was actually genuine. "And what's that going to get me, exactly? If I say I told you so, is that gonna make you any less hurt? Little burn," he added, spraying the scrape on her back with the antiseptic from the first aid kit.

"Ow! Mother f—" Scarlett's muscles flexed as her spine went bow-string tight, and she sucked in a breath on an audible inhale. "No," she said after a second. "It's not going to make me any less hurt. But climbing the tree was stupid. Obviously."

"Climbing the tree was impulsive," he corrected, an unwelcome pang arrowing deep into his gut at the fresh memory of her falling from the branches. "But saying I told you so won't change the fact that you did it. Seems like the only thing it *would* do is add insult to injury, and I'm fairly certain you won't leap before you look again. At least, not where apple trees are concerned."

"I won't." She tucked her chin to her chest, not even flinching as Eli dabbed at the welts on her back, even though by now, they'd damn near doubled in size. "I just . . . Mallory's my best friend. *FoodE* means everything to her. I came here to get her a blockbuster story that will bolster her business, and I wanted the perfect shot."

"I get that," Eli said, and as fucked up as the admission was, he did.

"Really?" Clearly, she was as shocked about the whole thing as he was. But whether it was her straight-up honesty or the uncharacteristic softness in her voice, something pushed the truth out of his mouth and into the space between them.

"Last week I bet a rival farmer five thousand dollars that Cross Creek would make more money than his family's farm this harvest."

Scarlett turned to stare at him over her shoulder, realization beginning to spread out over the surprise on her face. "Is *that* why you've been working like a madman? To try and make good on a bet?"

Eli's gut knotted, but since he wasn't about to get gabby about the love/hate thing he had going on with his brother—or anything else, really—he went with, "That's most of the reason, yeah. It's kind of a long story. Anyway, I get where you're coming from, wanting that perfect shot. I'd love a perfect solution right about now, myself. I can't really blame you for throwing your all into trying to get that. Although"—he paused with his hands halfway over the first aid kit, hardening his tone by just enough to hammer his next words home—"you do something impulsive that could put you in harm's way again, me and you are gonna have words, and they won't be 'happy birthday.' There's a thousand different ways to get hurt around here, and I'm none too interested in showing you any more of 'em firsthand. You got it?"

"Yeah." Scarlett gave up a small nod. "I've got it. I promise."

"Good." Eli turned back toward the supplies laid out over the table. Patching her up the rest of the way took only a few quick moves; after all, baking soda and water might be an old-fashioned remedy for swelling, but it was an easy fix that worked the same as all those fancy drugstore creams. With a few gauze pads and some well-placed medical tape, she was good to go.

"All set," he said, taking a step back and reaching for the discarded packaging littering the table's worn, honey-colored surface.

But as quickly as he'd created the space between them, Scarlett stood up and closed it. "We could help each other out, you know. I understand that you think getting in front of the camera is a bad idea," she added before he could cut her off with a *thanks, but no thanks*. "But it sounds as if you need the word of mouth, and I damn sure need something more to send to Mallory. I don't want to sensationalize what you do, or turn farming into a joke. I really am here to make Cross Creek look good."

Eli's thoughts winged back to the shots she'd taken of his old man in the kitchen, realization working a path through his brain. "I know."

"You do." Her reply was little bit question and a lot more disbelief, but he looked her in the eye to cancel out both.

"I do."

"Then take a leap of faith and trust me to do my job. Let me film you in a video segment. Nice and easy, just an introduction to you and Cross Creek. What do you say?"

Ah. There was the Scarlett he knew, brash and bold and right god-damn to it. But the more Eli tumbled her request around in his head, the less he could make his refusal stick. The truth was, he needed more than hard work to get ahead of this bet. He needed a risk.

He needed Scarlett.

"*If* we do this"—he crossed his arms over his chest, staring at her through the overbright sunlight spilling in through the kitchen win-dows—"then I have a couple of conditions."

"Name them," she said, knotting her own arms without so much as a blink even though, considering her recent injury, the move had to hurt.

Hell if that didn't make Eli's respect for her double. "I get that you want a connection to the farm, but I'm not talking about anything really personal. If it doesn't have to do with Cross Creek at least a little, my answer is 'No comment.'"

"Fair enough," she said, and although he got the feeling she'd probably push the envelope right up to the seal on that one, he'd fight the specific battles as they came. "Next?"

His heart gave up a yank, good and deep, but still, he didn't stand down. "I want to keep my old man's health scare out of the spotlight. He's made a full recovery, and he takes precautions to stay safe in the heat. No reason to remind anyone he wasn't less than a hundred percent."

"Oh." Scarlett's brows tugged in for a brief second before she answered with noticeably less moxie. "Of course. Anything else?"

Eli paused, but fuck it. If she could go all in, so could he. "Just one more thing. I'm not talking about this bet. Not on video, not in articles. Not on the record in any way."

Her white-blond brows shot up high enough to disappear beneath the long swoop of her bangs. "Oh, come on! We don't have to make it into a cheesy throwdown or anything, but two rival farms going head-to-head? It's click-me *catnip*."

Which was precisely why Eli refused to give it airtime. Bad enough that between Amber Cassidy and Billy Masterson, everyone in Millhaven already knew about the bet. But hanging the specifics out there for the whole Internet to see? Eli might need the win—more than a little bit, even—but he was going to get it fair and freaking square. No sensationalism. No cheating.

"The bet doesn't have anything to do with the farm, proper. You'll have to find your blockbuster someplace else."

"And you're going to let me?" Scarlett challenged.

Unease crept into Eli's chest, but only for a breath. Being in front of the camera, talking about a livelihood he didn't love and a farm where he didn't belong, wasn't ideal—or hell, even something he wanted a little bit. But he'd been hiding in plain sight at Cross Creek for years. Shit, he was the high lord of the dodge and deflect.

He was also fresh out of other options. Fall Fling was three weeks and one day away, and he needed to draw people's attention to the farm so they could sell as much produce as humanly possible and out-earn Whittaker Hollow. He *needed* to win this bet.

So Eli did the only thing he could.

With his very best cocky smile perfectly in place, he said, "Absolutely, darlin'. In fact, why don't we go ahead and knock the first one out right now? If we're gonna scratch each other's backs, there's really no time like the present."

CHAPTER NINE

Thankfully, Scarlett's second trip to Cross Creek's apple grove was less eventful than her first—at least in terms of bodily harm. Her back might not have stopped throbbing out a steady beat of *ow-ow-ow* on the drive back up the lane, and yeah, her pride was still riding shotgun right there next to it. But she'd finally gotten somewhere with Eli. No way was she going to scale back for a little thing like pain now.

Although holy hell in a handbasket, yellow jacket stings *hurt*.

"So, a couple of things about shooting video," Scarlett said, chasing the prickle on her cheeks with an all-business smile as her shoes shushed through the grass. "Baby here is a multitasker, so we don't need a different camera for recording."

Eli squinted through the sunlight, ambling to a stop in front of a row of apple trees, which—Scarlett fought the urge to do a full-on fist pump as she sight-measured the ratio of shadows to natural light—provided just as perfect of a backdrop now as they had half an hour ago. "You named your camera Baby?"

Nope. Not skipping a beat. Not even for that smooth, sexy, aw-shucks grin.

Mmmkay, maybe half a beat. But seriously, Eli's mouth should come with some kind of disclaimer. Full, firm lips framed by the barest hint of honey-blond stubble. A hard indent at the top for a touch of rugged appeal. The lift at the corners that was as sinful and delicious as warm butterscotch over ice cream . . .

Work. Video. Focus. Right this second, you great big hormone casserole! "Yes," she managed, sucking in a deep breath and lowering her backpack to the swath of grass between the first two rows of apple trees. Her stings and scrapes burned at the movement, and the pain set her determination in granite and her brain into "go" mode. "I named my camera Baby. Anyhow, even though we'll use the same equipment for video and stills, the process for shooting is actually quite different. In order to film as much useable footage as possible, we'll do most if not all of each video segment in one fixed place."

"You want me to sit still in front of the camera like we're doing an interview?" His smile grew instantly dubious, and at least here, she could reassure him.

"Yes, but don't worry. The videos will still be candid and casual, and Mallory will edit everything so only the very best of what we film goes online. It's just that action video—the kind where a camera person moves with the subject as he or she does something—can be tough to shoot well with only one camera, especially for someone who's more accustomed to taking stills, like me. So in the interest of not making the folks at home either watch your back for half the segment or feel like they're on the Coney Island Cyclone . . ."

"I'll need to park it while you record the videos."

"Exactly," Scarlett said. "Another added bonus of stationary shooting is that we get to pick the best lighting and background. And unlike action video, *that* is something in which I'm definitely well versed." Looking at the grove around them, she scanned a couple of possibilities before nodding him closer. "What do you think of sitting on the stepladder in front of this tree right here?"

Eli's lips parted as he pulled back to pin her with a whole lot of *whaaaa?* "I get a say in that?"

"Sure. I mean, I am the photographer, so I have to pick the spot I think will work best in terms of light and logistics. But I'm not the only expert. Cross Creek is your farm, Eli, and you've already shown you've got a great eye for framing things up. You should get a say in how people see the place."

"Oh." Although the single syllable came out wrapped in surprise, he still walked over to glance at the display on the back of her camera as she aimed it at the spot in question. "Hey, that does look kinda pretty, with the way the sun is slanting down through the branches," Eli said. "You can really see a lot of the apples from this angle, too. That'll be good power of suggestion for when we open the grove next week for pick-your-own."

How about that—his eye *was* pretty sharp. His brain? Even sharper.

Scarlett smiled. "Okay. Do me a favor and stand a couple of feet in front of the tree so I can frame up the shot and make sure everything works as well as we think it will."

She stepped back a handful of paces as Eli moved toward the low-hanging canopy of branches, adjusting Baby's settings a little here, a little more there . . . *annnnd gotcha.* "Perfect! The colors look great through the glass. I think we have a winner. Now all I have to do is get the camera attached to the portable tripod, and we'll be ready to start."

Tugging the hardware from her backpack, she unfolded the aluminum tripod, locking the legs into place and anchoring Baby in with a snap while Eli grabbed the stepladder. The tree—this one yellow jacket-free, thank God—offered just enough shade to keep him from sweating or squinting, and honestly, Scarlett couldn't have come up with a better background if she'd custom-ordered one from Photographers-R-Us.

Didn't hurt that her subject was drop-dead gorgeous, either.

Her pulse sped, and sucker that she was, the rest of her went along for the breathy, tingly, well-hello-there ride. "So, ah, like I said before, if it makes you more comfortable, you can pretend you and I are just having a conversation. I'll ask you a couple of open-ended questions to get the ball rolling, but Mallory will eventually edit them out."

"Won't that make it seem like I'm talking to myself?" Eli asked, brows lifted.

But Scarlett shook her head. "With how she'll put the end product together, it'll actually seem like you're talking to the viewer, which is what we want. Speaking of which . . ." She stepped a few feet to the left of the camera, looking at Eli across the sun-strewn space that separated them rather than on the digital display. "You're going to want to keep your focus right about here instead of looking directly at the camera while we talk. That will keep the segment engaging and personal— think more 'casual back and forth' than 'job interview.'"

His nod roughly translated to *that makes sense*. "So you want me to focus on you," he said, leaning back against the bar serving as the stepladder's handle.

"Oh." She paused. She'd only meant to stand in the spot long enough to give him a reference point, then slide back behind the camera—hello, comfort zone—while they actually filmed. But now that Baby was all locked and loaded, she didn't technically have to be behind the glass once she hit "Record." What's more, she didn't want to give Eli even the slightest reason to balk.

So Scarlett kept her Converse planted firmly in the grass. "Sure. Since we're really just having a low-key interaction, why not. You can focus on me. Are you ready?"

"As I'm gonna be," Eli drawled, and she had to admit it. With that mischief-maker smile and those rugged, all-American good looks, the camera was going to love him.

The audience? *They* were going to eat him up with a spoon.

"Alright. Then let's get rolling." Scooping in a deep breath, Scarlett tapped the button to start recording, then moved back to her spot beside the camera. "Why don't you go ahead and introduce yourself and tell me a little bit about Cross Creek."

"Okay. My name's Eli Cross, and I help my old man"—he paused just long enough for his shoulders to tighten beneath the red cotton of his T-shirt, his eyes flicking to the camera lens for a split second before returning to hers—"Tobias Cross, and my brothers, Owen and Hunter, operate our family's farm out here in Millhaven, Virginia."

He went on with a few facts about the size of Cross Creek Farm and their location within the Shenandoah Valley. Although his smile was perfectly metered, his shoulders kept to their high-and-tight position around his neck, and his delivery all but hollered "infomercial!" and damn it, she needed something to put him at ease so he'd trot out all that charm of his.

"You've lived here at Cross Creek your whole life," Scarlett prompted, and Eli gave up a nod.

"Yes, m—" He pressed his lips together, shifting his weight over the stepladder. "All twenty-eight years."

She paused in an effort to let him elaborate, but after a beat or two, the stillness drove her nuts. "And what's it like to live on a family-run farm out here in the Shenandoah Valley?"

"It's right nice, I suppose."

Another pause, and Scarlett nudged again. "Can you tell me a little bit about daily life?"

"Sure. Some seasons are busier than others. Right now, with the harvest coming, we're expecting some long days and great fall produce."

Pause number three lasted longer than the other two combined, and gah. Maybe if she went for something more direct . . . "And how about your role here at Cross Creek?"

Although she hadn't thought it possible, Eli's shoulders locked down even harder. "The daily work varies depending on what crops are in season and how many head of cattle we've got on the back half of the property, but I do whatever needs done, I guess."

Once again, the silence extended between them, with Eli looking at her expectantly for the next question and her unease churning faster by the second. He'd been fine right up until she'd started recording, and while he wouldn't be nearly the first subject to go from zero to awkward in the click of a button, he was the one she had to put at ease in the here and (preferably right) now.

Scarlett lifted a hand. "Okay, Eli. Let's put a pin in these questions for a second. I know being in front of the camera can be a little over-whelming at first—"

His suddenly genuine smile sent a ripple of shock through her belly. "Do you? And when was the last time you were on this side of the lens, huh, bumblebee?"

Her laughter flew out in a hard, involuntary pop. "You did *not* just call me that."

"Oh yes, I did. You said no 'ma'am,' and I honored that one. Anyway, bumblebee suits you." Eli paused to look directly at the camera, all mischief. "She buzzes all over the place. Y'all wouldn't even believe it if you saw her. In fact . . ."

He levered up from the stepladder, and oh no. No, no. What the hell was he doing?

"Eli," she started, but he squelched the protest with a ridiculously engaging grin—the exact one she'd been trying to coax out of him for the past five minutes straight.

"C'mon, Scarlett. You just got done telling me how nice and easy this was gonna be. 'Piece of cake,' she said." Another look at the camera, and sweet God in heaven, how could he break every single rule of filming and still be so freaking appealing? "Why don't you come see for yourself how the spotlight feels? Then you and I can tell everyone at home what Cross Creek is like together."

The word *no* formed in her brain, hot and fast. This segment wasn't about her being at Cross Creek; hell, of all the people in the galaxy, she probably belonged on the farm the least. But for the first time since they'd returned to the apple grove, Eli looked relaxed, his

Caribbean-blue eyes crinkling at the edges and his dimples flashing in all their sexy glory, and oh, screw it.

Scarlett needed him out of his shell. There were worse ways to get him there than hopping into a video frame for a few minutes, especially when Mallory would just edit her out later.

"Okay, fine," she said, ignoring the pull of the medical tape beneath her T-shirt as she lifted her hands in mock surrender and crossed the grass to the spot where Eli sat in front of the tree. He angled his body just enough to face her without turning too much of his shoulder to the camera, the solid foot of their height differential and the taller-than-average lift from the stepladder bringing them within a few inches of being face-to-face even though he'd settled back into place and she remained standing.

"Happy now?" Scarlett asked, unable to keep the smile from either her face or her words as she gave up an exaggerated *ta-da*-style twirl in front of the camera.

"As a matter of fact, I am," Eli countered. "But I've got a head start on you in front of the camera, which doesn't seem polite. You want to introduce yourself and tell everyone a little bit about why you're here at Cross Creek?"

Although he gestured to Baby with one hand, his flirty little grin stayed trained right on her, and Scarlett had to hand it to him. He was good.

But sadly for him, so was she. "I'm Scarlett Edwards-Stewart, and I'm a photographer for *FoodE* magazine." She paused just long enough to match his flirty little expression. "I'm here to give everyone their own personal taste of Cross Creek farm life."

"That's the truth," Eli said, his laughter rumbling out, rich and smooth. "You've been giving everything 'round here an honest go in order to get these articles just right. I know we had a little bit of a false start with the apples earlier, but I was thinking maybe now we could show everyone out there how easy apple picking is. Especially since our crop here is comin' in so nicely this season."

Although Scarlett's stomach did an aerial backflip at the reference to her epically stupid tree-climbing maneuver, Eli's gaze remained wide open and steady on hers, so she gave up a nod. "Okay. I'm game."

He shifted slightly against the stepladder, reaching up for the nearest tree branch. "These here are Jonagold apples." A quick turn of his wrist had one dropping right into his palm. "We also have Galas and Staymans, but the Jonagolds tend to come into season early and they're real nice to eat out of hand."

"Isn't Jonagold kind of a funny name for them since they're red?" Scarlett asked, leaning in to trace a nearby apple with the pads of her fingers.

Eli laughed. "Yeah, actually, I guess Jonagold is a bit of a misnomer when you think about it. But like a lot of the specialty produce we grow here at Cross Creek, these babies are actually hybrids. They're a cross between Jonathan apples and Golden Delicious, so they've got a great sweet-tart flavor even though they inherited more red than gold on the outside. However"—reaching just over her shoulder, he plucked another apple from the branches with a soft pop—"they did get something from the golden delicious side of things."

"And that is . . . ?"

Curling the fingers of his free hand around her wrist, Eli turned her palm face up, delivering one of the apples in his grasp while holding onto the other. "Go on and give it a smell."

Whether it was the spark in his gaze or the hot hint of a dare in his words, Scarlett couldn't be certain. But something made her cup the apple between both hands and raise it to the spot just below her lips.

"Ohhhh." She closed her eyes, inhaling until her lungs tapped out. "It smells like . . ."

"Honey."

Eli's voice layered over hers as they spoke at the same time, and Scarlett let go of a laugh as her eyes fluttered open to look at him.

"Okay. So what are the rules for picking them?"

"Lucky for us, there are only a few out-and-out rules, and the hardest one is to wait till they're in season. We're comin' up on the very beginning of fall, and the crops tend to change pretty quick. We've still got a week or two left of sweet corn and blackberries, but these apples here are just coming in."

He proceeded to show her—and the camera—a couple of easy tips for discovering whether an apple was ripe enough to be picked, along with how to twist the fruit from the branches to preserve the growth buds rather than going for a straight-up tug that might damage the tree. After liberating about a dozen apples from the branches in front of them and giving one a taste test at Eli's flirty insistence, Scarlett slid out of the frame to grab the crate, asking questions all the way. Eli sat back against the stepladder, his shoulders loose and his words even looser as he told her about everything from how to graft and bud apple trees for maximum fruit growth to what hours Cross Creek would be open next week in case local folks wanted to come pick their own or shop for already-picked produce at their roadside farm stand. Finally, she turned off the camera and put it back in the insulated safety of her bag, pivoting on the heel of her Converse to hit him with a smile that came up from her toes.

"Come on, admit it," Scarlett teased as she walked back over to the swath of shade being cast down by the apple tree. "That wasn't so bad."

"It was better than getting stung by a yellow jacket," Eli flipped back, his easy grin taking any heat out of the words.

She did her best to work up a glower, but funny, she couldn't make it stick. "You're hilarious. Really. You should take that show on the road."

"And miss all the glamour of farm life? Not a chance."

Pushing up from the stepladder, Eli grabbed the rough-hewn crate Scarlett had used to collect her apples, methodically adding to the pile. She slipped beneath the branches a few feet from him to use her new-found skill set to start picking the apples that were ready, finding a comfortable rhythm as she alternated between scanning the branches and liberating the fruit. Tiny pops of sunlight filtered through the thick umbrella of apples and foliage, sending flashes of green and gold rippling over the grass, and Scarlett felt so at ease that her thoughts took the bullet train right out of her mouth.

"So do you have any writing experience?"

"No. None. Why do you ask?"

Eli's speed-of-light answer took her by surprise. "I didn't mean it as a bad thing," she qualified. "It's just that you're a bit of a natural with words."

The fact that he'd popped off with *misnomer* in casual conversation was brow-raising enough. That he'd done it in such an easygoing way that anyone listening would A) instantly grab the meaning if they weren't familiar with the word, and B) not find his use of heightened vocabulary either forced or pretentious in the least? Yeah, that was pretty freaking impressive.

His shoulders rolled like a lazy ocean tide, lifting and lowering beneath his faded-red T-shirt as if they'd been born for the maneuver. "Nah. I'm just making it up as I go. Today must have been my lucky day, is all. Or maybe it was my on-screen company. You weren't so bad yourself."

Scarlett's brows took a one-way trip up. "Nice try, smooth talker. But the way you owned that segment was way more than luck."

"If you say so, bumblebee," he answered, prompting yet another round of warmth to bloom over her cheekbones.

"I'm not getting rid of that one, am I?"

Eli lowered a handful of apples into the crate at their feet before shaking his head. "Not a chance. Anyhow, did you still want that shot?"

"What shot?" Her brain did one of those rewind-playback-type deals in an effort to follow the conversational boomerang, and he pointed up to the softly rustling leaves overhead.

"The one you climbed the tree to try and get. In case you think it'd be a good match for the video."

Scarlett tried—she really did—to keep the shock from her face, but it was a complete and utter no-go, because first of all, he was right, a panoramic shot of the apple grove would be a perfect complement to the segment they'd just filmed. But more importantly . . . "I thought you said no more dangerous stuff."

"I said no more impulsive stuff that could get you hurt," he corrected, but her shock, it seemed, wasn't done taking control of her mouth.

"You were pretty clear that tree climbing applies."

While Eli eked out a nod, he also didn't concede. "Yeah, but me going to grab a nine-foot ladder from the storage shed and holding it steady so you can climb up and get the picture you were after doesn't."

Holy. Shit. "You would do that?"

"Of course." His mischievous grin turned into something a lot softer, but hell if it didn't arrow right through her anyway. "I told you. I'm not trying to keep you from doing your job, Scarlett. I really do get it."

"I know," she said, because as weird and unlikely and downright crazy as it was, she did. "Thank you."

In a flash, Eli was back. "Don't thank me yet, bumblebee. See, these CSA orders still need to get filled, and now that I know you have mad apple-picking skills . . ."

Scarlett couldn't help the laughter welling up from her chest, and what's more, she didn't want to. "Go get the rest of the crates, cowboy. But do yourself a favor and hurry up. Like you said, these apples aren't going to jump off the trees in surrender, and I've got a ladder to climb."

CHAPTER TEN

As much as it chapped his ass to admit it, Eli was having fun. Which was really saying something, considering there was a not-small amount of cow manure in his immediate future. But ever since he and Scarlett had shot that video segment this morning in the apple grove, then laughed and joked their way through the rest of his enormous to-do list and her even bigger to-shoot list afterward, he'd felt oddly at ease. Granted, the spotlight still wasn't his happy place, but being in front of the camera hadn't been the *worst* thing going—at least not after his defenses had impulsively dared him to dare Scarlett into the frame. Their back-and-forth had made it just easy enough to slide into his cocky comfort zone and relax in front of the camera, and while he was never going to forget that the thing was rolling, at least maybe the segments would make up for the Whittakers' stroke of good luck this week.

Stupid fucking peaches.

"Okay," Scarlett said, her smile ushering Eli back to reality as she fell into step next to him on the footpath leading to the horse barn. "What's next?"

Eli laughed. "You know, it's a good thing I've seen your back, otherwise I'd be tempted to look for the battery pack."

"First of all"—her blond brows arched, but the smile playing on her lips damn near canceled out her sass—"you really need to have a come-to-Jesus meeting with the pot and the kettle if you're going to give *me* a raft of crap for working hard."

Eh. She kind of had him dead to rights there. At least as far as recent events were concerned, anyway. "Fair enough. What's second?"

"I'm not *all* work. I took a break five hours ago, right after we got done in the apple grove."

Her satisfied, take-that smile lasted for all of a heartbeat before Eli met it with a snort.

"A for effort, but no. Going up to the main house to download and send raw video footage to Mallory totally doesn't count as a breather."

"Oh, come on!" Scarlett's shoes crunched over the gravel as she stepped toward him to nudge his shoulder with her own. "I was in the house for ten whole minutes."

He returned the favor of the nudge, albeit gently because of her yellow jacket stings. "It was more like eight. Still no."

Scarlett—being Scarlett—went for round two. "But I had lunch *and* took a bathroom break while the footage downloaded."

And Eli—being Eli—met round two with a smirk so good, the thing tasted like cold beer on a Friday night. "Nice try, but no joy. You wolfed down a salad and a protein bar over the kitchen sink," he pointed out, and she huffed out a sigh that was probably as much concession as he was going to get.

"Okay, so I was excited, and I wanted to get everything to Mallory as soon as possible. But seriously, there's no way the footage of you talking about apple picking didn't turn out really well. I think the stills of the grove came out great, too, although I'll still have to edit those later before I can send them out. And I'll probably skip e-mailing her the test shots of you scowling."

"Hey! You said those were just to measure the light," Eli argued. "And for the record, I don't scowl."

He'd meant to deliver the words with conviction, but the soft chuckle that had managed to well up and escape from his chest pretty much trashed the intent. Scarlett's corresponding laughter filled the warm, dusty air around them along with half the cornfield to their right, sending a handful of sparrows shooting upward from the bright-green stalks. Not that she seemed to care what the sparrows thought of her.

"Pardon me while I call bullshit," she said, pointing to the equipment around her neck. "The camera never lies."

Annnnd reality check. Eli's knuckles whitened over the plastic gallon jug of water and the pair of apples in his grasp, his heart knocking harder against his ribs at the reminder. Time for the old bob and weave. "Right. Well, we're not done working just yet, but I did save the best for last."

"There's something better than picking apples and harvesting sweet corn?" Scarlett asked, and huh, she actually seemed more serious than sarcastic.

"Yup," he said, slipping his gaze over the faded-yet-sturdy wood-planked horse barn with a grin.

It took all of three footsteps for Scarlett to cave. "Are you going to tell me what it is, or were you hoping I'd sprout mind-reading abilities in the next two minutes?"

Eli fought the urge to flinch at the mere suggestion of her being able to take a look-see into his melon. "Neither." He measured out a smile and popped his chin at the open entryway to the horse barn. "How about I show you instead?"

Covering the rest of the distance to the horse barn took less than a minute, and he led the way past the double-wide, ten-foot doors and into the blessedly cooler space. Eli slowed his pace for a few steps, both to allow his eyes the courtesy of adjusting to the barn's well-shaded interior and to take in the musty-sweet scents of hay and feed.

But Scarlett didn't so much as pause to bat a single platinum lash. "*This* is the best part of the day?"

"Mmm-hmm. This here is our horse barn."

"But there's nothing in it," she said, stopping in the center of the aisle in front of the first stall to turn a quick circle.

Eli looked at the rectangular stalls, five on either side of the packed-dirt center aisle. The rafters were a good fifteen feet up, with the wooden half walls dividing each stall measuring in at about his sternum, and for as big as Clarabelle was girthwise, she wasn't a champ in the height department. Add that to the facts that the cow occupied the very last stall in the horse barn and Scarlett was going at warp speed as usual, and yeah, it wasn't exactly a shocker that poor Clarabelle had been overlooked.

"There are no horses in here," he qualified, but again, he didn't elaborate.

And again, he could've counted off Scarlett's wait time in nanoseconds. "Seems to defeat the purpose of having a horse barn, doesn't it?"

"We used to keep a few here and there, but horses are expensive to care for, and they don't serve much functional purpose on the farm like the cattle and chickens. Now we mostly use the space in here to store spare equipment and feed, or to keep a handful of goats from time to time. But the barn isn't entirely unoccupied."

Kicking his work-bruised boots into motion, he made his way down the aisle. Although it probably burned her up to no end, Scarlett matched his slow, easy stride, until finally, they reached the last shadowy stall in the barn. Eli's smile grew at the sight of the cow lazily chewing hay in the corner, and he popped the latch to swing the door wide on its creaky hinges before stepping over the threshold of the stall.

"This is Clarabelle," he said, turning toward Scarlett.

Only she wasn't right on his heel, as usual, because she'd screeched to a halt a good five steps behind him.

His heart did a flash-bang in his chest. In truth, Eli hadn't known how Scarlett would react to the big Jersey brown; after all, if there hadn't been so much as a goldfish in Scarlett's past, then she damn sure had probably never clapped eyes on an animal as large as Clarabelle. The cow might be as sweet as Tupelo honey with those huge black eyes and that slow, gentle demeanor of hers, but she wasn't exactly conventional. Or small. Or . . .

Shit.

"Scarlett?"

A second unglued itself from the clock, then another, and another, and still, Scarlett stood nailed to the dirt floor in front of Clarabelle's stall. Eli's brain spun, scrambling for something—Christ, anything even partway decent would do the trick—to back his way out of what had clearly been a spectacular fail of an idea.

And then her entire face lit with pure, uncut happiness, her Christmas-morning smile making a direct hit in the center of his sternum and rendering him 100 percent useless.

"Oh." Scarlett splayed a hand over the front of her loose black-and-white top, just above where her camera rested over her breastbone. "Oh my God. Eli, she's so pretty. Can I . . . is it okay if I take some pictures of her?"

Thankfully, Scarlett was so entranced by the sight of Clarabelle that she didn't seem to notice the fact that his voice box had gone on a complete walkabout with the rest of his faculties. "Uh," he grunted, and awesome. He was officially a Neanderthal. "Yeah. Yes." Eli straightened, giving himself one last mental bitch-slap before blinking himself back to the horse barn once and for all. "Of course. She's actually quite the attention hog."

As if to prove the claim, Clarabelle shuffled over, lowering her head to brush against his arm in a clear bid for affection, and he had to laugh. "Okay, old girl. Smile for the camera."

Eli stepped aside, placing the gallon of water in the opposite corner of the stall as Scarlett's camera sounded off in a series of click-*click*s. After a few minutes' worth of taking photographs from various angles, she straightened, carefully replacing the lens cap and thumbing the power switch to the "off" position. Another couple of moves had her gear stored safely in her candy-apple-red camera bag and the bag placed out of harm's way on a peg outside the stall.

"I take it we have to feed her and make sure her water and bedding are clean, just like we did with the chickens," Scarlett said, stepping back over the threshold and tugging the stall door shut.

"Yes and no. Clarabelle spends most of her day grazing in the field adjacent to the henhouse, so she doesn't need much by way of food or stall cleaning." Thankfully, their immediate surroundings were remarkably fragrance-free right now, although Eli knew all too well how those circumstances could turn on a dime with nine and a half cents to spare. "But she does need eyes on her every day, along with plenty of water and TLC."

Scarlett edged closer. "TLC," she said, and he traded the apples in his hand for the two stiffly bristled brushes sitting on the ledge by his shoulder.

"Yup. You want to help me groom her?"

"Sure." Reaching out, Scarlett took the brush he'd extended in her direction. "Oh! These bristles are kind of hard. Won't they hurt her?"

Unable to cage it, he let go of a laugh. "You'll climb a tree clear to the top with no never mind for your own personal safety, but you're worried about brushing my cow too hard?"

One platinum-blond brow arched. "Do you want my help or not, cowboy?"

Eli's laugh lingered, and he ran his free hand over the short, wiry hair on Clarabelle's back. "No, the brush won't hurt her. Clarabelle's skin isn't thin like a person's, and life can get pretty dirty out in the pasture, so the sturdy brush is a bit of a necessity."

"Okay." Scarlett stood across from him, her olive-green eyes missing nothing as she watched him for a minute before mimicking his movements on Clarabelle's other side. "Like this?"

Clarabelle chuffed out her approval before Eli could answer, angling toward Scarlett, and at least his lapdog of a cow had good taste. "Look at you," he teased, tipping his chin at Scarlett's busy hands. "You're gettin' the hang of everything around here. Pretty soon you'll be ready to run the whole farm."

"Hardly." Scarlett scoffed, although the sound wasn't unkind. "Anyway, in case you haven't noticed, I'm not exactly a stay-in-one-place kind of girl."

"You're staying here at Cross Creek for a month," he pointed out. Hell, he'd stayed here his whole life, even though half the time his mind was in other places.

"Which is actually unusual. I don't normally stay on location—or anywhere, I guess—for quite so long, but Mallory really needed the help."

Eli paused, midbrush. Surely she couldn't mean *anywhere*, anywhere. "I could see how a month-long shoot would be out of the ordinary, but what about in between jobs? Don't you stay at home in New York for more than a week or two when you're not on location? Or when you shoot locally?"

He'd finally sucked it up a few nights ago and checked out her website, and hoo boy, Hunter hadn't been embellishing when he'd brought up Scarlett's credentials. A photographer of her caliber had to have a forty-foot list of people interested in hiring her for freelance work. Hell, she could probably stay in New York indefinitely if she really wanted to.

Which clearly, she didn't, because her next words were, "I don't really do a ton of local shoots. At least not extended ones. And I'm rarely ever not on location."

"I'm all for going whole hog when it's necessary," Eli said, mostly because she was sure to give him a healthy dose of crap if he didn't. "But don't you get tired, going so fast all the time?"

Scarlett's laughter sent a shot of surprise all the way up his spine. "Oh, I get exhausted. That's part of the thrill, though. There's never a shortage of places to go snap pictures of, and I love it enough to do it till I drop."

"And you don't worry you'll miss that perfect shot because you're constantly running around at Mach 3?" Okay, so his brain-to-mouth filter had decided to malfunction on that one. But he'd hung the question out on the line. No sense in trying to back his way out of things now. "I mean, Clarabelle here weighs about twelve hundred pounds and you nearly missed seein' her."

"I might move fast, but I'm not blind," Scarlett said with a shrug. "I'd have found her eventually. What I worry about more is what I'd miss if I weren't moving at all."

A smirk twitched hard at the corners of his mouth, and ah, the comeback was too good to pass up. "Sorry, does that ever happen?"

She pressed her lips together, but not before he'd caught sight of the sassy-sweet smile that had bloomed there. "Funny. And while it's true I might not have seen Clarabelle at first"—Scarlett paused to offer the cow an apologetic smile and an extra pat behind the ears—"if I'd decided to rest on my laurels in New York rather than hauling my cookies down here to Millhaven, I never would've seen her, period. That seems like the bigger shame of the two."

Cue up a whole lot of *whoa*. "Guess I never thought of it like that," Eli admitted.

"Most people don't. But I belong behind the camera. If I have to be busy in order to make that happen . . ."

She trailed off with a fluid lift and lower of one shoulder. Eli knew he wouldn't get a more seamless shot at a subject change—for Pete's sake, the ability to dodge and deflect when it came to the topic of belonging was practically stamped into his DNA.

So it was really freaking weird when, instead of dropping the subject like the thermonuclear potato that it was, he asked, "So how did you figure out you belonged behind the camera?"

"Oh." She blinked, but only once before keeping up the pace with both her brush and his question. "Well, I obviously moved around a lot before I was adopted. All my foster homes were within New York City limits, but I was still in a new place every year."

"I can't even imagine that," Eli said, and Jesus, could he jam his size twelve any farther into his cakehole? "Sorry. It's just that—"

"You've lived in Millhaven your whole life, and the concept of all that moving around without a place to call home seems weird to you?" Scarlett gave up a look so open and honest, he had no choice but to nod. "Believe me, small-town upbringing or no, you're not the first person to think my circumstances are strange. Don't worry."

Eli lifted the hand that wasn't busy brushing Clarabelle, and Scarlett continued with ease. "When I went to go live with my dads, I had a hard time adjusting. Even though Bryan and Miguel were fantastic— and still are—I didn't really feel like I belonged with them. Not all the way, anyhow."

The words struck swift and deep, like a sucker punch right to the chin. *Cover it up, jackass.* "With how much you moved from place to place before they adopted you, I suppose it makes sense you'd have a hard time feeling at home," Eli managed.

She nodded. "I actually moved around a lot after they adopted me, too. My dads both work for a humanitarian aid organization, so we spent a lot of time in other countries."

"Wow." The idea seemed so foreign, yet something oddly exciting turned over in Eli's chest. "How did you go to school?"

"I was home-schooled. We did most of it on the road. I actually got my high school diploma when we were in Peru," she said, as if it were the most natural thing in the universe, and hell if that didn't explain her obvious wanderlust. Along with her difficulty finding a place to belong. "Don't get me wrong, I was probably more comfortable traveling all over the place than most kids would've been, but I still never felt quite like I'd found a place that was perfect for me. Of course, like most dads, mine worried."

"They sound like good parents," he said, and Scarlett's smile answered before she'd even spoken a word.

"They're the best. They wanted me to find something I loved so I'd feel like I fit in better, so we went the activities route."

Ah. Eli ran a palm over Clarabelle's warm, sturdy body one last time before stepping back to return his brush to the shelf. Pulling a pocketknife from its well-worn spot in his Levi's, he grabbed one of the apples he'd freed from the stash he and Scarlett had picked earlier, slicing through the fruit with a soft *snick.*

"Let me guess." He handed half of the apple to Scarlett, flattening his palm to offer the other half to Clarabelle. "You picked photography."

"Nope," came her quick reply, and God, leave it to his partner in crime to keep him on his damned toes. "Actually, at first it was piano, which was a huge crash and burn, then dance, where I discovered my distinct lack of both rhythm and coordination. Should I just feed her the whole thing?" Scarlett dipped her chin at Clarabelle, who had unceremoniously finished the half of the apple Eli had just given her and was nosing her way toward Scarlett in a very obvious search for seconds.

He nodded. "Her digestive system is made to handle the core. Just don't curl your fingers when you feed her, or she'll think they're part of the deal."

"Got it." Passing over her brush so she could cradle the apple between both palms, Scarlett extended her hands, and the throaty laugh that worked its way past her lips did nothing to keep his pulse in line or his dick in check.

Eli cleared his throat in an effort to get his brain—and his other, more southerly parts—back online. "I've gotta say, I feel you on the no-dancing thing," he told her, pointing to the spot where his Red Wings met the hay scattered over the floor of the stall. "Even though my boots say otherwise, I'm pretty sure both of my feet are lefties."

Scarlett stepped back from Clarabelle, tucking a strand of wayward hair behind the row of tiny silver hoops and studs climbing halfway up her ear as she slid back to the topic with ease. "After piano and dance were both a no go for me, I didn't really want to try anything else. Once bitten, and all. But then when I was thirteen, I picked up a camera, just on a whim. It was just one of those PHD deals—"

At the look of confusion he must have been broadcasting in hi-definition, she added, "Push Here, Dummy. Complete point and shoot, not a whole lot of skill required. Anyway, after two days with that thing, about a hundred and fifty still-life shots of everything from our fruit bowl to our front stoop in Brooklyn, and far too much cash for one-hour developing, I was a goner. I've been all in ever since."

"You were all in at thirteen?" Eli asked, although God, he probably shouldn't be surprised.

"Oh yeah. I worked my butt and most of my other parts off for all four years to get into the fine arts program at Yale."

Just when he'd been certain there was no more shock to be had from this woman, his what-the-fuck barometer exploded. "As in, Yale University. In New Haven. The third oldest institution of higher learning in the entire nation." Christ, no wonder she'd been able to bust him quoting Walt Whitman.

"Mmm-hmm. That's the one." If Scarlett's nod was any sort of gauge, she was completely unfazed by both Eli's reaction and her wildly impressive Ivy League alma mater. "They have the best photography program in the United States, and I didn't see any point in anything other than going big." She paused. "Did you go to college?"

Every last one of his warning bells clanged, and he supersized his smile as he selected his words with near-surgical precision. "Operating a farm is more of a hands-on kind of thing."

"So none of you have gone?" she asked.

Eli grabbed the out and ran like hell. "Hunter had the chance to go away to college—he was a hell of a running back in high school. He could've gotten any one of a half dozen scholarships to about as many schools. But Cross Creek is a family business, and he's never wanted anything other than to stay here."

"I get that. This is where his passion is," Scarlett said. She waited until Eli had emptied the gallon of fresh water into the trough on the far side of Clarabelle's stall before adding on, "Most people feel like they belong in a place, I think. I'm just the odd man out because my place doesn't stand still."

His heart went for broke in his chest. He needed to shut up, or wink or smirk or dish up some flirty little innuendo. Most of all, he need *not* to ask . . . "Doesn't being the odd man out make you doubt what you picked?"

A tiny crease appeared between her brows, but only for a second. "Not really, no. I'm used to making my own normal, and while I love my dads, the only place I've ever felt really, truly at home is behind the camera. So while I might have come from all over the place, it's cool. I belong all over the place, too."

In that moment, with Scarlett standing in a patch of sunshine filtering in from the high, glassless window behind her and giving up a completely unvarnished smile, Eli almost forgot how to breathe. But then her smile shifted, becoming a self-deprecating version of itself, and she stepped back with a soft laugh.

"Anyway. I'm sure that probably sounds really hokey to you, having been born and raised here at Cross Creek. Of course you belong in one place."

The admission that he'd never felt like he belonged on the farm was right there on the tip of his tongue, brashly begging for release. Before he could let the words loose, both Scarlett's cell phone and the two-way radio at his hip went ballistic.

"Oh!" she murmured at the same time Eli came out with a muttered curse.

"What the . . ." With his heart in his windpipe, he unlatched the door to Clarabelle's stall and ushered Scarlett to the main space of the barn, not wanting the chatter or the static from the two-way to spook the poor animal. "This is Eli. Everything okay?"

"Copy that. Everything is fine." Emerson's voice threaded past the white noise hiss of their radio channel. "But did you place some kind of ad for apple picking that I don't know about?"

If there was a blue-ribbon medal for the world's most bizarre question, Emerson had just won the thing, hands-frickin'-down. "No," Eli managed past his confusion, moving closer to the empty stalls in the heart of the barn to give Scarlett some privacy to continue her call. "I only just realized we'd be good to go for next week's pick-your-own this morning. Why?"

"Because there's been a ton of buzz about it on the Cross Creek Facebook page over the last couple of hours. Everybody and their mother wants to know when they can come pick apples, and our website hits have gone through the roof since lunch. People keep talking about some video of you."

"But that's impossible." Eli stared at the two-way in his hand, his brain chock-full of *say what?* But the sensation took a backseat to the press of his pulse against his ears as he looked across the barn and caught sight of the shell-shock taking over Scarlett's pretty features.

After a quick "over and out" to Emerson, he covered the packed-dirt floor between him and Scarlett in only a half dozen strides. "Scarlett? What's the matter?"

"Nothing, I . . ." She held up her cell phone. "That was Mallory."

"Okay," he led, and for once, he was grateful for Scarlett's jump-right-in tendencies.

"She thought the video footage was great. Really great. In fact, she loved it so much that she didn't want to sit on it until Tuesday, when the next set of articles was supposed to go live. So she did the editing and went ahead and posted the segment a couple of hours ago."

Eli's jaw unhinged. "Damn, that was fast."

But before Eli could rewind enough to come up with something more eloquent, Scarlett said, "Yeah, hold that thought. Apparently, Mallory felt the biggest personal connection came from the part of the video where you and I were both in-frame together. I had no idea she would even *consider* doing anything with that footage other than scrapping it, but—"

"*That's* the part she put online? With me and you, goofing around?"

Scarlett nodded. "Yes. And believe it or not, that isn't even the most shocking part of what she said."

When all he could do was stare, she continued. "I guess some food blogger with a pretty big following happened to catch the link to the video when Mallory posted it on *FoodE*'s Twitter page. The blogger retweeted the link, and then some other people in her network retweeted it, too, and Mallory said the video is getting, um, a lot of traction."

People keep talking about some video of you . . . "Wait," Eli said, his heart beginning to pound in earnest. "How much traction are we talking about, exactly?"

Scarlett lifted the phone still pressed to her palm, a smile starting to maneuver past the stunned expression on her face as she held the thing out to show him a screen shot of *FoodE*'s Twitter page. "I don't have specific numbers, but it looks like as of ten minutes ago, we were officially trending."

"Are you . . ." Eli trailed off, unable to shove the rest of his thoughts past all the shock having a hoedown in his gray matter.

"Absolutely serious," Scarlett answered without skipping so much as a breath or a beat. "The video of you and me picking apples is pretty much going viral, Eli. We may have done it inadvertently, but it looks like we found our blockbuster."

Her smile became a full-fledged bubble of laughter, and she pushed up to her toes to throw her arms around his neck.

And out of sheer instinct, he kissed her.

CHAPTER ELEVEN

Two thoughts filled Eli's brain as he slanted his mouth over Scarlett's. The first was that kissing her should feel impulsive and reckless and crazy. The second?

Was that the first thought could take the direct path to hell, because Scarlett felt fucking flawless in his arms.

Their lips touched for only a second, two at the most, before Scarlett pulled back slightly to stare at him. Dread trickled into his belly on a reality chaser, and Jesus, Mary, and all the saints, had he seriously just kissed her?

"God, Scarlett, I apologize." Eli blinked. "I was out of line. I—"

Before he could speak or react or even form a scrap of thought, she pressed up to kiss him back.

For a sliver of a second, Eli stood stock-still, locked into place. Although the connection of their mouths was the same as it had been only seconds ago—just lips on lips, barely moving—this kiss was different. It wasn't born of shock or excitement or impulse. It stemmed from want. Hot and pure.

And he wasn't holding back.

Eli shifted forward, increasing the contact between their bodies in a hot rush of movement. With a sweep of his tongue, he parted Scarlett's lips, coaxing them open just enough to capture the taste of her exhale.

Her breath drifted out on a sigh that Eli felt against his chest, and yeah, *closer.*

He explored her mouth in slow, deliberate strokes. Lowering one hand to the column of her neck and spreading his fingers wide, he hooked his thumb beneath the angle of her jaw to hold her steady while he pushed harder against her lips. Scarlett made a sound in the back of her throat, caught somewhere between a moan and a fierce, feminine growl, sending a relentless ripple of want all the way down Eli's spine as he kissed and licked and searched.

Closer.

As if she'd formed the thought a fraction of a second before him, Scarlett altered her grasp on his shoulders, pressing forward for motion rather than contact. They moved a handful of steps until his back hit a solid surface—barn wall, probably—but at this point, she could've backed him up against a bed of flaming barbed wire and he wouldn't have cared one whit. The only thing that mattered was that Scarlett was still flush against him, her mouth under his mouth, her firm, full breasts on his chest. He wanted to taste every part of her all at once.

Starting with that sharp tongue.

Eli sucked her lower lip into his mouth, teasing the skin there until she opened wider to let him in. She met his every move, her tongue sliding over his in hot strokes, and her teeth nipping and teasing with just enough pressure to make his cock jerk behind the fly of his Levi's.

Fuck. Yeah. *Closer* wasn't going to be enough.

"Scarlett." Eli broke off from her mouth with an exhale that came from deep in his throat. Starting a trail of open-mouthed kisses that got harder as they descended, he coasted his mouth over her jaw, unable to keep from lingering by the soft spot just below her ear before continuing his path over her neck.

"Ah," Scarlett moaned, more sound than actual word. "God, do that again," she demanded, and suddenly, he found himself loving the hell out of the loose neckline of her shirt.

"You're bossy."

The grin he'd buried in the hollow of her throat doubled as she answered. "You already knew that. Now hurry up and kiss me. Right . . . there."

Her fingers closed over the cotton of his T-shirt, forming hot fists at his shoulders, and once again Eli was done holding back. He swiped his tongue over the indent between her collarbones, gripping her hips to maximize the tight, hot connection between their lower bodies. His cock throbbed in response, the friction of Scarlett's body—so soft and sweet despite the demanding, almost primal push of her hips against his—taking him from desire to reckless need in less than a breath.

Eli lifted his head, his lips so close to Scarlett's that he could feel her breath as she let out a tiny moue of frustration.

"You want me to keep kissing you?" He dropped his gaze to her slightly swollen mouth, his hand sliding from her hip to her rib cage before his brain registered his libido's command to move.

Scarlett met his stare with a bold one of her own. "Yes."

"Then say it."

Her brows edged upward, and she tested him with her silence. But that dark want welled up again to dare his hand higher, his fingers cupping her breast with only enough pressure to tease.

"Eli—"

"No," he interrupted, his heart slamming an insistent rhythm in his chest. "I'm bossy, too, Scarlett. I want to hear you say the words." His thumb inched higher, so close that he could feel the hard edge of her nipple through the thin cotton of her top and the even thinner lace of the bra he'd seen earlier. "I want you to tell me what you want"—his thumb slipped closer to the tight peak, his cock growing even harder as his next words formed in his mouth—"and exactly where you want it."

But then Scarlett fractured his control with a single, simple word.

"Eli," she whispered against his skin. "I want you to keep kissing me." Her gaze dropped to the connection between his hand and her body, her smile instant and wicked.

"And I don't want you to stop at my mouth."

He closed the slight space between them out of sheer instinct, crushing his mouth to hers in a near-punishing kiss. Curving his fingers more firmly beneath Scarlett's breast, Eli ran the pad of his thumb over her nipple, dark satisfaction rippling low through his belly as she arched into his touch on a moan. The sound was so deliciously wild that he repeated the move just to hear her make it again. Their kiss grew more intense, rough with need, and Eli crushed his mouth to hers so hard his lips ached. But God, Scarlett felt so reckless and crazy and perfect, it was all too easy to forget how they'd gotten here, what they should be doing . . .

Good Christ, what *was* he doing?

Reality crashed into him like a gallon of ice water, and every single part of him froze before his eyes flew open and he shifted back with a start.

"Scarlett." This time, her name was an apology. But dammit—*dammit!* He'd literally just gotten the break he so desperately needed. He should be focusing on the farm now more than ever, but instead, he'd been T-minus six seconds from impulsively stripping Scarlett naked and making her scream his name in the middle of the freaking horse barn.

Had he lost his ever-loving mind?

Scarlett's eyes fluttered open on a delay. For a second, her expression was dazed, completely caught up in the moment that passed. Then her dark-green stare filled with understanding just as Eli's gut filled with the dread of having put it there.

"Are you . . . oh." She lifted her fingers to her mouth for a second before pressing her lips into a hard line. "You stopped on purpose."

"Yeah." He ran a hand over his crew cut in a move that would've been a jab of frustration had he actually had enough hair for the movement. "Yeah. I did."

Scarlett's eyes flashed with an emotion he couldn't quite name but knew he didn't like. "So you think us kissing was a mistake," she said.

"It was"—*Impulsive. Sexy. The hottest kiss anyone has ever laid on me, bar fucking none*—"probably not a good idea," he managed, clamping down on his inner voice with a shake of his head. He needed to get his brain back online, and he needed to do it five minutes ago. "We were both excited about the video segment being a hit and got caught up in the moment, but I shouldn't have been so forward. I'm sorry."

"And you believe that? You believe this was just some heat-of-the-moment thing, and that we should forget it ever happened?"

Scarlett looked at him, and of all the times she could've bucked her penchant for broadcasting her emotions without apology, she had to choose *now* to go the unreadable route?

Eli paused, the word "no" burning a hole in his rib cage. But he couldn't lose track of what was important now. He had to get Cross Creek back in the black so he could go back to normal, and normal didn't include a woman who could so easily blow the composure he'd spent the last ten years of his life crafting. No matter how insanely hot their kiss had been.

So Eli said the only thing he could.

"We're going to have to work together on these video segments for the next three weeks, and that really needs to be our focus. So yes. I think we should forget this ever happened."

A heartbeat passed, then another before Scarlett took a full step back over the packed-earth floor.

"You got it, cowboy. Already done," she said, pivoting to pick up her camera bag before walking out of the barn without so much as a backward glance.

◆ ◆ ◆

Scarlett burrowed deeper under the hand-stitched quilt that had come with her borrowed bed, trying like mad to talk herself into going back to sleep. But the clock on her also-borrowed nightstand read 3:45 a.m., and if she were going to drift back off to dreamland, she'd have done it an hour ago.

Instead, she was lying here at the most obscene hour Saturday morning had to offer, torn between supreme frustration and the sort of insistent want that could only be quelled by an ice-cold shower or a white-hot roll in the sheets.

Cold shower for the win.

Throwing the covers from her legs with a curse that would make a sailor turn crimson, Scarlett got out of bed and padded the six requisite steps to the bathroom. She had a full day in front of her with today's farmers' market. Might as well get a jump on things.

Even if, despite that kiss and diss, what you really want is for Eli Cross to get a jump on you.

"Oh, for God's sake," she muttered, yanking back the shower curtain and cranking the faucet handle as far toward the "C" as she'd be able to bear. So the kisses she and Eli had shared had been hot enough to qualify as a fire hazard, and maybe she'd been just a teensy bit brash when she'd told him not to stop at her mouth. But he'd made it wildly clear that he wanted to focus on the work and nothing but the work, and in truth, that wasn't an entirely terrible plan. The video clip of the two of them had—however unexpectedly—gained a metric ton of exposure for both Cross Creek and *FoodE*. Maybe the kisses really *had* just been nothing more than heat of the moment excitement.

That had made her climb him like Mount Everest. And beg him to put his mouth on her. In all. The right. Places.

Scarlett swiped her toothbrush from the vanity's barely there ledge, scrubbing her pearly whites with more enthusiasm than the job probably required. Everything was working out as planned. Hell, there had been so many hits on the page of Cross Creek's website that linked to

Camden Valley's farmers' market that she'd had to grab a ride home from Emerson at eight last night because all four Cross men had still been cramming their box truck full of produce with no sign of stopping. Mallory was getting the exposure she needed for her magazine. Eli had agreed to do more video segments with Scarlett to keep it that way. Cross Creek was sure to have a banner day at today's market, where she'd likely snap an SD card's worth of fabulous images.

What she really needed to do was forget those kisses just like she'd said she would and keep her eye on the damned ball.

With one final swish, she finished brushing her teeth and got into the shower. Scarlett made quick work of getting clean, then getting dressed, and by the time she'd added a hi-there with both her hairbrush and her mascara brush, she was past due for a caffeine fix. She made her way to the kitchen to start the process of making a latte big enough to do the backstroke in, flipping her cell phone into her palm while she waited for her espresso machine to work its magic.

Oh my God, woman, you are a fucking genius! read the first in a string of text messages from Mallory, and okay, Scarlett had to admit, there were worse ways to start a day.

She leaned back against the counter, a tiny smile edging at the corners of her mouth as she read on. The video of you and Eli—who is freaking adorbs, BTW—is still bringing in a high volume of steady hits to FoodE's site. Mallory followed up with some numbers that made Scarlett's eyes go wide, and holy crap. She made a mental note never to underestimate the power of some well-placed tweets.

At any rate, I know you are asleep right now but wanted to say definitely send me whatever video you shoot tmw at the FM as soon as it's a wrap. I've had over a dozen food bloggers ask when it's coming and I want to give ppl round two ASAP to keep them clicking!

The espresso machine let out a soft beep—hello, elixir of life—and she pushed off the Formica, quickly glancing at the last message in Mallory's one-sided text stream.

And srsly, call me when you can, b/c I need the dirt on Farm Boy! Pls tell me all that flirting isn't just for show. At least one of us should be getting laid!

Scarlett's stomach squeezed, and she sent up a fast-but-fervent prayer that Emerson had left a giant bottle of scotch in one of the kitchen cabinets when she'd moved out.

"Come on," she whispered, putting her phone down and turning toward the fridge to grab the soy milk and get the hell on with her morning, once and for all. She and Eli might have to flirt for the camera and for the people who showed up at the farmers' market today, but it was all in the name of work.

Speaking of which . . .

Two lattes and a piece of wheat toast later, Scarlett had gone through all the photos she'd sent to Mallory over the course of the last week, dividing them by subject and cross-checking the ones of produce against any information she could find in her notes on Camden Valley's farmers' market. She was tapping out the last of her list of things to photograph today when a knock sounded off at her door. Her heart did the samba in her chest, but she pressed a hand over the front of her dark-green tank top to cover the commotion. Eli had said he wanted to stick to business. She could totally do that. They'd be professional. Polite. Work only.

But the perfectly professional, perfectly polite greeting Scarlett had worked up in her head completely disintegrated at the sight of Eli standing on her doorstep with a charming-as-hell smile on his face and a brown paper bag in his hand.

"Morning." He extended the bag, looking hotter than anyone had a right to. Seriously, who made a hoodie and a pair of banged-up jeans sexy? At five o'clock in the *morning*? It just wasn't right.

"What's this?" she blurted as she took the bag from his outstretched hand, and God, could she be any more graceless?

If Eli was bothered by her distinct lack of a filter, though, he sure didn't show it. "This is a vegan breakfast burrito." He paused, tipping his head slightly as he added, "And we can add that to the list of things I never thought I'd say."

Scarlett blinked, trying to piece the words together in a way that made sense. "You bought me a vegan breakfast burrito?"

"No. I made you a vegan breakfast burrito."

The shock pumping through her veins must've taken a detour over her face, because Eli took one look at her and backpedaled. "Okay, sort of. I went up to the main house an hour ago to get a bunch of crates that didn't fit in the box truck, and Owen was making breakfast burritos. I helped him come up with one for you that fits the bill."

"Why?"

Scarlett clamped down on her lip just a second too late to bite down on the overly bold question, but to her surprise, Eli just laughed.

"What, is breakfast some sort of sacrilege once you cross the Mason-Dixon Line or something?"

Seriously, she needed to build some sort of immunity to that here-comes-trouble smile of his. Either that or she was going to have to head back to that cute little town where she'd gotten her coffeepot for some cute little batteries to fuel her cute little vibrator.

"No! Nope, mmm-mmm," she barked, chasing the burn from her cheeks with a sweep of her fingertips. Sure, Eli was good-looking. (Fine. He was sex on a stick. Potato-potahto). But they needed to stay professional, and anyway, she was here to capture all the compelling aspects of his family-run farm. Current emphasis on *family*.

Scarlett cleared her throat and wrenched her thoughts back to the straight and sex-free narrow. "I mean. Um. Breakfast is perfectly normal in New York, along with all the other places I've been this month. I was referring more to the all-together-now thing. Your family just seems a lot closer than most."

An odd expression whisked through his eyes, but his cocksure grin took over again before Scarlett could be certain she'd seen the blip, let alone try to identify it. "Yep, that's us. We Crosses are thick as thieves."

Shouldering her camera bag, then the backup bag she'd had waiting by the door, Scarlett nodded. "I know. Don't get me wrong—I think all the family powwows you guys have are great. Breakfasts. Saturday dinners. They're just way outside of my wheelhouse, is all."

Eli reached out, clearly meaning to take one of the camera bags from her grasp, and after a second's worth of her hesitation, he said, "I know you can manage both, probably in your sleep. But leaving you with all the gear and me with the burrito bag seems a little out of balance, don't you think?"

"I suppose," Scarlett answered slowly, handing over the secondary bag as she grabbed her keys and followed him over the threshold. "Thank you. For the help and for breakfast."

"You're welcome. The farmers' market runs from seven to two, and sometimes things can get a little hectic. You never know when or if you'll be able to slip in a decent meal, so we tend to kick things off with something pretty hearty just in case."

Hell if that didn't make a boatload of sense, not to mention help to explain why Owen and Eli would get up so damned early to actually make breakfast rather than simply grab and go.

Scarlett moved to the passenger side of his pickup truck, lifting the paper bag with one hand before using the other to open the door. "So what's in it?"

"Potatoes, onions, red bell peppers, and cilantro—all fresh from the greenhouse and cooked in canola oil—and some black beans and salsa. Along with salt and pepper and some cumin Owen dug out of the spice cabinet," Eli said, getting into the truck beside her.

"Wow." She took the foil-wrapped burrito from the bag, her mouth starting to water at both the smells and the description of her breakfast. "That's totally vegan."

He pulled out onto the main road, his smile obvious in his words even though his face was mostly hidden by the predawn shadows. "I told you it was."

"No, no." Scarlett closed her eyes, a pang unfolding in her belly as she scrambled for a do-over. "What I meant was, not a lot of people who aren't vegan know what really *is* vegan. Much less how to make a meal that legitimately qualifies. It's actually impressive."

"Oh. Well, don't give me too much credit. I just Googled 'vegan breakfast burrito' and you got lucky—we had most of the stuff in the pantry. Sorry to say we were fresh out of tofu crumbles and soy cheese, though."

Eli named the products with such a straight face that Scarlett had no choice but to cave in and laugh. "You're not just trying to butter me up because we have to share screen time together, are you?" She waved a hand through the air to erase the question as soon as it had launched. "You know what, don't answer that. This burrito smells fantastic, and it was really nice of you to make me breakfast. Thanks."

"You're welcome," he said, tipping his chin at her but keeping his eyes on the road in front of them. "And for the record, yes."

Scarlett unwrapped one corner of the burrito to take a bite, fighting back a moan as the flavors and textures registered with her taste buds. The heartiness of the potatoes mixed in with the light, bright burst from the cilantro to make a perfect play on opposites. But the peppers refused to be outshined, and she took another three bites before she finally slowed down enough to speak.

"Yes, what? And holy Moses, can your brother cook," she managed past the party in her mouth. God, even the salsa had just the right ratio of flavor to kick.

"Glad you like it. The yes was to answer your question. The burrito is partly a peace offering. Not because we're shooting more videos, but . . ." Eli paused just in time for Scarlett's pulse to start double-timing through her veins. Especially when he finished with, "I didn't mean to make you uncomfortable yesterday in the horse barn."

"You didn't make me uncomfortable," she said, then amended with, "Your delivery might have pissed me off a little"—because brain-to-mouth filter or no, she wasn't scaling back on the truth—"but in the end, you're right. Us kissing *was* pretty impulsive. We've got three weeks' worth of video segments in front of us, so we should probably stick to business."

"And you're okay with doing that, even though I pissed you off?"

Although Eli asked the question with all his usual clear-and-present charm, something in his voice told Scarlett he really cared about her answer.

So she gave up a grin along with the truth. "Yeah, cowboy. You and I are cool. Just as long as you promise me one thing."

"And that is?" he asked.

"You'll show me how you and Owen made this burrito. Seriously. I've had breakfast on six of the seven continents, and I'm here to tell you, this thing is insane."

Eli's laughter filled the cab of the truck, warming her all the way through before settling into that cocky smile of his.

"You got it, bumblebee. Just make sure you finish your breakfast. If the last twelve hours' worth of traffic on Cross Creek's website is any indication, you're gonna need all the energy you can get."

CHAPTER TWELVE

Scarlett leaned back against the side panel of Cross Creek's box truck, 99 percent certain her leg muscles had been replaced by old rubber bands and even older glue. But since the crack of dawn boasted practically nonexistent natural light, she hadn't been able to snap any useable shots since she and Eli had pulled into Camden Valley's pavilion nearly an hour ago. Pitching in to help the Crosses set up for the farmers' market until she could get to work on her own stuff had been a no-brainer. Of course, right now her calves were tag-teaming with her lower back to give her no-brainer a whole lot of grief, to the point that Scarlett had no choice but to admit the truth.

Working on a farm definitely wasn't the tranquil cakewalk she'd expected it to be.

Now that she finally had a bit of daylight on her side, Scarlett took advantage of her brief respite on the sidelines to check out her surroundings. The pavilion was part of a larger park area, with ball fields and playgrounds and picnic tables on either side. Although the vendors had been able to drive all the way up to the pavilion via a narrow access road—thank God, because the mere thought of hauling all those crates from the parking lot made Scarlett consider crying outright—the main entrance was gated on the other side of a gently rolling hill. Railroad tracks formed the area's back boundary, separated from the rest of the park by a small commuter lot and a passenger platform.

The vendors for today's market—maybe thirty or so in all—had parked on the perimeter of the pavilion, which was protected from the elements by a fixed roof spanning four oversized columns in each corner. Scarlett grinned as she realized the sun would still have plenty of opportunity to slant in and brighten things up, and yeah, time to throw back a couple of ibuprofen and get going. The sooner, the better.

But before she could move so much as an aching muscle, a frosty water bottle appeared in her direct field of vision, sending a hard shot of relief all the way to her toes even as she tabled the go-go-go message pumping through her brain.

"Best hydrate," came Tobias Cross's warm-yet-gruff voice as he settled in next to her with a smile. "Or Owen will give you a wheelbarrowful of grief."

Scarlett grinned, unable to do anything but. "That sounds like first-hand knowledge."

"Might be," Tobias answered, but his wry smile said she'd hit the truth jackpot. "But I can't blame him for lookin' out, I s'pose."

She paused to crack the top off the bottle of water he'd passed over, taking a deep draw of its contents before she leaned back against the box truck and replied, "For whatever it's worth, Eli's the same way with me when we're running all over the farm."

"Is he now?"

The way Tobias's salt-and-pepper brows drifted up toward the brim of his Stetson suggested Eli's actions surprised him. Which made the two of them even, since Tobias's surprise shocked Scarlett right back.

"Mmm-hmm. Not that I'm complaining—all that bugging has probably saved my bacon a time or two. I get a little wrapped up in the moment when I'm shooting, and I don't like to slow down. I guess doing what you love can make hours feel like minutes."

"That does seem about right."

Although his smile stayed in place, it grew more wistful as he sent his gaze over the tables beneath the pair of oversized red canopy tents Owen and Eli were still stocking with last-minute crates of produce, and the sentiment in Scarlett's chest took the springboard route directly out of her mouth.

"I'm really grateful for your allowing me to visit Cross Creek for such an extended shoot," she said, her stare following his to the nearby hustle of last-minute preparations before the market opened. "I know having a stranger in your midst can't be easy. Especially one with a camera and a direct line to the Internet."

The lightning-fast wink Tobias sent in her direction was proof positive that Eli came by his charm honestly. "Well, I guess it's lucky for us you're not a stranger anymore, now isn't it?"

Scarlett's stomach squeezed. God, the Crosses' uber-inclusive dynamic was so outside of her wheelhouse. But since she refused to offend Tobias by saying so, she went with, "You just have such a tight-knit family. I appreciate that you're willing to let an outsider in."

For a heartbeat, he remained quiet, and her heartbeat accelerated with the worry that she'd somehow managed to offend him anyway.

But then he pushed off the side panel of the box truck, tipping his caramel-colored hat at her as if the pause had never happened. "Well, we're right happy to have you. 'Specially since Emerson tells me these stories of yours are startin' to take off."

Scarlett thought of the stats Mallory had texted her earlier, along with the correlating response Eli had told her Cross Creek's social media pages had been getting, and her pulse tapped faster for a completely different reason. "The photos and articles on *FoodE*'s site definitely seem to be gaining the traction we'd all hoped for."

Her eyes darted to the spot by the checkout station where Eli had carefully stored her gear next to the food scales and the cash box. Her fingers twitched with anticipation, all the colors and textures and shadows and contrasts around her insistently whispering with the need to be framed up and caught on camera, and she slid her hands into the pockets of her cutoffs in an effort to conceal the urge to not eat or breathe or stop until she'd taken pictures of pretty much every last thing under the tent in front of her.

Tobias's laughter welled up in a rusty burst. "Guess we should go on and get started. Sun's up, and I expect you're itchin' to snap a photograph or two."

Busted. A flush crept from her cheeks to her temples, but she didn't try to hide it. "What gave me away?"

"Darlin', I mean this as a kindness, but you are an open book. Plus, I've been around long enough to know passion for somethin' when I see it. Now go. Grab that camera of yours and take pictures of whatever suits you."

Smiling, Scarlett thanked him one last time for the water before covering the dozen or so steps between the box truck and Cross Creek's tent. She geared up easily, her excitement at the prospect of a day-long shoot as much a part of her muscle memory as the movements themselves, and equally vital. Knowing she had the luxury of time on her side since she'd be working in a relatively fixed space, Scarlett made the judgment call of sticking with just her primary camera for now. She could always swap out her glass and make other adjustments as the sunlight shifted around the tent, and anyway, she was going to get dangerously close to spontaneous human combustion if she didn't start taking some pictures, stat.

Her sneakers shushed over the smooth concrete on the pavilion floor as she moved farther beneath the tent. Lifting her camera to her eye, Scarlett measured the elements around her, taking a few test shots before a rumble of familiar, masculine laughter worked its way from her ears all the way down her spine.

"Smart to snap pictures of the produce while you can, bumblebee. They're gonna open the gates in five minutes, and I heard the parking lot is already jam-packed."

She lowered Baby, her brows pulling downward in confusion. "Who told you that?" Eli had been right here in the pavilion, with the parking lot well out of sight, since before the sun had come all the way up.

Not that his cocky smile would be deterred by such details. "He did," Eli said, pointing to his brother, Owen, who lifted his hands in explanation.

"My buddy Lane is Millhaven's sheriff. He comes down here to the farmers' market on Saturdays to help out with traffic and things like that whenever he can. He texted me a few minutes ago to say he hasn't seen the parking lot this full, this early, all year."

"Wow." Scarlett's lips parted over her surprise. "That's a good sign, right?"

Eli waggled his brows, gesturing to the tables in front of them with a flourish. "That's a *great* sign. Unless you're a Jonagold. Or a watermelon. Or one of Owen here's fancy-schmancy heirloom tomatoes. Or—"

"Okay, okay. We get it," Owen said, a small smile breaking past his normally serious demeanor. "And for the record, those tomatoes are Cherokee Purple, Marvel Stripe, and Brandywine. In that order."

"'Course they are." Eli paused for just a beat before he jokingly added, "Show off."

"Mmm." Owen's smile had an extremely short shelf life, disappearing even more quickly than it had arrived, and wow, that brotherly tension thing sure hadn't taken a hike since Scarlett had last been around both Eli and Owen together.

She took a half step toward Eli, whose shoulders had gone rigid beneath his navy-blue T-shirt. Time to lighten the mood, and fast. "Well," she said, letting her own smile pick up the luster Owen's had lost. "Seems Camden Valley has way better cell service than Millhaven if Lane was able to text you with such good news, Owen."

Both men blinked at her, but Eli found his feet first. "Eh, that's not saying much. Most parts of Siberia have better cell service than Millhaven."

Owen's expression remained unreadable for only a second longer before sliding into a wordless *good point*. "Hopefully we'll be too busy to even think about cell service today. Although I did promise Emerson I'd try my best to get on Cross Creek's social media sites to do a little promo of our specialty selections."

"She's not coming?" Scarlett asked, and Eli shook his head to the negative.

"Not today. Emerson has MS, and the heat and the car ride don't always make the trip out here to the farmers' market easy on her."

"Oh!" Scarlett's chin snapped up, a bolt of surprise filling her chest. "I'm sorry. I didn't know."

"Don't feel bad," Owen said. "It's not something she advertises."

Admittedly, Scarlett's knowledge of the disease was limited, but still . . . "Living with an illness like that must be tough."

"Yeah, but Emerson's tough, too," Eli pointed out. "She comes out to the market when she can, and that turns out to be more often than not. But she has a physical therapy practice in town in addition to the help she gives us at Cross Creek, and sometimes all that work can knock her out."

Scarlett's respect factor for the woman quintupled, just like that. "God. I can't imagine having to juggle two jobs and a health condition like multiple sclerosis all alone."

"Emerson isn't alone," Owen said, his voice gruff but his gray eyes kind. "We all pitch in to give her a breather when she needs one, just like she helps out at Cross Creek when she's feelin' up to it. Hunt is holding down the fort at the farm today, too, so he's nearby in case she needs anything."

Wow. Scarlett knew Hunter and Emerson weren't married, but the Crosses' support for her put a triple knot in their already tightly knit family dynamic, for sure.

Scarlett looked down at the camera around her neck, the idea in her mind going from zero to out-loud in less than three seconds. "Since you two will probably be really busy helping customers today, I can post updates and pictures to your social media accounts. I mean, I won't be able to edit the photos as carefully as I would for a magazine spread or anything," she amended, but Eli just laughed.

"Uh, news flash. You're a professional photographer. Your unedited photos will still kick the ass of anything Owen or I would shoot with our cell phones and throw on Cross Creek's Twitter feed."

Owen nodded in agreement, and Scarlett split her smile between the two of them.

"Fair enough. But as long as you guys are okay with hooking me up as a temporary admin on Cross Creek's social media pages, I'm happy to help," she said. Another idea popped into her mind right on the heels of the first, and *yes*, even better. "I can text Mallory and have her share everything on *FoodE*'s accounts, too."

"That's a great idea," Eli said. "A couple of cross-promoted posts will entice more people to come out *and* keep them tuning in to the magazine for the next video segment."

God, he must be the one who handled the marketing when Emerson needed a break, because he was seriously a ringer on the media side.

"Actually, I couldn't have said it better myself." Scarlet turned toward the tables full of produce, trying to break the fifty-way tie in her head over what to put online first, but then Eli threw her for a loop.

"Are you sure you're okay adding social media detail to your list of things to do today?" he asked, leaning in as Owen moved to the other side of the tent where Tobias was pouring some water into a plastic bowl he'd brought along for his dog, Lucy.

Scooping up her camera, Scarlett managed a laugh. "I know we haven't been working together for too terribly long, but the fact that I like to multitask cannot possibly be a shock to you."

"No," he agreed, pausing long enough for her to frame up a shot of the cardboard containers of green beans on the table in front of her—click-*click*. "But doing direct marketing for Cross Creek is above and beyond the deal we have with you and Mallory, and you already helped us set up for the market when you didn't have to."

"I'm here for the authentic experience, remember?" Shifting, she took another shot, then another, the movements loosening the ache from her overtired muscles. "Doing as much as I can while I also do my job is what gives the photos and the articles that personal connection. Anyway, taking pictures *is* part of our deal. Posting them online only takes me an extra second or two. Here, look."

Scarlett's fingers were in the back pocket of her cutoffs before she'd even finished the sentence, her cell phone in hand before she'd taken her next inhale. "Instagram has some crazy-good filters for a social media site, and we can cross-post to Twitter from there, too. All I need to do is take a shot"—she sent her stare over the produce beneath the bright-red canopy, pausing over the pretty pile of tricolor peppers sitting next to the green beans. Click-*click*—"do a little creative cropping to make sure the composition works"—a few slides of her thumb had the job in the past tense and the image centered with just the right ratio of subject-to-background—"choose a filter to make all the colors pop"—she scrolled through her choices before ah! Yeah, Clarendon was perfect for all these warm reds and yellows, with a little sharpening to pull in the gleam from the growing daylight—"and voilà! All I need to do now is to make things official."

"I see," Eli said, and wait . . . how had his cocky smile resurfaced at double its usual strength? "And what are you going to write for the text portion of the post?"

"Oh." Good freaking question. Mallory had always been the writer. But come on. Scarlett had a brain in her head—one that had earned her a degree from one of the most competitive Ivy League institutions out there. She could come up with 140 characters to back up her photo. Or wait, was it 120?

Shit.

"I guess I could just keep it simple and give up the facts, like our location and the market's hours," she offered slowly, but Eli made a face like he'd smelled something decidedly past its prime.

"Sure. That'd be spectacular. If you want the posts to be as scintillating as the instruction manual for an office printer."

Scarlett's belly squeezed behind the dark-green cotton of her tank top. Although she hated to admit it, the point was sadly valid, so she tried again.

"Okay. How about if I just look at what Emerson posted last week and recycle that?" There had to be at least a nugget or two of goodness in there. The woman did a huge portion of Cross Creek's PR, for God's sake.

Not that the suggestion seemed to impress Eli. "Emerson's good, but you need to do better than repurposing her copy. The words are as important as the photo, and they both have to be fresh, otherwise the post just turns into white noise. Here." Eli reached for her phone, his fingers turning out to be just as nimble as hers. "All we have to do is enter Cross Creek's password"—*tap, tap, tap*—"load the picture. Nice"—he paused to slide her an appreciative grin—"and come up with something quick and catchy that'll make Cross Creek stand out in the crowd."

Eli tapped an index finger against his bottom lip, but the unnervingly sexy gesture lasted only seconds before his eyes lit up and he returned his attention to her phone. Fifteen seconds' worth of keystrokes later, he passed the thing back over, and Scarlett found herself torn squarely between laughing out loud and being ridiculously impressed.

The laughter won out by a hair. "'Cross Creek Farm—today's peppers are so fresh, you'll want to slap them'?"

"You won't forget it, will you?" Eli asked. "Between the tagline, the great photo, and the link to the market, that should work for at least a little exposure."

Scarlett glanced down at the tweet on her phone, which had already gotten two likes and as many retweets, and her curiosity stirred faster. "What about Facebook? We have a little more room there for text, if you want me to just add on to this a bit."

"Ah, we have like two minutes before anyone will make it over the hill from the parking lot. I can totally come up with something for you real quick. No sweat."

He moved his fingers in true "gimme" fashion as he reached out to reclaim her phone. Her interest went from a slow burn to a simmer when he did exactly as promised, easily expanding on the original copy. But then her simmer turned into a full boil when she realized why the tone of the messages seemed so oddly familiar.

It was a spot-on match with the copy she'd read on Cross Creek's website, to the point that she'd bet the bank the same person had written them.

A person who, from the look of things . . . was Eli.

"Wow," Scarlett said, her heart pumping faster to keep up with her racing curiosity. "And you seriously don't have any sort of writing experience?"

Eli's cocky smile hitched, so slightly that if she hadn't seen the genuine thing about three dozen times this week, she probably wouldn't have even noticed.

"You got me. I'm actually a Rhodes Scholar."

His answer arrived with all his usual charm, those baby blues flashing and that distracting-as-sin mouth shaped by his trademark playful smirk. But he hadn't answered the question—in fact, now that she thought about it, he'd gone out of his way to *dodge* the question. Which left Scarlett with a question of her own.

Why would Eli hide the fact that he was a damned good writer?

She opened her mouth to ask exactly that, but something deep in his expression made her trap the words between her teeth.

Getting Eli to open up enough for a simple video segment on a farm he knew inside and out had been like trying to squeeze rainwater from rocks. Getting him to talk about something he so clearly wanted hidden?

Not going to happen. No matter how badly Scarlett found herself wanting to know.

"Ah. Well, I guess that explains it." She worked up a smile, lifting her cell phone in salute. "Thanks for the help with the posts. I'll catch you at lunchtime to do our next video?"

His brows arced up, clearly delineating his surprise, but still, he said, "You bet, bumblebee."

And then he walked away.

CHAPTER THIRTEEN

Eli knew that after the last four hours of nonstop movement, he should be happy. No, scratch that. He should be *ecstatic*. Less than two minutes after the front gates for the farmers' market had swung open, they'd seen a steady stream of customers at Cross Creek's tent, asking for and buying everything from asparagus to zucchini. Between him and Owen and their old man, they'd sold every last Jonagold they'd been able to spare from the trees—including the ones he and Hunter had picked by the light of his F-150's headlights at eight thirty last night—and more than half their other produce had practically flown out of the crates. Eli had chatted up dozens of folks who had seen yesterday's video online, and paused for as many selfies with Scarlett, who had stayed true to her promise of keeping up with social media along with taking what looked to be a ton of new pictures for *FoodE*. Hunter had even called in to say that Cross Creek's Internet traffic still looked as great as the last of the sweet corn he'd harvested for this week's delivery to the Corner Market, who had increased their order for fall produce. So yeah, Eli should definitely be ecstatic.

Except for the fact that he was a fucking idiot.

The thought panged through him from chest to conscience, and he turned toward the box truck to grab a fresh crate of watermelons even though he'd replenished the three beneath the tent less than an hour ago. Okay, so he hadn't meant to be so fast and loose with the writing thing when he and Scarlett had talked this morning. But between the hell-yes feeling of bringing in desperately needed business for Cross Creek and flirty banter with a smart, sexy woman, Eli had felt good—really, *truly* relaxed—for the first time in weeks.

Then he'd just had to go for the icing on the feelgood cake and sneak in a little wordsmithing, and bam! Scarlett had picked up on his passion in two seconds flat.

Which might not be so bad, except for the fact that in that tiny sliver of time after she'd asked if he had writing experience, Eli had wanted nothing more than to tell her the God's honest truth.

He was the only Cross in three generations to not want to work the land in the Shenandoah Valley. He wasn't a farmer. In his heart, his blood, in every last one of his bones, he was a writer.

Yeah. Make that a *colossal* fucking idiot.

Reaching into the back of the box truck, Eli hooked his fingers beneath the rough-edged hand slots of the wooden crate in front of him. He'd made a mistake, letting Scarlett grab a glimpse of who he really was, but it had been exactly that—a mistake. One he wouldn't be making again.

Dodge. Deflect. Move the hell on.

Eli slid a glance at the sun, double-checking the hour against the time stamp on his cell phone. Although the farmers' market would still be going strong for another few hours, foot traffic had slowed enough for him and Scarlett to head off to a quiet spot in the park to shoot today's video as promised. With one last deep breath, Eli made his way back to the tent, his cocky cover hammered into place. But then he caught sight of Scarlett, who stood face-to-overly-made-up-face with Millhaven's biggest gossip over by the crates full of sweet corn and summer squash, and oh hell, nothing good could come from this in any way.

"Oh my Lord in *heaven!*" Amber Cassidy threw her perfectly manicured hands in the air just as Eli walked into earshot. "Scarlett, right? Scarlett Edwards-Stewart."

Scarlett lowered the camera from her face, blinking at the sight of the tall, thin blonde, whose shellacked-on jeans and four-inch platform heels earmarked her more for a *Girls Gone Wild* video than a Saturday morning farmers' market. "Um, yes?"

"I've been wonderin' when I'd *finally* get the chance to finally meet you!" Amber purred.

Scarlett took a step back on the concrete, her olive-green eyes going round with obvious confusion, and Eli swooped in for damage control.

"Ladies. Where are my manners?" He dialed his smile up to eleven as he lowered the crate of watermelons next to the others already on display, then stepped behind the table to stand beside Scarlett. "Scarlett Edwards-Stewart, this is Amber Cassidy. She's a local from Millhaven."

Scarlett's lips parted, which did little for Eli's cocky cover. "Oh! I wasn't aware anyone from Millhaven even knew I was in town before yesterday."

Amber laughed as if Scarlett had just suggested they all sprout extra heads and start a sing-along. "Well bless your *heart.* Of course I did! The Crosses might be keepin' you all to themselves up there at the farm." She paused to flicker a shame-on-you glance in Eli's direction, and his smile grew just a touch harder to reconcile. Damn, Amber was really pouring it on like warm molasses. "But I've known you were visiting all week, honey! That convertible of yours is tough to miss."

"You noticed my car?" Scarlett asked, and Eli swallowed the curse in his throat. Of course, Amber would pounce on an unfamiliar vehicle with out-of-state plates in the parking lot at the Twin Pines. Just like, of course, the idea of that sort of small-town familiarity was probably as alien to Scarlett as little green men in a galactic battleship.

Eli leaned in for the assist. "Amber's a bit of a social butterfly," he offered, but funny, now that her surprise had worn off, neither the scrutiny nor the spotlight seemed to bother Scarlett.

"Wow," she said to Amber, her smile polite yet not tight or forced. "Looks like you're really in the know."

Amber nodded sagely, her bottle-blond hair refusing to move despite the action. "And, of course, I saw that *cute* little video on that fancy-food website. Y'all are just two peas in a pod! It's so *exciting* to have a celebrity staying in our little ol' town."

Now *that* threw her. "Oh, no," Scarlett protested with a startled laugh. "I'm glad to be here, taking pictures of Cross Creek Farm for *FoodE*, but I'm definitely not a celebrity."

Amber's expression said she wasn't even buying the argument wholesale. "Look at *you*, not wanting to be all braggadocios. But it's okay. You can trust me with the truth, girl."

From just the recent shots she'd posted on her website, Eli knew Scarlett could legitimately claim the celebrity status Amber offered, just as he'd bet dollars to doughnuts Amber knew it, too.

Only Scarlett didn't budge. "Sorry to disappoint you, Amber. What you see is what you get. I'm really just a photographer."

"A *famous* photographer," Amber corrected. "I saw online that you've taken pictures of all sorts of celebrities." She ran a hand over her bright-purple tube top, smiling as if she was primed and ready for a close-up of her own. "Between you and me, I was all *set* to be a fashion model. I was a finalist in the Miss Cook County pageant three years in a *row*."

Eli's gut sank like a stone sliding down a steep grade. Yeah, Amber might be far more annoying than downright cutthroat or mean, but her small-town experiences probably seemed lame to a woman like Scarlett. She'd been to six of the seven continents, for Chrissake.

Yet she didn't show any signs of boredom or irritation when she looked at Amber and said, "Those pageants can be pretty competitive. That's quite an accomplishment."

"*Isn't* it?" Amber beamed. "But you know, then my true passion showed itself, and I couldn't ignore the call."

"Oh? And what did you do instead of going into modeling?"

Amber's chest puffed out within a half inch of a wardrobe malfunction. "I'm an artist over at the Hair Lair." She pronounced the word *ar-teest*, and seriously, Eli couldn't make this up if he tried. "We're right on Town Street in downtown Millhaven," Amber continued, gesturing to Scarlett's tousled blond-on-blond hair. "You should come on down and see us before you go back to New York. I could fix those dark streaks right up for you, good as new."

"Actually," Scarlett said, not skipping so much as a single beat. "They're lowlights. My stylist put them in on purpose. Thanks for the offer, but I love the way they look."

"Oh. *Oh.*" But rather than looking chagrined, Amber dished out a sympathetic stare. "Well aren't you *sweet*. I could never pull off that sort of hairstyle, but look at you."

Something hard and strangely proprietary turned over in Eli's gut, and he interrupted without knowing he would. "I think Scarlett's hair looks sexy."

Both women gave him the brows-up treatment, which he guessed he deserved. Not that he hadn't been honest—Scarlett's bold, edgy looks turned him on like Friday-night lights at a football game. But saying so out loud, in front of the town freaking crier? He was seriously losing it.

Amber rebounded with a flashy smile. "Oh, you would, Eli Cross," she said, turning her knowing gaze back toward at Scarlett. "He is such a *flirt*. But I guess you knew that, now didn't you?"

Before Scarlett could answer or Eli could swap the topic to something safer, like oh, say, juggling chainsaws, Amber said, "Anyhow, I'd best be makin' my rounds. I promised Greyson I'd stop on over at Whittaker Hollow's tent to pick up some peaches. Did you hear they had a big ol' bumper crop this week? Kinda makes things *exciting*, if you know what I mean." She paused to give Eli a wink so obvious the damn thing had probably been visible from outer space. "Anyway, it was *super* nice to meet you, Scarlett, and the invite to the Hair Lair is good anytime in case you change your mind. See y'all soon!"

Eli counted off the seconds until the woman was out of earshot before releasing an exhale and chancing a look at Scarlett. "Sorry about that. Amber's mostly harmless, but she can be a little, um. Much."

"Eh, she didn't seem so bad."

Scarlett's shrug was so honest, so *not* what he would expect out of any woman in the face of Amber Cassidy's obvious efforts to kick-start the gossip mill, that his surprise popped out before he could cage it. "We are talking about the same woman, right? Nosy blonde, too much makeup, was just less than polite about the way you wear your hair?"

"Oh, don't get me wrong," Scarlett said, a wry smile hooking at the corners of her mouth as she slipped her camera's lens cap into place with a soft snap. "I'm not saying I want to jump on the BFF train with her, and a tiny, awful part of me would love nothing more than to Photoshop a nose onto her ass just to see the meltdown."

A laugh barged past Eli's lips. "That'd be just desserts."

"But even though Amber is pretty annoying, she also seems upfront about who she is. So while I might not *like* her personality-wise, at least I can respect her."

The words dove right into his solar plexus, knocking his breath loose on a huff. "You respect Amber Cassidy?"

"I don't love the whole pot-stirring thing, but I respect that she's forthright, in her own way," Scarlett said with a shrug. "As far as her throwing a little shade about my hairstyle . . . well, the truth is, I can't be everybody's favorite flavor. And while I may not be perfect by any means, I'm not going to live by anyone else's standards, either. I've got to be my own brand of perfect if I'm going to be happy."

Eli's pulse pressed hard and fast at his throat. He was sailing head-long into dangerous water, he knew, just like he also knew he needed to come up with a cocky comeback and a freshly minted subject, the sooner the better.

But Scarlett was so matter of fact, so right out in the open with herself, that instead he asked, "Are you always so unapologetic about who you are?"

"Yes." Scooping up her backpack, she slung the strap over her delicately inked shoulder, waiting for Eli to grab his own bag before asking right back, "Aren't you? I mean, that whole cocky-charming thing you do is pretty relentless."

He gestured across the tent to his old man that he was taking a break, which thankfully gave him a couple of seconds to land on his feet. "Relentless, huh? For the record, most of the time 'charming' is a compliment."

"Relax, cowboy. I didn't say I don't like it." Scarlett followed him toward the main thoroughfare of the pavilion. "It's just not something a lot of people can pull off without seeming disingenuous."

Eli shouldn't flirt with her. He *shouldn't*. But all it took was one look at Scarlett's sassy little smile, and his dick outmaneuvered his defenses for control over his mouth.

"You like my charm?" he asked, a dark thread of satisfaction uncurling in his chest as her cheeks pinked with a sexy-as-hell blush.

"You made an apple-picking video go viral on the Internet, Eli. Everybody seems to like your charm."

"Ah, but that's not what I asked you, now is it, bumblebee?"

For a second, he thought she might balk. But then her chin hiked into that stubborn lift he knew all too well now, and good Christ, he liked this woman way more than was proper.

"Yes," Scarlett said, his attraction to her instantly doubling as she looked him directly in the eye. "I like your charm."

"And I really do think your hair is sexy." Reaching out, Eli tucked an errant, bright-blond lock behind the row of tiny hoops and studs climbing her ear. Of course, it had a mind of its own just like its wearer, sliding right back where it wanted to go as soon as he moved his hand. "And for the record, *we* made an apple-picking video go viral on the Internet," he reminded her. "Charming or not, I couldn't have done that without you."

Laughing, she lifted her hands in concession. "Fair enough. We do make a pretty good team."

They walked for a few minutes in comfortable quiet, with Scarlett taking in all the vendors and Eli taking in Scarlett. Her genuine interest was contagious, and even though he knew every vendor like the back of his work-callused hand, seeing the way *she* was seeing them made his brain start sparking with all sorts of ideas and words. Now that Cross Creek was getting more online exposure, they could probably do with adding an in-depth article or two to their website. He could write up something seasonal and update it weekly—or no, if he could figure out a way to tie Cross Creek's article to whatever Mallory was going to post on *FoodE*, he could even—

"Yoo-hoo. Anybody home in there?"

Eli registered Scarlett's voice and the soft brush of her fingers over his forearm all at once, and he realized—clearly too late—that he must have missed whatever she'd asked him at least twice.

"I'm sorry," he said, and dammit, how had they reached the end of the pavilion already? "Guess I got a little lost in thought. I apologize for being rude."

Scarlett's throaty laughter took him by surprise, even as it heated a path down his spine. "Must've been a hell of a thought. And no apologies. Thinking isn't rude."

"No, but ignoring you is," Eli countered. Leading the way from the pavilion over to the network of paths branching out toward the picnic areas, he said, "So please. Ask again."

She gestured over her shoulder, where the tent bearing Whittaker Hollow's logo was still visible beneath the pavilion. "I was just curious what the deal is with this bet. And before you get all tight-lipped about it, I'm keeping my end of our bargain. Unless the camera's rolling or we're discussing Cross Creek's operations directly, anything you and I talk about is off the record."

Eli's brows shot up. "So you want to know about the bet I made with Greyson Whittaker just for shits and giggles?"

"Unless you'd rather talk about the merits of prime lenses or the difference between JPEGs and RAW files. Which *I* could do all day, but I really don't think—"

"Okay, okay." The laughter welling up from his chest scattered any unease he might've had about the topic of this dumbass bet. "We can talk about the bet. Although the whole thing is stupid, really."

Scarlett's soft snort called him out right off the bat. "There's nothing stupid about five grand."

Annnnd point. "I guess I should say the way we got to the bet is stupid. The rivalry between Cross Creek and Whittaker Hollow goes back for decades. Think the Hatfields and the McCoys, only not as cuddly."

"Ouch," she said. Their footsteps measured out a few more seconds on the asphalt as Scarlett followed his lead toward a more secluded path, where the glossy-green leaves and the gentle breeze that rustled them was totally at odds with the topic of the rough-edged grudge between families. "Was there some kind of blowout that triggered the whole thing?"

"You know, I'm not really sure. My old man doesn't talk about it much." Okay, so his old man didn't really get chatty about *anything* all that much. Not that Eli or his brothers pushed. They were, after all, a family full of men, and farming men on top of it. If everyone was upright, working hard, and not trying to throw punches, all systems were assumed to be a go.

Eli shook his head and continued. "Anyhow, Greyson and I are the same age, and we're both the youngest, but he's got three sisters, none of whom are interested in operating Whittaker Hollow. So he's got a lot to prove, and rivalry or not, his old man is junkyard-dog mean. Greyson's not too far from that particular family legacy."

"He sounds like a real prize." The words slid between Scarlett's teeth, and Eli laughed long and loud at the euphemism.

"Oh, he's a complete asshat. We've pretty much hated each other since birth, and I'll admit, we got into more than our fair share of scuffles back when we were in school. The fact that our families own and operate the two biggest, most productive farms in the county and half the Shenandoah Valley besides doesn't help matters. Greyson got to shooting his mouth off like a two-dollar pistol at the farming co-op a week and a half ago, and he threw down this stupid bet that his family's farm would make more money than Cross Creek between then and the town's Fall Fling event in a couple of weeks."

"And you shot your mouth off right back and took the wager." Scarlett paused, her lashes fanning wider in sudden understanding. "Is that why there's all that weird tension between you and Owen? Because of this bet?"

Unease trickled into Eli's chest, pushing his heartbeat faster against his ribs. But her question had been straightforward enough, and more to the point, she wasn't stupid. Scarlett had been witness to damn near every minute Eli had spent with his oldest brother over the last eight days. The tension between them was thick enough to spread on toast.

And what's more, he was sick of keeping it all bottled up.

"The bet is part of it, yeah," Eli said carefully, because while a little venting might feel really freaking good right now, he also wasn't going to let loose with *all* the whys behind his love/hate relationship with his brother. "Owen's none too happy I picked up the gauntlet Greyson threw in my face, and he's not shy about reminding me that he's pissed. I'm sure you've noticed he takes the farm real seriously."

Without even the smallest hitch in her voice or her steps, Scarlett said, "Spoiler alert. Owen's not the only one who takes Cross Creek seriously. You dragged me all over—what did you call it? Ah, right—hell's half acre this week, trying to bring in more business. Anyway, you were just standing up for the farm when you took the bet, right?"

"I was, but Owen doesn't see things that way."

"There's another way to see them?"

Eli exhaled in realization. Scarlett didn't have any brothers or sisters—hell, she'd told him herself how foreign sibling relationships were to her. And as much as his had deep, dark layers he wasn't about to talk about with anyone, *including* his siblings, Scarlett had promised they were off the record. Blowing off a little more steam couldn't hurt.

"There is," he said. Scanning the picnic areas dotted along the winding path in individual alcoves, he spotted a table farther away from the others, beneath a cluster of oak trees. Scarlett fell into step beside him as he changed course from the neatly paved path to head for the privacy of the alcove, and they covered the grassy, partially wooded space side by side.

"Okay." She put her gear safely at the other end of the picnic table before settling in on the bench across from him, propping her elbows over the weathered wood. "Explain it to me."

"Ever since Owen and Hunter and I were little kids, there's always been this sort of unspoken way of doing things around the farm," Eli said, making Scarlett's brows dip in confusion.

"You mean the way you split up who does what?" she asked.

"Sort of. I mean, my brothers and I all know how to do the important stuff, and a lot of that has to be done together."

She tilted her head, clearly processing. "Like when you harvest corn for the feed distributors."

"Exactly." Not even his old man could do the high-caliber tasks like that single-handedly. "But the other tasks and responsibilities fall under this weird sort of umbrella. Owen's the serious one, and he's always lived, slept, and breathed for the farm. He's never made any bones about wanting to run the place when our dad retires."

Okay, so Eli couldn't imagine a scenario in which his old man would retire completely, but farming was backbreaking work. At some point, he'd hand over the bulk of day-to-day operations to Owen, just as his old man had done with him. Cross Creek was Owen's legacy, and always had been.

"I can see that," Scarlett said slowly, a ray of sunlight catching in her hair as she nodded. "Owen *is* pretty focused. Plus, he's obviously devoted to Cross Creek."

"He's also the innovator," Eli said. "Owen loves the farm, but at the same time, he wants to make it bigger and better."

Her expression balanced between surprise and recognition. "So that's why he's always in the greenhouse. He's working on the specialty produce to help Cross Creek pioneer new territory."

Eli wrestled the urge to laugh. Of course, Scarlett was sharp enough to make the connection with ease. "And brushing up on new technology. And researching the best soil-to-fertilizer ratios for every plant under the sun. And trying to figure out how to build, staff, and maintain a fixed structure on site that would replace our roadside farm stands. But yeah, you've got the idea. If it has to do with Cross Creek, it's not just on Owen's radar. It's in his blood."

"How about Hunter?" Scarlett asked, and now Eli did laugh.

"Classic middle sibling. Hunt's the peacekeeper, the guy who we can all count on to split the difference and keep his head on the level." Christ, Hunter had kept Owen and Eli from knocking knuckles so many times he probably should have been sainted. "He's just as serious about Cross Creek as Owen, though. He's never wanted to do anything but work the land. Well, that and be with Emerson." At Scarlett's brow lift, Eli added, "They were high school sweethearts."

"Ah. Another thing that makes perfect sense, given how they look at each other." She paused, shifting her weight on the silvery, weather-worn bench beneath her. "So Owen is the serious one and Hunter keeps the peace. How about you? Where do you fit into the mix?"

Although her movement had been slight, it had closed some of the space between them, with only the scant width of one table board now separating his hand from her elbow. Scarlett leaned forward, her chin on her long, folded fingers, her green eyes honest and wide open and so wildly pretty that Eli edged closer, too.

"Behind my brothers, I'm afraid. Don't get me wrong. I like Cross Creek well enough," he said, because *fuck*, despite it all, he really did. "But being the charming youngest brother has its disadvantages sometimes."

"I find that hard to believe." Not a question, but straight to the point all the same.

So that's just how Eli answered her. "With four men operating the same farm, someone's got to be the extra."

A laugh worked its way up from her throat—he could see it forming at the edges of her mouth in the tiny creases around her eyes. But all at once, the gesture crashed to a halt. "Wait . . . you're serious?"

"Sure." He should feel vulnerable, he supposed, laying the truth out there like the Sunday paper. But it *was* the truth, one anyone who spent enough time looking at the Cross family could see.

Ever since Eli could remember, they'd been the patriarch, the prodigy, the peacekeeper . . .

And the pariah.

"You work pretty hard to be an extra, don't you think?" Scarlett asked, and his defenses kicked his shoulders into a shrug.

"Everything's hard work when you operate a farm, and the truth is, I don't love it the way my old man and brothers do. All four of us have got a role. Mine's just to do whatever no one else is doin'."

For just a breath, she sat without speaking, an odd sort of confusion flickering through her stare. But then her expression shifted, and she asked, "It's been just the four of you, then? Since you and Hunter and Owen were little?"

The question surprised Eli just enough to make him pause, and Scarlett bit down on her lower lip hard enough to leave tiny, curved indents on the skin there.

"You know what, forget I asked. You've already said you don't want to talk about it, and I shouldn't have—"

He closed the space between his hand and her elbow in an instant, her skin so smooth and warm that he couldn't pull back if he wanted to.

And he didn't.

"Since I was four," Eli said, and funny, the words didn't stick in his throat the way he thought they would. "My mother died of breast cancer."

Scarlett's breath pushed out on a whisper-soft puff that he heard as much as he felt on his cheek. "Oh my God. Eli, I'm so sorry."

"Thanks. I am, too."

The steady *thump-thump-thump* of his heart turned his pulse into a whoosh of white noise against his eardrums. This was the tipping point—the part of the conversation that always went from zero to sympathy-awkward in less than two nanoseconds. Although Rosemary Cross's death didn't come up as a topic of conversation but once in a blue moon, especially around Eli or either of his brothers—or worse yet, their old man—everyone in Millhaven knew the story.

But rather than gloss over the subject with some overused platitude, Scarlett simply dropped one hand to cover his and held on tight to his stare. "She must have been really young if she died when you were only four."

"She was thirty-seven when she was diagnosed. She died later that same year." Again, the admission came out more easily than he'd expected. Which was pretty messed up considering how much dust had collected in its corners.

Scarlett's fingers remained a sweet, steady pressure on his. "I don't know what to say. I'm sure that was really difficult for you. And, oh." She broke off. Inhaled. Then whispered, "For all of you."

The unvarnished words, the pure emotion in her green-gold eyes that matched them, loosened the tension gripping his chest, at least enough to allow him to breathe.

"Screenings back then weren't nearly as common or advanced as they are now, and my mother's cancer was extremely aggressive. By the time she and my old man found out how sick she really was, it was too late to even do more than one round of chemotherapy."

Of course, Eli had learned that bit from Millhaven's longtime town physician, Doc Sanders, after fifteen years of not being able to call up one single memory of his mother and not having the heart or the balls to ask anyone who shared his last name. The details of her death hadn't helped him remember her, though—not even in scraps and clips, the way he remembered kissing Missy Tremaine on the playground in the second grade or falling off his dirt bike and breaking his wrist three days before his sixth birthday.

They did, however, remind him all too well that he should be able to remember at least *something* about her just like everyone else in his family did, and dammit—*dammit!* Eli needed to throw the brakes on this conversation right now, otherwise Scarlett was going to see the one thing he was desperate to keep hidden.

He wasn't just the extra. He was the odd man out. He didn't belong.

And the guilt was eating him alive.

"Right. Anyway, we should probably get to this video, huh?" Eli shifted, fully prepared to slide his hand from beneath Scarlett's with a cocky smile and an ironclad vow to keep his trap embroidered shut from now on.

Only she curled her fingers over his and refused to let go.

"Don't. Please."

It was the *please* that froze him into place, the soft, small word arrowing all the way through him and stealing any deflection he could possibly put together. For a second—or maybe it was a minute or an hour, because fuck if Eli could feel anything other than the warm, unyielding pressure of Scarlett's hand on his—he said nothing, sitting perfectly motionless on a picnic bench that might as well have been light-years away.

But still, Scarlett didn't blink. "I know talking about your mom must be difficult, and we can change the subject if you want. But don't do that."

"Do what?" Eli managed past the tight knot in his throat.

"Don't hide," she said. "I meant it when I said I like your charming side, Eli. But this"—she paused to draw an imaginary loop between them with the index finger on her free hand—"this side of you is real. It's honest. And I like it even better. So please, no matter what we talk about, don't hide."

Eli knew the words should scare the hell out of him as much as Scarlett's beautiful, wide-open stare and the sure-and-steady grasp on his hand that marked what she'd said as true.

But they didn't. So he tightened his fingers around hers right back and said, "Okay."

CHAPTER FOURTEEN

Scarlett sat back against the well-cushioned love seat in her apartment, her eyes on her laptop screen and her mouth curving up into the world's most gigantic smile. But as goofy as it was, the expression was warranted.

Five days had passed since the farmers' market, and each had been better and busier than the one before. The second video clip she and Eli had filmed—along with the accompanying articles on *FoodE* and the extra content the Crosses had put on the farm's website—had garnered even more reach than the first. Both *FoodE* and Cross Creek had seen so much increased business after the segment had gone live that Mallory had needed to reinforce her skeleton crew with a temporary assistant and Hunter had needed to literally run to the cornfields to pick whatever he could by hand in order to restock yesterday's roadside stand. Scarlett had taken hundreds of new photos to go with this week's articles, along with pitching in at the farm stand to help Eli with customers and crowd control.

Involuntarily, her cheeks warmed. Although Eli had been his usual cocky self whenever the camera was out or his brothers were around, he'd also kept the promise he'd made to her on that picnic bench. While none of their one-on-one conversations had been quite as personal as that first one—God, Scarlett's heart still thudded and ached when she remembered the look on his face as he'd talked about his mother—she and Eli had worked together with growing ease, brainstorming ideas for articles and laughing and trading both stories and banter so seamlessly that Scarlett couldn't deny the truth.

Between his smart observations, his clear devotion to the farm, and that borderline-mischievous smile that kept threatening to reduce her panties to a white-hot afterthought, she liked Eli Cross a *lot*.

Scarlett's hands froze over the keyboard perched across her lap. Okay, so Eli was sexy as hell, and quick-witted enough on top of that to flip every last one of her *oh hell yes* switches. The attraction wasn't one-sided—last week's toe-curling kiss was proof positive of that. But she'd come here to take pictures. To save Mallory's magazine. Hell, as pretty as Millhaven was, she gave herself T-minus any day now before she started to get twitchy for her next adventure, anyway.

She belonged behind the camera. Which meant her time with Eli had an expiration date in the very near future.

Which *really* meant she shouldn't be sitting here fantasizing about what his cocky mouth could do when it wasn't caught up in a smile.

"Oh for God's sake," Scarlett murmured, closing the folder of today's Cross Creek photos with a heavy sigh. She and Eli had gotten rained out of their chores on the farm this afternoon, so she'd already edited and sent this morning's shots to Mallory. Still, Scarlett loved her job like most people loved eating and sleeping. She could always find something to crop or edit or sharpen.

Inhaling deeply, Scarlett scrolled through the photo folders on her laptop—no . . . no . . . no . . . *a-ha!* Although she'd sold the best shots from last month's film festival to an entertainment magazine, she could still edit a few of the rest. Publicists and agents could always be counted on to want great photographs of their clients. Even if said clients suddenly looked awfully slick and over-polished as they flashed across her laptop screen in their designer tuxedos and $10,000 watches. Whatever happened to a good, old-fashioned jeans-and-T-shirt combo, with broken-in denim hugging a pair of work-muscled thighs and faded cotton clinging to all the right places . . .

A knock sounded off at the front door, sending Scarlett's pulse through the rafters and a blush tearing over her face. Both sensations, however, were quickly chased off by a hard shot of suspicion. She could literally count the number of people she knew in Millhaven on one hand, and while a glance at the clock told her it was barely past dinnertime, she still wasn't expecting anyone.

Unease bubbled harder in her chest as the knock came again—you could take the girl out of New York, blah, blah, blah—but the feeling faded instantly at the sound of the voice that followed.

"Scarlett? Are you there? It's me, Emerson."

"Oh!" Blinking back her surprise, Scarlett pushed her way up from the love seat, pausing to rest her laptop on the tiny coffee table before padding across the floor to flip the deadbolt and swing the door open.

"Oh, good! You're home," Emerson said, offering up a genuine smile. "You remember my friend Daisy, right?"

She gestured to the petite blonde standing next to her on the rain-splattered threshold, and Scarlett's confusion doubled even as she nodded.

"Yes, of course." They'd met at the farmers' market, where Daisy had been selling her homemade beauty products. "Is, um, everything okay at Cross Creek?"

"Are you kidding?" Emerson's laugh wiped out any possibility of a negative answer, and she gestured to the narrow overhead ledge keeping her (sort of) sheltered. "It's been raining for the last four hours. Everything at Cross Creek is coming up roses."

At the mention of the weather, Scarlett's flush made a repeat performance. "God, sorry. Come on in." She ushered the two women into her apartment and shut the door, realizing only after the fact that the living room looked like a hurricane had whipped a path of destruction directly over the carpet. "Sorry it's kind of, um, untidy. I was catching up on some work."

But Emerson just shook her head, her auburn curls swishing over her shoulders. "Actually, this looks about the same as when I lived here."

"She's not just saying that to be polite, either," Daisy added with a pixie smile. "Trust me."

Scarlett laughed, because it was exactly what she'd been thinking, and Emerson lifted her hands to signal *guilty as charged*.

"Yeah, I can't lie. I have nothing on Martha Stewart. Anyway, sorry we just showed up on your doorstep. We tried to call you but . . ."

Daisy made a sound suspiciously close to a snort. "We'd have had better luck with smoke signals than cell service around here."

"Pretty much," Emerson said. "But we were just hanging out for the evening, and since Daisy lives a few doors down, we figured we'd drop in and see what you're up to."

"Oh. That's awfully nice of you." Scarlett smiled, although the gesture didn't last. She wasn't used to being in the same place for too terribly long, much less having guests wherever said place happened to be. Surely there was some sort of protocol for this kind of thing, right? People talked all the time about girls' night in like it was gospel. Well, people other than her, anyway. Even Mallory, who was married to her job like Scarlett, mentioned going to her coworkers' apartments from time to time for Netflix marathons and wine.

Drinks, drinks! Yeah, that was a good jumping-off point. Or—*shit*—it would be if Scarlett had anything in her fridge other than soy milk and raspberry jam. But before she could open her mouth to ask whether anyone at least wanted a glass of water, Daisy let out a small chirp of surprise.

"Oh my God." Her bright-green stare was fixed roundly on the image splashed over Scarlett's laptop a few feet away. "Is that Grant *Kirkpatrick?*"

Emerson sent a discreet elbow to Daisy's ribs, sending the woman's chin up about three inches. "I mean! I'm sorry. I don't mean to be nosy, but . . ." Daisy trailed off for a second before mouthing *Grant Kirkpatrick!* at Emerson.

Relief whooshed through Scarlett's chest. She might suck as a hostess, but work? She could talk about *that* all day. "No, no, it's fine. I'm the one who left my laptop open. And to answer your question, yes. That's Grant."

Now even Emerson looked a little starstruck. "You seriously have photos of Grant Kirkpatrick just hanging around on your laptop?"

"Mmm-hmm. Do you want to see them?"

"Holy crap, is that even a question?" Daisy blurted, but then she backpedaled. "I mean, only if that's okay."

Every once in a while, Scarlett had to hold to an exclusive nondisclosure agreement that made showing images to anyone a bit sticky, but . . . "Sure. These were taken at a public film festival about three weeks ago, and the exclusive images have already been released."

"Wow," Emerson murmured after Scarlett had scooped up her laptop and the three of them had settled in side by side to click through the first dozen-or-so photos. "So do you, ah, know him?"

Scarlett laughed. "I'm good, but not that good. I've shot probably a half dozen movie premiers and other events where Grant has been in attendance, though. He's a nice guy."

"A nice guy," Daisy echoed with a self-deprecating laugh. "God, between you knowing A-listers like Grant Kirkpatrick"—she paused to swing her glance from Scarlett to Emerson—"and you having dated pro football's MVP, I am definitely the odd woman out."

A bolt of shock rippled up Scarlett's spine. "You used to date Lance Devlin?" Talk about the last thing she'd have expected from the down-to-earth woman sitting next to her.

"Yeah, that's a long story," Emerson said with a wink. "It's best told over alcohol."

Daisy sat back against the cushions of the love seat and let out an audible breath. "Ooooh, I could go for a drink."

Scarlett darted a glance at her kitchen cupboards, and ugh, she really was terrible at this hostess thing. "I'm sorry. I don't have anything here other than water or soy milk. But we could go to the liquor store," she offered.

Emerson's headshake said a beer run was better in theory than practice. "Not unless you want to haul your cookies to Camden Valley."

"Or"—Daisy arched a brow, the glint in her eyes completely at odds with her delicate features—"we could just go to The Bar. They have plenty of liquor."

"That's a *great* idea," Emerson said, brightening. "I can call Hunter on the landline at the cottage. I bet he and Eli and Owen would be up for meeting us for a beer or two. We can make it a family affair. What do you say, Scarlett?"

Scarlett's heart stuttered. An impromptu drink or two in her little living room was one thing. An event—even a casual one—that had the F-word attached? That was a whole different ballgame.

"Oh, no. I don't want to intrude on a family thing. Really. You guys go and have a great time, though. I'll catch that story from you another time, Emerson."

"You will not."

Scarlett pulled back, full to the brim with surprise. "Pardon?"

Emerson didn't budge. "You will not," she repeated, all kindness. "Cross Creek has had an incredible week, and your photos are a huge reason for that success. That makes you part of the group. Plus, something tells me Eli won't be unhappy to see you, and despite all that bad-boy swagger, he's really a good guy."

The air in Scarlett's lungs stopped short. "Eli and I are . . ." She broke off in search of the right word, but hell if she could find one that was both accurate and acceptable for use in mixed company. "We aren't a thing."

"Okay," Emerson said, the lack of argument sending a ribbon of surprise through Scarlett's belly. "You're still not intruding, and we still aren't taking no for an answer."

Scarlett nearly said it anyway. But all at once, she realized the truth.

She didn't want to say no, and she didn't want to stay in and work. Just for tonight, she wanted to be part of the group.

And even if it was also just for tonight, she *really* wanted to see Eli.

"In that case," Scarlett said, her heart fluttering faster even though her mind was 100 percent made up, "just give me five minutes to change. But the first round is on me. No arguments."

◆ ◆ ◆

All it took was one look across the dimly lit interior of The Bar for Eli to know he was in deep fucking trouble. The place was more crowded than usual for a Thursday night, likely thanks to the rain that had made harvesting every field in Millhaven either difficult or downright impossible. Greyson Whittaker stood over by the jukebox with Billy Masterson and Moonpie Porter, leaning against the far end of the scuffed-and-scraped mahogany bar, with attitude to spare. The country music blaring from the overhead speakers was as loud as the tiny white lights dangling from the rafters were soft, and the beer flowed readily from tap to table.

But it was the sight of Scarlett, sitting on the other side of the bar in a tight black miniskirt and a smile that could make a dead man sing, that was going to be Eli's undoing.

"Nice of you to finally grace us with your presence, you goddamn slacker," came a familiar, joking voice from beside him, and Eli grabbed the chance for distraction with both hands.

"I took the time to shower. You know, with soap and water." He lifted a brow at Hunter, whose smile was admirably close to Eli's in the cocky department tonight. "You might want to give it a shot sometime."

"I clean up just fine," his brother said, shaking Eli's hand and leaning in for a shoulder bump in greeting. "And oh by the way, I'm also the one of us who's getting laid, so . . ."

Eli simultaneously laughed and thrashed the urge to send his gaze back to the spot across the bar where Scarlett sat between Daisy and Emerson. "Details. I'm still the best looking of the three of us. Speaking of which"—he spun a stare over the groups of people clustered at café tables and along the length of the L-shaped bar—"where's Saint Owen?"

Eli registered Hunter's oh-hell expression two seconds before he heard Owen's throat clear from behind him, and seriously, how did his oldest brother manage to slide into his blind spot every single time?

"I'm right here," he said, the look on his face marking him as none too amused at the nickname. "Took you long enough to make your way out."

"Yeah," Eli said. But since he couldn't exactly follow up with "Sorry, but I was up to my adverbs, writing a new article for Cross Creek's website," he pasted on a smirk instead. "This place looks busy."

Hunter nodded. "Rain'll do that. Plus, Thursday is ladies' night."

Unable to keep his stare in check any longer, Eli let his eyes drift back over toward the spot where Scarlett sat at a café table with Emerson and Daisy Halstead, her legs crossed in a provocative knot and the four-inch heel of her strappy sandal hooked over the bottom rung of her bar stool. Anyone else would stick out like a swear on Sunday wearing a skirt and heels in The Bar, but when Scarlett threw her head back and laughed at something Emerson had said, then lifted her two-for-one draft beer to her bow-shaped mouth for a nice, long draw, she looked for all the world like she'd never belonged anywhere else.

Scarlett chose exactly that moment to shift her glance in his direction, their eyes locking hard enough to send a current of want on a hot path down Eli's spine. The sensation met an untimely end, though, when Owen let out a low curse.

"Please tell me that look doesn't mean what I think it means."

Although Eli's heart had just dumped directly into his gut, he scraped together a bored expression. "I'm not about to pretend to know what's going on in your brain pan, brother."

"Well, then, let me spell it out for you. What I'm thinking is that it looks like you're getting a little too friendly with the woman who's got the fate of our PR in her hands right now," Owen said with just enough frost in his tone to turn Eli's fingers to fists.

He made a noise in his throat that was less than polite, but come on. "You've got to be fucking kidding me. First you told me not to piss Scarlett off. Now you're telling me not to be nice to her? Jesus, Owen! Make up your damn mind."

"I'm not telling you not to be nice to her. I'm telling you not to sleep with her," Owen growled back.

"I'm not!" Not that he didn't *want* to be sleeping with Scarlett. Or hadn't thought about it no less than four dozen times since he'd dragged himself out of bed this morning. Because he most definitely had, but . . . "Anyway, whether or not Scarlett and I are sleeping together is beside the point, because there are only two people who get a say over who I have sex with. One of them is me, and I can damn sure promise the other one's not you."

Hunter inserted himself between them on the floorboards before Owen could answer or Eli could back up his words with something decidedly more convincing. "Okay, you two. That's enough chest thumping for tonight."

"But—"

Eli's protest collided with Owen's, but Hunter shot them both down with a quick "ah!" Looking at Owen first, he continued. "Scarlett's a very nice woman, and no one wants to piss her off. Including Eli, I'm sure." Swinging his steely gaze at Eli, he added, "And everyone here knows how important Cross Creek's PR is. No one's going to do anything rash to jeopardize it."

His tone added a nonverbal *right?* to the mix, and Eli knotted his arms over his chest in an equally wordless reply.

"So now that we're all on the same page," Hunter continued. "Can we please just cut the crap and go have a beer? Because we've had a great week at the farm, and I'd hate to end it by fixin' to take you out to the parking lot to knock some damned sense into both of your asses."

To Eli's absolute surprise, Owen nodded. "You're right."

"Come again?" Hunter asked, voicing a prettied-up version of the "what the hell?" that Eli had been just about to let loose.

Owen tugged a hand through his hair, letting his palm rest on the back of his neck as he blew out a breath. "I said you're right, okay? We *have* had a better week than any of us could've hoped for, and . . . well, I guess I just don't want anything to happen to make us lose the ground we've gained. That's all."

"Do you really think I'd sleep with Scarlett and then blow her off?" Eli took care to keep the sharp edges from his voice—not because he was unoffended at his brother's implication, but this was the first semi-decent conversation they'd been able to forge in ages. Being pissy right off the bat wouldn't help. Even if it was warranted.

Owen hesitated, but then sent a look around the bar; specifically, at the four—shit, make that five—women Eli had very casually dated within the last year. "Monogamy isn't exactly your bag, Eli."

"Fair," he allowed after a second. "But neither is being a dick."

Hunter nodded. "You've gotta admit, he has a point, O."

"I'm not saying I think you're a dick. I'm . . ." Owen broke off, a rare flicker of emotion moving through his serious gray eyes. "I'm looking at the bigger picture. This momentum we're gaining doesn't just have the potential to get us out of the hot water of the bet you made with Greyson. If we play this exposure right, the increased business could be our ticket to serious growth."

A pang of understanding hit Eli right in the gut. "You think we can make the fixed-structure farm stand happen if we keep going like this."

"No."

The word hiked both Eli's and Hunter's chins upward in surprise. But then Owen said, "I've run the numbers. If we can sustain the sort of business we've seen this week, I think we can make *anything* happen."

"Whoa." Hunter's jaw unhinged in a glint of day-old stubble. "Are you serious?"

Under any other circumstances, Eli would've laughed at the irony of the question. But right now, he was far too busy fielding all the *holy shit* winging around in his gray matter.

Owen loved Cross Creek the way Eli loved writing. It was his livelihood. It was his *life*.

And if they played their cards right, it might just take off like a rocket.

"I get it," Eli said slowly, his heart pounding harder as he looked first at Scarlett, then at his brother through the dim overhead light spilling down from the rafters. "I don't want to fuck this up, either."

Owen followed the path of Eli's glance, tipping his head ever so slightly in Scarlett's direction. "Then do me a favor and don't," he flipped back, and wait . . .

"Was that a joke?"

The corners of Owen's mouth went from a twitch to a definite half smile. "I do have a sense of humor on occasion. I'm not as slick as you, I know," he added, but Eli shook his head and laughed.

"Actually, that was pretty good."

"Thanks." Owen's smile stuck around for another beat before his expression slid back into more serious territory. "Look, I'm not saying I won't ride your ass when it comes to the farm, especially now that we've got so much on the line. But as for the rest . . . just be sure to use that big ol' head of yours for something other than a hat rack, okay? Especially when it comes to a certain blonde across the bar."

Eli opened his mouth, fully intending to go for the default. A maneuver his brother had clearly been expecting, because he beat Eli to the one-two by adding, "You can save the no-big-deal routine. You were right about your personal life being none of my business, and anyway"—Owen shot a split-second glance at Hunter—"after seeing the look you and Scarlett shared a couple of minutes ago, neither one of us is buying it anyway."

Hunter gave up a *sorry dude, but yeah* nod, and shit. Eli had nothing. "Okay," he said, because A) Owen wasn't wrong about the eye guzzling, and B) it was about as close to hugging it out as he and his brothers were going to get in the middle of The Bar.

"Cool." The slight softening of Owen's steel-gray stare was the only acknowledgment of what had passed between them, but Eli saw it all the same. "I'm going to run and grab a round. You in?"

Laughing, Eli jumped right back into bravado-as-usual. "If you're buying, I'm drinking."

"'Course you are." Owen let go of one more smile before heading over to the bar. Eli turned to take a step toward the table where Scarlett was now chatting with Michelle Martin and a few other locals, but Hunter's brow lift stopped his movement midstep.

"Dad didn't raise any dummies, but you're swingin' at a hell of a curve there, brother. You sure you know what you're doing?"

Eli looked at Scarlett just in time to catch her bright, beautiful smile right in the chest.

"Nope," he said.

But he walked over to her anyway.

CHAPTER FIFTEEN

Two beers and one hour later, Eli's resistance to Scarlett's miniskirt (and her laugh . . . and the stories about her travels . . . and he didn't even want to get started on how good she'd smelled when they'd hugged hello) was pretty much toast. But they'd had a great time hanging out and celebrating Cross Creek's great week, along with *FoodE*'s success. He could handle sitting next to her without making a complete ass of himself.

Scarlett leaned in from her seat next to him to put her empty pint glass on the table, and Christ on a cracker, how could any woman smell like fresh-cut flowers in the middle of a goddamn country bar?

"Hey, you guys." The distinctly female voice brought Eli back to reality with a snap, and he turned to look at the dark-haired waitress to whom it belonged. "Sorry you've had to self-serve up till now, but my shift just started. Can I grab anyone a refill or something from the kitchen?"

"Cate?" Owen's beer bottle hit the table with a graceless thunk, and he scrambled to cover the move with a smile. "I didn't know you were working here. I thought you were waiting tables at Clementine's."

"I am. I mean, not right now, obviously." She gestured to the bright-red half apron tied around her waist and her matching T-shirt bearing The Bar's logo just below her left shoulder. "But I picked up a few extra shifts here to make ends meet."

Concern flickered over Owen's face, and huh, looked like Eli wasn't the only one with a soft spot for a pretty woman. "Oh. Well, it's nice to see you out."

"I'm not out," Cate replied, her smile tightening slightly, but enough. "I'm working."

"Right. Right, of course," Owen said.

Silence crept over the group like a solid, heavy weight. But Eli knew all too well how little he liked poor-you sympathy when it came to the subject of his mother. Cate's story might be way worse, but hell if he was going to remind her of it by treating her with kid gloves.

"Hey, that's awesome news that you're working here at The Bar now," he said, tacking on a wink to make extra sure the distraction made a direct hit. "You'll pretty the place up, for sure."

Cate's lips twisted in a wry smile, scattering the tension at the table. "Shouldn't you save all that sweet talk for the camera, Eli Cross?"

Segue, party of one, your table is now available. "Speaking of which, have you met our resident photographer?" Eli asked. At Cate's head-shake, he added, "Cate McAllister, this is Scarlett Edwards-Stewart."

"It's great to meet you," Scarlett said, her stack of bracelets jingling softly as she extended a hand toward Cate.

"Likewise. We don't see a whole lot of famous people out here in Millhaven."

"Oh God, I'm definitely not famous." Scarlett's self-deprecating laughter chased off what little unease remained from the earlier conversation, and Cate murmured a quick "nice to meet you" before offering up one last smile and departing for the bar.

"I'm sorry, did I miss something?" Scarlett asked as soon as the brunette was out of earshot, and Eli exchanged a glance with Hunter, who exchanged a glance with everyone else at the table, before he answered.

"Cate's husband and nine-year-old daughter were killed in a car accident three years ago."

Scarlett's lashes fanned up in a snap, sympathy filling her dark-green stare. "That's awful."

Owen nodded, taking a longer-than-usual sip from his beer before saying, "Brian and I were pretty good friends in high school. We've all known Cate since . . . God, forever. They were that couple everyone wanted to be."

"She seems to be doing okay, all things considered," Emerson offered. "Doc Sanders and I had lunch at Clementine's last week, and I talked to Cate for a few minutes. Actually, she asked if we needed any help with our filing and clerical work, but we've already got Nurse Kelley taking care of that. I'm glad she was able to pick up a few shifts here at The Bar, though. I hope she's not having too rough a time."

Hunter and Daisy both nodded in emphatic agreement while Owen knocked back the rest of his beer in one go, and yeah, time for a new subject, stat.

"Looks like everyone in town is a little starstruck by our famous photographer," Eli said, gesturing to the groups of people around the bar, nearly all of whom he'd caught in various stages of staring or whispering tonight.

Scarlett shifted over her bar stool, the edge of her heel brushing his calf with enough contact that he felt it, yet lightly enough to drive him crazy in the best possible way. "If I'm famous, then so are you."

"Ah, Eli's more like notorious. His reputation precedes him." Hunter waggled his brows at Eli, who offered his brother a nice, long look at his middle finger.

"I'm not *that* bad," he argued, and jeez, did everyone at the table have to laugh so loud, so quickly?

"Dude. You conned Dad into letting you get a pet cow for your sixteenth birthday."

Scarlett's eyes sparkled at the same time her chin did that lift thing that meant nothing good for him. "He what?"

Hunter's smile went full-on mischievous as he swung the expression in Scarlett's direction. "He didn't tell you the story of how he fast-talked his way into getting Clarabelle?"

"No." Scarlett lifted the end of the word just enough to twist it into a request, but oh no. No way was he going to get tossed under the Cross family nostalgia bus just for grins.

"Hunter," Eli warned, but his brother shook his head.

"Oh, come on. It's priceless."

"Classic Eli," Owen agreed from across the table, and for once, it didn't sound like a barb.

Emerson chimed in with, "I love this story. I can't believe you didn't tell it to Scarlett!"

Before Eli could protest or promise murder, Hunter jumped in and started doing exactly that. "So you know we have a cattle farm on the back half of the property, right?"

"Sure," Scarlett said. Even though their old man had hired a cattle manager decades ago to run that end of their farm, all four Cross men still kept up with the daily operations on both parts of Cross Creek's business. "Eli took me up there twice this week and filled me in on all the basics of how things operate."

The lift of Owen's brows clearly translated his surprise, causing Eli to remind him, "You told me to show her the whole farm."

"Well done, then," Owen murmured, and even though Eli paused for a second to wonder whether there was something stronger than beer in his brother's cup, he kept his trap clapped shut so Hunter could get story hour over with.

"So you know that every spring, we get a pretty big round of cattle." Hunter placed his half-empty beer on the glass-littered table in front of them, clearly more interested in putting Eli on the hot seat than in drinking. The jackass. "But we're not a dairy farm. We just raise the cows for a certain amount of time before they're sold to distributors."

Scarlett paled at that, her vegan side likely not a happy camper at the reminder that most of Cross Creek's cows grew up to be cheeseburgers, and Eli took full control of the chance to interrupt.

"Do we seriously have to tell—"

"Yes," came the chorus of answers from around the table, the loudest of which was Scarlett's, and jeez, Eli knew when he'd been beat.

Apparently Hunter did, too, because he opened his yap and kept right on going. "Well, this particular spring, when we got our round of cattle, the guy making the delivery asked Pop if he knew someone willing to take a baby Jersey cow. She couldn't have been but two months old."

"Two and a half," Eli muttered, and Owen took the opportunity to grab the conversational baton and run like mad.

"She was a tiny thing. The momma cow had died during the birth, and the calf had to be bottle-fed. She was sweet, to be sure, but we had no reason to take a cow that needed daily hand-feeding. Pop got on the two-way radio and asked me if I knew anyone who'd want her, but of course, I didn't. He was all set to say no when Eli caught wind of the conversation we'd had."

A smile played on Scarlett's lips, and all of a sudden this story wasn't so bad. "Then what happened?"

Hunter grinned. "He came flyin' on up to the back half of the property on one of our four-wheelers, looked Dad straight in the eye, and said, 'Hold everything! That's my cow!'"

Scarlett's smile became a full-on laugh that slid right under Eli's skin. "He did not."

"Hand to God," Hunter promised. "There he was, barely a minute over sixteen years old, about as filthy as a person could be from working in a bunch of muddy fields, putting the full court press on our old man for that cow. He swore up one side and down the other we'd never even know she was there. He'd feed her—"

"And groom her daily," Owen added.

"And pay her vet bills and everything." Hunter laughed, although the sound wasn't unkind. "Pop argued for a coupl'a minutes, but Eli's mind was done made up. Clarabelle was his cow, and she wasn't leaving Cross Creek property come hell or high tide. I think he even threatened to lie down in front of the trailer."

"Hey." God, Eli wanted to squash the smile tugging at the corners of his mouth. He really did. But it was an exercise in futility. "If you're gonna tell the story, at least get your facts straight. I said I'd *stand* in front of the trailer."

Owen grinned, capping off the story with a flourish. "But of course he didn't have to. He charmed Dad into keeping ol' Clarabelle, and she's been living the high life in that horse barn ever since."

"Your brothers are right," Scarlett said, turning toward him on her bar stool. "That's a fantastic story."

"My brothers are something." Eli paused to sling a stare at both Owen and Hunter that substituted "assholes" for "something," although the laugh that came after probably made the whole bit a tough sell. "But I'm glad you enjoyed the story."

"You know what else I bet Scarlett would enjoy? Dancing."

The mischief-making flash in Emerson's smile registered just a beat too late for Eli to work up any damage control, and seriously, was his *entire* family trying to kill him?

"Oh, I uh—"

"Yes!" Daisy exclaimed, looping her arm through the crook of Owen's elbow with a meddling smile of her own. "Come on. We'll all go."

Eli was all set to dive into round two of his protest when Scarlett slid her high heels to the floorboards beside him.

"I have two left feet, too, remember? But it's a slow song, and there are already a bunch of people on the dance floor, so we shouldn't be too bad off. Probably," she added.

He studied the open space by the jukebox, where the rest of their group had already coupled off and started to sway to the low, slow twang of the song filtering through the speakers. She was right on both counts, and anyway, as bad as he was bound to be at it, dancing with her sounded kind of nice. "Okay, bumblebee. They're your toes."

Leading Scarlett across the bar, Eli stopped at the outer edge of the makeshift dance floor, turning to frame her waist with his hands. She slipped against him and folded her arms over his shoulders, her palms pressing hotly just below the back of his neck, and forget "kind of nice." Dancing was fucking *spectacular*.

"I'm glad you decided to come out tonight," Scarlett said, pulling back just far enough to be able to look at him clearly.

"You should probably reserve your judgment until after you survive the next three minutes on the dance floor," he teased, and her laughter in response didn't make concentrating on his feet any easier.

"I'll be glad no matter what. I'm not used to this whole group/family thing. But it's a whole lot easier with you here."

Surprise combined with some deeper emotion he couldn't quite name, both making his heart beat faster behind the navy-blue cotton of his T-shirt. "If you feel out of place, you sure don't show it."

Scarlett made a sound in the back of her throat, half scoff and all sexy. "It's sweet of you to humor me, but come on. I even got the dress code ass-backward."

"Are you kidding? You could be wearing a flour sack and you'd still be far sexier than any other woman here."

Eli realized his egregious breach of brain-to-mouth filter about two seconds after Scarlett's eyes rounded like dinner plates, and shit. Shit, shit, *shit!*

"You think I'm the sexiest woman in the bar?" she asked. The rational part of his brain screamed with all the reasons he needed to back-pedal, to come up with some glib answer, to *not* pull her even closer against his body from shoulders to chest to hips.

But instead, he looked at her and told the truth. "I do."

Her smile made the admission worth every goddamn syllable, and that was even before she pressed up to place her answer just inches away from his mouth.

"Good to know the way I feel about you is mutual. Now what do you say we make a really good excuse and get out of here so I can prove it?"

CHAPTER SIXTEEN

Thankfully, Eli was excellent at both making excuses and driving really, really fast. They didn't talk much on the way back to the Twin Pines, which was okay with Scarlett. She'd already said the thing that had been front and center in her brain—and all her other parts—ever since she'd seen Eli walk into The Bar tonight.

She wanted him. And she was done waiting.

The headlights of Eli's truck threw shadows over the faded pavement of the parking lot as he pulled into his usual spot in front of his apartment. Quiet filtered into the truck, punctuated by the creak and sigh of the now-still engine and the soft rustle of denim and cotton against leather as they both shifted against the front seats of the truck to look at each other.

"Hey," Eli whispered, a curl of pure want unraveling in Scarlett's belly as he dropped his eyes to her mouth for a beat before raising them back up to meet her stare.

"Hey."

"Are you sure—"

She pressed forward to cover his mouth with hers before he could even finish. A ragged groan collapsed from the back of his throat, daring her to skip every pleasantry in favor of parting his lips with a deep, suggestive sweep of her tongue.

"Yes," Scarlett murmured, her lips still touched against his. "I'm very sure. But unless you want to do this here, we really need to get out of your truck."

Eli didn't hesitate. In a rush of movement, he was out of the driver's side, rounding the front of the truck to pull the passenger door wide on its hinges. Laughter welled up from her chest as he reached up to slide both hands beneath her arms, lifting her from her elevated seat and bringing her feet down to the pavement beside him.

"Better?" he asked, angling her back against the cool side panel of the door he'd just pushed shut. He pressed against her body, the hard plane of his chest and the brush of his even harder arousal sending all sorts of *yes, yes, yes* messages between her thighs, and she leaned in to meet the delicious friction of both.

"Mmm." Scarlett's head drifted back as Eli slid a slow, sexy-as-hell kiss over the column of her neck. Her fingers flexed hard on his shoulders, which made his tighten over her waist in return, and oh God, if they didn't get behind closed doors *right now* . . .

"Your place." She flattened her palms over his chest, buying just the smallest amount of space and sanity. "Go."

He paused to flick a lightning-fast glance at his front door. "My place is—"

"Closer. Eli, please. The town gossip noticed my rental car in the parking lot. There's no way people didn't see us leave together, and we're not going to make it all the way to my place with our clothes on. I don't want to end up on YouTube, here."

"Good point."

They took the dozen or so steps needed to reach his threshold in various stages of kissing, touching, and laughing. Things got a little tricky for a minute at the end of the trip—in Eli's defense, getting a key successfully into a lock while unrepentantly making out against the door in question had to be a challenge. But finally, he twisted the knob, and the front door gave way to the cool, dark interior of his apartment.

"That's better," Scarlett said. She gave her eyes a minute to adjust to the shadows, quickly discovering that Eli's apartment had the same footprint as hers. Turning toward him, she reached out to wrap her arms around his neck and pull him flush against her as she returned her lips to his. The want pulsing between her legs became an insistent demand, and she started moving backward toward the hallway leading to his bedroom.

But the rush of cool air on her body stopped her in her tracks.

"Where's the fire?" Eli asked from the spot where he still stood, a few steps from his closed and relocked front door.

Scarlett laughed. "Can you really not figure that out, cowboy?"

"All I meant was we don't need to go so fast."

"I like fast." She closed the space between them, skimming her hand up the solid, denim-wrapped length of his thigh as proof.

A muscle ticked in his jaw, barely visible in the ambient light filtering in through the curtains. "I see that," he grated. But still, he didn't move.

"I want you, Eli." Her heart pounded faster, her sex throbbing *right now, right now, right now* with every beat. "I don't want to wait."

To her utter surprise, he threw his head back and laughed. "Oh, darlin'," he said, his sexy drawl sliding over her skin like silk and sin. "Believe me, I want you, too." His hands coasted over her shoulders. Her rib cage. Her hips. "But I only just got started, and I'm not about to miss a single part of you."

Scarlett's want-soaked sigh spilled past her lips before she felt it fully form in her chest. "There's only one part I'm really concerned with at the moment."

"You really want to go that fast?" Eli dropped one hand lower, the calluses on his fingers rasping over the hypersensitive skin on her bare inner thigh as he pushed beneath her skirt, and oh *God*, she couldn't tell whether she was going to die or scream or fly apart first.

Somehow, she managed to slip a "yes" past her lips, and he pinned her with a glittering stare.

"If you need to come quick to get it out of your system, I can get you there in the next ninety seconds. But make no mistake. I intend to go slow after that, just to watch you come even harder the second time."

Scarlett's moan in response was all the encouragement Eli needed. The hand on her thigh trailed higher, the glint in his eyes turning darker and more wicked as he lowered his stare to the suggestive contact.

"Do you have any idea how hot this skirt is?" he asked, his ragged tone turning her nipples to hard, tight peaks against her shimmery gold top.

"You like it?" While Scarlett didn't normally give a flying fig what anyone else thought of her, she'd definitely noticed the raised eyebrows from half the patrons at The Bar tonight.

But Eli seemed to have his brows up for a whole different reason. "'Like' is a little weak for how I feel about you in this skirt."

"Yeah?" Wetness bloomed between her legs, making her even bolder than normal. "Tell me."

"This skirt looks like it was made for you." Hooking his free arm around her waist, he pulled her close, anchoring her lower back firmly against his forearm and splaying his fingers wide against her opposite hip. "So sexy. It makes me wonder what's underneath it."

Eli's fingers moved higher still, playing lightly at the juncture between her leg and the border of her panties, and Scarlett was helpless against the thrust of her hips in search of his touch.

"Go ahead and find out."

"You really do live in the moment, don't you?" he asked, coaxing her feet apart with a gentle yet intentional push of one boot.

Unable to make her mouth form an actual word—*damn*, she wanted him so much—Scarlett simply nodded. Eli flexed the fingers at her hip, his other hand a hot, sweet weight between her legs.

"Well, then. Far be it from me not to keep my word."

With nothing more than a turn of his wrist, he shoved the lace of her panties aside and slid a finger all the way into her heat. Her inner muscles clenched out of sheer instinct, and the sudden, erotic pressure sent a shockwave deep into her center.

"Oh." Scarlett turned her nails against the tops of Eli's shoulders. A heavy exhale slipped out of him, coasting a path all the way past her ear and melting into her skin before he began to move the hand between her legs in a slow, deliberate rhythm. The sensation was too much and not enough all at once, rippling through her and pulsing along with her rapidly beating heart.

"Jesus, Scarlett. You are . . ." He finished the thought with a sound in the back of his throat, part appreciation, part something dirtier that Scarlett liked even more. Eli's movements grew more purposeful, a second finger joining the first inside her, spiraling her desire into outright need. Her clit throbbed harder with each shift in contact, and her breath tangled in her lungs as he slid his thumb directly where she ached for it.

"Don't stop. Please." She ground against his hand to hammer the words home. But he didn't need any encouragement, thrusting into her core with as much need as she had for him to fill it.

"So beautiful," he whispered, his strokes growing faster, harder, even more flawless. "Take it, beautiful. Take everything you need and come for me."

The words detonated deep in Scarlett's body, triggering a release that flew through her in wave after hot wave. She arched up, her lower back bowing against the support of Eli's forearm, her toes pressing into the carpet beneath them. He held her steady the whole time, his arms growing stronger as her knees weakened, and she rode out the pleasure with one last cry.

Slowly, her senses recalibrated—the whispering rush of the air conditioning, the clutch of soft cotton between her fingers, the rapid rise and fall of Eli's chest against hers. Eli drew back, an unspoken question flashing through his stare, but Scarlett answered it out loud.

"Yes." God, did that husky, honeyed voice belong to her? She lifted her chin, sliding her mouth over his before stepping toward his bedroom. "I'm still sure."

The three words were all he needed. Desire rebuilt in her belly, sparking stronger with every step as he led her over the carpet and down the narrow hallway. Not stopping until they'd crossed the shadowy threshold to his bedroom, Eli turned, his fingers finding her shoulder and tracing a slow line to her wrist. The gesture wasn't overtly sexy; in fact, the barely there contact was actually almost sweet. But then he lifted her wrist to his mouth, his lips parting over the wild hammer of her pulse point, and that weak-in-the-knees feeling slammed back into her, full force.

"Ohhh." Scarlett shuddered out a sigh, surprised at the deep sensation that could come from a move so seemingly innocent.

Eli trailed his mouth higher. "See?" he asked, shifting to press his mischievous smile against the sensitive spot of her inner elbow. "There are so many places I want to touch you."

"But I want to touch you, too."

Eli stilled, but now it was Scarlett who didn't hesitate. Reaching out, she cupped the smooth skin on his hardened jawline. She stroked her way softly toward the curve of his ear until he shuddered, and a bright lick of desire unfolded inside of her at his reaction.

"Don't you see?" She stroked again, her breath growing heavier as he kissed higher up her arm in return. "I don't just want to feel good, Eli. I want to feel *you*."

He moved all at once, reaching down to pull his T-shirt over his head in one swift yank before returning the favor with her top. They traded pieces of clothing until nothing stood between them but his dark-gray boxer briefs and her black lace bra and panties, and Scarlett's pulse hammered faster at the sight of him in the moonlight slanting past the blinds. She'd known Eli had to be packing some serious musculature—the outline beneath his clothes as they'd worked side by side for the last two weeks had been indicator enough.

But now that he stood nearly naked in front of her, she realized her imagination, as wild and vivid as it had been ever since Eli had kissed her in the horse barn, hadn't done him justice. Shoulders chiseled like a Michelangelo gave way to a broad chest, the sun-bronzed, work-hardened expanse of his abs tapering to a deep "V" around his muscle-wrapped hips. His fully erect cock pressed a clear outline against the cotton of his boxer briefs, and sweet Jesus, Scarlett had never wanted anyone under her hands or inside her body so much.

One look at the glint in his eyes told her the desire was mutual. "Come here," he said, the two gruff syllables making her breath catch in her chest. His hands were on her the second she took the step, bracketing her rib cage and guiding her back until her legs hit his bed. The covers were rumpled but soft, and she slid between them, inhaling a scent that was part laundry line, part cedar, and part something uniquely Eli.

"I'm still a man of my word." Lying down beside her, he drew her face-to-face, his mouth brushing over hers. "You're fucking gorgeous, Scarlett. I won't rush through having you."

"Okay," she said, a smile hooking at the corners of her lips, so decadent that Eli could probably taste it. "But I'm a woman of my word, too, cowboy. I want to touch you, and I'm done waiting."

They both pressed forward with equal measure, meeting in a hard, hot kiss. Eli explored every part of her, from the places she ached to the ones she'd never even thought of as erogenous, and Scarlett touched him in return—her fingers brushing his collarbone, his navel, the hard length between his legs. His kisses dropped from her mouth to her shoulder to her chest, his mouth hovering over the breast he'd cupped with one heavy palm.

Yes. There. Right there. All of her need seemed suddenly focused in that one place, the slide of the feather-light lace on her sensitive skin and the provocative promise of Eli's lips so close to her nipple making her desperate. At her needy exhale, he traced the tip of her lace-covered nipple with his tongue, making her fingers go tight over the spot where they rested at his hip.

"Ah." The noise drifting out of her was more moan than actual word. But rather than slow down or scale back, Eli repeated the ministration once, then again. And again, Scarlett exhaled, arching her back to seek out more contact. He gave it readily, reaching around to free the clasp on her bra, tugging the straps from her shoulders in the same move. His fingers cradled her breast, his lips closing over her nipple to lick and suck and taste, and the feel of his mouth on her bare skin sent sparks dancing through her field of vision.

"Eli." Scarlett meant to move, to go faster, to touch him, too. But oh God, oh God, she couldn't do anything but slow down and feel every second of his touch. With a swirl of his tongue, he sucked her again, harder, then faster, then so softly she was sure she'd die or come or both. Testing the weight of her breast between callused fingers, he added the slightest graze of his teeth on her already-throbbing nipple.

"You want more?" The cool air of his whisper sent another shot of lust pulsing through her core, and Scarlett didn't think. Just spoke.

"No." The word stopped Eli cold, and she spoke quickly to reassure him. "I don't want more, but I do want *you.*"

Curling her fingers around the waistband of his boxer briefs, she lowered them in a decisive pull. His cock sprang free, and Scarlett's heartbeat spiraled faster at the sight of his nakedness. She closed her fingers around him, his length hot and hard against her palm as she began to pump her hand in an up-and-down glide.

"I want to feel exactly what I was just feeling, only I want to feel it with you inside of me. I don't want more. I just want you. Right now."

A low curse tore past Eli's lips, but God, she found it darkly sexy. He thrust in time with her movements, the flex of his muscles combining with the ragged sounds of his breathing to make her sex grow even slicker behind her panties. A push of her free hand had Eli on his back, and with a nimble shift of her weight, Scarlett was straddling his thighs. Her thoughts slowed, breaking through the lusty haze of endorphins as she realized she'd have to backtrack to his truck to get the stash of just-in-case condoms she always kept in her wristlet. She might be right-here, right-now with regard to every other aspect of having sex with him, but no matter how much she ached for Eli to fill the need that had once again become a demand deep between her legs, no way was she not taking five in the name of safety first.

Thankfully, Eli turned her thoughts into reality. Reaching back to open the drawer of his nearby nightstand, he grabbed a condom, sheathing himself in a few seconds' worth of careful motions. Scarlett propped herself higher on her knees, sliding from Eli's body just long enough to take off her panties.

"Eli." Her clit pulsed along with her heartbeat, the delicate friction of her movements making her want to whimper as she returned to the frame of his hips. He looked at her, one lingering circuit that traveled from her eyes to her wet, waiting sex, and God, it turned her on more than any tease or touch.

She eased back, the blunt head of his erection nudging at her entrance. Slowly, Scarlett angled her hips to take more of him, the pressure sending tremors through her center to the pit of her belly and between every last one of her ribs.

Eli groaned, and somehow the sound was reverent. He levered his hips to fill her in one final push. For just a breath, Scarlett was helpless to do anything but register the sensations rioting through her, each one growing hotter and more intense than the one before.

Then Eli began to move, and she lost what little control she had over her thoughts.

Wrapping his hands low around her waist, he lifted her body, just by an inch before lowering her back into place. Scarlett's inner muscles clenched, her need deep and hot and endless. She adjusted her weight, pressing forward as Eli thrust, retreated, then thrust again. On an exhale, she caught his rhythm, leaning in even farther to grip the bedsheets on either side of his shoulders. Her hips canted back, and he pushed up against her even though he already filled her to the hilt.

"Yes." The word spilled out of her, the only thing she could manage. They moved together, Eli's strong, wide hands holding her steady as he moved beneath her over and over. His breath grew sharper, his movements less smooth, and oh God, she wanted *all* of him.

"Yes. *Yes*," Scarlett said. Release built low in her belly, dancing just out of reach. But Eli heard her, offering her desperate need no quarter as he slipped his hand between the tight press of their bodies, his thumb circling her clit. Between the merciless strokes where they joined and the blunt pressure of his cock stretching her so completely, Scarlett was lost. She gasped as her orgasm took control of her, making her tremble and cry out.

"Scarlett." Her name, shaped by such ragged sounds, made her sex clench again. This time, Eli lifted her up nearly far enough to part their bodies before thrusting deep enough to steal her breath. He moved with nothing but sheer intensity, their hips meeting with a slap of flesh on flesh, until suddenly, he went completely rigid, then climaxed with a guttural moan.

Everything slowed save Scarlett's heartbeat. Her body went loose, and her joints became liquid as she dropped over Eli from shoulders to chest to the spot where they were still locked together. The brightness of her pleasure ebbed away bit by bit, slipping into the night like the moonlit shadows on Eli's walls. After an amount of time she could only guess at—and probably poorly—he moved her carefully to his side and murmured a quick "be right back."

Scarlett's thoughts rebooted in a series of breaths, and even though she knew she should get up, find her clothes, and start rummaging up something to say to keep them from the inevitably awkward small talk that almost always arrived post-sex, she couldn't force herself to move.

Nothing about this felt awkward.

"Hey. You okay?" Eli asked, his words a soft rumble from the doorway. Although he'd paused to throw on a pair of shorts, his muscles still stood out in the low light, as nuanced and beautiful as if someone had drawn him.

"Are you kidding?" She laughed, because honestly, she felt too fucking good to do anything but. "I just had two otherworldly orgasms, and got to watch you have one of your own. I'm pretty sure saying I'm *okay* would be the understatement of the freaking century."

His quick burst of laughter marked his surprise at her no-holds-barred truthfulness, and he slid under the covers next to her. "Otherworldly, huh?"

"Mmm. I should've known that would go right to your head."

"Oh, it's gonna go somewhere, alright. I just hope you weren't planning on leaving this bed any time soon."

Eli kissed her just in time to capture her shock full-on with his mouth. "Seriously?" Scarlett asked. "You want me to stay?"

His expression softened for a split second before his mischievous half smile took over. "The way I see it, we've got nearly seven hours before daybreak. Seems a damn shame to waste 'em apart when we could be doing something much more fun together."

The suggestion sent a pang through her belly that quickly headed south. "I like the way you think, cowboy."

"Oh, stick around, bumblebee," Eli said, kissing her lips just once more before starting to move lower. "There's plenty more good ideas where that came from."

CHAPTER SEVENTEEN

Eli woke up in slow stages. Which wasn't anything groundbreaking or even beyond the realm of completely normal. But the soft, warm body next to him definitely *was* out of the ordinary. The fact that said body belonged to Scarlett, who—oh by the way—was not only next to him but also as naked as the day she was born and holding his leather-bound, special-edition copy of *The Complete Works of William Shakespeare* in her bed-sheet-covered lap?

Screw out of the ordinary. This was downright fucking insane.

And judging by the curiosity in her shrewd, gorgeous stare, all his ugly truths were about to be right in the middle of it.

"Uh," Eli grunted, his heart pinballing off every last one of his ribs, even as he tried to cover his expression with a whole lot of nothing-doing. "Morning. It is morning, right?"

"Oh hey." Scarlett smiled through the soft glow of the hallway light, which she must've turned on at some point between when he'd finally drifted off a handful of hours ago and now. "It's about a quarter to five, but I couldn't sleep. I hope I didn't wake you."

"No. I . . ." He trailed off. He didn't regret any of the night he and Scarlett had spent together, not laughing with her over a few beers at The Bar, and *certainly* not the incendiary sex they'd had not once but twice after that. Not even the odd sense of calm he'd felt as she'd finally settled in at his side and fallen asleep had rattled him. But she was at Cross Creek to tell stories, the more personal, the better. If she found out his was the biggest doozy of them all . . .

"We don't have a whole ton of time before we have to leave for the farm. We should probably just go ahead and get moving."

"We should," Scarlett said. Only she didn't move from her spot beside him. Instead, she gestured to the book in her lap. "I didn't mean to pry, but this was on your nightstand, along with two journalism textbooks, a writer's notebook, and a pretty-well-loved copy of *Leaves of Grass* by Walt Whitman. They're kind of hard to miss."

Eli scraped in a breath. *Smile. Cover. Don't panic.* "Doorstops," he said, tacking a brittle grin over the lame excuse for an explanation.

Of course, she didn't buy it for a second. "You need two book-cases' worth of doorstops for the three doors you have in this entire apartment?"

Eli followed her gaze to the pair of low, stuffed-to-the-gills book-shelves lining the wall beside his bed, his gut doing its best imperson-ation of a corkscrew.

You could tell her.

The whisper came from some hidden place within him. Looking at Scarlett, with her platinum hair framing her face like an untamed halo and her green eyes that seemed not only to see everything but to *get* everything, Eli knew the voice wasn't full of shit. He could tell her; hell, a part of him was goddamn dying to let loose with the words. His defenses hadn't been finely honed for kicks, though, and they forced one shoulder up into a shrug.

"Yeah. Something like that."

The sheet tucked around Scarlett's body rustled softly as she turned, not away but closer toward him. "I'm a little torn here. I'd like to help you out if you need a sounding board, and my gut is telling me that you do . . . but you're not talking. If you want me to back off—"

"They're mine. The books are mine. The journals, too. They're . . ." Relief pumped through him, as palpable as any touch. "Mine. All of them."

"So you're a writer?" she asked gently, and even though his brain told his mouth to form the words "you know what, forget I said anything," his gut overrode every syllable.

"You know the way you feel about photography? How you love it and want to be taking pictures no matter what?" At her nod, Eli continued. "Well, that's how I feel about words. Writing, specifically, but obviously reading, too. I just . . . when I'm writing about what's going on around me, I feel more like myself than when I'm doing anything else. The words are just *it* for me." He heard himself a half second later, and okay, yeah, he'd officially done a double gainer into a great big pool of crazysauce. "Which sounds like I should be hugging it out and getting in touch with my inner light, or whatever, and *that* sounds epically stupid, I know."

Scarlett folded her lips together, and if he had to guess, it was to hide the smile that had managed to sneak over her face anyway. "That doesn't sound stupid at all."

But man, now that he'd popped the cork on his feelings, they wouldn't stop flying out. "Maybe not to you." Eli ran a hand over his crew cut, letting it rest on the back of his head before turning more fully toward her on the bed. "Photography is your passion, and it's how you make your living. You travel all over the world, and you take pictures. You do what you love."

"Clearly, you write." Scarlett gestured to the stack of journals lying on top of the bookshelf nearest to them, and irony pushed a laugh right out of him at her choice of words.

"Not so clearly, I'm afraid."

Understanding dawned on her face. "Nobody knows."

Eli closed his eyes. Took a breath. And told her the balls-out truth.

"I've loved writing since I was in high school. I spent four and a half years and all my savings getting my BA in journalism online, and I've written every last shred of copy for the farm's marketing and advertising for the last eight seasons under a handful of different guises. But no. Nobody outside of this room knows that."

A sound left her throat, some combination of disbelief and conviction. "I don't understand. Your family is close. For God's sake, you're knit more tightly than a Christmas sweater. Plus, I've read the stories and all the copy on your website, and they're really good." Here, her shoulders tightened into a determined line. "Why would you hide something this big from your father and brothers?"

Eli held the urge to laugh between his teeth. Christ, if only it were so easy. "Because what I told you the other day wasn't bullshit, Scarlett." The truth—and the reality that went with it—sent his pulse moving through him in a cold rush. "Each one of us has a purpose on the farm, a place. Owen's the serious one, the prodigy. Hunter's the middleman, the peacekeeper, and I . . . am the extra. The one with no specific place on the farm."

"Do you want one? Or do you want something else?"

The question was so honest, so simple as it fell from Scarlett's lips that Eli answered without thinking.

"No. Not always, but it's not that easy. And that's precisely why I just smile and shrug and do enough to get by. I don't have any other choice but to live up to being the extra. I can't be anything else."

"Of course you can," she said, and funny how a whisper could hold so much certainty. "Just because your passion isn't farming doesn't mean you have to be excluded. It's okay for you to love something different."

Eli's laugh held neither humor nor heat as it filled the small space of his bedroom. But this was his truth, and he knew it all too well. "No, it's not. For three generations, every single Cross has farmed our land. My grandfather did it with his son, just like my old man does it with us. Farming is what we do. *That's* our legacy. You asked me the other day about the tension between me and Owen."

Scarlett nodded but didn't interrupt, and hell if that didn't make it even easier to let the words shovel on out.

"Part of it is over the bet with Greyson. But the deeper part stems from the fact that Owen has always thought I'm just a screwup. He's never thought I take Cross Creek seriously."

"First of all, that hardly seems true. At least, not from where I sit," she said, shifting toward him on the bedsheets. "Secondly . . . no disrespect to Owen, but why do you care what he thinks?"

Something that looked a lot like defensiveness glimmered through her olive-green stare, and ah hell, he hated to disappoint. Then again, he'd gotten pretty fucking good at it over the last decade, and anyway, no matter how much he might want to, Eli could no sooner change his reality than rearrange the stars in the night sky.

"Because he's right. I'm not saying I don't love Cross Creek, or that I don't work hard enough at the farm to get by," he added quickly, because Scarlett's imminent protest was sunrise-clear in the sudden set of her shoulders. "Because I do. But I just feel comfortable there. Like I'm treading water. My brothers and my old man . . . they feel something else. They *love* it. It's their passion, and I don't feel that way."

"So you just charm your way past the fact that you don't feel what they feel." Her words arrived without judgment, but they bull's-eyed into his sternum all the same.

Eli blew out a breath to try and displace the squeeze. "Pretty much."

"Have you ever thought about leaving Millhaven? I mean, you have your degree, right? You could always—"

"No."

His answer was too fast and loaded with sharp corners, and *shit*, this wasn't how he wanted any of this to go.

Taking a second to be sure his voice would stay steady, Eli said, "Look, I know it probably makes no sense to you. You're awful sure of who you are. But I can't leave Cross Creek, and I can't tell my brothers—or worse yet, my old man—that I'd rather be writing than farming. I'm already the outlier."

Ah, but you candy-coated that one, now didn't you? Outlier wasn't exactly accurate. Outlier implied that he was just a few steps away from belonging. That he was happy blending in, that he was content enough to fake his way through a lifetime there, and everything would turn out just fine.

After all, what sort of Cross didn't belong on the farm at all, even as an outlier, other than the disloyal sort?

"Okay."

Scarlett's voice boomeranged him back to reality in an instant, rattling his heartbeat. "Okay?"

"Yeah, okay." Sliding Shakespeare back to the scuffed oak of the nightstand, she kept the bedsheet tucked beneath her arms and swung one leg over Eli's waist so he had no choice but to look her directly in the eyes. "Look, I'm not going to cut any corners here, but I don't think you're expecting me to. I like you. I like spending time with you, and I like having sex with you."

Despite the seriousness of their topic of conversation, the fact that she was damn close to being locked over his lap wasn't lost on Eli. "I like being with you, too."

Although Scarlett smiled, her expression remained wistful in the soft light filtering in from the hallway behind her. "You're right. Hiding what you love from your family doesn't make any sense to me. But I'm not the one in charge of that choice, so frankly, it doesn't have to. You and I have two more weeks together, and we still have a job to do. As long as you're straight-up with me, I'd really like to spend that time with you."

"You're not going to say anything about me being a writer?"

Scarlett shocked the hell out of him with a laugh. "That would kind of make me an asshole, and while I'm pretty brash . . . I'm not interested in spilling secrets that aren't mine for the telling."

Foot, meet mouth. "Sorry. I didn't mean to suggest—"

She interrupted him with a quick slide of her lips. "Don't worry about it. You confided in me, cowboy. I know you don't think I'm a jerk. And for the record, I'm glad you did."

"Yeah?" Eli asked, and all of a sudden, he realized just how thin his bedsheets were. He lifted his hips just enough to share the knowledge with Scarlett, who let out a throaty murmur. "How glad?"

"Glad enough that if you keep doing that, we're going to be late," she said, her eyes drifting shut as he thrust against her again, this time with more suggestion. She might be from a completely different world, a world to which she'd return in fairly short order. But Eli liked her. He *trusted* her.

They had two weeks. He'd be a goddamn fool to waste a single second.

"Maybe. But we could save a little time if we shower together. Now c'mon, darlin'. Time's a wasting."

Eli sat back against the driver's seat in his truck, wondering how on earth he'd gotten so fucking lucky. Between the Friday-afternoon sunshine streaming down from the cloudless blue sky, the season high for weekly revenue *and* website hits that Owen had confirmed a couple of hours ago, and the pretty girl sitting beside him as he headed to town, Eli couldn't deny the truth.

He was happier than a pig in a puddle, and it was mostly Scarlett's fault.

"So tell me about the co-op," she said, her bright-blond hair blowing around her face despite the navy-and-white bandana she'd knotted over her crown in an effort to keep it in check. She'd finally broken down this week and invested in a pair of real-deal work boots, although the fact that she insisted on pairing them with cutoffs more often than not still made Eli shake his head. But from the sprinkle of freckles over the sun-kissed bridge of her nose to the plaid shirt she'd stolen from his closet this morning and thrown over her T-shirt to ward off the predawn chill, Scarlett looked perfectly at home in the front seat of his truck.

How about that? His big ol' idiot grin went for a double. "The co-op is essentially one-stop shopping for farmers. They stock everything from tractor parts to fencing supplies, and whatever's not on the shelves, they can order for you. The co-op's also the place to get your fertilizer and feed for pretty much all manner of livestock, plus they carry things like milk replacer for baby animals who have to be bottle-fed."

"And that's what we're going for today?" she confirmed. "Feed, right?"

"Yes, ma'am." Eli lifted a hand from the wheel in concession at her raised-brow stare. "Sorry, habit. Yes, we're picking up feed, along with a few other things. I've got a fence to mend out by the apple grove, and your chickens have to eat."

That brought her smile back. "My girls do get hungry," Scarlett agreed. At the top of the week, she'd taken it upon herself to commandeer henhouse duty completely. Despite multiple offers to help, Eli had been summarily (albeit kindly) shut down. In fact, other than to put a practiced eye on the birds to confirm that none of them looked sick or hurt as he herded them in for the night, he hadn't needed to go anywhere near the henhouse at all.

Eli pulled onto Town Street, tilting his head at the rows of brick-and-clapboard buildings on either side of the cobblestone-lined thoroughfare. "It was probably dark when you drove by this last night with Emerson and Daisy. But this here's Town Street. There's Doc Sanders's office, and Emerson's physical-therapy practice is around back. Clementine's Diner is right across the way—she makes the best home fries you ever tasted, even if they are cardiologically perilous."

Scarlett laughed. "I'm guessing they're not quite vegan."

Eli resisted the urge to tell her that Clementine's not-so-secret rec- ipe involved a skilletful of bacon grease and half a cup of hand-churned butter, besides. No sense in sending her over the edge. "Ah, that's a negative, although if you asked her real nice and offered up some ideas for alternative ingredients, I bet she'd be willing to turn up a new recipe for you."

"You think so?" Scarlett blinked her surprise through the free- flowing sunlight in the truck. But really, the answer was a no-brainer.

"Sure. Clem's as nice as they come." She'd been feeding everyone in Millhaven for the last two decades, just like her mother had before her.

"I'm sure she is, but I'm pretty much a random stranger." Scarlett paused for a wry twist of her lips. "And I'm likely to be the only vegan in town, besides. Nice or not, I wouldn't expect her to adjust her menu or her tried-and-true recipes just for me."

Eli let the *nope* winging around in his brain make an appearance on his face. "First of all, you're not a stranger anymore. Secondly, just because you wouldn't expect Clementine to fix you something special doesn't mean she wouldn't be happy to do it."

"Really?"

"Really. Vegan cuisine might be a little out of Clem's wheelhouse." Okay, so that was probably a euphemism and a half. The only thing Scarlett hadn't been wrong about was the likelihood that she was the only vegan within a thirty-mile radius of downtown Millhaven. Maybe more. "But it's diner policy that if you come into the place hungry, she's not gonna let you leave that way."

"Oh," Scarlett said, her pretty smile matching the equally pretty flush spreading over her cheeks as she sat up taller in the passenger seat. "Well, then. Vegan home fries it is. What else has Town Street got?"

Eli barely had to look through the windows to know every last inch of their surroundings, and he gestured to the pair of storefronts ahead. "The Hair Lair is right there, home of hair dye and fresh gossip, both served up by Amber and Mollie Mae Van Buren. Oh, and there's the barber shop, where I betcha Curtis Shoemaker and Harley Martin are sitting right out front on the bench, trading stories about the good old days."

He tapped the F-150's brakes, slowing just enough to tip his baseball hat at the two older men, who were more reliable than Old Faithful.

Scarlett's brow-lift was back in all its sweet-and-sassy glory. "Do you know *everybody* who lives in this town?"

"Yeah," Eli said, painting the word with the tone equivalent of *well duh*. "You're either born and bred and buried in Millhaven, or you beat feet the minute your high school diploma hits your hand, and you never come back. No in-betweens."

"None at all?"

"You didn't learn the definition of 'no in-betweens' at Yale?" He let out a chuckle, unable to keep from ribbing her. "I hate to break it to you, but you might have gotten robbed just a little on that one."

Jesus, even with her mad face on, Scarlett was still freaking cute. "Ha-ha. What I meant was that it's just a little tough for me to wrap my head around staying in one place, forever and ever, amen."

Eli's fingers tightened over the smooth leather of the steering wheel, but he managed to keep his smile intact. "You feelin' antsy to leave us already, bumblebee?"

"Actually, no," she said, looking as weirdly surprised at her answer as he felt. "The farm is beautiful, and there's a lot more to this job than I expected. Slowing down, at least a little"—she qualified with a sheepish shrug—"in order to get both *FoodE* and Cross Creek closer to where they deserve to be has been pretty great."

"Yeah. It has." Eli tamped down the flicker of unease sparking in his gut. He hadn't just fallen off the turnip truck. He knew damn well Scarlett couldn't stay in Millhaven, just as he knew he couldn't leave. There was no sense in dwelling on the things he couldn't change.

And so he didn't. Reorienting himself with the here and now, Eli spent the next few minutes finishing his rundown of Millhaven's landmarks, answering the rapid-fire string of questions he'd not only come to expect from Scarlett but also grown an odd sort of affection for. Not even the sight of Greyson Whittaker's Silverado in front of the co-op could put a damper on his mood. Eh, mostly, anyhow.

Eli tugged open the glass-and-chrome door to the farm center, letting the bells strung across the top of the frame do their thing before gesturing Scarlett over the threshold. Her head was on a swivel less than two seconds later, taking in the oversized bags of fertilizer and top soil and seed stacked around the perimeter of the place, along with the shelves of smaller equipment and supplies forming four aisles running front to back. His shoulders tightened ever so slightly at the sight of Greyson leaning against the front counter—did the guy *seriously* not have anything better to do with his day than jaw with Billy Masterson?—but he took a deep breath to loosen them as he stepped forward.

"Hey, Billy, how's it going? I need to grab fifty pounds of chicken feed, plus a dozen five-and-a-half-foot T-posts if you've got 'em."

"Sure thing," Billy said, but he didn't back up the words with any movement to speak of, choosing to gape at Scarlett like a fresh-caught bass instead, and hell. For as much as Eli wanted to grab what he'd come for and get the hell out of Dodge, not making a round of introductions at this point would be skirting the boundaries of rude.

"Billy, this is Scarlett Edwards-Stewart. She's spending some time with us at Cross Creek."

Billy's head moved up and down on his beefy neck as Scarlett reached out to shake his hand. "So I hear."

"So everyone hears," muttered Greyson, and the breath Eli pulled in this time was a whole lot sketchier than its predecessor.

Scarlett, however, didn't bat so much as a single eyelash, even though she'd certainly heard Greyson just as well as the rest of them had. "Pleasure to meet you, Billy."

"Yes, ma'am," he said, prompting her to give up a genuine laugh.

"Please. Just Scarlett," she said, and Eli had to give her credit. Her smile stayed sweet as spun sugar when she turned toward Greyson. "And you must be Greyson Whittaker."

His surprise showed in one brief, dark glint. "Didn't realize I was wearin' a name tag." One corner of Greyson's mouth kicked up into a half smirk that made Eli want to bury his fist in something (liiiiike that half smirk, for example), but Scarlett simply shrugged.

"Just a lucky guess. Billy, is it okay with you if I take a few pictures?" She lifted the camera from the front of her T-shirt that read OKAY, BUT FIRST COFFEE in big, bold letters, gesturing to the sun-filled aisles to her right. "If any of them run online, I'll credit the co-op, of course."

"You want to take pictures of the co-op," Greyson confirmed, his black brows shooting high enough to do a disappearing act beneath the brim of his Harley-Davidson baseball cap.

Scarlett paused, already checking the light meter and fiddling with the settings on her camera. "Sure, why not?"

"Seems a little . . . basic for a famous photographer, is all."

Both Greyson's tone and his expression were far too close to impolite for Eli's liking. Adrenaline bloomed in his veins, urging him to remind Greyson what manners looked like.

But once again, Scarlett remained steady. "Ah, basic is in the eye of the beholder." She left her eyes on Greyson's for a full beat to let the subtlety of the barb sink in, then returned her smile to Billy. "So, am I cool to take a few shots?"

"Oh, ah, yes, ma'am," Billy managed past a laugh he looked to be doing his best to try and swallow. "Help yourself."

"Thanks so much."

Eli let himself watch her move halfway down the aisle before allowing his grin to step up to the plate. "Guess she's got you all figured out, huh?"

"You know, I've gotta hand it to you, Cross." Greyson knotted his arms over his chest just tightly enough to bare the edges of the tattoo beneath the left sleeve of his T-shirt. "You played me pretty good."

A hard pang of irritation spread out in Eli's chest. "What the hell are you talking about? I didn't play you."

"Right," Greyson spat, his dark eyes flashing as they followed the path Scarlett had just taken down the aisle housing all the canning supplies. "Because you had no idea some big-deal photographer was gonna come blow up the Internet with pictures of Cross Creek when you put your co-op tab on the line."

Oh for Chrissake . . . "I didn't, actually, but that's really beside the point, since you're the one who threw down the bet in the first place. Anyway, Scarlett and I have a deal. All her coverage is on Cross Creek, and Cross Creek only. If word of the bet gets online, it won't be because she or I hung it out there."

"Why would you make a deal like that?" Greyson asked after a pause.

Eli, however, didn't hesitate so much as a nanosecond in response. "Because. Not that you're familiar with the concept, but I intend to beat you fair and square," he said. "And I've got no interest in you crying foul when I do."

Greyson's momentary silence said he was clearly sidestepping the insult in order to process the intel, and Eli had to give the asshole a sliver of credit. At least he wasn't stupid 24/7.

Till he opened his cakehole again, anyway. "I see. And is that the only *deal* you've got with Miss Fancy Pants? Or are you getting *in* her fancy pants, too?"

Eli's mind flashed back to the night he'd spent with Scarlett and the sexy-sweet promise she'd made to spend the next two weeks with him, but only for a second. "That falls square under the category of none of your damned business, now doesn't it?" he bit out, stepping just a hair closer to Greyson than was cordial.

Of course, Greyson pushed off the counter to meet him halfway. "That's a no," he snorted. "If you were tapping that, you'd be hoarse as a crow from the bragging."

Anger snapped, hot and vicious in Eli's chest, tempting him to plow his fist right into the center of Greyson's face. His fingers twitched, his muscles coiling with just enough tension to turn the thought into action.

But instead, he loosened his fists and exhaled. "Do yourself a favor," he said, notching his voice to its lowest, meanest setting. "Stop talking about Scarlett and walk away from me. Right. Fucking. Now."

Greyson's black brows winged upward, sending Eli's gut toward his knees and his adrenaline to a full percolate. But just when he was sure Greyson would push his luck and they'd end up fixin' to kick each other's asses once and for all, the douchebag took a step back.

"Whatever. Bring in all the highbrow city girls you want. Whittaker Hollow's making a killing, just like we have been all season. We're still the better farm, and in two weeks, everyone in town—and now, all over the Internet, besides—will know it."

"We'll see," Eli promised, his molars still locked together even after Greyson had given up his back and walked away.

CHAPTER EIGHTEEN

"Hey, bumblebee. How do you feel about a field trip?"

The question caught Scarlett so off guard that she nearly dropped the crate of butter lettuce balanced between her palms. "I've been in Millhaven for three weeks now," she pointed out with a sassy smile. "I'm pretty sure you've shown me everything the town has to offer."

"Everything, huh? It's only been a week since we branched out from the farm and started exploring Millhaven, proper. And in today's case, beyond," Eli pointed out, leaning one hip against the tailgate of Cross Creek's box truck and tipping his head at the pavilion in front of them, where the famers' market was in full swing. "You sure you've seen it all?"

She laughed and bit back the urge to remind him that she usually changed locations the way most people changed their pants. "Well, let's see. We've covered Town Street from stem to stern. I took some incredible shots of the preparations for Fall Fling on the afternoon we spent in Willow Park."

"If you do say so yourself," Eli teased, and oh hell, that slow, easygoing grin was borderline not fair.

But God, she loved everything about it. "You also took me on that driving tour to show me where everyone's farms are located, plus I spent that afternoon taking candids of your entire family, including Emerson.

Truly, there cannot be anything in the county I haven't clapped eyes on by now."

Eli ran his hands over the front of his jeans before lifting them in admission. "Okay, okay. You've seen everything. But that's why we'd be leaving town. Jeez, I figured an Ivy Leaguer like you would get the ins and outs of the whole 'field trip' thing."

He hooked air quotes around the words and a smile over his oh-so-sexy mouth, and dammit. *Dammit!* How was she supposed to combat *that*?

"A field trip, huh?" Her wanderlust, which had been oddly dormant for at least a week now, perked up and stretched through her like a cat in a patch of sunshine. "I thought you were a stick-close-to-home kind of guy."

"I am," he agreed. "But you're not."

Scarlett lowered the small crate full of produce she'd just snapped some stills of for Mallory's article on fall salads, making sure it was safely in the back of Cross Creek's box truck before turning to look at Eli. "True," she agreed slowly. "But what about the farm?"

"Technically, today *is* a work day," he said, gesturing to the pavilion in front of them, where the farmers' market was in full swing. "But it's also Saturday. Since we don't have to be back at Cross Creek until Monday morning, I thought I'd take you to our cabin in the mountains for the rest of the weekend."

"Your cabin in the mountains," she repeated, her belly double-knotting at the unspoken *no coffee maker, no Wi-Fi, no civilization whatsoever but almost certainly bears* embedded in his words.

Eli laughed. "Relax. I know who I'm asking. There's heat and AC and full plumbing, and yes. We can bring your coffee maker."

"Am I that transparent?" she asked, unable to keep a wry smile from poking at the corners of her mouth.

Luckily for him, Eli chose to sidestep the question. "The property is about ninety minutes from Millhaven. It was originally a hunting cabin, but now it's more of a fishing/four-wheeling/drinking-beer-and-relaxing kind of cabin."

"That is more my speed," Scarlett agreed. "Minus the fishing part, anyway. I take it the place belongs to your father."

"And my grandfather before that. We've had it for about thirty years, and my old man finally bit the bullet and had the place fully renovated last year. Although the cabin itself is pretty small, it sits on about twenty-five acres. The nearby trails all have great scenic hiking routes. I thought it would be kind of cool to spend some time there—you know, in case you had the urge to take a couple hundred thousand pictures of the Shenandoah trail."

Good God, she really *was* that transparent. "That sounds like a great idea. I'll bet Mallory would love some extra landscape shots to supplement this week's features."

Eli nodded, as if he'd been thinking the exact same thing. Which, knowing his head for journalism, he probably had. "We can do another video from up there if you want, too. The cabin isn't technically part of Cross Creek property, but . . ."

"I'm not certain anyone watching will split hairs," Scarlett said. She and Eli had done two more videos this week to make five total, and even though things had leveled out a bit in terms of visibility, both *FoodE*'s website hits and Cross Creek's local sales were still seeing steady, solid numbers.

"Okay, then," Eli said. "If you got all the shots you needed of the produce, we can go ahead and head out now."

She blinked past her surprise. "It's only noon. Are you sure?"

"Mmm hmm." Eli gestured to Cross Creek's double-wide canopy tent, where the better part of his family milled around, helping customers and chatting with the locals Scarlett had come to know quite well in her trio of trips to Camden Valley. "I've already hashed out the details with my old man, and Hunter and Emerson have the next couple of hours under control here. We have to pass through Millhaven on our way to the cabin anyway, so we can swing by your apartment and grab whatever you'll need for the next couple of days."

Scarlett grinned, and even though she knew she shouldn't tease him, she felt too good not to. "You went out of your way to arrange a getaway for just the two of us."

Although his cheeks colored just slightly, Eli pinned her with the full, flirty force of his baby blues. "What can I say? You may be an acquired taste, but I'm a little sweet on you, Scarlett Edwards-Stewart."

"Is that a compliment?" she asked after she was done laughing, and Eli slipped an arm around her waist, pulling her close and pressing a kiss over her temple even though anybody walking by could see them.

"Yeah, that's a compliment. So do you want to get away with me?" His mouth lingered on her skin just long enough to send a shiver up her spine, and she melted into his touch like snow in a soft rain.

"Yes. I'd love to get away with you for the weekend."

"Of course, you would," Eli joked. "After all, I *am* the charming one."

Before Scarlett could work up an appropriately smart-assed response, or even get done laughing, her cell phone chimed merrily from the back pocket of her cutoffs. "You just got saved by the bell, smooth talker."

He stole another quick kiss, then turned toward the pavilion, probably in an effort to give her some privacy to take her call. "Tell Mallory I said 'nice timing.' Come find me when you're done, and we can head out."

"Okay." She watched Eli take a few steps over the grass—selfish, maybe, but the man had an ass like Roman sculpture, and she was, after all, only human (and also horny). But her phone was on ring number three, so she slid the thing into her palm, her grin going for broke as she registered the name and number on the caller ID. "*Olá, meu belo amigo!* Rafael, how are you? How's life in São Paulo?"

Her longtime friend and Brazilian newspaper contact's chuckle filled the line as if they were separated by mere feet rather than almost five thousand miles and two time zones. "Life here in paradise is good, but it's waiting for you, *minha querida*. Do you have any particulars on your arrival in a few weeks?"

Scarlett swallowed past her suddenly dry throat. "I have a flight itinerary," she said, her mind whirling back to the travel plans she'd booked before she'd even come to Cross Creek. God, those few clicks online felt as if she'd made them a hundred years ago. "I'm on a job here in the States for another week or so, but after that, I'm headed your way, as promised."

"Yes, I saw some of your latest work on your Twitter feed. The farm you're shooting looks lovely, but I know you. You must be going out of your mind. Have you really been there in the middle of all that corn for three whole weeks?"

"I have," Scarlett said, her wanderlust picking a solid fight with her libido. "This job has been great actually."

Okay, so it was a two-ton understatement. But she couldn't exactly tell Rafael that she'd barely thought about leaving Virginia for over a week now, let alone cop to how down-to-her-toes good she'd felt spending every waking moment with Eli, a man who'd only ever been to one state in his entire life and never planned to leave. Raff would never believe her.

No matter how true the words were.

"Well, you've got your work cut out for you here, I'm afraid." Rafael's voice grew more serious on the other end of the line. "I just lost the reporter who I'd scheduled to work with you. His *mãe* fell ill two days ago."

"That's awful. Is she okay?" Just because Scarlett didn't have a mother herself didn't mean she didn't get that other people did, and that they cared deeply for them on top of it.

"It looks as if she will be, but she's got a long road ahead. He had to cancel indefinitely."

"Do you want to postpone the articles we have scheduled?" Scarlett asked, her heart torn between the *yes* and *are you fucking crazy, girl?* pumping alternately through her chest.

But Raff put a quick end to the conflict. "Of course not. For you, I'll pull something out of my hat. No worries, sweetheart. Just send me your itinerary when you can, eh?"

"Sure," she said.

But as Scarlett lifted her gaze at Eli, looking perfectly comfortable and even more perfectly happy as he knelt down to give his dad's dog, Lucy, a nice, long scratch behind the ears, she knew she'd lied to Rafael.

For the first time in her life, she wasn't sure at all.

◆　◆　◆

Scarlett stared at Eli, absolutely convinced she'd either gone hard of hearing or batshit crazy.

"You want me to blindfold myself with this bandana?" She held up the square of bright-red cloth in question, staring at him from the passenger seat of his truck.

His mischievous smile didn't budge. If anything, her skepticism only kicked it into higher gear. "Just for a few minutes, and I promise there's a method to my madness."

"I thought you said we were only a few minutes away from the cabin." One beat passed, then another before realization dropped on her like a great big duh-shaped anvil. "Ah. That's why you want to keep me in the dark. Because we're almost there." God, she'd been so preoccupied by her earlier conversation with Rafael that her brain was seriously turning into tapioca.

A fact that clearly wasn't lost on Eli. "You keep up all that quick thinking and I'm going to have to change your nickname to Sherlock.

Yes," he added, before she could raise a brow over a playfully back-handed comment of her own. "That's why I want to keep you in the dark. I know you're visual, and the thought of being in the dark gives you the shakes."

Hell if he didn't have her dead to rights there. But come on. She was a *photographer*. She'd been guilty of framing up her breakfast in her head more than once. "I'm not a fan," Scarlett agreed.

"Trust me. This will be worth it, and besides"—Eli slipped one hand over hers while keeping the other firmly on the steering wheel—"I've got your back."

An odd pang settled in Scarlett's chest, but rather than making her uncomfortable, she began folding the bandana into a blindfold.

She *did* trust him. A lot.

And it felt really, really good.

"Okay," Scarlett said a few seconds later when the cotton was sufficiently folded into a thick band and knotted around the back of her head. They rode in comfortable silence for another few minutes, and she used the opportunity to let the rest of her senses recalibrate. The smooth vibration of pavement beneath the truck's tires became a bit bumpier after a slow turn, the sudden pop and crunch of gravel confirming that they must be getting really close to the cabin. The truck came to a stop a minute later, with Eli quieting the engine, and instinctively, Scarlett reached up to remove the bandana so she could finally see where they were.

Eli's fingers closed around hers before she could so much as loosen the fabric, the brush of his callused fingers sending a ripple down her spine. "Whoa. Slow down, bumblebee."

"But we're here. How am I supposed to figure out where I'm going?" Her two left feet weren't limited to dancing. Surely she wouldn't make it more than five steps without sprawling directly on her ass if she kept this blindfold in place. Plus, the drive out here had been chock full of breathtaking scenery, the bright-blue sky serving as a flawless backdrop for the rolling mountains and the trees that were just starting to be touched by fall.

"You're supposed to let me help you," Eli said. The rustle of fabric and the open-slam combo of the door told her he'd gotten out of the truck, the shift in temperature a few seconds later signaling that he'd opened the passenger door. Thanks to the higher elevation, the weather wasn't nearly as warm here as it had been in Millhaven, and she shivered a little at the cool breeze skating over her bare arms.

"We're on gravel." Eli's hands closed around her rib cage, easing her to her feet. "It's mostly level, but I'll keep you steady just in case."

Scarlett inhaled, her lungs filling with air so fresh she'd swear no one had ever breathed it before. "Oh." The murmur was mostly sound slipping past her lips, but Eli still chuckled in response.

"Yep. The Shenandoah air will do that to ya." His body tensed, his arm tightening around her shoulders by just fraction. "I guess you've probably been to a lot of mountains, though."

"None that smell like this," she said, all truth. The second breath felt even better than the first, sliding through her lungs and amplifying her heartbeat in her ears, and Scarlett slowed her pace to better take in every nuance even though she couldn't see anything.

Crisp. Earthy. Vital.

Each sensation washed through her on the heels of the one that had come before, all combining to stir the promise of what she couldn't yet see. Eli's body was solid and warm as he guided her step by step. Gauging distance by paces rather than sight was more difficult than she'd expected—God, she missed her most trusted tool—but finally, he said, "Okay. Two paces in front of us is a set of stairs. Just three headed up, with a railing to your right. There you go."

Scarlett's hand found the rough-hewn railing after a second's worth of reaching through thin air. The stairs were easy enough to navigate with Eli's help, her boots thumping against what sounded like wooden planks in a steady one, two, three before the jingle of keys rang out.

Click, twist, squeak . . . Each sound filtered in to heighten her awareness even more. The musty-sweet scent of the air inside the cabin filled her nose, and she paused again to register the different sounds and smells.

"You ready to keep going?" Eli asked, his voice rumbling softly past her ear.

Scarlett nodded. "Yes."

Continuing to take in the gentle creak of the floorboards and the shift in natural light brightening whatever was on the other side of the bandana through the cloth, she heel-toed her way into the cabin, her anticipation swelling as Eli came to a stop beside her.

"Okay. This ought to be just about right." He wrapped his palms over her shoulders, angling her a little farther to the left, where the daylight turned the cotton over her eyes to a bold, brilliant red. Scarlett's chest squeezed, rising, falling, then rising again to the rhythm of her excitement. She shivered as Eli's fingers slid up into her hair, unfastening the bandana with one fluid twist, and for a second, all she could do was blink at the kaleidoscope of light and colors and shapes.

And then she saw what was in front of her—really *saw* it—and all the air left her lungs on a hard whoosh.

"Oh. *Oh*," Scarlett gasped. Her pulse tapped through her, hard enough to weaken her stance over what turned out to be gorgeous, honey-colored floorboards. The room around her was cozy enough—a small, two-story family room surrounded by a stone hearth and fireplace on one side, and a navy-blue love seat/overstuffed-chair combo on the other, all under the span of a rustic, wood-beamed ceiling.

But it was the view outside the wall of windows lining the entire back of the room that had Scarlett speechless.

"The Shenandoah mountain ridge is about seventy miles long, give or take, and it spans from here in Virginia all the way to West VA," Eli said, his voice reverent even though his words were pure fact.

Scarlett stared, unable to speak. Her heart fluttered against her ribs as she took in the skyline, the silhouette of taller, smoke-and-moss-colored mountains in the distance turning the tree-covered hills in the valley below them an even brighter, almost impossible green. Every color, every texture, and every shadow was amplified in its detail, and she was helpless to do anything other than stand still and slowly drink in every last part of the view.

"Eli, it's . . ." She searched for a word that would do the scene in front of her—the feeling *inside* of her—any sort of justice, but had to settle on "gorgeous."

He let out an exhale, shockingly soft. "I may be biased, but I happen to think this is the most gorgeous part."

And then, all at once, Scarlett realized Eli wasn't looking out the window at all.

He was looking at her.

CHAPTER NINETEEN

The only thing Eli had ever done on sheer, undiluted instinct was write. Everything else came with varying degrees of dodge and deflect, of cautious moves and cocky cover-ups. But in that moment, with Scarlett looking so wide open and beautiful that she knocked the breath right out of him, Eli didn't speak or think or hold back.

He brought his mouth down on hers in one swift move.

For a time-stopping second, she stilled beneath his touch, a noise of shock riding out on her exhale. Then her arms shot around his shoulders, her lips opening readily as she deepened the kiss. She felt so vibrant, so right, and so fucking *good* in his arms that all Eli could do was pull her in tighter.

More. More. *More.*

The blunt edges of Scarlett's fingers dug into his shoulder blades in response. The sound drifting up from her chest was part moan, part sigh, part something primal that shot straight to his cock, and he kissed her even harder just to make her do it again.

"Ohhh." Her tongue darted out, sliding over the inside of his bottom lip before she followed the path with the edge of her teeth. Although the cautious part of Eli's brain warned him to slow down and savor the moment, some new, reckless voice welled up to cancel it out.

He didn't want to savor the moment. He wanted to grab it and let it grab him in return, to take the moment and really *live* it without scaling back.

He wanted Scarlett. Hot and hard and fast.

Right goddamn now.

Keeping his arms banded around her rib cage, he swung her around, pressing against her from chest to hips as they moved to the nearest available surface. Her lower body connected with what turned out to be the back of the love seat, and Eli lowered his hands to palm the curve of her ass. He spent a greedy second letting his fingers take in the feel of her—the friction of her soft denim cutoffs on his work-callused skin, the firm, sexy muscles flexing against his hands from underneath. But he wanted more—Christ, he wanted *everything*—so he lifted her up, resting her solidly on the back of the love seat in order to get it.

"Oh God, yes." Scarlett widened her knees, but only long enough for Eli to fit himself against the cradle of her hips before she knotted her legs around his waist. He lost the fight with his moan, his cock throbbing at the direct contact with the hot seam of her body. Scarlett's fingers took a nimble trip to the back of his T-shirt, the tightening of her hands into fists Eli's only warning before his shirt had been tugged over his head and flung to the floorboards.

"Your body is like a work of art," she whispered, sending a slow, green gaze from his shoulders to the spot where his hips were notched tightly against her own.

Of all the things she could have said, he'd expected that the least. "Careful," Eli warned after his surprise wore off. "That'll go right to my head, remember?"

But Scarlett just lifted one slim shoulder in a shrug. "Let it. There's nothing wrong with embracing the truth, and the truth is, you're sexy as hell."

He laughed at the absolute irony of this woman calling *him* sexy. "Pretty sure it's the other way around, darlin'."

"You don't believe me."

"I believe I want you." Dropping his mouth to her neck—how could anyone's skin be so ridiculously soft and so damn hot at the same time?—Eli started kissing a path toward her collarbone, fully intending not to stop until he'd taken off every last stitch of Scarlett's clothing and made her scream out his name right where they stood.

So he was pretty fucking shocked when the next thing he knew, she'd slipped from the back of the love seat to swing him around, her feet planted firmly over the edge of the area rug beneath them and his back pressed hard against the upholstery.

"You want me right now?" A glint of wickedness mixed in with the smile pulling at her lips. Scarlett ran her hands over his shoulders, bringing them to the slight space between their bodies and running them over his chest before moving lower.

"Yes," Eli grated, although somehow, it didn't seem a strong enough word.

"Do you trust me?"

"Yes."

Although his answer was all instinct and 100 percent true, hearing it out loud sent a bolt of shock through him.

Not Scarlett, though. Her eyes were completely steady, her expression sure as she whispered, "Good. Now come here."

But rather than sliding out of her cutoffs and panties while he made a lightning-fast grab for the condom in his wallet, she pulled the bandana from her pocket.

Jesus, this woman would *never* stop doing the brashest thing possible. "You want to blindfold me?" His cock jerked its approval, already rock-hard against the fly of his jeans, and Scarlett's soft, throaty laugh did nothing but make him impossibly harder.

"There's a method to my madness," she said, smoothing the bandana into one long strip before reaching up to knot the fabric snugly into place.

Eli bit back the irony threatening to spill out of him in a chuckle—he'd known his earlier comment was going to come back to haunt him. He'd gone the blindfold route to surprise her with the unbelievable view from the cabin, so she'd slow down and really see it, but . . . "You sure this isn't just payback?"

"Maybe a tiny bit," she admitted, a smile coloring her voice. "But this will be worth it, and you don't have to worry." She lowered her fingers from behind his head, skimming them down his bare arms, then placing his hands on either side of the love seat so he could get his bearings. "I've got your back."

Now his chuckle did escape. Damn, she was good at turning the tables. Maybe a little *too* good, because she'd not only just used all his words against him but also ensured that he really couldn't see a thing. Reorienting his senses against the blindfold-induced darkness, Eli reached out to pull Scarlett close and finally get what he'd wanted ever since they'd walked in the door.

Only she wasn't standing in front of him.

"Scarlett." His cock throbbed beneath the layers of his jeans and boxers as he registered the warmth of her exhale over his abdomen, and—oh fuck—exactly how she'd changed her position to get it there. "I'm not sure this is a good idea."

It was ironic as hell, of course, because what she was poised to do was a *stellar* idea. But as sharp and hot as the desire in his belly was, he wouldn't last more than two minutes with Scarlett's smart mouth on him.

Of course, she didn't hesitate. "You said you want me, right?"

"Yes, but—"

"No buts." Her fingers brushed over his, the contact warm and oddly sweet. "I want you, too, Eli. So please. Let me have you."

His heart drummed in his chest. He knew he should tell her this was a bad idea—his self-control was already running on fumes. But

Christ, he wanted her without borders or limits or holding back. He wanted every last dirty, delicious thing she felt compelled to do to him.

So he let go and let her in.

Scarlett's fingers moved from his hands to the top edge of his jeans, the sudden loosening of the denim from his hips signaling that she'd freed the button from its mooring. Eli's breath hitched at the sound of his zipper being lowered, then coalesced into a moan when her hand lingered on his denim-covered cock. Hot, impulsive want raked down his spine at the feel of her touch, every slide and sound and smell heightened by the fact that he couldn't rely on the sights that went with them. The slightly rough texture of the upholstery under his hands, the silky glide of Scarlett's hair brushing over his skin as she kissed a path across his belly, the deep, herbal scent of her shampoo that drifted up with every move—each one shot through him with white-hot intensity. Her fingertips trailed up to his waist, skimming a path to the point of his hip even though he felt the touch in a dozen other places besides, and sweet Jesus, not only was he going to die on this spot, but he was going to love every second of the trip.

"Scarlett," he bit out, and even her name tasted like uncut want on his tongue. "You're killing me here."

She laughed, just a soft puff of sound. "You want more."

Nothing about it was a question, which worked out great, since his answer was just as definite.

"Yes. God, *yes*."

"Good. Because I don't want to stop."

In a few economical moves, Scarlett slid his jeans, then his boxers from their low-slung resting places before shifting to one side to let him toe his way out of his boots. The thought of her, fully clothed while he was so thoroughly naked, sent a pulse of lust-filled want from the base of his spine to his balls despite the fact that he couldn't actually see the image branded in his mind.

But then she parted her lips over his cock, and screw not being able to see. Eli couldn't breathe or think or even remember his goddamn name.

"*Ah.*" His muscles went bowstring tight, his brain desperately trying to keep up with the raw sensations screaming through his body. Scarlett slid one hand over his hip, holding him steady while the other joined the play of her mouth between his legs. Circling her fingers around the base of his cock, she learned him with bold strokes and slow slides of her lips and tongue. Eli gripped the edge of the love seat, trying like hell to steel himself against the warm, wet pressure of her mouth.

But his mind's eye showed him everything. The fall of white-blond hair spilling over her lean, muscular shoulders. The contrast between her soft, creamy skin and his work-hardened body, inevitably tan from a season's worth of exposure to the sun. Her perfectly pink lips moving in sinful strokes as she sucked. Licked. Tasted. Took.

Scarlett's movements became more rhythmic, full of intent, and Eli's muscles damn near locked down from the tension of his restraint. Restraint that was further tested when she pulled back to murmur, "It's okay, Eli. You don't have to hold back."

The words slammed through him, and he pulled the blindfold from his eyes and Scarlett to her feet before he had any notion that he was going to.

"That's just it," Eli said, cupping her shocked-as-hell face between his palms. "I don't want to hold back. I want *you.*"

Reaching down, he grabbed the hem of her tank top, yanking the fabric over her head, and God help him, Scarlett actually moaned in response.

"I want to see you." Another quick turn of his wrist, and her cutoffs fell to the floor. "I want to watch your face as I bury myself inside you until you lose your mind." The flush on her cheeks—which was already the sexiest shade of pink Eli had ever seen—deepened at his words, and he bent to claim her mouth in a rough kiss before adding, "And I want my eyes on you when I lose mine right after. No halfway. No holding back. I want to fuck you, right here." He hooked his thumbs beneath the lacy strings at Scarlett's shoulders, then the ones at her hips, sliding the last of her clothes from her body and leaving her bare. "Right. Now."

Her chest rose and fell rapidly against his, her lashes tipped in gold from the sunlight spilling in from the windows. Pressing up to her toes, she brushed her lips over his, her eyes wide open and wicked as she said, "Then go ahead and fuck me. Right now."

Eli's movements were a combination of reflex and pure want. Pausing only to pull the blanket from the arm of the love seat and the condom from his wallet, he led Scarlett beneath the windows spanning the back of the house. He draped the blanket over the floorboards, wrapping his arms around her rib cage before guiding her down beside him. She looked so perfect with the sunlight on her skin, illuminating her tight, rosy nipples, the soft indent of her navel, the snug juncture where her calf met the back of her knee.

But he'd have to explore those places later. Right now, he only wanted one thing.

Everything.

One quick but careful movement had the condom in place, and Eli parted Scarlett's thighs with a press of his palms. Covering her body with his, he slid the head of his cock along her folds, the slick feel of her readiness knocking a groan from deep in his chest. Raw pleasure gripped him as he thrust forward to fill her in one unrepentant stroke. Her inner muscles clenched around him, turning his need hot, desperate, and ah, *God*, he couldn't hold back.

But Scarlett didn't hold back, either. Arching her lower back, she lifted her hips from the soft cotton beneath them, fitting herself to his cock until he was seated inside of her with no room to spare. The pressure sent sparks through his field of vision, and Eli savored it for just a fraction of a second before he started to move. He pulled back as far as possible without withdrawing from her core altogether, only to bury himself deeply; once, then again and again.

"Eli." His name tore from her throat, sounding like sex itself. Whatever else she'd meant to say was lost on the gasp that followed, and the noise shattered the last of Eli's control. He filled Scarlett's sex in long, penetrating strokes, levering his hips against hers over and over again. She met each thrust, moving with him in rhythm, her fingers digging in to his sides, then splaying wider over his ass. Her knees fluttered farther apart, her lower back bowing off the blanket in a deep curve as he pushed into her heat.

Christ, she was so beautiful, so pared down and perfect beneath him, that he gripped her even harder, pistoning into her without gentleness. Her cry in return only made him more reckless, and when he changed the angle of his hips to bring his cock flush with the swollen knot of her clit, he felt her begin to tremble from the inside out.

"That's it," Eli murmured. "No holding back. Let me see you come undone, baby."

Scarlett's body tightened, one bright, delicious squeeze of pressure around his cock so intense, it bordered on pleasure/pain. Release built in the deepest part of his belly, but he didn't slow his movements. Eli worked her through every moan, every shudder and scream, and each one triggered something hot a needful within him. His climax rushed up from between his hips, rolling through him in wave after wave, until finally, he lowered himself over Scarlett's body, pressing against her from forehead to belly.

At some point, his breathing slowed, the rapid rise and release of his chest coalescing into a normal rhythm. But despite the fact that Eli knew he should pull back, at the very least to give Scarlett some breathing room, he didn't. Instead, he tightened his arms around her rib cage to hold her even closer. No halfway. No holding back.

And while he also knew that should scare the ever-loving hell out of him, he felt too damn good with her in his arms to care.

CHAPTER TWENTY

"Okay, cowboy. You win."

Eli looked up from his spot in front of the fireplace in the bedroom, unable to crank down on his surprise. "Can I get that in writing? Notarized would be cool, too. Or hey, maybe a nice plaque—"

"Eli."

Funny how it only took the single word of warning for him to fold like last week's laundry. But come on. Not only had Scarlett delivered the word in question with a sexy smile tipping her lips, but she was stretched across the bed in the cabin's master suite in nothing more than a gauzy white tank top and a pair of short-short-style panties that made arguing with her an act of pure fucking idiocy.

"Alright, no plaque. But can I at least ask to what I owe the honor?" Eli crossed the room—although admittedly, the act only took three steps—stopping to bend down and brush a kiss over Scarlett's mouth before parking himself on the floorboards beside the bed.

"Slowing down to really look at the landscape and trails out here gave me perspective I wouldn't have found if I'd tried to rush through everything," she said, turning over onto her belly and burying her smile against his bare shoulder as he leaned back to face the fire he'd just started in the fireplace. "Coming up here was an incredible idea."

"Ah. Well, then, I couldn't agree more."

After they'd finally gotten up and gotten dressed a handful of hours ago, they'd taken a leisurely predinner hike around the property, during which Scarlett had snapped at least two hundred photos, as predicted. He'd snuck in some quality time with his journal while she'd downloaded the images and edited a few for the magazine, then spent two totally laid-back hours hashing out story ideas with her after that as they laughed and ate. The more he listened to Scarlett talk about the places she'd been and the photographs she'd taken, the brighter his own words had become in his head—to the point that he'd added three extra pages of notes to his journal as they'd talked—and hell if that hadn't made this a perfect day.

A day he wanted to hold on to and have over and over again, even though he knew it was impossible.

Eli's stomach knotted at the thought. Bending his knees, he propped his bare forearms over his jeans-clad thighs, staring into the flames and trying to mash down on his unease. Yes, his perfect day had involved two things he knew he couldn't keep. But it wasn't like he could control that, much less change it.

Christ, he wanted to change it.

"Hey." Scarlett's voice cut through his churning emotions, bringing him back to the orange-and-gold firelight in the room. "Are you okay?"

"Sure," he said, because old habits and all that crap. *Dodge. Deflect.* "I'm fine. Why do you ask?"

She pushed off the mattress to slide into the space beside him on the floorboards, pinning him with a wide-open stare that took a chunk out of his defenses. "Because you look like someone just kicked your puppy. Or I guess in your case, it would be your cow. Either way, the last thing you look is fine."

Her honesty tagged him in the chest, prompting his own truth right out. "Today was the best day I've had in . . . I don't know how long."

"Okay," Scarlett said, her brow furrowing softly in confusion. "Me, too, but I'm not sure why today being so good is a bad thing."

"That's exactly the point. Today wasn't a bad thing. Today was a fucking *great* thing."

The words hung between them for a beat, then two, before Scarlett's breath kicked out on an audible exhale. "Except you weren't at Cross Creek."

Eli laughed, but God, he couldn't stick any humor to the sound. "Not even for a minute. Hunter, Owen, my dad—it would never even occur to them that a perfect day could happen without the farm. But not me." Guilt flashed through him, sharp and hot. "I actually had to leave the place in order to have one."

For a minute, the only thing that passed between them was the crackle and hiss of the fire. An ache, stronger than usual, but not unfamiliar, centered in Eli's chest, and ah hell, he never should have opened his mouth in the first place.

A fact that was grand-slammed home when Scarlett broke the silence in the room with, "Have you given any more thought to putting your writing out there?"

"Of course I have," Eli said, surprising himself with the admission even though it was the unvarnished truth. But Scarlett knew the score—shit, she was the *only* one who did. And anyway, trying to pretty up the reality of his situation was like putting lipstick on a three-hundred-pound hog. No matter what he did, it was still a big, fat problem he couldn't get around. "I think about putting my writing out there every damned day, Scarlett. But there's no way I can actually do it."

"Technically, you already have," she pointed out. "There are dozens of stories and in-depth articles archived on Cross Creek's website, and you wrote every one of them. So if the work is already online for the whole world to potentially read, why is it such a big deal to send a few of the articles to editors who might be looking for a freelance writer?"

Even though her tone painted the question as genuine, frustration still swelled in his chest, fueled by the push-pull of his reality. "Because even though they're extended pieces, writing all those articles for Cross Creek was easy—I was already on the farm. I didn't have to leave to do the work. But I can't go halfway on writing about anyplace else. You know better than anyone that freelance journalism almost always requires travel."

Some emotion Eli couldn't identify whisked through her dark-green stare, there and gone in nearly the same instant. "I do know that. But it's close to the end of September, which means things will slow down for a while at the farm, right?"

"Yeah," he said slowly, his shoulders tightening against the hand-sewn quilt draped over the bed's side rail. The truth was, with the exception of the cattle farm and the work they (okay, Owen) did in the greenhouse, Cross Creek was pretty quiet from November through March. "After the harvest, the work load changes some."

"Which makes right now the perfect time to try and pick up a couple of small freelance jobs."

Even though Eli knew Scarlett's intentions were pure—not to mention that she wasn't wrong about the timing—the implication of her words still sliced through him like razor wire.

You are extra. Cross Creek can do without you.

Leaving the farm to write, even temporarily, would prove just how much of an outlier he'd always been. And *fuck*, he owed his father and brothers better than ditching out on them.

Eli's pulse hammered faster in his veins, and he searched desperately for a cocky enough comeback to cover up this conversation. "It's not that simple."

"It's also not that difficult. You have a degree, Eli, and your work speaks for itself. You're qualified to be a writer, and it's what's in your heart. You *can* do this."

She slid her hand over his, her eyes glittering green and gold in the firelight, and his chin snapped up with the force of his realization.

The words weren't a bossy demand. They were an affirmation. A promise.

Scarlett saw him. And she believed in him.

Eli's heart pounded, so hard he was certain the damned thing would spring free and end him right there on the floorboards. "I already told you," he said, his voice sounding as ragged as he felt. "My family can't know about my writing."

"Bullshit."

He blinked, the two syllables rattling through his brain like pennies in a glass jar. "Beg pardon?"

But rather than stand down, Scarlett stepped up. "Bullshit," she repeated with conviction even though her tone carried all the gentleness of a whisper. "Look, I don't have any siblings—hell, for ten years, I didn't even have any parents—so I may not be the best judge of family dynamics, but I know what I see. Yes, you and Owen have had your differences, but your family loves you, and you love to write. I'm trying to understand your hesitation"—her fingers squeezed over his as proof of her support, and God, how could such a small movement make him want to tell her *everything*? "I really am. But you have a chance here. Why won't you take it?"

In that second, with Scarlett's hands on him and her belief in him both so strong, Eli's finely tuned defenses turned to dust, and the answer rushed out of him before his brain even realized he wouldn't push it away or cover it up.

"Because when I said my father and brothers can't know I write, it had nothing to do with the fact that I don't think they'll support me, Scarlett. I can't tell them because then they'll know I don't belong where they do. At the farm. Where I'm *supposed to*."

◆ ◆ ◆

Scarlett sat glued to the floor next to Eli, her stomach between her knees and her heart wedged in her throat. This whole time, she'd assumed he'd stayed at Cross Creek out of a sense of duty to his family's business, and clearly, that was part of the equation. But what he'd just said—the raw emotion on his face as he'd said it—had stunned her into place. Eli hadn't *just* kept his passion for writing hidden all this time because of obligation to his family's farm.

He'd done it because he felt guilty that his passion was for something else.

"Oh, Eli," she started, but God, she had no idea how to finish. So Scarlett did the only thing she could think of.

She kept her grip on his hand steady and listened.

"I love Cross Creek, I really do. But I've known since high school that I don't belong there. I thought I could live with it—I mean, to see the way my old man looks at something as simple as the sun coming up over the east field . . . Christ, it's as if nothing else exists but him and the land. My brothers get that same look. But I never felt it. Not for the farm, anyway."

There—*there* in the glimmer of those ocean-blue eyes—was the wild confidence Scarlett had come to find so captivating. "You do feel that way for something, though. Just like your father and brothers do. Surely they'd understand."

Eli's laugh was soft and joyless as it slipped into the gold-and-gray shadows between them. "I have no doubt they would."

Scarlett's surprise knocked into her, an almost palpable push to her chest. "I'm sorry, I don't follow."

"We might be four men who don't exactly go the hot-chocolate-and-hugs route very often"—he paused here to lift one bare shoulder—"or, you know, pretty much ever. But I'm not brainless. I know my family loves me . . . even though Owen has a funny way of showing it sometimes," he added. "If I told them I'm a writer, I think they'd be okay with that. Once they got over the shock, anyway."

"So why not take the plunge if writing is what makes you happy?"

"Because I'm already the fuck-up." Eli jabbed a hand over his crew cut, hard enough that if his hair had been longer, his fingers would've tangled there. "I'm the one Cross who doesn't want the legacy our entire family has been built on for three generations, and I owe Hunter and Owen and my old man better than to leave."

Scarlett's heart clattered against her rib cage, and she dropped his hand to slide into the space in front of him. "You are not a fuck-up."

"You don't understand—"

"No." She wanted to give him room to air out whatever he needed to, she really did. But no way was she letting that stand. "You have a different passion, and a different way of looking at Cross Creek than your father or brothers. But you are *not* a fuck-up, Eli Cross. You're still good enough to be part of your family, even if you love something else."

"When I said I was the black sheep of my family, I *meant* it," he argued, his voice suddenly brittle enough to shatter. "I don't belong on the farm. I don't have a specific set of responsibilities there like everyone else. I don't love the work. I don't live on the property. Christ, Scarlett, I don't even remember my own damn mother!"

The words arrowed all the way through her, squeezing her heart and stealing the air from her lungs. "What?"

"I don't have a single memory of my mother. Not one. Hunter remembers. Owen sure as shit remembers. And, of course, my old man remembers every detail." Eli broke off, his eyes darkening to a near navy-blue with emotion as he whispered, "They tell stories of her with me. How she'd bandage my banged-up knees and how she'd sing me to sleep at night. And I just nod and say I remember, but the truth is, no matter how hard I try, no matter how badly I fucking *want to*, I don't. How can I possibly be good enough to belong in my family if I can't even remember the woman who put me there?"

Scarlett's throat knotted over the sound that wanted to leave it at the raw, ragged emotion in his words. She was out of her depth, she knew. She had no mother, no barometer whatsoever for this sort of family dynamic. But she did have something more powerful. Something she believed in beyond the shadow of a doubt.

She had the truth Eli had showed her over the better part of the last month.

"You were a little boy when your mother died, Eli. But just because you don't remember her doesn't mean you didn't love her, and it doesn't mean you're not a good man, with a good heart."

He tried to look away, just the smallest drop of his chin, but Scarlett cupped his face between her palms, steady and sure. "And just because you want something different than farming doesn't mean you're not part of your family. It simply means the part that belongs to you doesn't look like anyone else's. Your part belongs to *you*."

Her pulse pressed a hard beat against her throat. But scaling back now simply wasn't an option, not when Eli so clearly needed to know what she knew.

So she said, "Your part is cocky and confident, but it's also kind and smart as hell. It might not belong at Cross Creek, but your part in your family has been waiting for a long time. The only thing left to ask yourself is if you're ready to take it."

"I want to." Eli blinked, as if he'd been as shocked as Scarlett to hear his answer. "But I've spent so long covering up who I am, I don't even know where I'd start."

"I'm going to Brazil." Scarlett's cheeks burned, and God, just once, she'd love for her brain to function ahead of her mouth.

"What? When?" Eli asked, the muscles in his jaw flexing beneath her fingers.

She lowered her hands, taking a breath in an effort to make her thoughts fall in line. "In a few weeks. I have a good friend who runs a newspaper there." She paused, but screw it. Watering down her tenacity when she needed it the most was just plain stupid. "A good friend who just so happens to be looking for a freelance reporter to work the story with me."

For a second, confusion settled between Eli's brows. But then . . . "Holy shit." His shoulders smacked against the quilt-covered side of the mattress behind him. "You're not seriously suggesting—"

"That you come with me to Brazil," Scarlett confirmed, and finally, *finally*, her brain caught up to her mouth. "Look, I know it sounds crazy—"

"Scarlett, please. My throwing a dozen resumes out to editors in Richmond or Washington, DC, is crazy. Me going to Brazil with you is—"

"A really good idea," she interrupted back. Okay, it might be a tiny bit crazy, too, but it wasn't as if that had ever stopped her before. Especially when the crazy idea had merit. "Look, Rafael needs a reporter to cover the local part of a traveling festival, and you'd be perfect for the job; plus, it's a short-term assignment, so you'd be gone for a week, tops, including travel time. This is a win-win, Eli. It's one story, no big deal, and we'd cover it together, just like we've been doing at Cross Creek."

"Except that we'd be in South America," Eli said, and although his tone could've easily swapped "the dark side of the moon" for "South America," Scarlett couldn't help but notice he hadn't punctuated the fact with a great, big *no*.

She proceeded with care. "Yes, we'd be in South America. But São Paulo is beautiful, we'd have a local contact with us who speaks Portuguese, and more importantly, you'd be doing what you love."

"I appreciate the thought here, but . . ." He paused, his expression unreadable in the low light. At least until he said, "My family stuff aside, I don't want a freelance job unless I've earned it aboveboard."

"Well good, because that's the only way you're going to get this assignment," Scarlett told him "Raff and I might be friends, and, of course, I'll give you a great reference. But my rec will only go so far.

He's a savvy businessman, and he's not going to hire anyone whose work doesn't stand up."

"And you think mine will."

Reaching out to skim her fingertips down Eli's forearm, she let her touch linger on the wild rhythm at his wrist before pressing her palm against his. "I do. I've read the pieces on Cross Creek's website, and they're not just fluff. I believe you deserve the chance to see what a good writer you are, and that you're an even better man. But as great as I think the idea of giving Rafael your work is, you have to want to take the leap. I can't make the decision for you, and I don't want you to make it for me."

He looked at her, hope and fear and about sixty other emotions swirling through his stare. Although it twisted her heart and nearly drove her bat-shit bonkers in the process, she waited out each one, watching Eli as he watched the firelight over her shoulder, until finally, he shifted his gaze back to her.

"I don't know if I'm a good enough writer to cover the Cook County Fair, let alone a festival on another continent," he said quietly. "Even if I am, I don't know how the hell I'd tell my family I'm putting in a rush job for a passport and hopping a flight to Brazil, and I don't have any idea how they'd react on the off chance I'd find a way to say it. But there's one thing I *do* know."

Scarlett swallowed past dry lips. "And that is?"

"It's time for me to figure it out. Go ahead and tell Rafael I'll send him whatever he needs to consider me for the job. If he's game, you and I are going to Brazil."

CHAPTER TWENTY-ONE

Three days later, Eli was still vacillating between feeling like he'd won a Nobel Prize and wondering whether he'd lost every last shred of his already dubious sanity. But as soon as Scarlett had reached out to her friend Rafael the other night from the cabin, the guy had asked to see a portfolio of Eli's work, then followed up with both a phone interview and some back and forth via e-mail. Rafael had seemed impressed with Scarlett's recommendation, not to mention *really* impressed with the writing, and had promised to be in touch as soon as possible.

Which meant that life as Eli knew it had the potential to go ass over teakettle any frigging second now.

The creak and bang of the screen door on the back of Cross Creek's main house brought him crash-landing back to reality. Despite all the nerves doing the jump and jangle in his gut, the sight of Scarlett with her camera around her neck and a wooden bucket in each hand knocked a laugh right out of him.

"I take it you're ready to feed the chickens," Eli said, nodding down in a wordless *may I?* before slipping one of the buckets from her grasp and falling into step beside her.

She grinned, albeit sheepishly, and Christ, she was beautiful. "I am. Sorry I'm running so late today. I got caught up in a project while you and Owen were out in the greenhouse getting things ready for today's farm stand. God, it's got to be, what . . ."

Scarlett fumbled for her cell phone, but before she could even get her hand to the back pocket of her jeans, Eli had already eyeballed the position of the sun where it hung, low and fat over the east field.

"Eight-thirty. Give or take."

Her laugh was just as pretty as the grin that had paved the way for it. "Right. I forgot about that magic trick you do with the time."

He was tempted—not a little—to let her be impressed. But in the end, the smoke and mirrors just didn't seem right. "As much as I'd love to take credit for working magic, sight-measuring the sun to tell the time is really just a learned skill."

"So it's kind of like instinct," Scarlett said.

Eli nodded. "Yeah. I suppose that's as good a way to think of it as any."

"Mmm." Their boots—hers a pair of rubber Wellies with bright-pink-and-blue koi fish printed all over them—crunched over the gravel path for a few seconds' worth of paces before she continued. "You know, you're going to get a chance to add to that arsenal of instincts when we go to São Paulo."

His pulse did the two-step in his veins, but he took a deep breath of early fall air to counteract the *thump-thump-thump*. "You're awful confident," he said, simultaneously loving the reply of her smirk and wanting to kiss the expression right off her lips.

"I get it from you."

Damn, he had to give her that one. "Well, I'm glad one of us feels like me getting this job is a slam dunk."

Her brows shot up toward the gold-blond fall of her bangs. "You don't?"

And here he was, right back in dicey territory. "I think I can *do* the job," Eli said slowly, but oh, screw it. Scarlett would just see right through him if he tried to dodge the truth. What's more, for the first time in . . . well, ever, he didn't want to.

He'd been hiding for far too long. Brash or not, it was time to admit the truth.

He was a writer. And he wanted the chance to say so, out loud in front of God and everybody.

"I just really want the job," Eli admitted. "Guess I'm feelin' pretty nervous."

Without slowing her footsteps on the path, Scarlett reached out to wrap her the fingers of her free hand around his. But before she could say anything to accompany the gesture, Eli's cell phone sounded off in a buzz-and-beep combo that sent his heartbeat through the stratosphere.

"Jeez!" he blurted, stopping short on the path and lowering the egg bucket in his grasp before fumbling the thing out of his back pocket. *Oh, shit.* "It's Rafael."

Scarlett's eyes went dinner plate wide. "Are you going to answer it?"

"I probably should." Check that. He *really* should.

So why the hell couldn't he make himself press the icon?

"Eli." Scarlett squeezed his hand—just one quick pulse, but man, it was everything—before stepping back. "Answer the phone."

"Okay, yeah." Setting his resolve, he tapped the screen to take the call. "Hello. Eli Cross."

Time slowed and sped up all at once. Afraid he'd lose the precarious thread of cell coverage he'd managed to Hail Mary his way into in order for the call to reach him in the first place, Eli kept his Red Wings cemented in place on the sun-strewn gravel. His conversation with Rafael turned out to be short and sweet, though, and five minutes later, the call ended as unceremoniously as it had begun.

"Well?" Scarlett asked, making her way back from the spot by the main house where she'd moved to give him some privacy, even though if he knew her at all, it had probably damn near driven her nuts. As soon as Eli looked up at her, her cheeks flushed pink with excitement and her stare bright and wide open with possibility, the reality of what had just happened sank all the way into his brain.

"I got the job."

There was a split second of silence, and truly, Eli was just as stunned as Scarlett seemed at hearing the words out loud. But then she let out a gleeful whoop, jumping into his arms to kiss his face and laugh that unfettered laugh he felt in his blood and his bones and all his other places besides, and just like that, shit got even more perfect.

"I knew it. I *knew* it!" Scarlett pressed her grin to his mouth, then his cheek, then back to his mouth again. "Oh my God, congratulations! I'm so happy for you."

"I'm happy, too," Eli admitted, trying to steady his hands and his thoughts even though his adrenal gland was making it a tough row to hoe.

She pulled back, but only far enough to look him in the eye. "Have you thought about how you're going to tell your dad and Owen and Hunter?"

His heart tripped against his sternum. He hadn't wanted to dwell on it too much, in case Rafael decided to come back with a *thanks, but no thanks*. "Not really. I mean, I'll only be gone for a week, and at that point we'll be done with the final harvest. But we're not there yet, and there's still this bet with Greyson to contend with."

"You deserve to tell them and be happy. You've done everything in your power to win the bet and do right by Cross Creek," Scarlett said, and even though Eli knew she was right, he still shook his head.

"Yeah, but that doesn't mean we're gonna. Look"—he slipped a quick kiss over her lips, mostly for courage—"Don't get me wrong. I want to tell my father and brothers about this trip right now. I do."

Her eyes remained steady on his despite the ultra-bright sunshine spilling down over both of them. "So why don't you?"

"Because shooting my mouth off without thinking of the consequences is what got me into this mess with Greyson in the first place, and I can't make that mistake twice. If I tell my family I want to leave now, chances are, they'll be happy for me." He brushed off the silent *I hope* whispering down from the back hallway of his brain. He'd get to that worry soon enough. "But they'll be distracted by it, too, and I can't do that to them as we head into the last three days of the harvest. Especially not with so much on the line."

Scarlett tipped her head in concession. "Telling them isn't going to be a small deal."

"I know I have a lot to figure out in terms of how I'm going to work this. Still, saying anything before Fall Fling just doesn't feel right. It's only a few more days, and I've already put in a rush request for my passport." It was the first thing he'd done when he and Scarlett had gotten back from the cabin. "I'm ready to tell my family I'm a writer. I just have to do it on my own terms."

"Okay," she said, and Eli's surprise took control of his mouth in one fell swoop.

"You're not going to try to convince me to go all in and just tell them now?"

Scarlett simply shrugged. "If you're asking me if I wish you'd make the leap and be who you are, then the answer is yes. But how you do that—and when—isn't up to me." An odd, nameless emotion pulled at her features, gone before Eli could even bet good money he'd seen it. "As long you're not having second thoughts."

"What? No." The words flew past his lips, automatic and hot. "No," he repeated, this time with more control. "I'm not having second thoughts."

"Alright. Then you'll tell them when you're ready, and I won't say anything until you do."

Scarlett pressed up to kiss him one last time before picking up the bucket she'd temporarily abandoned beside the dirt-and-gravel path. Eli bent down to mirror the gesture, and they made their way toward the henhouse, side by side. Although his gut churned with so many emotions that he couldn't pin one down for love or money, he felt oddly light, as if a boulder he hadn't known he'd been carrying had suddenly been lifted from across his shoulders.

Funny, the sensation was suddenly nothing compared with what went whipping through him as he watched Scarlett approach the grassy area surrounding the faded-red henhouse.

"Good morning, Parsley! Hello, Lavender," she cooed as the chickens all chattered their way over to her, ruffling their feathers and pecking happily at the air. "Oh, don't shove, Thyme. It's not ladylike. Yes, Buttercup, I see you, too. Good morning, sweetheart."

Eli stared, unable to check his surprise. "You named the chickens?"

"Of course," she said, greeting a few more of the birds, who were now conversing in a series of soft squawks, as happy as girls in a schoolyard. "They're my ladies. Anyway, you named Clarabelle."

"Yeah, but there's only one of her." The henhouse held upward of fifty chickens, for Pete's sake. Not that *that* little nugget seemed to be any sort of roadblock for Scarlett.

"I know you guys have the birds tagged and numbered to keep track of everybody, but I see them every day. Calling them by number felt totally impersonal. Well, except for Nine over here, because she likes it. Don't you, sugar?" Scarlett asked, pausing to kneel down and slide her hand deftly over the back of a gray-and-white hybrid who clucked her pleasure at the attention. "Seriously, I had no idea these beauties had so much personality. They even give hugs!"

He barked out a laugh, much to the dismay of the chickens gathered around Scarlett's crazy, colorful boots. "Did you get into the stash of moonshine Owen keeps in the top kitchen cupboard in the main house?"

"No," Scarlett said, attempting what she'd probably meant as a frown, except the pure honesty on her face turned it into a smirk at best. "I'm absolutely serious."

"Oh, so am I," Eli promised. "Rumor has it old Harley Martin makes that stuff right in his bathtub. It's a complete out-of-body experience. Right up till you start prayin' for death, anyway."

Not even Scarlett's sigh could make a dent in her pretty factor. "I see the girls and I are just going to have to prove you wrong, cowboy." She handed over her camera, waiting for Eli to loop the thing around his neck before she waggled her brows and moved a few more steps through the shade of the chicken yard. Squatting down beside an old tree stump, she clicked her tongue against the roof of her mouth. "Come here, Buttercup. Of course, you want some sugar, don't you? You're such a love."

Eli had a smart-assed retort all cued up and ready for launch . . . but then the words stopped cold in his throat. The big, tawny-colored Rhode Island Red she'd greeted a minute ago came strutting across the grass, fluttering her way up to the low, flat plane of the tree stump. For a minute, Scarlett simply sat there, with her knees pressed against the soft earth and her arms outstretched in a loose, empty circle. But then the chicken moved closer, as if drawn to the lilt of Scarlett's encouraging murmurs, and Eli's brows took a one-way trip up.

"There you go," came Scarlett's near whisper, her voice sliding out like honey over oven-fresh cornbread, warm and rich and so damn sweet. "Come give me a hug."

She waited for a beat, then two, for the hen to settle into the cradle of her arms. Closing her embrace ever so slowly, Scarlett rested her fingertips on the bird's back, running a soft touch all the way down her wings before lifting her hands to repeat the process. The chicken leaned into Scarlett's embrace, pressing her feathered belly even closer against Scarlett's shoulder with each stroke.

But what floored Eli most wasn't that she was actually hugging a chicken, or even that she'd grown so comfortable, so perfectly at home at Cross Creek over the last month, that she'd realized chicken hugging could even be a thing.

No, it was the look on Scarlett's face that was doing him in, so wide open and unabashedly beautiful that he couldn't have taken his eyes off her if the world were burning down around them. Eli's heart folded in half, putting the air in his lungs at a premium. He knew—Christ, he *knew*—the feeling commandeering every last part of his common sense should scare the hell out of him.

But instead, he found himself wanting every reckless, crazy, beautiful thing about Scarlett, and in that moment, with his boots in the grass and his heart in his throat, Eli knew he was falling in love with her.

Although biding her time for the rest of the day had nearly driven her around the bend, Scarlett waited until Eli had headed out to help Hunter bale the last of the hay in the west field before she made her way back to Cross Creek's main house. Aside from one more set of photos that she'd promised Mallory from the Fall Fling festivities, her work at Cross Creek was done in the official sense. *FoodE* had seen a steady increase in traffic, subscriptions, and advertising dollars, and the numbers had continued to grow stronger with each published article and every passing day. Likewise, Cross Creek had seen its busiest farmers' market in three seasons last Saturday, along with having added yet another local contract for greenhouse produce to their books. Scarlett had found herself just as giddy about the farm's success as she felt for Mallory's saved business—there was no way one could've gone down without the other in either direction, really—so she'd come up with a little surprise to thank the Crosses for letting her elbow her way into their lives for the month.

"Okay. Time to make some magic," Scarlett murmured, shifting her weight from one foot to the other on the porch boards as she nudged the front door open with care, pausing first to listen, then to toe out of her dusty (but super cute) work boots before crossing the threshold into the house.

"Hello?" she called out, tacking on an, "Anybody here?" just to be sure she wasn't sneaking up on anyone, or worse yet, intruding where she didn't belong. The comfortable quiet she got in reply told her she was good on both counts, though, so she tiptoed past the foyer and into the Crosses' small, formal living room. Kneeling down, she slipped her fingers beneath the sofa, reaching around until she hit pay dirt, aka the stack of slim, silver picture frames she'd snuck in to the house and stashed there earlier this morning.

Scarlett glanced at the window, wishing like hell she could do that mind-meld, what-time-is-it thing with the sun that all four Cross men seemed to have ingrained in their DNA. As it stood, she was left to stare down the lacy pattern of golden light drifting in through the curtains and pull her cell phone from the back pocket of her jeans for a time check.

Three-thirty. Right. Time to act fast.

Working with quick fingers, she removed the back of the first picture frame, then reached into the padded envelope she'd slipped beneath the sofa along with the frames. A tiny bit of trimming with the portable cutting blade she'd brought from her apartment for this very purpose, and *yessss*.

Scarlett grinned. Flipped the frame over to inspect the fit of the double-matted black-and-white photograph. Grinned even bigger.

"Perfect."

She repeated the process with the other picture frames, filling them one by one until only a single photograph remained in the envelope. Pushing to her feet, she padded over the cream-colored area rug, carefully lifting the one silver frame she hadn't brought with her from its resting spot on the side table. The snap of the frame fasteners and the rustle of the aging photo paper that had been pressed against the glass became the backdrop for her swiftly moving heartbeat, a low, bittersweet ache centering itself between her ribs as she finished her task and placed the frame back on the table, then arranged all the others around it.

Scarlett looked at the photos, the squeeze in her chest going for a double as her mind tumbled back to all the Cross family breakfasts and dinners—the ones she'd found so foreign at first. Of course, that had been before she'd grown accustomed to the way Eli always razzed Owen about his cooking and Hunter never forgot to cut a few flowers for the table because Emerson had remarked—just once—how pretty they were. With a bittersweet sigh, Scarlett let her gaze linger on the photographs; the natural smiles, the embraces, the support and belonging so effortlessly shared in each simple glance.

She'd been mistaken a minute ago, when she'd thought the first photograph was perfect. As flawless as the composition was, with just the right ratio of shadows and light, of subject and background, she hadn't realized the one thing that had been missing.

That photo had been by itself on the table. But now that it was with all the others, exactly where it belonged?

Now it was perfect.

"Well, now. This is a right nice surprise."

Tobias's voice dumped Scarlett back to the living room, shock kicking through her in a hard burst despite the slow, smooth cadence of his accent.

"Oh, jeez!" Her chin whipped up, one hand clapping over the front of her mostly clean T-shirt to keep her heart from vaulting right out of her chest. "Mr. Cross, you took me by surprise."

"Sorry 'bout that. Didn't know anyone was up here just yet." He tipped his Stetson at her, his smile reaching all the way up to the sun-weathered creases around his eyes. "You workin' on some business for Miss Parsons?"

Scarlett steadied herself with an inhale. "Actually, I was working on something for you."

"Were you now?" His surprise showed only in the slight lift of his salt-and-pepper brows, but she countered it with a definitive nod.

"I wanted to thank you for letting me come to Cross Creek and take all these photos and videos," she said. "You've all been so kind, but I know it couldn't have been easy to have a stranger in your midst all month."

"I don't reckon any of us think of you as a stranger. Least of all, Eli."

The mention of Eli's name was enough to send a flutter of happiness through Scarlett's belly, and she had no choice but to let loose with the smile winding its way over her mouth. "I suppose not. But still, I wanted to do something to thank you, so"—she stepped aside, revealing the frames she'd lined up over the side table—"I chose some of the portraits and candid photos I took and made you an album of sorts."

Her excitement grew along with her smile, and she gestured to the picture frames as Tobias stepped closer, the surprise on his face plain. "There are photos of each of you individually, and then a few of everyone in pairs or small groups. I included Emerson, too," Scarlett said, because in truth, it had seemed terribly wrong not to. "But I have to admit, the picture of you with Owen, Hunter, and Eli is my favorite."

Okay, so it was an understatement. She'd let out a God's honest gasp when she'd first seen the shot of the Cross men standing on the porch steps, their arms thrown around one another and their faces caught up in candid laughter. They looked so happy, so much like a *family*, that she'd known in that instant how to thank them for their hospitality.

"You've got a mighty fine eye," Tobias said, the compliment sending a flush of warmth over Scarlett's cheeks.

"Thank you. You've got a mighty fine family."

Shifting back, she watched as his gaze lingered over each photograph, her palms growing slick at her sides when he reached the very last one in the row.

"I took the liberty of scanning the picture of you and Mrs. Cross that you already had in here," Scarlett said, and oh God. Borrowing the photo, even for the few minutes it had taken to scan the image for some digital sharpening and reprinting, had been a really brash move. "I didn't mean to overstep my bounds. I know the picture must mean a lot to you, and I didn't alter the original. It's right there in the frame, behind the one I reprinted. And it's a lovely shot. The original, I mean. But I . . ."

Am babbling, chided her inner voice, and oh, fuck it. Brash was all she had. "I didn't know your wife, but I know she was loved. I know she's missed. She's part of your family, so I thought she belonged here. With all of you."

"Ah," he said, after the longest minute of Scarlett's life. "Looks like you have a mighty fine heart to go with that eye of yours."

Relief sailed through her, swift and sweet. "You like the photographs?"

"They are . . ." Tobias paused, so long that Scarlett began to wonder whether he would finish the sentence at all. But then he said, "Well, they're somethin' special, just like the gal who took 'em. Rosemary would have loved every last one of these. Thank you."

"You're welcome," Scarlett said.

As she moved forward to meet his fatherly embrace, she didn't feel like a product of everywhere and nowhere all at once, and she didn't feel like a stranger.

In that moment, Scarlett felt like she belonged at Cross Creek.

CHAPTER TWENTY-TWO

Eli stood at the entrance to Willow Park and pondered the merits of getting drunk off his rocker. But even though it was technically after five o'clock, he still had a whole lot of evening in front of him, including an annual harvest celebration after which he had to tell his family he was leaving the country and a $5,000 bet he had a decent chance of losing in front of the entire town.

On second thought, getting drunk sounded like an outstanding fucking plan.

"Dude." Hunter looked at him through the waning daylight filtering down through the trees, his arms crossed over the front of his crisply ironed button-down shirt. "Don't take this the wrong way, but you look like someone just took a serious piss in your Post Toasties."

Owen nodded his agreement from the spot where he stood on Eli's other side, and Eli laughed, but only because right now, it was either that or cry. Or, apparently, get sauced.

"Seriously, Hunt? There cannot possibly be a right way to take that. You dick," he tacked on, because hello, pride.

"Hunter has a valid point," Owen said, lifting a hand before Eli could call him a dick, too. "Albeit maybe not the smoothest way of making it."

"Okay, okay," Hunter allowed, turning to shift his gaze from Owen back to Eli. "Still. It's Fall Fling. The harvest is officially over. We had an incredible month at the farm, and you're keepin' company with a pretty girl who, for some reason beyond my understanding, seems to like putting up with you."

"Funny." He put his thoughts of exactly *where* he'd be spending time with Scarlett aside, choosing to go with the lesser of two thorny topics. "Aren't either of you the least bit worried I might lose this bet?"

His brothers answered in unison. "No."

"Huh?" Considering the high volume of what-the-fuck running amok in his veins, the single syllable was the best Eli could deliver. But he'd handed every last one of their financial records for the month over to Loretta Masterson, CPA, not even five hours ago. And since the woman was currently standing by the grassy area where Harley Martin was fixin' to serve up some of the best pork barbecue on the entire Eastern Seaboard, Eli was bound to be faced with the repercussions of having shot his mouth off in very short order. "You're not worried at *all*?"

Hunter answered first. "Don't get us wrong. Losing this bet won't mean anything good for Cross Creek. But either way, you busted your ass for the farm, Eli, and a lot of good came out of that."

"If we lose—which for the record, I don't think we will," Owen added. "Then it won't be for lack of trying. No matter what, you did all you could, E. We all did. And we did it together."

Eli let out a breath and rocked back on the heels of his boots. "I guess you're right."

"I want that shit in writing." Owen's grin flashed, fast and wide. "Now can we please stop standing here like patience on a monument and grab some lemonade?"

Eli started to snort until he realized his brother was heart-attack serious. "Since when do you drink lemonade over beer at Fall Fling?"

"Since Cate McAllister started pouring it," Hunter interjected with an exaggerated waggle of his brows that turned Eli's snort into laughter and Owen's grin to a scowl, lickety-split.

"I thought I'd show some support for Clementine's Diner, that's all. My wanting lemonade doesn't have anything to do with who's serving it up," Owen protested, crossing his arms and looking anywhere other than the lemonade stand set up by the park's entrance, where the pretty brunette was indeed pouring drinks right alongside Clementine Parker.

Oh, it was too good to pass up. "Sell stupid someplace else, brother. You like that woman."

But whatever retort Owen made—hell, the rest of the park, the state of Virginia, and the whole freaking universe—disappeared when Eli caught sight of Scarlett.

She was standing with Emerson and Daisy beside a cluster of picnic tables, a frosty beer bottle in one hand and a smile on her lips. The hem of her flowy white dress swished just above her knees, the low, loose neckline showing off a string of bright-turquoise beads along with her smooth skin and the inky edges of her tattoo. A handful of tiny, white wildflowers peeked out from the strands of her platinum hair, and when she pressed up to the toes of her brown ankle boots to hug Owen's friend Lane hello, the deep-down, genuine happiness on her face made Eli's heart swell and stop all at once.

Then Scarlett's eyes found his across the softly lit park, her smile becoming something else altogether, and what his heart did no longer mattered, because the damned thing didn't belong to him anymore.

"Whoa." Owen's voice brought Eli partway back to Willow Park, and the clap Hunter placed on his shoulder finished the job. "Looks like maybe you've got a lesson to learn about the pot and the kettle, little brother."

Hunter laughed in agreement. "You've got it so bad for that woman, ribbing you wouldn't even be enjoyable, E. And believe me, that is saying something."

Old, ingrained instinct warned Eli to cover up his feelings. Lord knew he was chock full of 'em right now, and anyhow, giving his brothers emotional ammo wasn't really on his list of *sure, why not*. But with this bet and his decision to leave Millhaven and everything else cycloning through him, the only thing he knew for sure was how he felt right now. In this moment. About this woman.

He was impulsively, impossibly, head-over-boot-heels crazy about her.

And he didn't care who saw it.

"Yeah. I really do," Eli said, giving each of his brothers a quick nod before kicking his feet into motion. He kept his eyes on Scarlett, feeling every inch of her gaze in return as he crossed the grass. Murmuring something to whomever was standing beside her and passing off her beer, she broke away from the group, walking toward him until they met beneath the low-hanging branches of a weeping willow tree.

"Hey! I was wondering when you'd get here." She slipped her arms around his shoulders, and hell if it didn't feel as if they were exactly where they belonged. "I had a lot of fun taking pictures of the last-minute preparations while the daylight was still good, but I missed you."

"I missed you, too. You look . . ." Eli quickly realized that despite his more-than-decent command of the English language, he wasn't going to turn up a word for how beautiful she looked, so he let the rest of the sentence hang.

Although he'd have thought it impossible, the smile Scarlett gave up made her look even prettier than she had a moment ago. "Thanks. So do you."

He looked down at his plain old T-shirt and jeans with a laugh. "I look like I always look."

"Yeah, but don't you know by now? I like you just as you are."

Eli tightened his grip on her waist, the soft cotton of her dress sliding under his fingers and hinting at the warm skin beneath. The paper lanterns and tiny white lights that had been strung through the tree branches around them cast a golden glow over Scarlett's face, but something deeper lit her up from the inside out. She looked so flawlessly at home, so undeniably happy right there with her hands bracketing his shoulders and that tenacious smile promising sin and salvation on her lips, that letting go of her wasn't an option. In a move that was pure Scarlett, she started swaying in his arms to some imaginary song, and Eli pressed his forehead to hers, swaying right back.

"Hey, you two," came Owen's voice from a few feet away. "Smile."

His cell phone was already up, not giving them much choice in the matter, and Scarlett turned toward Owen and laughed.

"I've got to admit, I'm not really used to being on this side of the camera," she said, posing for the picture anyway.

"Ah, you're a natural," Owen said, glancing down at the photo he'd just snapped. "And definitely the prettier of the two of you."

Eli grinned without loosening his hold on Scarlett's waist. "No one likes a hater."

"Yeah? How about a loser?"

In an instant, Eli's grin vanished, his jaw clenching so hard he was half-sure his molars would surrender. "Greyson." He made sure his tone painted the word interchangeably with "asshole" before turning to look at the spot where the guy had just slunk from the growing shadows. "I'd say it's nice to see you, but that'd be more fiction than fact."

"Good, because the feeling's mutual, and I ain't here for a social call. Miz Masterson said she's ready to announce who won the bet whenever you and I are."

He rocked back on the heels of his work-battered boots, a smirk growing beneath the three days' worth of dark stubble he wore on a permanent basis, but for as much of a ruckus as Eli's heart was making against his rib cage, he'd take now over never.

"Fine by me, as long as you're up for it."

Greyson snorted. But instead of answering, he surprised Eli by turning toward Owen. "You comin' to watch your brother lose five grand on behalf of your precious farm?"

"No."

The word, so definitive, sent a soft gasp past Scarlett's lips and Eli's gut into a free fall.

"Figures," Greyson said, although there was no denying the lightning-fast pop of surprise that had sent his chin a few inches higher at Owen's answer. "See, Cross? Not even your brothers think you've got a snowball's chance of winning this thing."

Before Eli could tell Greyson to just get on with it, Owen shocked the shit out of him by stepping forward rather than back.

"There you go putting words in my mouth. I guess that probably shouldn't surprise me, seein' as how you're so full of piss and wind, but let's set the record straight, shall we?" Owen paused, his stare steely and unyielding as Hunter appeared beside him. "The reason I said I wouldn't come watch Eli lose five grand is because I don't think it's gonna happen. But even if it does, that's fine. I stand by my brother just like I stand by our farm. Win or lose."

Shock sandbagged Eli to the spot, his pulse ramping up even faster as Hunter nodded with just as much certainty as Owen had.

"Me, too."

"I stand by Eli, too," Scarlett said, her spine unfolding to its full height to punctuate the affirmation.

Greyson blinked, just once, before lifting one shoulder in a haphazard shrug. "So you have a cheering section. How cute. I'm still fixin' to beat you, so what do you say we skip the rest of the pep rally and get on with it?"

"Fine by me," Eli said. Wrapping his fingers around the hand Scarlett offered and falling into step beside her and his brothers and Emerson, he followed Greyson farther into Willow Park. A not-small crowd had amassed over by the temporary stage set up for the evening's festivities—good *Christ*, Billy Masterson's mouth needed a good, old-fashioned duct-taping—but it was far past time to face the results of this bet, good or bad.

Amber Cassidy pulled out her phone, looking for all the world like she was getting ready to live-tweet every last detail, line by line, and please God, let them be good.

"Eli. Greyson." Miz Masterson looked at them both over the thin wire rims of her glasses, and Eli (begrudgingly) gave Greyson a lick of credit for tugging the baseball cap from his head and giving up a "ma'am" to match his own. "I s'pose you boys are wanting to know who won this bet that's had the town in a twist all month."

"Yes, ma'am." Eli nodded. A hush rippled over the crowd, making it that much easier for him to hear the thunder pounding in place of his heartbeat. The staccato thump cranked even faster as he caught sight of his old man on the outskirts of the throng of folks gathered on the grass, but still, he said, "We're ready."

Billy's mother lifted her brows. "Well, I don't mind telling y'all that for the first week or two, you were darn near neck and neck. But in the end, one farm did come out on top." She split her gaze between Eli and Greyson, finally smiling in Eli's direction, and holy shit. "Congratulations, Eli. Cross Creek won. You pulled in more revenue than Whittaker Hollow."

Everything around him stood suspended for just a fraction of a second before the words—and exactly what they meant—cut a path past the adrenaline in his veins. But then Greyson's eyes closed as he bit out a swear that lacked volume but not intensity, and Scarlett was squeezing Eli's fingers into next week while his brothers let out simultaneous victory cries, and "holy shit" became the biggest understatement that had ever taken a tour through his gray matter.

They'd won the bet.

Eli exhaled in a hard breath of relief as a wave of chatter burst through the crowd, snapping him back to real time. "Thank you, Miz

Masterson." He shook the woman's hand, pausing to exchange a pair of swift glances with his brothers and an ear-to-ear grin with Scarlett before turning toward Greyson.

"Listen," Eli said. "About the money—"

"Guess you're gonna want that check tonight," Greyson interrupted quietly. But for all the bad blood between the two of them (and fuck, there had been a *lot*), Eli knew there was only one answer he could give up.

"Actually, no." His voice dropped a register, turning the conversation nearly private in the din of the crowd that had begun to disperse around them, and he took a few steps from his brothers and Scarlett to ensure no one would overhear what he was about to say. "I don't want the check tonight."

Greyson's shoulders hitched, clearly signaling that he hadn't expected the reply. "Real kind of you to wait till Monday."

"I don't want to wait until Monday, either."

"Not sure I follow."

Greyson looked at Eli as if surely his brain had dimmed to half power, and hell, maybe it had. But that didn't stop Eli from coming out with the truth.

"Look, you and I got into a pretty serious pissing contest the day we made this bet, and that probably wasn't the brightest idea either of us ever tilled up. But we did it because we both believe in our farms, and there's no harm in that. Cross Creek may have made more money than Whittaker Hollow, but as far as I'm concerned, you and I are square."

He extended his hand. For a long, drawn out beat, Greyson just looked at him, and dammit. *Dammit.* Making a production out of this so wasn't on Eli's agenda. Especially since he knew better than to think that Billy and Amber and a good chunk of the Twitterverse were that far away.

"No," Greyson finally said, his expression unreadable. "Fair's fair. I owe you the five thousand, so the five thousand is what you'll get."

Eli stared at him through the waning daylight, dropping his voice another register even though everyone in the park seemed to be giving them a wide berth. "Look, you don't have to worry. I'm not going to tell anyone we didn't actually exchange the money."

"I know you're not, because I'm giving you every dime before this party's over."

"I don't want it," Eli replied, but Greyson simply shook his head.

"Then you're a bigger fool than you look."

Eli's molars met with a clack. It figured the guy would play jump rope with his last happy nerve while they got this hashed out. "I was a fool to take the bet in the first place."

"Just like I'd be a fool not to make good on a wager I knew I could lose," Greyson said, pride flickering through his stare. "You'll have the money tonight."

With that, he shook Eli's hand and walked away.

"Everything cool?" Hunter asked, appearing at Eli's side a second later with Owen on his heels. "We figured y'all were settling up and didn't want to intrude, but . . ."

Eli waved off the rest with a headshake. "Yeah, everything's fine." Or at least it would be when he tore up the check Greyson had probably gone off to write. "Wait. Where's Scarlett?" he asked, swiveling his gaze around the park and coming up empty.

Owen laughed. "She said to tell you she'd catch you after our broment"—he lifted his hands, quickly adding—"her word, not mine. She went to go take some pictures of Harley's barbecue and Miss Clem's apple cobbler. But Emerson and Daisy went with her, so don't worry."

Funny how she'd realized he'd want a minute with his brothers even when he hadn't realized it himself. But someone was still missing, and had been from the get.

Eli swallowed, his throat suddenly tighter than was comfortable. "And, ah. How about Dad?"

"I'm here."

The old man's gravelly voice hit him like a gut punch, and Eli turned to see his father standing a few feet away on the grass. "I guess you heard we won the bet."

"I did," his father agreed. "I'm proud of you, son."

"You shouldn't be," Eli said, and meant it. "I never should have taken that bet in the first place."

A small smile moved over his old man's face. "A lesson I reckon you've learned. Which is why I'm proud of you."

Eli looked from his brothers to their father, his chest tugging in a thousand directions. Scarlett had been right. His family did know him, and they knew exactly who he was, regardless of all the things he'd kept from them in the past.

He really did owe them everything.

"Thanks, Pop. That means a lot to me."

"Ah," his father said, his eyes filling with a rare shot of emotion. "Enough with all this serious business. Now go find that pretty girl of yours, would you? I may not be young, but the night is. Go on and make it one to remember."

Eli nodded, his smile as inevitable as the sun slipping low over the horizon and the crickets beginning their nighttime symphony. "Now that sounds like a plan."

CHAPTER TWENTY-THREE

Scarlett laid back against the passenger seat of Eli's truck and wondered how on earth a night sky could get so ridiculously clear. Even through the window, the velvety-black canvas stretched infinitely overhead, littered with stars ranging from faint smudges to brilliant bursts of light. Her wanderlust kicked with the reminder that there were hundreds of places to see, thousands of places to explore beneath the sprawl of the night sky, and that she'd shelved all of them for an entire month now.

She sighed. Cross Creek was beautiful in ways she'd never expected. The things she'd uncovered there, even more so. But she didn't belong in one place—she never had. It was past time for Scarlett to follow her passion to the next thing.

And Eli was going with her.

"You okay over there?" His voice rumbled through the interior of the truck in a living embodiment of *speak of the devil*. Not that she should be surprised Eli had guessed how deep in thought she was. Or that the look he was currently giving her through the soft glow of the dashboard lights made the whole mischievous devil thing realllllllly freaking fitting.

"Mmm." Scarlett's heart tapped faster as the warmth in her belly spread out and traveled south. "After tonight, that doesn't seem like a fair question."

Eli let out a soft laugh. "True. Tonight has been pretty perfect so far. But you know, the night's not over. I'm thinking we could make it even better."

"More perfect than all that dancing and laughing and incredible food?" At the height of the evening, Scarlett hadn't been able to tell what had made her sides hurt more—the reminiscent stories from every member of the Cross family, or the recipe for vegan apple cobbler that Clementine had nailed perfectly and made just for her.

"More perfect than that," he agreed. "As it turns out, there's a place here in Millhaven you haven't seen yet."

Scarlett straightened against the leather seat back. She'd been so preoccupied with looking up that it had been a while since she'd looked *out*. Not that she could see much of anything other than the slim ribbon of asphalt within reach of the truck's headlights. "Where are we?"

"Technically?" He waited for her to nod before continuing. "We're on the stretch of land between Pete Hitchcock's farm and Curtis Shoemaker's property. Nobody really knows who owns it, and since it's way the hell out here in God's country, there ain't but a handful of people who know it's even here."

Eli turned off the paved road, angling the truck carefully onto a dirt path that couldn't be much wider than Scarlett's arm span, and whoa, he really wasn't kidding about the God's country part. "I see," she said, trying again—and failing again—to see anything out the window. "And *not* technically?"

He drove on for a few more seconds before pulling beneath a copse of trees she'd come to recognize as red oaks.

"Not technically, you and I are smack in the middle of one of the best places on earth. Come on. I'll show you."

Sliding from the driver's seat, Eli rounded the front of the truck just in time for her boots to hit the soft grass beside the passenger door. The cool air on Scarlett's bare legs was proof that the evening had long since surrendered to nighttime, and she wrapped her arms around herself with a shiver.

"I'm not sure you'll be showing me much of anything," she said, only half-kidding as she closed the door behind her to cloak the two of them in pure, deep darkness.

"Oh ye of little faith." The smile hung in Eli's voice as he pulled the flannel shirt from his shoulders, wrapping it snugly around her own before lacing his fingers through hers. "Your eyes will get used to the dark, and anyway, we're not going far."

He proved to be a man of his word a few seconds later when he stopped at the back of the truck, lowering the tailgate and jumping up into the bed.

"Wow. You weren't kidding." Scarlett laughed, following him into the back of the truck, where he'd popped open one of the two large storage containers built in by the cab.

"About the not going far part? Nah. But I will argue your claim that you won't see much."

"How's that?" Her eyesight was good, but come on. Millhaven boasted a whole new level of pitch black at night. Especially this far from town.

Eli closed the storage container with a metallic bang, unfurling what looked like a huge, thick blanket over the bed liner at their feet. "You can answer your own question, bumblebee. All you've gotta do is c'mere and look up."

He sat on the blanket, which turned out to be a well-cushioned featherbed, stretching his long, denim-clad legs in front of him. Scarlett didn't think twice about settling in next to him, her smile growing even bigger as he shook a quilt out over their bodies to ward off the chill, then leaned back against the featherbed to wrap his arms around her rib cage.

But as soon as she looked all the way up, her smile became a gasp.

"Oh, *Eli*. Look at the sky."

Scarlett stared, unable to disguise her breathlessness. Once again, something she thought she'd seen—something she *had* seen, that had been right above her for hours, even—stunned her into place when she slowed down to adjust her perspective. The shadows surrounding her and Eli on the ground made the stars above them look that much brighter, illuminating each one in a way that was both bold and beautiful. A flawlessly carved crescent moon hung not far over the tree line, its delicate, silvery curve offset by twin pinpoints and its light adding to the ambient glow being cast over the truck bed. The sky itself was the sort of lush color only found in nature, some combination of purple and black that had no name. But rather than being extravagant or gaudy in its presentation, the scene over her head made Scarlett prickle with awe, as if the stars and the sky simply went on forever with all sorts of promise of what lay beneath them.

"I knew you'd like it," Eli said, his voice gently bringing her back to the warm circle of his arms. "I come out here from time to time to think. On clear nights like this, the sky seems to show you how big the world can be."

Scarlett pressed closer against him, breathing in the spicy, masculine scent of his soap, his skin. The world *was* big. Enough that in three weeks, they'd be under the same stars in Brazil.

The thought sent a thrill all the way through her. "Kind of makes you think the possibilities are endless, huh?"

"No. You do that."

"What?" Her heart sped faster beneath the gauzy cotton of her dress.

But Eli was steady and calm. "I don't need the sky to remind me what's possible," he said, dipping his chin to look at her. "I have you."

He lowered his lips to hers. The kiss was deceptively gentle, just a light brush of mouths, a slight hint of contact. But the intensity of Eli's words—of the pounding in Scarlett's chest at what they *meant*—turned the connection deeply passionate. With a hot exhale, she reveled in the feel of the kiss, the juxtaposition between the soft pressure and his firm lips, the slow, intimate glide of his tongue slipping out for a taste of her. Where before she'd have rushed, moved faster, hotter, harder, and tempted Eli to do the same, now Scarlett didn't. Instead, she took in his movements, letting herself feel each one, second by second.

And oh God, she felt everything. Hooking his hands in her hair, he pulled her closer, bringing their bodies flush and warm under the folds of the quilt. The sinewy flex of his shoulders stretched and released beneath her fingers as she met his embrace in a provocative push-pull that belonged solely to them, unique as a signature. Every sweep, every press and nibble and stroke of his lips and tongue made her hungrier for the next, until she was certain he could kiss her for a month and still, she'd want his mouth on hers this badly.

"Eli." His name flew out of her, unchecked. He parted her lips farther in response, the sinful swipe of his tongue making her sex turn slick behind the thin cotton of her panties.

"Do you have any idea how hard it is for me to resist you when you say my name like that?" Eli asked, his lips curving into a seductive smile over the question.

The heat between her legs doubled. "You don't have to resist me. I want this. I want *you*."

To her shock, his smile turned into the low rumble of laughter. "Darlin', 'want' doesn't come within a country mile of how hard I'm achin' for you right now. But I don't just want you here."

Eli reached beneath the quilt to trail a finger over her sex, and even with the barrier of her dress and her panties between them, Scarlett cried out with want.

The sound turned his stare even darker in the scant starlight. "I want you here." His hand trailed up her body, his touch reverent as he returned it to her face, his fingers grazing her temple. "I want you here," he whispered, stroking his thumb over her bottom lip as if he were committing every nuance to memory. The move, which by all accounts should have been tame—sweet, even—was more erotic than if he'd torn off her panties and pushed his cock inside of her until she could no longer think.

Yes. This. Yes. Scarlett opened for him readily, her tongue darting out to trace the blunt edge of his thumb. A moan grated up from Eli's chest, but still, he didn't hesitate with his touch, his hand moving lower until his fingers opened to cover the wild rhythm of her heart.

"Most of all, I want you here. I'm not trying to resist because I don't want every last part of you." He paused to prove it with another punishing kiss. "I'm trying to go slow because I do. I want all of you."

Although the words made Scarlett's pulse press even faster in her veins, she answered the only way she knew how.

With the truth.

"Tell you what, cowboy." The sexy, silk-over-gravel lilt to her voice sent yet another ribbon of want uncurling through her, but she refused to hold back. "You go on and take whatever you want, however you want it. I'm right here with you. I'm yours."

Eli moved before the words had fully disappeared into the hush of the night around them. Wrapping one arm around her shoulder and the other around her waist, he guided her to her back, settling her against the downy softness of the featherbed. For a minute, he did nothing but look at her, his long, slow glance as powerful as any touch as it traveled from her eyes to the loose neckline of her dress, then over her breasts and belly before lowering to the spot where the quilt covered her legs.

"You are so beautiful," he said, leaning in to let his breath coast over her neck. His mouth hovered for one tantalizing second before he made contact with her skin, stringing a line of lazy kisses from behind her ear down to the slope of her shoulder. It occurred to Scarlett to answer, to kiss Eli back, to touch him, too. But she'd promised to let him have her, and what's more, she wanted him to.

Scarlett let her eyes drift shut. Pressing against her side, Eli kissed his way over her collarbone, then the soft divot where her throat met her chest. The swell of her breasts was only half-covered by her dress, and he paused just briefly before sliding his tongue over the rapidly beating pulse point at her neck.

"Ah." The sigh barged out of her without her brain's permission, but the hot, sharp exhale only seemed to spur Eli on. With only a few deft moves, his fingers made quick work of the tiny buttons marching down the front of her dress, then the front closure of her bra, exposing her from shoulders to navel.

Now Eli cut out a breath. "So beautiful," he repeated. He kissed gently down the center of her chest, the smooth skin on his jaw creating just enough friction to turn her nipples into hard, aching points as he turned his attention to the curve of one breast. Scarlett kept her eyes squeezed shut, staying right there in the moment as she'd promised even when his lips closed over one nipple and she was sure she'd lose her mind. She arched into his touch, her shoulder blades lifting off the feather bed and her fingers closing over the sleeve of his T-shirt, gripping tight. Cupping her breast with one hand, Eli swirled and sucked and licked. Scarlett's breath grew thicker in her lungs, her clit aching harder with every move of his mouth, until finally, he broke away from her body.

"Jesus, Scarlett. You taste just as hot as you look."

She fluttered her eyes open. Pale moonlight draped over her skin, the tight peaks of her nipples standing out in relief against the smooth curve of her breasts. Eli kissed his way lower, propping one palm on either side of her hips as his mouth continued its southerly slide.

"Eli." It took every last scrap of her remaining restraint not to buck into his suggestive touch. The hem of her dress had rucked up around her thighs beneath the quilt, and Eli reached down to follow the path of the fabric with one hand.

"I'm not done tasting you." His stare was all promise, and oh God, Scarlett had never wanted anything so deeply in her life. She widened her knees at the same time Eli tugged the quilt from her body. Two fast moves had her boots off her feet, one more bringing him low over the frame of her hips.

"Scarlett." One whisper. A pair of tiny syllables he'd said probably hundreds of times before now. Yet this time, right here under the stars and all the possibility in the sky, the sound of her name on Eli's lips found all her deepest places, turning them brand new.

She parted her knees even wider in clear invitation, and—thank *God*—he didn't scale back. The hem of her dress became a pool of white fabric at her waist as Eli pushed it up to settle himself in the cradle of her hips. His shoulders fit firmly beneath the backs of her thighs, the fingertip he trailed over the seam of her sex sending shockwaves of pleasure sparking up her spine.

"So sexy," he murmured, his lips brushing the cotton of her panties right where she ached. "But I want you." His tongue pressed a path over her sex, making her panties even wetter and the friction between the fabric and her hypersensitive clit almost unbearable. As if he sensed the need radiating out of her, Eli pulled back to curl his fingers beneath the top of her panties. "Which means these have to go."

He removed them in one long pull. A shaky exhale warmed Scarlett's inner thigh, surprising her with its softness.

Then Eli lowered his mouth to her body, and she couldn't feel anything other than breath-stealing pleasure.

At first, he didn't move, simply letting his lips and tongue rest against the seam of her in a connection both hot and soft. But then his tongue edged up in a wicked taste, and need pulsed through her so darkly that her movements weren't her own.

"Eli, please." Scarlett canted her hips at the same time he pushed deeper to meet her. "Please don't *stop*."

He didn't. Parting her folds with his fingers, he kissed her intimately, exploring her body with bold strokes of his tongue. Pleasure built almost immediately between her legs, beckoning fast and bright, and she couldn't hold back. Scarlett thrust against Eli's mouth, her climax rushing closer by the second. For half a second, she walked the tightrope between need and release. Then he closed his lips over her clit in a slow, suggestive pull, and she flew apart under his tongue.

Ragged breaths passed, and dazedly, Scarlett realized that time probably did, too, as Eli lightened his touch by degrees. But he didn't move from between her legs, and finally, when she dropped her chin to her chest to get her bearings, she found him staring up at her with more desire on his face than ever.

"You okay?" he asked, the question kicking the corners of her mouth into a smile.

"Yes." Scarlett shifted her weight, fully intending to pull him toward her and undress him so she could return the favor and then some.

Eli didn't budge. "Good."

"Good?" she repeated, unable to get anything else past the confusion taking root in her brain.

"Very. See, I'm not done with you yet. When I said I wanted all of you, I meant it."

He ran the tip of his tongue over her folds, and *God*, she'd never seen anything so wantonly sexy. As if he'd never stopped, Eli returned his attention between her thighs, kissing and licking and loving her until desire rekindled in her belly. Scarlett reached down to splay her fingers over the back of his neck, not caring how lust-driven her moans must surely sound or how brash she looked as she held him close.

That was the heart of it, though. The thing that made her more wild for him than anything he could do to her body. Scarlett wanted all of him. Not only for her but also *with* her.

"Eli. Come here."

He looked up, his eyes glittering as he met her stare, but she didn't even think twice.

"If you want all of me, come here and take me. But let me have you, too." She shifted forward, pulling him in until they were heart to slamming heart.

"I don't just want you. I want you and me."

Eli dropped his forehead to hers, nodding even as he slanted a kiss over her lips. He quickly shed his clothes, pausing only to take a condom from his wallet and sheath himself before wrapping the quilt around his shoulders and covering her with his body. Fitting his hips against hers, Eli slid his cock over her entrance, just once before thrusting all the way into her heat.

All of Scarlett's breath rushed out on a gasp, and for a second, she thought the sensation, the pressure, the raw pleasure, would be too much. But then he began to move, and just like that, too much became not enough. Eli filled her in long strokes, one hand on her shoulder, the other gripping her hip. Her clit throbbed in time with his movements, ripples of need spiraling through her with each thrust and retreat.

All too soon, her need became an undeniable demand. Scarlett met every push of his hips, every press of his cock as he filled her over and again. Her orgasm crashed into her, her sex squeezing and releasing in waves of undiluted bliss. The moans tearing from her throat changed the tempo of Eli's movements, and he pistoned into her, harder, deeper, until his body went rigid over hers.

"You and me, Eli," she whispered, arching up from the feather bed until he was flush inside of her, filling her to the hilt. "I want all of you, too. Please."

The tension in his muscles unraveled on a shudder, his fingers digging into her as he came with a broken, guttural shout. Scarlett rode out every ragged breath until Eli's fingers loosened from her hip and her shoulder. Reaching up, she gathered him into her arms to pull him close.

"You and me," she whispered.

And as she looked up at the stars over his shoulder, Scarlett knew the sky was right.

Anything was possible.

CHAPTER TWENTY-FOUR

Eli stood on the front porch of Cross Creek's main house with his keys in his hand and his heart in his windpipe. The sun, which should have been smack in the center of the sky at this point in the day, hid behind a bank of thick gray clouds that finally matched the cooler October weather.

He sank a little deeper into his blue-and-green flannel shirt, fiddling with the bottom button as he stared at the whitewashed porch boards extending out from beneath the welcome mat. Both Hunter's and Owen's trucks were lined up in the drive beside the house, which meant everyone was already here.

The irony of being last in yet again sure as hell wasn't lost on him.

"Eli."

Scarlett turned from the spot where she'd stood next to him for the last five minutes. Her tone didn't push, although he heard the unspoken "it's time" in her voice, and he blew out a rickety breath.

"I know," he said quietly, because Christ, he really did. "Telling them is the right thing to do, and now is the right time to do it. But no one's called a family meeting since . . . well, ever. They've got to know something major is up."

"They probably do," Scarlett agreed. "But just because something big is happening doesn't mean that thing is bad. This trip to Brazil is a *great* thing. Look"—she stared up at him, her gaze warm and sweet and so fucking sure—"I'm right here with you. Show your family who you are, Eli. It's time."

He dropped his chin just a fraction before nodding. She was right. Yeah, he was ten pounds of nerves stuffed into a five-pound sack, but he wasn't going to get more ready by standing out here on the porch boards.

He was a writer. And for as much loyalty as he owed the family who stood by him no matter what, it was time to tell them the truth.

"Okay." Sliding a deep breath into his lungs, Eli reached out for the doorknob, ushering Scarlett over the threshold before following her into the house. The telltale clink and clank of kitchenware filtered in from the back of the house, punctuated by strains of laughter and the low, smooth cadence of voices volleying in conversation. Before, it might have struck him as exclusionary that such easy happiness could happen without him being a part of it. But he *was* a part of it.

He didn't have to be at Cross Creek to belong.

"Hey! We were starting to think you two got lost." Emerson grinned out a greeting from the spot where she stood, sweetening her cup of coffee at the butcher-block island.

"Or waylaid," Hunter added with a good-natured smirk, dropping his voice low enough to keep the comment out of the earshot of their old man, who stood over by the pantry with Owen.

"Hunter," Emerson chided at the exact moment Scarlett coughed out a laugh, and Eli offered his brother a smile to go with his single-fingered salute.

"Okay, okay. Pardon my manners." Hunter reached out to shake Eli's hand, then turned to give Scarlett a big hug. "It's good to see you guys. Even if the invite to meet up on a Sunday was a surprise."

Eli's pulse stuttered, doubly so when Owen made his way to the island to add, "Yeah, it was. We just saw you last night."

Concern flickered through the unspoken question in his brothers' stares, mirrored by both Emerson and his old man, and looked like *now or never* had turned into just plain *now*.

"Yeah. About that. I asked you all to come out here because there's, ah, something you should know." The air threatened to leave the room, so Eli hauled in a big ol' lungful of the stuff and blurted, "I wrote all the extended articles on Cross Creek's website, and I've written all the ads and copy, too. Everything that's ever been put to paper for the farm for the last ten years . . . is mine. I spent four and a half years getting my bachelor's degree online in journalism, and I did it because I want to be a writer."

No, that wasn't quite right.

He planted his boots into the kitchen tiles and stood as tall as he could. "I *am* a writer."

For a minute that lasted easily a month, the room was filled with nothing but silence and stunned stares. Eli gripped Scarlett's hand, and although he had no memory whatsoever of reaching for her, she held him back just as tightly.

Hunter broke the excruciating quiet first. "So all those friends of yours, people you knew who were freelance writers . . . for the last decade, that's all been you?"

Eli's brain hit fast-forward, his thoughts moving almost too fast for his mouth. "Yes, but I never took any money from Cross Creek for my writing," he said, his gaze moving from Hunter to Owen to their father. He'd had to be downright cloak-and-dagger about rerouting payments back to the farm more than once, but he'd always been meticulous about not taking a dime for his work.

"That's why you insisted on dealing with your contacts personally," Owen said, realization trickling over his expression. "The whole time, it was you doing the writing."

"Yeah. I . . ." Eli swallowed past his sandpaper throat. "Yeah."

"Can I ask why you never said anything?" Emerson looked at him from across the butcher-block island, her voice soft and her coppery brows knit in question. "I mean, the work is excellent, Eli. You've written dozens of in-depth articles and earned a college degree. You should be proud."

"I am," he said, the answer as automatic as the rapid-fire heartbeat that accompanied it. "I'm proud of the writing. The rest is kind of, ah. Complicated."

Here, Eli paused. Complicated was the world's biggest understatement, and hell if—despite having run through this no less than a billion times in his head—he had any clue how to properly explain how he felt.

But then Scarlett leaned in from beside him to whisper a simple, "It's okay," and Eli opened his mouth to let loose with the truth.

"I love Cross Creek. I don't regret a single day I've worked the land, and I wouldn't trade them for anything. But I've never felt like I belong here. It's not because of anything any of you did," he rushed to add, and fuck, he was botching this. "It's just that while I love Cross Creek, I don't love farming. Not the way the three of you do."

He looked at his father, who had been noticeably silent since Eli had dumped the writer bombshell in everyone's laps. While he looked far from angry, there were emotions simmering in his stare that Eli couldn't identify, which pretty much turned waiting for the old man to say something into an anvil in the center of his chest.

Owen scrubbed a hand over his five-o'clock shadow, his shock still plain as sunrise on his face. "Jesus, E. I had no idea you felt like you didn't belong at the farm."

"I worked real hard to keep it that way," Eli said, and Hunter made a sound of sudden understanding.

"All that fast talk and no-big-deal attitude was a cover."

Eli nodded. He'd blown the lid off the topic. Not going the full-disclosure route now would just be stupid. "Most of the time, yeah. I figured being a bit of a slacker was better than coming out with the truth."

"Not feeling like farming is your passion, I get," Owen said, although when Eli—along with nearly everyone else in the kitchen—shot him a look akin to *is your ass on crooked*? He shook his head and went for a lightning-fast rephrase. "Just because running Cross Creek is what I've always wanted doesn't mean the farm is for everyone. I understand that. But you honestly feel like you don't belong here? With us?"

The guilt on Owen's face sent a corkscrew through Eli's gut, but he firmed his voice to be sure his next words found their mark. "My feeling like the odd man out was my own doing. You're my family, and we have a legacy. I owe it to you to be a part of this farm."

He looked at each of them in turn, and even though it was easily the hardest thing he'd ever done, Eli held his old man's stare as he said, "But I realize now that I owe it to myself to do what I love, too. And deep down, what I love isn't farming. It's writing."

"So what does that mean, exactly?" Emerson asked. "There can't be many jobs for writers in Millhaven. We don't even have a newspaper. Are you going to leave?"

And here came the crux of it all. "Yes and no. I've been offered a short-term freelance job with Scarlett in Brazil, and we're leaving in four days."

Owen took a step back from the island. "You're leaving in four *days*?"

"The trip is only for a week," Eli qualified quickly. "I'd never leave you guys in the lurch here. Scarlett and I are covering one story, and then I'll be back in Millhaven. But I'm hoping this leads to other freelance offers."

"How long have you known about the job?" Owen asked, still clearly trying to get his head around things.

"As a possibility? For a little while. I would have told you sooner, but the actual offer just came together. I know this seems sudden—"

"'Sudden' is a good word for it," Hunter said, slow and skeptical. "Don't get me wrong, I think your wanting to write is great. But you're not talking about a quick jump to Lockridge here. You've never been on a plane. Hell, you've never even been out of the state. There's got to be a crazy learning curve to a profession like travel journalism. You sure it's a good idea to go so big right out of the gate?"

For a second, Eli hesitated. Truth was, he *wasn't* sure. He had no way of knowing what this trip to Brazil would bring, and he was taking a gigantic, reckless leap into the unknown by going.

Before he could get some sort of answer past his tripping pulse, Scarlett lowered his hand and stepped up to the kitchen island.

"I know a trip like this seems overwhelming," she said. "And that's because frankly, it is. But I've read Eli's articles. I know what a job like this entails. Going on assignment in another country might seem brash. It might *be* brash. But he can do this job. He's got what it takes."

Eli's throat knotted at hearing her conviction out loud, and finally, his voice came back online. "I'm not going to pretend I have all the answers or that any of this will be easy. I want this trip to turn into a lot more. I want a career in travel journalism. But even more, I need you to know who I am. I can't cover it up anymore."

"Then don't."

Although his old man's reply wasn't loud or laced with obvious emotion, it sliced through Eli all the same.

"I'm so sorry, Pop," he started, but his father cut the rest of the apology short with a shake of his head.

"None of that, now. You're the first Cross to earn a college degree, and you did it while working on the farm, to boot. You've got a lot to be proud of, but not one thing to be sorry for."

Eli let go of a shaky breath that didn't get any easier when Hunter, Owen, and Emerson all nodded in agreement. "But the farm is our legacy, and I owe you so much. You're not upset I don't want to fulfill it?"

His father paused. "If you're askin' whether I wish you loved Cross Creek the way I do, then I can't lie. Of course I do," he said, crossing the kitchen until less than an arm's length remained between them. "But if you're askin' if I'm disappointed in who you are, the answer's no. Your legacy is what you make it. What you just did, bein' honest even though you knew the truth would make waves? That took an awful lot of guts."

The sudden emotion welling in his old man's eyes hit Eli like a wrecking ball, and he cleared his throat twice in an effort to give his voice the highest possible odds of not breaking.

"I know operating this place while you're a man down isn't going to be easy," he finally managed.

But his father's answer brooked no argument. "We'll cross those bridges when we get to 'em. For now, sounds like you've got a trip to plan."

"Thanks, Pop." Christ, the words seemed far too simple for the feeling in his chest right now.

"Thank you, Eli. For not coverin' up who you are."

After a beat, Hunter borrowed a page from Eli's throat-clearing playbook. "So I guess that kind of makes this your bon voyage party, huh?"

"I'm only gonna be gone for a week," Eli pointed out, still trying to process the thoughts churning through his brain and the relief/happiness/holy-shit-did-that-just-happen churning through his gut.

Emerson sniffle-laughed, swiping at her face with the back of one hand, and Hunter slipped one arm around her before breaking into a huge grin.

"Well, yeah, but Owen was threatening to make a big ol' pot of chili this afternoon. Seems like a waste not to raise a beer or two along with it now that we have a reason to celebrate."

Eli snorted, and guess his cockiness hadn't *all* been a cover. "You just want an excuse to throw a few back on a Sunday afternoon."

"Possibly," Owen allowed, stepping in to clap him on the shoulder with a grin. "But come on. You've gotta admit, you're giving us a helluva good one."

Eli sobered. "You know my leaving means more work for you, even though I'll be back in a week." He might be extra around Cross Creek, but that didn't mean he didn't bust his ass.

"Yep." Hunter didn't so much as blink in the gray daylight filtering through the windows behind him. "But I don't give a lick. I'm proud of you, little brother."

Owen chimed in. "Me, too."

"And me," Emerson added.

There was no help for Eli's grin, especially when he heard Scarlett's throaty laughter from beside him.

"Okay, okay," he said, edging in close to give her hip a playful bump with his own. "I know you're dying to, so go ahead and say it."

"Say what?" She blinked, her eyes all olive-green innocence.

"I told you so," they said in unison, and he couldn't help himself from pulling her in close.

"I know. You *did* tell me. But be careful what you wish for, bumblebee, because now, you're stuck with me."

She pushed up on her toes to brush a kiss over his cheek. "Sounds like a plan to me, cowboy."

They all fell into orbit around one another in the kitchen, each of them chopping or slicing or stirring in preparation for a killer lunch. True to his promise, Hunter threw a bunch of beers on ice while Scarlett and Owen had a chili cook-off, hers with beans and greenhouse veggies and his with ground beef and a blend of spices he swore he'd take to the grave. Emerson asked Eli about his degree, then some more about his writing, and everyone else joined in, both listening and voicing their curiosity. Conversation moved easily as Scarlett peppered in some knowledge about freelance writing, and finally, *finally*, Eli was able to breathe all the way out in relief.

He was going to Brazil with Scarlett. In four days' time, he'd be living the dream he'd stuffed down deep for ten long years.

Just as he and Emerson got some corn bread in the oven, the doorbell sounded off from the front of the house. Eli's chin lifted in surprise, and he gave his old man the same quizzical expression that both of his brothers currently had plastered over their kissers.

"You expectin' anybody, Pop?" he asked, brows up. With all of them already sardined into the kitchen, he'd have been shocked as hell to hear anything resembling a yes.

"No," his father confirmed. "But that doesn't mean Nathan isn't coming up with some news about the cattle."

Ah. His father was old school, always preferring face-to-face communication with their cattle manager.

"Alright. I'll go talk to him, then. Make sure everything's copacetic."

"Someone give Webster here two bits for the big word," Hunter said, and Eli had no choice but to laugh.

"Hilarious. I'm thinking of a pair of real fancy words right now. I'll give you three guesses as to what they are, and the first two don't count."

The doorbell sounded off again, prompting another laugh from Eli. "Saved by the bell. Literally," he said, making his way out of the kitchen and down the hallway to the front door. But rather than finding Nathan on the other side of the pine as expected, Eli found himself gaze-to-gaze with a brunette wearing too much eye makeup and a defiant-as-hell frown, and whoa, talk about a shocker.

"Can I help you, ma'am?" Eli kept his slow smile in place even though the woman—who come to think of it, looked younger than he'd thought now that he'd gotten a good look past all the stuff on her face—still scowled.

"You're Eli Cross, right?"

She knotted her arms over her threadbare hoodie, her bright-blue stare tagging him in some deep part of his subconscious. Eli was certain he'd never met her—score one for small-town living. Yet something about the young woman was so familiar, he couldn't help but feel as if he knew her, or at the very least, recognized her.

"Yes, ma'am, that's me," he said, and God, how did he *know* her? "And who might you be?"

Her scowl slipped for a split second to reveal her features more genuinely, and wait . . . this couldn't be right . . .

"My name is Marley Rallston." The woman slid her hand to her hips, her eyes blazing as her scowl came back in full force.

"It looks like I'm your sister."

CHAPTER TWENTY-FIVE

No less than a thousand thoughts and feelings went on an immediate rampage in Eli's brain, each one pushed faster by the rush of blood against his ears, turning his heartbeat so fast that he was momentarily dizzy.

"Uh." Not eloquent, but it was the only word he could shove past his lips. He needed to tell the woman—Marley—she was wrong. He couldn't possibly *have* a sister, much less one he didn't know existed. "I think there's been some kind of mistake."

"Nope. Well, not about this," she clarified, and although her expression might qualify as a smile, it was really more of a baring of teeth. "My mother's name is Lorraine Rallston."

"Miss Lorraine?" The name slid out from a rusty, unused corner of Eli's mind. He hadn't heard it in ages, decades really, and despite the woman having been best friends with his mother, Eli only knew of her from secondhand anecdotes and ancient, small-town gossip. "She used to live here in Millhaven, but she moved away."

Marley's laugh was quick and joyless. "Twenty-four years ago, to be exact."

Eli's brain tilted like an old carnival ride, but no. No fucking way. "Are you trying to say—"

"Tobias Cross is my father."

Anger flickered, sudden and hot, in Eli's chest. Cross Creek had gotten an absolute landslide of press lately. Cherry-picking the Internet for vague details like the name of a woman long gone from Millhaven couldn't be that hard. He didn't know who this woman really was, or why she'd popped up on their doorstep slinging attitude and accusations, but right about now, he didn't really give a shit.

"Look," Eli said, doing some arm crossing of his own. "I'm not sure what you're after, or where you got your information, but I'm here to tell you, there's no chance in hell—"

"Eli."

His father's voice arrived from behind him, quiet and a gunshot all at once. Eli turned to see his father standing on the floorboards a few feet away, his face loaded with sadness and regret, and Christ, none of this made any sense.

Then with seven little words, his father yanked the rug out from beneath everything Eli had ever known.

"Marley. It's nice to finally meet you."

"Pop?" Eli blinked, absolutely certain he'd misheard his old man. They'd been a family—*this* family—forever. Marley might bear an uncanny resemblance to his father with those blue eyes and dark hair and the strong set of her jawline, but that was all it was. Coincidence.

And yet, his old man knew who she was. Without asking.

Holy. Fucking. Hell.

"How's your mother?" his father asked, but apparently, it was the wrong question, because Marley's body went rigid, hurt tearing a path through the anger on her face.

She stabbed her heavy-soled black boots into the welcome mat, her chin snapping up in a defiant lift. "She died three months ago. Not that you care."

"What?" Eli's father paled, clearly surprised by the news, and this entire conversation was officially surreal. "How?"

"Pancreatic cancer," Marley said slowly, her tone slapping the words with a heavy dose of *duh* despite the tears rimming her heavily made-up eyes.

His father's throat worked over a swallow. "I'm sorry. I didn't . . . I didn't know she was sick."

"I bet." She looked up at the porch eave over her head, and Eli would bet she was trying her damndest to keep those tears from spilling. "Anyway, the morning my mother died, she told me all about you. Which, I've gotta admit, was a pretty big shocker, since she'd spent the last twenty-three years telling me you'd kicked the bucket just before I was born. But she made me promise to come see you, and whatever, after she died. So now that that's done and I did what she wanted, I guess we're good here."

Marley turned to leave, and his old man took a step toward her at the same time Eli took a step toward him.

"Wait," his father said, and to Eli's shock, she actually did. "Come inside, Marley. Please."

"Why?"

His old man slid a hand over the back of his neck, the look on his face telling Eli this was all too real. "Because you've come all the way from Chicago, and I'm sure you're tired. Why don't you at least come in and have a cup of coffee and a nice, hot meal?"

"Because I don't need you," she said, jamming her hands over the hips of her too-baggy jeans. "You sent my mother away after you knocked her up. You've spent the last twenty-three years denying you have a daughter, and you think you can fix that with a cup of freaking *coffee*? Hate to break it to you, but you don't get to have a Hallmark moment with me, old man. I'm not your charity case."

Eli's adrenaline spiked. He opened his mouth to tell Marley to watch hers, but his father lifted a hand to quell the *oh hell no* that had to be plastered all over Eli's face.

"I'm not offerin' charity. Just some food and a place to rest a spell. After that, you can do what you will."

"And I won't have to, you know. *Talk* to you?"

His old man shook his head. "Not unless you want to."

"I don't."

After a minute during which Eli considered throttling her and his father exercised the patience of Job, Marley huffed out an exaggerated sigh. "Fine. I guess I could use a nap and something to eat. But after that, I'm out of here."

"The guest bedroom's at the top of the stairs," his father said. "There are towels in the hall bathroom if you feel like washin' up. Supper's at five."

"Great."

Marley wrapped her arms around herself and crossed the threshold, but only when she'd made her way up all thirteen stairs and shut the door to the bedroom that had once been Hunter's did Eli turn to face his old man.

"Pop?" *So many questions . . . so many questions . . .* "Can you help me out here, because I'm not really sure what on God's green earth just happened."

"Why don't we go find your brothers," he answered, and for the first time in Eli's life, his old man looked truly broken.

"I need to have a conversation with the three of you that's long overdue."

◆ ◆ ◆

The instant Eli and Tobias walked back into the kitchen, Scarlett knew that whatever had gone down at the front door was far worse than some mishap on the cattle farm. The charming, easy smile that Eli had worn on his way out of the kitchen ten minutes ago was gone as if it had never existed, and Tobias . . .

Oh, God. What the hell had *happened*?

"Hey," Scarlett murmured, her heart hopscotching over her ribs. "What's the matter?"

Eli looked at her. But Hunter had already looked at him, and he was out of his kitchen chair before Eli could say a word.

"E? Pop? What's going on?"

Tobias sent his gaze from Hunter to Owen to Eli, and good Lord, what could make the man look so wrecked? "I hate to break up the party, but there's somethin' I need to discuss with the three of you privately, and it can't wait."

Although a thousand questions burned on her tongue, Scarlett swallowed them. "Of course."

"Why don't I give you a ride back to your apartment, Scarlett?" Emerson asked, slipping a hand over Hunter's forearm for a quick, reassuring squeeze. "Owen, you can bring Hunter back to the cottage later, right?"

"Yeah. Absolutely."

Owen's expression was as serious as Scarlett had ever seen it—which was *really* saying something—and she moved toward Eli to kiss him good-bye.

"Do you want me to wait at your place?" she asked quietly, concern pumping through her with every heartbeat. Whatever this conversation was about wasn't small. Eli would almost certainly need a sounding board when they were done. Plus, just because she wasn't a Cross didn't make her immune from worrying about the family she'd come to care for over the last month. They were the closest thing she had to a family herself, other than her dads.

"I don't know. Yeah," Eli quickly amended, pulling his keys from the pocket of his jeans and separating the one for his apartment from the rest. "I'll see you later."

Dread filled Scarlett's belly, swift and unrepentant, but she auto-piloted her legs toward the front of the house alongside Emerson. A battered Toyota with Illinois license plates sat in the drive next to Eli's truck, and Scarlett blinked first at the vehicle, then at Emerson.

"Whose car is that?"

Emerson's eyes went wide. "I don't know. I've never seen it before."

Scarlett scraped in a breath and took a total flyer. "Do you have any idea what's going on in there?"

"No," Emerson said. "But I'm sure we will soon enough."

"Yeah." Scarlett nodded. She knew Emerson was right.

So why the hell wouldn't this vise grip of dread ease up on her gut?

She climbed up into the passenger seat of Hunter's truck, her thoughts taking over as Emerson started the engine and pulled down the gravel drive. Her friend must have been as lost in both worry and thought as she was, because they remained silent for the entire fifteen-minute drive to the Twin Pines. Scarlett thanked Emerson for the ride, barely dodging the cold, fat raindrops just starting to fall from the sky as she made a mad dash for Eli's apartment. Shivering, she hit the light switch with the back of her hand, illuminating the small space.

Four minutes later, she was thiiiiis close to losing her mind.

"Okay," Scarlett whispered, not even caring that she was talking to herself, because at this point, she had to prioritize her crazy if she was going to make it through the evening. "You need something to do. Something to keep you busy."

Her laptop was at her own apartment along with the rest of her stuff, save a toothbrush and a spare pair of clean panties, but that was (sadly) just as well. She didn't have any photos to edit. She *could* still work, though—she and Eli were going to need some background on this traveling festival they were covering in Brazil. He'd given her an all-access pass to his laptop weeks ago, so she scooped it up from the coffee table and parked herself on the couch. Sliding her phone out of her back pocket, Scarlett went to open a new page of notes, but the damned thing scared the bejesus out of her by ringing in her hand.

"Gah!" She let loose with a string of top-shelf swear words. Her surprise didn't dissipate as she looked at the caller ID, though, and her hands were still shaking as she lifted the phone to her ear.

"Rafael? Is everything okay?" She wasn't supposed to talk to him for another two days, when they were scheduled to firm up all of her and Eli's flight plans, and solidify their final work itinerary.

The hiss of a long-distance connection echoed in her ear. "*Minha querida.* It's not like you to assume the worst," Rafael joked, and relief crashed into her hard enough to make her laugh.

"Sorry, I've just had a weird day. So tell me, what's up?"

"I do have news," Rafael said. "But I think you'll be pleased. I spoke with a friend of mine in Rio. Do you know Matteo Garza?"

Scarlett barely won the fight with her snort. "Yes. Of course."

Everyone in the industry knew Garza. He ran the biggest travel magazine in Brazil, with circulation to every city that owned a dot on the world map.

"Well, when he heard that I'd booked you to cover the leg of this festival that comes through São Paulo, he gave me a call. Seems he's looking for a team to do an extended magazine layout with print and online coverage."

Holy shit. "That's *huge*." Even for Scarlett, a job like that would be a bold-faced, big fat shouty-caps headliner for her résumé.

Rafael's laughter threaded over the phone line. "Precisely my feeling. He'd like to partner with my newspaper and you for the coverage. I told him I'd call to see if you and Eli would be interested, but—"

"Are you kidding me? Yes. God, yes!"

"Good. I will confess that he wanted a more experienced writer for the job, but I told him I didn't know how negotiable you'd be."

Scarlett's gut panged, but her shoulders remained firm against the couch cushions. "Nonnegotiable. Eli and I are a team. Where he goes, I go."

"I told Matteo I suspected as much," Raff said with a smile in his voice. "At any rate, I'll convey your availability to him, and we can plan from there. Of course, you and Eli will need to extend your travel dates as soon as you're able."

"Wait." Scarlett's brows tucked under the weight of the *whaaaaa* spinning through her brain. "Why would we need to change our travel plans just because we're working with Matteo?"

Rafael paused. "I'm sorry. I should have been clearer. Matteo is looking for coverage of the entire festival."

Okay, there was no way her ears were functioning properly. "But the festival lasts for a month. It spans every major city in the country."

"Yes," Raff agreed. "I know this will mean more research and travel, and obviously more of a time commitment, but I can assure you, you and Eli will be well compensated. This is truly a once-in-a-lifetime opportunity."

Scarlett pressed to standing, pacing the confines of Eli's dollhouse-sized apartment. Rafael was right. A chance like this was rare enough for someone like her with established ties in the media world. For someone like Eli? Yeah, he'd have to dive in headfirst, but a job like this could catapult him right to the center of the journalism map.

They'd planned to go for the week. A month wasn't *that* much different now that things were slowing down at Cross Creek. Anyway, they'd promised to be a team, the two of them together.

I don't just want you, Eli. I want you and me . . . you and me . . .

She belonged with him.

"No, no. You're right, Rafael. I'll go ahead and change the travel itinerary right now. You can tell Matteo that Eli and I are in."

CHAPTER TWENTY-SIX

Eli sat at the kitchen table in Cross Creek's main house, completely and utterly poleaxed. Scarlett and Emerson had left a little while ago, and despite several hundred variations of "What the hell is going on?" from both of Eli's brothers, their old man had simply sat at one of the four compass points of the farmhouse table, his hands wrapped around a mug of coffee that had gone otherwise untouched.

Eli had a sister. His father had been with another woman. Gotten her pregnant. Kept his daughter hidden from Eli and his brothers for twenty-three *years*.

How were they supposed to process this?

And more importantly, how the *fuck* were they supposed to recover as a family?

Finally, their old man spoke. "I have a lot to tell you boys, and most of it won't be easy to hear. I reckon you'll be angry. Hurt, even." He paused for a slow breath. "All I ask is that you hear me out till I've said my piece."

"Pop, seriously." Owen took the lead, which under the circumstances wasn't surprising. "What do you have to tell us that's so urgent?"

"You three have a sister. That's who was at the door a little while ago, and she may be stayin' for a bit. Her name is Marley Rallston. She grew up in Chicago with her mother."

Paralyzing silence ricocheted through the kitchen, and damn, Eli didn't find the words any easier to process the second time around.

"A sister," Hunter said slowly, as if their father had been speaking some long-dead language like Latin or ancient Sanskrit. "And she's in this house. Right now. Upstairs."

"Yes."

Owen's eyes flew wide, his shoulders smacking the ladder back of his chair as realization dropped his jaw. "Rallston. As in, *Lorraine* Rallston."

"What?" Hunter asked. "That can't be right. Miss Lorraine left Millhaven twenty-four years ago, just after Mom died. She . . ." The rest stopped short on a sharp breath out as his expression hardened with anger. "Oh my God. You had an affair with Miss Lorraine?"

"No." Their father's voice cracked across the table like thunder. "Let me make one thing real clear. I loved your mother. I love her still." He lowered his chin. "But I wouldn't wish watchin' a loved one slip away on my worst enemy."

The words sent twin pangs of sadness and confusion through Eli's gut, and neither played nicely with the betrayal already filling the space. Christ, they had a *sister*, and she'd clearly been conceived not long after their mother had died.

How could there be a good explanation for this?

"Why don't you start from the beginning," Eli said, and his old man gave up a small nod before sending his gaze around the table.

"You all know your momma got sick in a blink. We were blindsided. Me, Miss Lorraine. Everyone. The docs back then didn't know the sorts of things we know now, but even then, your mother knew. She knew she wouldn't live."

He stopped for a shaky inhale, and sweet Jesus, Eli wasn't going to make it through this.

As rattled as his father seemed, he continued. "One night, toward the end, she got real lucid. Peaceful, even."

"I remember that," Owen said, prompting a spear of jealousy through Eli's chest. "She wore that pretty white nightgown with the blue flowers on it, and we all ate ice cream in her hospital room. She even sang Eli to sleep."

Sadness lined their old man's face despite his faraway smile. "That was the night. After Addie Hitchcock took you boys home and put you to bed, your mother sat me and Lorraine down. She made us promise we wouldn't fret after she was gone. She said . . ." His voice tripped, and he cleared his throat before starting again. "She said she didn't want either of our hearts to go to waste. Told us we'd need to be there for each other. And then she was gone, and I was alone raisin' the three of you, and . . ."

"You were lonely," Hunter said. "I remember you sitting down here by the fireplace at night, in the dark. You tried to hide it from us, but you were lonely."

"I was a lot of things," he agreed quietly, dropping his gaze to where he'd folded his hands over the table in front of him. "And I missed your mother so much. I didn't intend for anything to happen with Lorraine, but it did."

At that, Eli's pulse tripped, and his brothers looked equally unhappy. The tension in the room thickened further as their old man added, "When she told me she was pregnant, I wanted to do right by her. I asked her to marry me so we could raise the baby together."

"What?" Hunter blurted, sitting ramrod straight in his chair, and Eli exhaled in shock so deep, his hands started to shake. Given Marley's spitting-mad attitude and the accusations that had accompanied it at the front door—not to mention how deeply his father had still been grieving at the time and how much a new wife and baby would have impacted their family—it was the last thing Eli had expected him to say.

He asked, "Then how did she end up leaving Millhaven?"

"Lorraine knew I didn't love her. That I could never love her the way she wanted. The way she deserved. So she decided to leave town."

Owen's brows rose along with the color on his cheeks. "Just like that? She was pregnant with your *baby*," he said, but their father shook his head.

"Not everything is cut-and-dried, Owen. I reckon her decision was far from easy, just like it was hard for me to let her go. It was her choice, though, and in the end, I respected that. We spoke from time to time, and I sent her money for Marley every month, from the day the girl was born until she turned eighteen. But on one thing, Lorraine was clear. She didn't want Marley to know about me, so she gave me a made-up name and told Marley I'd died just before she was born."

"And what about us?" Hunter asked, his arms knotting over his chest and his features hardening in a rare show of anger. "You weren't ever going to tell us we have a sister?"

"I wanted to. I did." Although his father's voice was barely more than a whisper, emotion wrapped over every word. "At first, you were too young. And then as you got older . . . so much time had passed. Marley didn't know, and Lorraine had made a life for them, so I just kept the secret."

Eli closed his eyes and let the irony swamp him. He knew what it was like to keep secrets—big ones—from his family. But for Chrissake, he couldn't even remember his own mother. He'd lived with the guilt of it his entire life.

Now he had not only a sister he didn't know, but a family he didn't recognize.

Owen shook his head, as if he'd been processing everything on a delay and it was just now sinking in. "It's been twenty-four years, Pop. I get not telling us when we were younger, but we're a family. You raised us as a *family*. We deserved to know we have a sister before she showed up on our doorstep as an adult."

"Speaking of which," Hunter said. "She *did* show up. What made Lorraine finally decide to tell her about you after all this time?"

A shadow flickered through the emotions already churning in their old man's stare at the same time Eli's gut dropped toward the kitchen tiles. "Lorraine passed a few months ago. I didn't know until today, but it seems she told Marley the truth just before she died. Lorraine had Marley make the same promise your momma asked of her all those years ago."

"To come find you so she wouldn't be alone," Eli said, a chill rushing down his spine.

"I'd guess that was the gist of it. Marley is . . . angry, though. I have a feeling this is going to get a whole lot worse before it gets any better."

"You can't really blame her for being upset," Hunter allowed. "I'm freaking upset, and I'm not gonna lie, Pop. I'm pretty angry, too. Owen's right. We're a family. We deserved to know about Marley."

Their father pushed back from the table, just slightly. "You did, and for that I owe all three of you an apology. I never meant to keep secrets from you. I wanted to honor Lorraine's wishes, but I was wrong not to tell you the truth."

His voice broke over the last word, startling the hell out of Eli. Tears formed in his old man's eyes, their presence slicing to the bone.

In his twenty-eight years, Eli had never, ever seen the man cry.

"Having a sister *is* a lot to process, Pop. For all of us," Owen said quietly, and Eli had to admit, it wasn't inaccurate. Marley's existence was a familial triple-whammy. "It's just gonna take some time to adjust and figure this out."

"I understand."

"But we'll do it," Hunter added, nodding across the table at their father. "Things might be pear-shaped right now, but we *are* a family. Mad or not, upset or not, we'll get through. Somehow."

Owen looked at the hallway, his doubt scrawled over his face. "In the meantime, Marley's upstairs. What are you going to say to her when she comes down?"

The dread in Eli's gut reached critical mass as their father shook his head in defeat, his work-hardened face wet with tears.

"I don't know, son. I really don't know."

◆ ◆ ◆

Scarlett bolted upright on the couch cushions at the turn and click of Eli's front doorknob. A handful of scrawled research notes fluttered to the floor, and dammit, she must have fallen asleep somewhere between Salvador and Recife.

"Hey." Her grogginess did an instant disappearing act as she took in Eli's rumpled flannel, dead-serious expression, and bloodshot eyes, and good *Lord*, he looked like hell. "What's the matter? Is everything okay with your father?"

"No."

Rather than following up, the tread of his boots called out a path to the tiny kitchen connected to his living space. A soft glass-on-glass clink said he was pouring a nice, stiff drink, and the healthy slosh of liquid that followed told Scarlett said drink was big enough to do the backstroke in.

"Okay." She stood, her heart thudding beneath her sleep-creased T-shirt. She needed to tell him about Rafael's news, but at the same time . . . "Do you want to talk about it?"

"I've just spent all night talking, so not really. No." Eli took a long swallow of what turned out to be Jim Beam, wincing. "I apologize," he said, replacing the half-empty glass on the Formica. "That was shitty. It's just . . . do you remember when the doorbell rang, earlier at the main house?"

Scarlett nodded. "Of course."

"That was my sister."

She replayed the words in her head, once. Twice. But yeah, those four words couldn't possibly go together. "I'm sorry. Did you say—"

"My sister," Eli repeated, throwing back the last of the bourbon in his glass. "So yeah. It's been a helluva night."

He spent the next fifteen minutes filling her in on the events of the evening, from Marley's arrival at the front door to the back-and-forth between her and his father to the heart-wrenching conversation that had followed between Tobias and his sons. Scarlett tried to keep her questions to a minimum, she really did. But given the holy-shit factor of so much hidden truth coming to light, the task was pretty much a monster, especially when he got to the part where Marley had finally come out of the upstairs bedroom to join them for dinner.

"So what did she say?" Scarlett asked, her shoulders still high and tight from the shock of it all.

"Not a damn thing."

Scarlett's lips parted, although for a second, no sound followed. "Nothing at *all*?"

"Nothing with more than a syllable," Eli amended. "She came down for supper right at five and muttered a hello to me and Owen and Hunter when we introduced ourselves, but she refused to even look at my old man, much less speak to him."

"Wow." A defensive ripple moved up Scarlett's spine. "That's a little cold, don't you think?"

Eli laughed without humor as he turned to pace over the linoleum. "Of course I do, but I'm his son. Marley only knows one side of things, and she won't even think about listening to anything he has to say. She's pissed and she's hurting and the one thing she doesn't want is the only thing she's got left. I don't think she's letting go of that any time soon. The whole meal was just intense."

"So how did you leave everything?"

"I wasn't kidding about my old man bein' the only thing she's got left," Eli said, lifting one dark-blond brow. "If I had to wager, I'd say every last thing that girl owns is in her car—which by the look of it is one head gasket away from the scrap heap in the sky. Hunter got her to agree to stay at Cross Creek for the time being, but I can assure you she did it out of necessity."

Scarlett's heart ached at the look on Eli's face. She closed the space between them, stopping him midpace to slip her arms around him and pull him in close. "I'm so sorry things are tough for your family right now, Eli. I don't know what else to say."

He let out a breath, his body going lax against hers. "It's just as well. I can talk about it till I'm purple, but that won't change anything. At least, not tonight. Look, I'm exhausted, so—"

"Rafael called me tonight."

Ah, *shit*. She'd totally jumped the gun. As usual. "I'm sorry," she added, biting her lip as she pulled back to look at him. "But he called with some great news."

Eli blinked. "Rafael. Crap, with everything that went on tonight, I totally forgot about Brazil."

"Well, Brazil hasn't forgotten about you," Scarlett said over a small smile. "Rafael got a call from a man named Matteo Garza, who owns and operates one of the biggest travel publications in South America. They want us to cover the whole festival in a series of articles. All of it. Me and you."

"All of it," he repeated, taking a full step back to pin her with a stare. "But the festival lasts for a month."

She let her arms, now suddenly empty, drop. "I know it might sound like a long time, but—"

"A long time? It's a fucking *eternity*. I can't be gone for a month right now."

The incredulous look on his face mixed with something darker, prompting a hard bubble of unease to rise in her chest. "We planned for this, Eli. Maybe not for this long right off the bat, but you can't be serious about not taking this job."

He froze into place on the two-by-two patch of linoleum between the kitchen and the living space. "Of course I'm serious! How could I possibly go to Brazil for an entire month right now when I need to be here, with my family?"

Scarlett paused, trying like hell to smooth the emotion from her voice. "I know a lot went on with your father tonight. But this trip isn't forever, and it *is* a once-in-a-lifetime opportunity. Taking this assignment could write your ticket. It could make your entire *career* start happening, right now." God, how could he not see how huge this was?

"It's not that easy," Eli bit out, his tone icing over and turning desperate all at once. "This is my family. My *father*."

"Your father who believes in you," she reminded him. "Your father who told you just today to be who you are and to take this leap." She gentled her voice despite the rock-solid seriousness in her words. "Please, Eli. This is everything you've wanted for the last ten years."

"I . . ." Eli broke off. "I can't leave, Scarlett. I can't."

She tried, only half-successfully, to drag a breath past the tangled knot in her throat. "But I told Rafael yes."

Eli's chin whipped up, his eyes going perfectly round before narrowing over her. "You . . . what?"

"I told him yes."

"For both of us," Eli confirmed, the expression lining his face suddenly unreadable. "You said yes for both of us."

Scarlett nodded. "We're a team, so yes. I didn't know about Marley when he called," she started, but Eli cut her off with a single lift of his hand.

"And if you had? Would that have made your answer any different?"

The question stopped Scarlett cold, turning her palms slick. She loved Eli. Loved the family for whom he so desperately cared. But she'd never in her life been anything other than balls-out honest, and what's more, she owed him so much more than to lie.

"No. It wouldn't. There isn't going to be another opportunity like this one, ever. I'd have said yes either way."

"Right. Of course you would've."

The words, the cold, callous tone that clung to them, hit her point-blank, stunning her into momentary silence. Finally, she managed a choked, "I'm sorry?"

A sound crossed his lips in a bitter approximation of a snort. "The thing is, you're really not, though. You're never sorry for anything. You live your life out of a suitcase, one big adventure after the next. I mean, you've said it yourself. You belong everywhere. Things like family don't matter to you. So really, why the hell *wouldn't* you say yes when the next assignment comes calling? Your job is the only thing that's important to you."

Scarlett's chest hitched at an unnatural pace, her lungs burning for air that wouldn't come. "Is that what you think? That I have no idea how to make those deeper connections like you do? That after all this time together, I don't care about you or your family or your farm at all?"

She paused, and for a brief, beautiful second, she saw the *no* flickering in his stare. Brash instinct moved her forward, and she reached out to take his hand.

"Please, Eli," Scarlett whispered, tears pricking behind her mutinous eyelids. But just like she belonged behind her camera, he belonged writing stories. They were a team.

They belonged together.

Her fingers tightened over his. "Don't lose this chance to be who you are. I know you feel indebted to your family, but we can figure—"

"No." His expression slammed shut, and he pulled his hand from hers.

"Eli—"

"*No*," he said, the word slicing to the bone despite being far from a yell. But no, this was far, far worse. "You don't know the first thing about how I feel, Scarlett. In fact, you don't know anything about me. Look, this writing thing was a fun idea in theory, but in practice, it's not going to work out."

Her heartbeat ricocheted off her ribs. "You mean you're giving up on it."

"I'm being realistic," he corrected, his arms forming an impenetrable knot over his chest. "Thinking I could leave the farm, that I could be a travel journalist—it was all just a pipe dream. I don't belong out there." Eli looked out the window, where the sky and the stars sprawled endlessly, and oh God. He wasn't just saying that. He *meant* it.

"I think you do," Scarlett whispered, because the brazen truth was all she had left.

But it wasn't enough. "No, *you* do. So go on and go to Brazil, Scarlett. I belong here. And you don't."

With that, he turned and walked away.

CHAPTER TWENTY-SEVEN

At four fifty-six the next morning, Eli turned off his alarm clock. Of course, he hadn't slept, so the feat was actually rather easy.

The getting-out-of-bed-to-face-his-locomotive-wreck-of-a-life part? Yeah, not so fucking much.

Eli stared into the shadows, a heavy ache centered right in the middle of his chest. His family had been pulled in a thousand directions last night, his old man worst of all. But that family had stood by him, through screwups and brash, mouthy decisions and everything else Eli had ever lobbed at them. He owed it to them to stay here at Cross Creek. Not to leave and become something else. And definitely *not* to impulsively get on a plane to Brazil and spend a month writing his head off with Scarlett.

Scarlett, who'd believed in him, too.

The only difference was, she'd been wrong.

Cursing, Eli tossed the covers from his legs and plodded toward the bathroom. He was going to have to get back to normal sooner or later. Might as well rip off the Band-Aid now. Plus, maybe they'd make some headway with Marley today. Maybe today would be better.

He looked down to see Scarlett's cherry-red toothbrush standing at attention right next to his plain blue one in the holder, and God dammit, today was going to suck worse than an industrial-grade Hoover.

Eli turned his back to the vanity for the duration of his tooth-brushing, then went to his room to get dressed. Yeah, he could've stood a shower, but he was only going to get dirty in his first fifteen minutes at the farm. Besides, no amount of soap and hot water was going to cover up the fact that he not only hadn't slept but also *looked* like he hadn't slept.

Of course, his brother was all too happy to point that out as soon as Eli stepped into the kitchen at Cross Creek's main house.

"Whoa, E. I know we all had a rough night, but you look like shit run over twice." Owen's brows rode up to the brim of his Cross Creek baseball cap, and Hunter opened the cupboard over the coffee maker to pull down an extra-large travel mug.

"Sorry to say so, man, but Owen's right. What happened to you?"

Eli laughed, because really, it was that or beat the hell out of something. "Well, let's see. This look here was actually caused by a combination of factors, but an overabundance of Jim Beam and a nasty breakup were probably the two biggest. Other than the obvious secret-baby-sister thing that's rippin' into our family, of course."

Hunter dropped the half-full mug to the counter with a thunk. "Ho-ly . . ."

"Shit," Owen finished.

"Yup. That about sums it up." Eli stepped in to take the mug from Hunter, because some coffee was better than none and he really hadn't been kidding about the bourbon. Smartly, his brothers let him take a pair of nice, long draws from the mug before saying anything else.

Not so smartly, Owen poked the sorest part of the wound right off the bat. "What the hell happened with you and Scarlett? You guys can't break up. You're going to Brazil, remember?"

"She's going to Brazil," he corrected, reaching for the coffee carafe to go all-in with his mug. "I'm staying here at Cross Creek. Where I belong."

Hunter looked at him, his confusion plain. "But you told us yesterday that you want to be a writer."

"That was before we had a sister who hates our old man. Speaking of which, where are they?"

Eli hoped the question would morph into a subject change, but Owen didn't budge by so much as a millimeter. The ass. "Both still sleeping. How come you're not going to Brazil?"

"Pop is still sleeping?" Surprise uncoiled in Eli's belly, waking him up along with the coffee. "It's five thirty on a Monday morning."

"It's after the harvest," Owen said. "I told him to sleep in and we'd cover him. Seriously, how come you're not going to Brazil?"

"Because I'm staying here instead."

But Eli's heart wasn't going to stop with this stupid twist-and-free-fall thing until he put the topic to rest once and for all, so he turned toward his brothers and said, "Look. The journalism thing was just an impulsive mistake. Slapping together a handful of articles for Cross Creek is in a whole different universe than traveling around the globe for the job, and the Brazil assignment got pushed from a week to a month."

Hunter's shoulders hitched in surprise beneath his thick canvas jacket, and Owen's wide-eyed expression matched. "Okay," Hunter finally said. "So a month is a bit longer than you were expecting. But—"

"No buts." God, Eli was so sick of this. He just wanted to get back to the farm and get on with his life. "The whole thing was a shit idea to begin with. You guys need me here. I owe it to Pop to stay here. And Scarlett didn't get that, so"—he pulled a breath into his ridiculous, traitorous lungs—"we broke up."

"Eli," Owen started, but apparently Eli wasn't done in the Big-Reveal department.

"I don't remember Mom."

Eli heard the words only after they'd launched, and Christ, emotions before breakfast *had* to be a bad idea.

"What?" Hunter asked, not unkindly. "What do you mean, you don't remember Mom?"

"I don't remember her at all," Eli confessed, guilt crowding his chest and his words. "I listen to you guys talk about her, and I try so hard, but . . . I can't remember. I should remember her, right?" He looked at Owen. "I should remember *something*. But I don't, and I just . . ."

"She used to read you bedtime stories in that big ol' rocking chair that's in Pop's room. You got too big for her lap after a while, but you asked her every night, and she never told you no," Owen said quietly, shocking Eli into stillness.

"And she used to mash up your peas and mix 'em in with your mashed potatoes to get you to eat them," Hunter added.

"That's disgusting," Eli said, but he laughed anyway.

"Yeah, but you bought it." Hunter grinned. "Hook, line, and veggies."

Owen laughed, too. "God, I'd forgotten all about that, but you sure did."

Surprise plucked a path up Eli's spine. "You don't remember everything?"

"Of course not," Owen said, his expression soft yet serious. "And just because you don't remember what we do doesn't mean you're any less of her son, E."

"It's not that I don't remember what you do. I don't remember *anything*." Guilt pulsed in Eli's gut, but Hunter shook his head to cancel it out.

"You still loved her, Eli. Owen and I remember *that*. Just because you can't remember her doesn't mean you didn't love her, or that you're any less her son than the rest of us."

He blinked in surprise. "I guess . . . I never really thought about it that way."

"You should probably start," said Owen, reaching out to place a quick, firm squeeze on Eli's shoulder. "You're part of this family no matter what."

"I know." Eli swallowed back the emotion threatening to spill out of him. "We have to stick together now more than ever."

Hunter glanced at Owen, the exchange done before Eli could unravel its meaning. "This thing with Marley will be tough, and it's gonna take some time, but we're gonna get through it. Pop will get through it. Even if you go to Brazil, and even if you become a travel journalist."

The words knocked into him with palpable force, but no. Eli wasn't going down this road. This was over. Said. Done. "I appreciate the sentiment, you guys. I really do. But Scarlett's leaving Millhaven later today as planned, and I'm not going with her."

"Eli—"

"If it's cool with you, I'd really like to just drop it and get to work."

For a second, Eli was sure his brothers would argue. But then Hunter said, "Okay. Just let us know if you change your mind."

"Thanks, but I won't."

Despite all that effort, as Eli kicked his Red Wings into motion and headed for the hayloft, his heart did the stupid twist-and-free-fall thing anyway.

◆ ◆ ◆

Six hours later, Eli was filthy, exhausted, and still trying to ignore the giant hole in his chest. He might as well be patching the thing with duct tape and glue for all the good work was doing, and dammit, there had to be a better way to get past this and move on.

Don't lose this chance to be who you are . . . you're good enough to be part of your family even if you love something else . . .

Right. Probably, he should've stuck with the bourbon.

Tugging the dust-covered work gloves from his hands, Eli headed toward the main house. The sun told him lunchtime was awful close, and even though he had zero appetite, he couldn't keep working if he didn't fuel up. And if he didn't keep working, he'd think about Scarlett, who had almost certainly packed her little yellow convertible to the gills and hightailed it out of town by now.

So, yeah. He'd eat a big fat sawdust sandwich if he had to. It was better than the alternative.

Eli toed out of his boots, abandoning them by the welcome mat. He was two steps inside the main house when Lucy ambled over for a hello, and he bent down to give her a good scratch behind the ears.

"Hey, pretty girl. Where's Pop? You keepin' him company today?"

Lucy trotted to the living room at the words. Concern rolled through Eli's gut, only dissipating halfway when he found his father sitting on the living room sofa, staring out the lace-curtained window.

"Hey," Eli said softly, not wanting to startle the man. He already looked like he'd been through the wringer, his jaw unshaven and twin shadows darkening the space below his eyes.

But his father looked up, scraping together the slightest of smiles. "Ah. Just the person I wanted to see."

Okay, *so* not what he'd expected. "Me?" Eli asked.

"Yes, you. Your brothers tell me you've decided not to take this trip of yours."

Eli exhaled, hard and fast. Of course they had. Gabby bastards. "You don't need to be worrying about that right now."

His old man's smile lingered for a few seconds longer. "I'm sure one day when you have children of your own, you'll understand this better, but you're my son. No matter what's doin' in my own world, I'm gonna worry over you. That's just the way of it."

"I'm sure you're worried over Marley, too," Eli said, but his father shook his head.

"That job's bigger than just today, I'm afraid. So right now, you're stuck with my concern."

Eli's gut tightened before dropping toward the floorboards. "Not sure there's anything for you to worry about with me, Pop. I decided to stay here at Cross Creek. It's not a big deal."

"It is when you're passin' on your dream in order to do it," his father said, and oh hell, Eli really wasn't going to make it through this conversation twice in one day.

"I'm not passing on anything," he argued, but his father shocked him with a wistful smile.

"You're just like your mother. Did you know that?"

For a second, Eli froze, unable to even speak. Finally, he asked, "Do you mean because I'm being stubborn?"

His old man's smile grew. "Ah, that, too. But I meant you lovin' to read and write."

"Mom loved to write?" Eli's heart started to pound. Could he really have something so fundamental in common with the mother he couldn't even remember?

"She did," his father confirmed. "Your momma was such a free spirit. It was one of the things I loved about her most."

His eyes crinkled slightly at the edges, signaling such a sweet memory that Eli didn't dare interrupt him. "She read darn near everything she could get her hands on. Kept a journal, too. Oh, she was always scribbling in that thing. Said she was just collectin' her thoughts, but the truth is, I think she had a bit of curiosity about bigger things. Just like you."

"I never knew she liked to write," Eli said, and his father nodded.

"That she did. You're so much more like her than you know. And *I* know she'd want you to follow your heart. No matter where it leads you."

Just like that, Eli dropped back to reality with a hard snap. "Going to Brazil was a bad idea. I don't belong there."

"And what about that girl of yours, hmm? What does she think?"

"It doesn't matter."

Eli registered the gravel in the words only after they'd disappeared into silence. But none of this rift with Scarlett was his old man's fault, so he eased up on his tone to add, "What I mean is, that's done. We had a, ah, difference of opinion, and she's going to São Paulo and I'm not, so yeah. It doesn't matter."

"Actually, I think it does." His father looked pointedly at the side table over by the window, and wait . . .

"Where did all these pictures come from?" Damn, there had to be a dozen of them at least.

One salt-and-pepper brow rose. "Scarlett printed them up to thank us for lettin' her stay at Cross Creek for the month."

The hole in Eli's chest grew another inch. Christ, that was so something Scarlett would do. *Had* done. "She got everyone in the family." There was even a shot of him with Clarabelle, and . . . his lungs squeezed. The picture of his old man with his mom.

"Seems she's pretty smart. You sure she's not right about this disagreement you two had last night?"

Of course, his father could read between the lines enough to know what had been the source of their blowout. "I'm not sure it's that easy," Eli said, but his old man just smiled.

"Ah, but I'm certain it's not that hard. I know you feel loyalty to this family, and that means more to me than you'll ever know. But you're overdue to be who ya are, son. No matter what's goin' on here at Cross Creek, and no matter how long you have to be gone to do it."

Eli's heart pounded faster in a last-ditch defensive maneuver. "Okay, but everything with Marley—"

"Will be here when you get back," his father promised. "Do you want to be a writer, Eli?"

He nodded. He couldn't cover up the truth. Not anymore. "Yeah."

"And do you love Scarlett?"

"Yes, sir. I do," Eli said without hesitation, realizing the gravity of the words as he spoke.

He loved her. He loved Scarlett. He loved her too-loud laugh and the fact that she hugged chickens and every brash, bold, in-your-face part of her that had pushed him to be who he was, even when he'd tried his best to fight it.

And now she was gone.

Eli bit out a curse, dropping his chin to his chest. But then he caught sight of the picture frames, each one glinting in the sunlight, and an idea sparked in his head, wild and insistent.

"Pop, can you call Owen and Hunter and ask them to come up here as fast as they can? I've got to do something, but I need all the help I can get."

CHAPTER TWENTY-EIGHT

Scarlett shouldered her camera bag, taking one last look around the fun-sized apartment she'd borrowed from Emerson. Somewhere right around two a.m., the concept of sleep became one of those things that was great in theory but impossible in practice, so she'd thrown in the towel and tidied the place from top to bottom as she'd packed. Everything had fit in the Volkswagen just as it had on the day she'd arrived, and funny how it seemed like it had been forever and five minutes ago all at the same time.

You might want to make that never, sweetheart.

Scarlett ran a hand over her breastbone, trying to cover the ache there. But she knew it wouldn't work—shit, she'd tried it nearly nonstop for the last twelve hours. The only thing that *would* work was punching her passport and getting back behind her camera, where she belonged.

Crossing the threshold, she locked the door and slid the key under the mat. It was a move she'd never dream of in New York, but then again, she'd text Daisy as soon as she made her first pit stop in Lockridge.

Time to hit the road. No matter how badly she didn't want to.

No matter how much it hurt.

Scarlett took one last look at the Twin Pines parking lot before kicking her block-heeled booties into motion across the asphalt, but she'd barely made it to her car before her cell phone buzzed in her back pocket. Her heartbeat rocketed in a moment of bold, stupid hope, but the sensation quickly flamed out at the sight of Hunter's phone number on her caller ID.

"Hi, Hunter. What's up? How's your dad?"

"He's hanging in there. Did I catch you on the road?"

"Sort of," Scarlett said, finishing her trip to the Volkswagen and going through the pleasantries with the door locks and the ignition. "I was actually just heading out."

"Well, I'm glad you're not too far away. I've got one of your lenses here at the farm. You must've left it by accident."

Surprise prickled through her. "Are you sure?"

Hunter's laughter moved over the line. "The only cameras we have around this place are the ones on our phones, so yeah, I'd say I'm pretty sure."

"Point taken," Scarlett said with a tiny smile. She was normally meticulous about her equipment, but she *had* stockpiled some lenses at Cross Creek. She must've missed one somehow. "I can come by and get it since I'm on my way out of town. I have Emerson's key, anyway."

"Sounds like a plan. I'll see you in a few."

After a quick trip back to the welcome mat, Scarlett aimed the convertible at Cross Creek. There was the possibility Eli would be there, she knew. But after last night, he'd made it clear that he belonged at the farm and she didn't, so even if he was, surely he wouldn't be champing at the bit to be anywhere near her.

By the time she pulled up the gravel drive leading to the main house, the pang in her belly had (mostly. Sort of) subsided. Eli's truck was nowhere to be seen, and she made her way to the porch to place a knock on the door so she could make the swap and get on the road before that changed.

To her surprise, it was Owen, not Hunter, who answered the door.

"Um, hi," she said, but he met her confusion with a grin.

"Hey, Scarlett. Hunter told me you'd be stoppin' by. Come on in, and I'll go get what you came for."

"Oh. Sure." Going into the house hadn't really been on her agenda, but she didn't want to be rude. Scarlett stepped into the foyer, but her feet clattered to a sloppy halt as soon as she reached the living room.

Eli stood front and center on the area rug with two huge duffel bags at his feet.

"Right." Owen's smile turned the slightest bit guilty, and Hunter's was a perfect match as he appeared beside his brother in the hallway. "Sorry, but we sort of lied to you."

"And by 'sort of,' we mean 'totally,'" Hunter added, placing a quick squeeze on her shoulder before following Owen back down the hallway and out the front door.

Scarlett crossed her arms over the front of her sweater, partly as a defense and partly because she was sure that if she didn't, her heart would do a triple gainer right out of her chest. "What are you doing here?" she finally managed.

"I'm here because I knew you'd be here. I know—" Eli broke off, pain and regret making a clear-cut appearance in his eyes. But they didn't stop him from continuing. "I know I said a lot of things last night that hurt you, and none of them were true. It doesn't change the fact that I said them, though, and for that I apologize."

She felt her stare go round and wide. "Okay."

"It's not okay, though. I said those things to push you away, but what I should've done instead was tell you the truth," he said. "I should've told you that I was torn over what to do and how best to help my family. I should've told you I was panicking that the assignment in Brazil got so big, so fast."

"Anything else?" Scarlett asked, hope flickering strong and sweet in her chest.

Eli nodded. "I should've told you that you were right about who I am. I've spent all this time worrying about belonging in a place, about not belonging at the farm, that I didn't see what was right in front of me. I don't fit into a place, Scarlett. I fit with a person. I fit with you."

Tears welled, sudden and hot, and oh God, her heart was going to pound right out of her rib cage.

"I thought I came from everywhere," Scarlett whispered. "My whole life, I thought I belonged everywhere, but I don't. I belong with you. My home—my heart, my *everything*—it's all you. I belong with you, Eli."

He moved to cross the living room, but she met him halfway, throwing her arms around his shoulders just before he pulled her in close in return. His lips brushed over hers, and nothing had ever felt so good or so vital in her life.

"I'm so sorry," Eli said, but she pulled back to look at him, shaking her head.

"You love your family. I understand. I love them, too."

He lowered his forehead to hers, the corners of his mouth edging up into a mischievous smile. "Speaking of which, I should probably tell you one more thing."

"What's that?" she asked.

"Everyone around here seems to think you're family, too. See for yourself."

He swung her toward the side table where all the photos she'd taken were lined up, but with one addition.

"Oh my God." Scarlett's tears began to fall in earnest, but she didn't care. "Is that . . .?"

"The picture Owen took of me and you two nights ago. You're part of our family, Scarlett. I love you."

"I love you, too, cowboy."

And as she pressed to her toes to kiss him, she knew they were both exactly where they belonged.

ACKNOWLEDGMENTS

Like all books, *Crossing the Line* is a collaborative effort, and I wouldn't have been able to write more than five words of it without the encouragement and dedication of many, many people. I owe endless thanks to my wonder-agent, Nalini Akolekar, who is as patient as she is fierce. Chris Werner and Melody Guy, truly, there are no finer editors than you. I'm so blessed to work with you both. To the entire team at Montlake Publishing, thank you for making me look so good and for being cheerleaders for this series. Also, an extra-special thank-you to Jessica Poore for showing me that carnitas and pancakes are a thing. (Trust me—they're a thing and they're fabulous!)

This book would not have had a heroine (specifically, *this* heroine) were it not for the fantastic Robin Gansle saying to me once upon a time, "You know what you should write one day? A photographer heroine!" I owe Scarlett all to you, and I promise never to Photoshop a nose onto your seat.

As an author, I'm fortunate beyond measure to have a support system that is both badass and beautiful. In no particular order other than random, I have to thank Alyssa Alexander, Tracy Brogan, Skye Jordan, Carrie Ann Ryan, Erin Nicholas, Scarlett Cole, Liz Talley, and Marina Adair, along with the incomparable Brenda Novak, for their incredible encouragement.

Robin Covington and Avery Flynn, you are far better besties than I deserve. Without you, this book simply wouldn't exist.

A huge shout-out to my online reader group, the Taste Testers. You make me laugh every day, and I am so grateful!

Lastly, to my ever-patient daughters, thank you for your continued excitement every time I take on a project, even though you know it will make our lives crazy. And Mr. K . . . you make writing heroes easy. Thanks for giving me my HEA.

ABOUT THE AUTHOR

Crossing the Line is the second book in The Cross Creek Series by Kimberly Kincaid, a *USA Today* bestselling author and a 2016 and 2015 RITA Award finalist who lives (and writes!) by the mantra "Food is love." When she's not sitting cross-legged in an ancient desk chair that she calls the "Pleather Bomber," she can be found practicing crazy amounts of yoga, whipping up everything from enchiladas to éclairs in her kitchen, or curled up with her nose in a book. Kimberly, who writes contemporary romance that splits the difference between sexy and sweet, resides in Virginia with her wildly patient husband and their three daughters. Visit her at www.kimberlykincaid.com or on Facebook, Twitter, Pinterest, and Instagram.